Darien

C. Iggulden is one of the most successful authors of historical fiction writing today. He has written three previous bestselling historical series, including the recent Wars of the Roses quartet. *Darien* is the first in his epic new fantasy series, The Empire of Salt.

Darien

Empire of Salt: Book One

C. F. IGGULDEN

PENGUIN BOOKS

PENGUIN BOOKS

UK | USA | Canada | Ireland | Australia
India | New Zealand | South Africa

Penguin Books is part of the Penguin Random House group of companies
whose addresses can be found at global.penguinrandomhouse.com.

First published by Michael Joseph 2017
Published in Penguin Books 2018
001

Copyright © Conn Iggulden, 2017

The moral right of the author has been asserted

Set in 12.15/14.4 pt Garamond MT Std
Typeset by Jouve (UK), Milton Keynes
Printed in Great Britain by Clays Ltd, St Ives plc

A CIP catalogue record for this book is available from the British Library

ISBN: 978-0-718-18647-0

www.greenpenguin.co.uk

MIX
Paper from
responsible sources
FSC   FSC® C018179
www.fsc.org

Penguin Random House is committed to a
sustainable future for our business, our readers
and our planet. This book is made from Forest
Stewardship Council® certified paper.

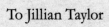

To Jillian Taylor

Acknowledgements

I haven't called on friends to accompany me to far-flung ruins for this one, nor on researchers to seek the names of Caesar's assassins. Instead, I would like to acknowledge some of the authors who filled my mind with colours in the first place – and made me want to write. Every writer is a reader first. We do it because we love it.

Please raise a glass to the thieves of time, to the storytellers:

David Gemmell, Raymond E. Feist, Orson Scott Card, Robin Hobb, Peter F. Hamilton, Philip José Farmer, Michael Crichton, Jim Butcher, Mark Lawrence, Terry Pratchett, George R. R. Martin, Piers Anthony, David Eddings, Robert A. Heinlein, Isaac Asimov, David Feintuch, Harry Harrison, Ursula Le Guin, Lawrence Watt-Evans, Warren Murphy and Richard Sapir, Brent Weeks, Robert E. Howard, L. Sprague de Camp, Stephen King, Sheri S. Tepper, Larry Niven, Poul Anderson, Lois McMaster Bujold and Spider Robinson.

Honestly, every name on that list is a greater joy than the last, read forwards or backwards. The world is a better place because they walked it once, or perhaps because they still do. Thank you, all.

Conn Iggulden

PART ONE

I

Risk

He was a hunter, Elias Post, a good one. The village elders spoke of his skills with enormous pride, as if they owned some part of his talents. The people of Wyburn looked to him to bring them meat, even in the darkest months of winter when other places lost their old and young.

The land around them was exhausted, though they still worked it hard, forcing some small crop from each scrub field, guarding slow-growing things from crows and ravenous pigeons. Sheep still roamed the bare hills. Doves pecked and glared in their boxes. Bees drowsed in lines of hives. It might have been enough to feed them all if some of the woods had not been burned and sown to grow oilseed for the city, earning silver over food. Elias did not know the rights and wrongs of those choices. When the grain store was down to a crust of years past, when the warrens were trapped out and empty, thin-fingered hunger crept into the village, peering in at old men as they rocked by the fire.

He'd gone out first when he'd been a boy, coming back to his mother in triumph with ducks clutched together or hares all tucked up under his belt like a skirt of grey fur. There was an abundance in the summers, but it was in the deep winter where Elias earned the praise of the village council. When the frost came down and the world was white and silent, he had been a sure source of venison and partridge, hares – even wolf or bear if the snows were deep. He drew his line at fox, though he trapped them to let the hares thrive. The meat was foul-tasting and he could not bear the smell.

As he reached forty, he'd been offered a place on the village council himself. He took pride in attending the meetings on the first day of each month. Along with his skills, there was an authority in him that grew each year, like a cloak he was made to wear whether he wanted to or not. He did not speak often – and then only when he knew the subject well enough to be sure of his judgement.

The one source of disagreement was his refusal to take an apprentice, but even then they knew his son would follow him when the boy was grown. What did it matter if Elias preferred to teach his craft to his own kin? There were always some who grumbled when every other hunter went into the forests and returned thin and empty-handed, with frost on their beards. Elias would come in then, hunched and bowed by the weight of a carcass draped over his shoulders, all black with frozen blood. He did not laugh or boast to the other hunters, though some still hated him even so. They were proud men themselves and they did not like to be shamed in front of their families, no matter how he shared the meat, in exchange for other goods or coin. They held their peace, for they were not fools and the village needed Elias Post more than the other hunters. No one wanted to be cast out, to have to go to the city for work. There were no good endings there, everyone knew that. When young girls ran off to Darien, their parents even held a simple funeral, knowing it was much the same. Perhaps to warn the other girls, too.

The plague had arrived that summer on the cart of a

potion-seller from the city, or so they said. It had first become a scourge there, where people lived too close and rubbed cheek and jowl with fleas and lice. No doubt it was a punishment for sinful couplings. You did not have to live long to know that healthy lives had hardly any pleasure in them. This plague began with rashes, and for most of them it was no worse than that. A few days of fever and itching before good health returned. They all began with that hope, only for some to lie cold and staring after a week of misery and pain. It was a cruel thing that year, and it knew no favourites.

When the proctors of the village met that autumn, they were not surprised to see Elias' seat standing empty. They murmured the name of Elias Post in sorrow and pity then. They had all heard. Wyburn was a small place.

His son Jack had gone in just a week, a little boy of black hair and laughter who'd been struck down and snatched from life, leaving a piece of river ice in his father's heart. The hunter had aged as many years as the boy had lived in that last night, sitting with him. Towards the end, Elias had walked a mile to pray at the temple outside Wyburn, that stood alone on the road leading to the city. He'd made his offering – a wisp of golden hay from the harvest. The Goddess of the reaping had turned her face from him, spinning on her iron chain. By the time he'd trudged back across the fields to his house near the village square, the boy was cold and still. Elias had sat with him for a time, just looking.

When the sun rose, his wife and daughters were weeping and trying not to scratch the welts that had risen on their skin, dumb with fear, pale as plucked flesh. Elias had kissed them all, tasting the salt of bright sweat. He'd hoped for the plague to take him, and when he slept for a while and woke again, it was almost a relief to discover his own welts swelling, his forehead damp. His wife had wailed to see him sick, but he'd gathered her in with their two daughters, a knot of arms and tears and grief.

'And what would I do on my own, my love? You and the girls are all I have left. Now that Jack is gone. I had one chance to be happy and it was *taken* from me. I will not be left alone, Beth! No. Wherever we are going, I will walk with you. What does it matter now, love? We'll go after Jack. We'll catch him up. We'll fall into step beside him, wherever he is. He'll be pleased to see us, you know he will. Why, I can see his face now.'

As darkness came, Elias found he could not bear to sit and listen to breaths crackling in the silence. He rose from his chair and stood for a time at the window, looking out on a moonlit road. It was an early dark then and he knew the tavern would be open. Yet it was not ale he wanted, nor clear spirits. He had no coin to waste on those and no taste for it. There were other things to be found in the light and the noise of a crowd.

He knew he would be thrown out or even killed by frightened men if they saw the raised patches on his arms and stomach. He grimaced, uncaring, driven wild by the itching. Perhaps it was murder he was considering, though he did not think it was. Some men were taken, others were spared. That was just the way of it then. They knew it was spread by touch; no one really understood the manner of it. There had been plagues before. They rose in summers and burned out in the cold months that followed. In some ways, it was as ordinary as the seasons, though that was no comfort to him.

Elias shrugged. An old shirt and a long coat would hide

the marks. There was a patch of swelling under his hair and another at the crook of his throat. In the mirror, it looked like a map of islands, white in a pink sea. He shook his head, then buttoned the shirt up high.

Hunting was clean, especially in the dark and the cold. He went out and he used his knack and he caught deer with his hands. It was a thing he had not shared with anyone, though he had hoped his son would learn the craft of it when he was older. That thought brought such a wave of grief that he could not bear to remain in the house. He pulled thick clothes from a reeking pile and yanked them on, adding a felt hat with a broken brim that would hide his face. He could not just lie down and die. That had always been a weakness in him.

There was medicine in the city, everyone knew that. There were doctors who could make the dead stand up and dance, so they said. Yet such miracles required more coins than a village hunter had ever seen. In the autumn, Elias butchered hogs on local homesteads and took away some chops and kidneys for his labour. Or he cut wood in exchange for a pot or two of honey. When he caught white or red foxes in his traps, he saved the skins and sold them all at once to a fellow a few miles downriver, for real silver bits. Elias had never been to the city himself, but he knew they had all sorts of learned men there, who could do just about anything. For money, anyway, not for kindness or for love. That was understood and he could accept it. The world owed nothing to anyone. He had made a living from it even so.

Elias kept his precious coins in a pot on the mantel, saved for the years ahead when he would not be able to hunt in the snow, when his fingers would not grip the knife too well. Perhaps too for when his knack would surely wither in him, like a man's sight or hearing. He touched the pouch in his pocket, its contents taken down and counted out on the kitchen table earlier that day. Perhaps he'd intended this thing all along, he did not know. The mind was a strangely complex beast, slow and deep, layer upon layer. His father had said he felt like a boy riding a great ox at times, without very much idea of what the ox was thinking.

The fruit of a dozen years of fur and meat trading could be held in one hand. Yet even his precious pieces of silver would never be enough, Elias knew that. Doctors were rich men. Rich men expected gold, with the heads of other rich men pressed into the soft metal. Elias had never seen a gold coin but he knew there were twenty silver to one noble – and they were somehow worth just the same. It was a little like the captains of the troops of soldiers who came through sometimes in the spring, looking for young men to recruit. Each captain lorded it over twenty men, telling them what to do and where to step. Elias wondered as he walked how many captains a general would command. A dozen? A score? Was there a metal they valued more than gold? If so, he had never known its name.

He considered this and other things as he made his way down the road towards the inn, his mind whirling in grief and anger and recklessness. He had worked hard and raised four. One had gone into the ground after just a few days in the world. Back then, he and his wife had been younger, more able to put it behind and try again. He'd told Beth they'd given one back, comforting his wife in that way. He said they'd paid the tithe of their lives in that grief.

It had not been part of the bargain for his son Jack to follow, nor for the itching plague to touch his daughters. Elias had known that most of those who grew sick survived it.

He'd been calm and utterly certain it would pass at first, denying what was happening right to the moment when he'd felt his son's hand had somehow grown cool. The flesh had kept its colour, but it always had been warm before. He'd known then.

He'd been teaching the boy how to read, letter by letter. It just wasn't possible that the lessons would stop, that he wouldn't hear one more halting word or feel the boy's laughing weight as he leaped on his father from a doorpost. Perhaps it was a kind of madness, but Elias felt no check or curb on him that evening, as if he'd seen his life through glass and understood at last that *nothing* mattered, but those he loved and those who loved him.

He knew that night was one of two in the year when farmers sold their wool. The great Harvest Eve was coming and that would be a day of celebration, where hams were cut thick and for one day the villagers drank one another's health and ate until they could hardly move. First came the wool sale, at the end of summer. There were men with real silver in the tavern that evening, pleased with themselves and drinking jug after jug of the rich brown ale.

Elias wet his lips with his tongue, feeling the cold air dry and tighten them once again. He had never used his knack amongst men before. That secret heart of him was for the deep silences, for the dark hills and the frosts. The thought of using it with eyes on him was akin to walking in with his buttocks hanging out of his breeches. He found he was sweating and began to scratch himself. No, not that night. He would just have to keep his hands still, no matter how much it was a torment. The whole countryside was alive with warnings of plague and they all knew his son had been failing.

He remembered then that the Goddess had turned her face away from him when he asked about his boy, Jack. Elias had to bite his lip for a time at that thought, until the pain made him shiver, anything rather than curse her. She might be deaf to those who needed her help, but she heard every word spoken ill. It was hard to pull his mind back from the furious words that simmered and seethed in him. He stumbled along to the light that spilled onto the street, drawn by the sound of laughter and the clink of brown pots.

Elias slipped in amongst the drinkers and talkers without his presence being noticed at all. He had never been a large man and he wore his beard short, with patches of grey. He had lived forty-four years in that town and if that was to be his last, there had been more good times than bad. He nodded to one or two he knew and swept past while they were still widening their eyes. No one had seen Elias in the inn before, not in all the years he had hunted. He was just not a sociable man. He would never be a proctor of Wyburn, though he might help choose the man who was.

At the far end of the room were the gaming tables Elias wanted, filled with the farmers he hoped to see. Despite his serious intent, his mouth twitched when he remembered his mother's words of warning about this very tavern and the vices it contained. She had been in the ground for a long time, in a hole dug by his own hands. He had packed up the earth twice to leave a mound in the years since, when it sank down. Still, her words remained in him.

Already there were piles of silver coins in front of the men at the tables. Elias dug in his pocket, gathering up the dozen he owned. He held them out as proof he had the right to stand there, looking for the leader, whoever it was. They were not men he knew, on the whole, though he had seen a few of them around the village stores. One of them had a harder stare than the others – and they were men used to wrestling a sheep out of thorns or a muddy ditch. Elias looked away when he felt the stranger's gaze crawl over his face, convinced there would be a cry of disgust and a shout of plague. The man looked more suited to being a whorehouse guard. Younger than the others there, he wore a smart yellow waistcoat over a white shirt that marked him out all on its own. White shirts were usually kept for funerals and marriages, if they were owned at all. The rest of the men wore the sort of colours that showed dirt only as a shine on hard-wearing cloth. The yellow and the white was a challenge in itself. Whoever he was, the fellow did not work the land.

Elias found his gaze trapped by the man's interest in him. Wide-shouldered, the stranger lacked the sheer bulk of the farmers at that table. He was more sheepdog than mastiff, Elias decided, more speed than brawn. Yet there was still a threat in the man's eyes that stopped Elias cold.

He held out his coins even so, tight between black-nailed fingers. He had not used his knack before in such a way and he felt his hand shake, uncertain until that moment that it would even work.

The young man shrugged and nodded to an empty chair. As Elias stepped towards it, he saw one of the new guns they made in the city was on the fellow's hip, a thing of black metal that looked sleek and oiled in its holster. It was said to make a great noise and to punch a hole through a side of beef. Elias looked at the thing in awe and fear and the weapon's owner caught his interest and smiled widely.

'You've seen my toy, my warmaker? Don't be afraid, meneer. My name is Vic Deeds. If you've heard of me, you'll know I do not draw it in this sort of company.'

'I am not afraid,' Elias said.

He spoke with such transparent truth that the man looked at him oddly. Before the gunman could ask any more questions, the cards were dealt and Elias seated himself and pushed his first coin into the middle. Beyond a few games at his kitchen table with his wife and son, he had never played in public. He sat with his back to the crowd and knew enough to clutch the squares of card very closely to his chest. He'd heard of men placing their friends behind other players to signal good or bad hands.

The game began with a bet, then a chance to improve the draw, then a final round of betting. There did not appear to be any limit for a given hand, so Elias knew he could lose everything he had in a single round. His first cards were worth nothing, so he placed them face down and waited for the rest of them to bring it to an end, struggling to find the calm he needed.

There. There it was. The knack was just as strong as it had always been. Even surrounded by people, with talk and laughter and men's backs knocking against his chair, it was there to be called upon. He felt a surge of confidence and smiled as each card was turned. When he looked up, it was to find the gunman's eyes on him once again, watching with a concentration that was unnerving, as if this Vic Deeds could see even the knack that had brought Elias to that godforsaken place, with all his hopes being slowly drawn out of the world a few streets away.

Mindful of his blisters, Elias dropped his gaze once more, grateful for the hat and the length of his hair as it fell forward over his face. He watched as a silver coin that had been his became part of another man's pile of winnings. It represented a week or so of trapping, just about. Still, Elias had called every card.

When the second hand was dealt, he used his knack again, but frowned, *reaching* as far as he could ahead. This hand would be slow as men hemmed and hawed and hesitated over bets. He could not look as far as he needed. Ruefully, Elias realised he would have to be in every round, then stretch his knack to the very utmost to see the results.

Two more passed before he won one, giving him back all he had lost and four more pieces of silver. The gunman grunted in irritation, having bet most of his own pile on a weak and losing hand. Elias gathered in the coins and wondered if he might faint from the pounding of his heart. If he could win enough, he might just borrow the Widow Joan's horse and ride to the city for medicine. If he spared neither the horse nor his own strength, he could be back in a few days with whatever his wife and daughters needed. He could. It was in his grasp.

As the next hand was dealt, he sensed it all crash around him. The man sitting on his right had been munching his yellow beard and watching Elias with a sour expression ever since he'd sat down. Without warning, the farmer put out his hand to touch Elias' coat. His fingers closed on air as Elias leaned back, his excitement fading into dismay as his dream broke into sharp pieces.

'What are you hiding up that sleeve, son?' the man said.

Half the table seemed to freeze and the gunman perked up, showing sharp white teeth. The old farmer didn't even seem to realise it sounded like an accusation of cheating. He pointed a bony hand at Elias.

'You're sweating hard and yet your coat is still on. That

old hat of yours has dust on the brim. It's not one you wear every day, is it? Show me your arms, son! If you're clean, I'll take your hand and beg your pardon. Hell, I'll buy you a drink even. But show me you ain't a plague-carrier first.'

Elias stood, touching a hand to the brim of his old hat.

'I don't want any trouble, sir. I just wanted to play cards.'

He winced at the voice from behind him before it called out, but the press was too great and his mind was fogged with weakness and fever. One of the men had lost all his season's profits that evening. As he shouted, he began to stand, his hands holding the edge of the table, about to tip it over in his anger and greed.

Elias knew it had been a mistake then, a wild fantasy that might yet cost him his life. So he *reached*, as the fight began all around him.

Vic Deeds sat back in his chair and watched a man not get killed. He had never seen anything like it in his life, and for most of his twenty-six years he had ridden with either thieves or armies – and sometimes with so little difference between them that he could not remember which it had been. Even with the spittle-flecked rage of the farmers taking swings at each other, none of them dared attack Deeds as he sat still, his hand resting lightly on a long pistol across his thigh. One of them even stumbled over his outstretched legs and tipped his hat in apology, but that was not what surprised the gunman. Most of the farmers sensed he was a killer, just as sheep would crowd together in the presence of a dog that would enjoy nothing more than tearing out their throats.

What had his eyes straining wide in disbelief was the small fellow who had bet hard on a risky hand and won a neat pile before they called him out on his plague. At least that part wasn't a worry. Deeds had watched as some sort of medicine was painted on his arm a few months before – and drunk a bitter glass of the stuff when he'd been told to. The army that had trusted him with new pistols had insisted. The syrup cost a fortune, that was the problem. It would probably never find its way to shit-kicking villages where they bought and sold damp wool.

As far as Deeds was concerned, it wouldn't hurt anyone to thin the herd, especially of the old and weak. That was only common sense and it wasn't his concern what the Twelve Families in Darien chose to spend their money on – or not. Still, his night had been ruined. He'd expected to make enough from the table to keep him in style for a month or two. Farmers who could not calculate odds were just about his favourite sort.

Deeds stared as the stranger moved around and through the crowd at the bar, as if he walked a path they had all agreed before. The hunter in his long coat took each step with care, pausing for a fist to pass before his face or a club to complete its swing. Delicately, like a cat, Elias turned aside from a spinning table, guiding it slightly with a palm against the polished wood so that it did not crash into a fallen man. It was like a dance to watch, but Deeds thought no one else had even noticed. They were all so busy with their set-tling of grudges and gleeful knockabout that they missed a dozen moments that broke every rule he understood about the world.

Deeds had not been a soft child and he was not a soft man. He made a lightning decision and raised his pistol when Elias was still two paces from escaping through the door to the road outside. Without hesitation, Deeds fired twice, the concussions enormous in the enclosed space, so that his ears rang with a high-pitched tone. The gunman's mouth dropped open as his mind caught up with what he had seen down the length of his barrel.

Elias had *looked* at him through the crowd before the first shot, turning just a fraction so that when it came, it passed him by. The second shot had compensated, Deeds relying on his instincts to aim and adjust at a speed to make an older man weep. He had seen it pass under the fellow's arm, between his body and the crook of his elbow. Behind Elias, the bullet had punched another brawler from his feet and Deeds could only look on in astonishment. They were no more than twelve feet apart. He had never missed at that range before.

At the door, Elias looked back through a cloud of gun smoke with a mixture of anger and sadness. In the sudden silence, he flung the door back with a crash and disappeared into the night.

2

New Boy

The old man had been a soldier in his day; so they said, when they were sure he couldn't hear. If it was true, it must have been forty years before. Tellius might once have had a barrel of a chest, but as the years advanced, his arms had grown as skinny as crow legs and about as scaled. Whatever the exact truth, he was quick to anger with the boys; that was well known. If you did not work, you were not fed. If you were not fed, your only hope was the great brick pauper's oven on Frith Street. Perhaps it was just bad luck that the city orphanage looked like a bakery kiln, but it did. There were very few windows in that place and the stories they told of it were not pleasant. None of the boys who stole for Tellius would have expected clean dormitories and a chance to learn their letters there.

Sometimes, friends they had known were taken up by the city guards, the new ones they called the King's Men. In the courts, those young lads had hidden their fear, with faces scrubbed mostly clean and their hair slicked down in one long shine. They'd promised to come back and tell the others what it was like, just as soon as they could get away. None of them had ever returned or been seen again. No, they stole because the alternatives could have been as dark as they could imagine. That was all the old man asked them to do and if they were not particularly clean, at least they did not starve. There was even the tale, oft told amongst them, that when they reached fourteen or so, Old Tellius would buy them an apprenticeship in a proper smithy, or with a pottery maker. No one ever asked him if that part was true, in case it turned out not to be. Such dreams were better untested, they all knew that. With care and polish, a good dream could give hope and comfort for years and years.

Tellius shuffled along the line of filthy, reeking boys. He held a felt bag with a drawstring as he went, pausing by each lad to see what they had brought back. His mind clicked like counting beads as they put a few coins in, or a brooch, or a silver pin. He had never been seen with an accounts book, nor even a piece of paper. Yet there had been times when he would snap out his long arm and snag-collar some lad with slow hands or who ate more than he ever brought in. Tellius would tap his own temple then – and while the boy squirmed, the old man would recite a list of everything the boy had brought to their workshop floor, almost as if it was all laid out on a table before him. Sometimes, he would even reach out and turn over an imaginary item to bring it closer. After that, he would send them out to starve on their own for a day or two, without even a stripe from the belt that they expected. The street was hard on those who had no one. Those who came back had learned a lesson, shivering and thin. Those who did not were sometimes found in the river.

Tellius wrinkled his nose as he went along the neat queue of boys, revealing his missing teeth and the tongue that always seemed a bit too large for his mouth, so it muffled his speech. He had to tuck it into his cheek when he wanted to speak quickly and it gave him a lopsided expression, a sardonic one, with one eye raised and gleaming and the other hidden in folds and eyebrow, all twisted up.

He looked at the boy last in line, who at least had not been stupid enough to try and pretend he had dropped something into the darkness of the bag. They'd all tried that once after a bad night. Some of them had a friend distract him just as they opened their hand, or even dropped a pebble in, to make the coins clink. Each time, Tellius had grabbed the scrawny wrist so hard it made them gasp. 'That will be your only chance, son,' he said then. 'Do better or go.'

The boy who had not moved was Donny, one of the least sharp of his lads and one Tellius knew he should really have sent back to the street. He certainly would have when he'd first arrived in Darien. The process had been gradual as the seasons and decades passed. Tellius hardly recognised even then how rarely he drove a boy away. It would have surprised him to be told he had not actually done so for years.

He did not think Donny held anything back – the boy was desperate to stay and the Goddess alone knew what he had run from to find comfort in that grubby family. Yet the world was cruel and there was one constant truth: Tellius could not make food appear from thin air.

'Nothing for me, Donny?' he said softly.

'Found a new kid,' Donny said in a rush. He knew he had used up all his chances. 'You said that was as good as. You *said* so.'

Tellius looked past him, though the truth was he'd noticed the new boy just as soon as he came into the room. There'd been a stillness there, while the rest of them rushed about and boasted and shoved each other. Tellius had known a few wounded dogs in his time, giving the room the same wary, sort of sullen look, with the threat of knuckles in it. He'd seen all that before, though the boy standing with Donny must have rolled in a privy midden to have accumulated the sheer amount of filth that caked him from head to foot. Tellius wrinkled his nose as he leaned in to have a look.

Donny glanced up and saw his distaste.

'We was runnin' and that. He dived into a shit barrow. I went under it. They ran past.'

'And why were you being chased, Donny? Strange thing to say, if you've got nothing to give me for my stew and to deserve your spot in the corner.'

'My razor was blunt and it didn't cut, like, so when I pulled a purse, she felt it . . .'

'And you ran,' Tellius said, sighing. 'Empty-handed.'

'But I brought you this one. I saw him and he looked hungry and I told him to come with me, 'cause I remembered you said a new kid was as good as a pearl earring.'

'All right, Donny. I know what I said. Go in and get your stew with the others. It's fish tonight. With pepper that will make your eyes stream.'

Donny ducked his head and scuttled off, ten years old and all elbows and bones, with freckled skin stretched so tight it looked as if it might split if he ever smiled.

Tellius turned to the new arrival.

'So. Who are you? Apart from bleedin' filthy.'

The boy stared back in silence, eyes large. He was as skinny as Donny and the powerful smell on him made Tellius cough and clear his throat. He didn't concern himself with their cleanliness and whatnot. But he was tempted to put this one into the rain barrel out the back, before he stank the whole place out. Tellius sniffed again, pleased his cold had returned and blocked one nostril at least.

'Something got your tongue? Eh? Do you speak?'

The boy shook his head, so that Tellius' enormous eyebrows rose a good inch.

'You don't *speak*?' he demanded.

The boy shook his head solemnly once again.

'But you can understand me?' Tellius said.

The head dipped slowly and came back.

'Goddess, I can't be dealing with this,' he muttered. He'd known boys who could not speak before, sadly. They were often ones with stories so dark he'd learned not to ask. He could not do anything about those poor mites. Some of them lasted. Some of them just vanished after a time. He could not be a father to them, Goddess knew. He could do only a little and if that was not enough . . . He bit his tongue quickly. The Goddess listened to old men who scorned her, everyone knew that. And she would come in the night's dark for that man and drag him from his bed. It was best to mind your tongue in the king's city of Darien.

'Donny and the other lads, they work for me,' he said. 'I only have this floor, which was my workshop a long time ago, but it's mine and I pay no rents. Nor taxes neither, since the building was condemned. So we sneak out the back when we come and go. I can't keep you if you don't work and if I can't *find* you work, you go out and you get me a day's wage with quick hands. You take a purse, or a shoe buckle, or a couple of nice chops for my dinner. Understand? You do all that and you'll get two meals and a warm bed and no one will hurt you. When you grow up, well, you can do whatever you like, though I have a few friends still who can always use hard workers. Oh, and you will have a bath in cold water, because you stink.'

The boy was watching him like an owl. Tellius smiled at him and would have reached out to ruffle his hair if not for the clotted mess it had become.

'So you'll need quick hands, lad. Or would you rather

be climbing into chimneys with a rag wrapped around your face? I need both sorts on most days, just to keep going. You've a strong stomach, looks like. Perhaps you could dig out the privy holes in rich houses. Well? Oh, yes. How about you just nod? Quick hands and thieving?'

Under the steady stare, Tellius wondered how much the boy had even understood. Perhaps he was one of those orphans who sometimes wandered into the city. Inspired, the old man reached into his pockets and withdrew an old apple, a thimble of green glass and a paper cork, still stained with red wine.

'Like this, lad. Quick hands.'

He tossed the three items into the air and juggled them with casual skill. He saw the boy's eyes focus sharply. Tellius tried not to smile in pride. The boy held out his hands.

'Oh, you'd like a try, would you?' Tellius said, handing them over. 'These things are mine though – I want them all back for . . .' He trailed off as the boy tossed them up exactly as he had done, settling quickly into the pattern. The old man watched for a while, but nothing fell and in the end he snatched them out of the air, leaving the boy patting nothing with a frown on his face.

'That was good . . . er . . . By Her Wounds, I'm going to need to call you something! I can't call you "boy" in this place, can I? What's your name, son? Do you know that much? Could you write it down? No?' The boy was shaking his head once more. 'No, I didn't think so. Well, I'm going to call you . . . Arthur. How does that sound? Arthur. It means like a bear, I think.'

The filthy boy looked up at him in silence until the old man sighed.

'Right. So you know how to juggle, which means you have

the hand-to-eye. But you're small, so you ain't going to be a soldier, not unless you spring up overnight. Still, I think you'll be a fine addition. Now I'll get Donny to show you the water barrel. You'll have to use the floor brush and a bucket. Be thorough, Arthur. There'll be stew for you, after, or none if you take too long.'

Elias stumbled away from the tavern into the darkness, but there was only one road in the village and it led straight through and away. He was just about weeping as he went, with all the fine dreams from earlier that evening like so many burned rags. He would not win enough to buy medicine. He would not race to the city on the widow's horse and save his wife and his daughters. Instead, he would watch them die, or die himself. The plague could take them all. Without the help of a city doctor, it was no better than throwing dice. It was what had changed his mind about just accepting his fate: the thought that he and his wife might die and leave the girls alone.

Somehow the misery of his failure was made sharper by the manner of it. He'd used his knack and it had failed him. He felt soiled by the experience, as if he'd committed some sin and shared something that had been for himself alone. He could still feel the eyes of that gunman on him, wide with disbelief as Elias *reached* and saw where to step to avoid the shots.

The worst moment had been when he used his knack and saw that the bullet would strike another man when he'd stepped aside. Though Elias had felt the plague in his gut and death on his shoulder, he'd still moved, unable even to die with his dignity intact. Shame seared him and then he came to a halt in the road, just a few moments before he heard footsteps scrape on the stones behind.

Vic Deeds had followed him in the moonlight, staying well back until he saw there was no threat from the staggering, weeping hunter in the darkness. Yet when Elias turned to face him, the young man drew both pistols and levelled them. Most of the new breed of gunfighters favoured one hand, but Deeds could shoot left or right equally. The truth was he liked to see men flinch when they heard his name.

It was not just the destructive power in his hands that made his heart beat faster. What Deeds had witnessed in the tavern had unnerved him. He knew he was good with the weapons. He'd made his guns fit his grip, over thousands of hours of practice. It made him frightening, even to swordmasters, their own hard-won skill all for nothing down the length of a barrel. Yet despite that, Deeds had watched a man dodge through a crowd and then ignore the threat of his bullets. He was not even sure what to say, but he knew he had to bring this particular hunter back to camp. The general was not a man to disturb with a trifle, Deeds knew that. He thought a man who could walk through gunfire was no small thing, no matter how he did it.

With an effort, Deeds holstered his pistols and raised his hands, showing empty palms.

'I'm sorry about drawing my guns on you. You startled me then, when you turned on me in the road. I mean you no harm, meneer, and I am heartily sorry if I came close to injuring you in the tavern.'

'You did not come close,' Elias Post said.

Deeds forced a smile and went on.

'I'm a man of my word, meneer. I give it to you now – I will not harm you, or try to. I did not begin that mess in there.'

'You shot at me twice, though,' Elias said. 'I don't know you, except what they say of you in the logging camps.'

Deeds decided not to ask what that was. Loggers had a nasty streak.

'I am a bondsman, just as you are, meneer. I work for the legion – for General Justan, if you know that name. He pays me my wages – aye, and a bonus when I please him. You are a hunter, are you not? You've paid a tithe on Goddess Day, surely? You've sent goods to markets? Of course you have. And there is peace, because the Twelve Families of Darien said there had to be laws across the land. General Justan pays for a few like me to hunt the men who won't play the game. He sends me when he hears there's been a killing or a feud. And I bring his vengeance. Or his justice. It is much the same. Think of me as a public service, meneer.'

'What do you want from me? I won't let you shoot me down, not tonight.'

'No, you won't, will you?' Deeds said, awed. 'Which is exactly why I am out here without even my coat to talk to you. What I want is for you to ride a few miles with me to the camp of the Immortal legion, to General Justan Aldan Aeris. Now you tell me what *you* want and we'll see whether we can find a way to make us both happy.'

Elias wiped his nose with his sleeve, leaving a shining trail.

'I have the plague, Mr Deeds,' he said, wearily. 'You don't want to be anywhere close to me.'

'So? I am immune to it, so they say. Would you like a doctor, then? Would that earn me a day of your life – in return for all the rest of it returned to you?'

'You know of a cure?'

Elias watched as Deeds nodded slowly. It took a huge

effort to smother the excitement that soared through him. He knew men like Deeds walked by while strangers died in the gutter. They did not stop and offer solace, or hold water to the lips of those dying. They did not look down at all.

'I need it. Not for me,' Elias said firmly. 'It's early in me still. For my wife and my two daughters.'

'Done,' Deeds said. 'On my honour, I swear it. I have a horse in the stable back there. He'll carry us both. If you come with me to the camp, I'll send the doctor and he will do what he can. Are you satisfied?'

Elias felt his heart thump in fear. The gunman was smiling and handsome as he put out his right hand. Elias dared not hope, but he could not help it.

'All right, though I can borrow a horse. You have one day, Mr Deeds. If you send the doctor to heal my family, I will see your friend.'

'Oh, he's not my friend,' Deeds said with a chuckle as they shook on the deal. 'But he will still want to meet you, I am certain of it.'

3

Quick Study

The rain made music of a sort, collected in a dozen metal cups and buckets as it dripped through tiles and old beams. The notes would jar and rattle, and yet every now and then they'd sound almost like bars of a song, half-remembered.

Tellius was enjoying the chatter and horseplay of the boys larking about in the huge old attic. He never spoke of his own childhood, or any part of his life before arriving in Darien. After all, it wasn't their business what he had done, nor who he had killed.

He had certainly not intended to teach the lads the dances of his youth, not at first. Tellius had learned the Mazer steps in an army camp fully half a century before, when he had been drilled in them to the point of blood-blisters and agony. Even in Darien there were legends of eastern legions leaping and flipping and stepping in complex patterns. Actually to picture such a thing made it all seem a flight of fancy. Over the centuries, the stories had become no more likely than tales of oracles or great beasts. Nine thousand miles over sea and land was further than they would ever travel. A different world, just about.

However the tradition had begun, back when the workshop was still making a profit and Tellius was a half-respectable mender and jeweller, it was certainly before the time of the oldest boys there. They'd just accepted it was the way it was.

They practised every morning before they went out to work, then Tellius made them all dance each seventh day, when it was said the Goddess had kicked up her heels for delight in the world she'd found. Not made. That was an older god, gone from the world. They said you could still hear his hymns in some parts.

When the new boy came back in, he had scrubbed himself so hard he'd left pink scratches on his face and arms. The ragged clothes were just as stinking and thick with dirt as they had been, but showed damp patches seeping through. His hair had darkened without the street dust, hanging over his face so that he had to sweep it back to see, making the gesture without a trace of irritation.

The boys had all finished eating and Arthur went over to the great cauldron, staring into its emptiness without expression. It looked as if it had been polished. He did not react when Tellius pressed a bowl against his ribs, with a piece of spelt bread wedged into some thick slop of fish, beans and gravy that smelled delicious.

'I kept one for you,' Tellius said. 'Won't do it again, mind, but I thought – first night. The boys are like wolves when they're sharp-set, all quick hands. So I kept a bowl back. Here, take it.'

The old man looked embarrassed by the gesture, holding it out as if he wished to step away. Arthur took it with a nod and folded himself then and there into a crouch on the ground, eating with his fingers and hiding the bowl from anyone who might steal its contents. Tellius shook his head. He'd seen street manners before, when meals were to be snarled over and forced down as quickly as they could be. He waited until the animal noises had lessened a touch before speaking again.

'Look there, Arthur, to what Donny is doing. You'll learn that in a while if you stay. It makes the legs strong.'

The boy raised his bowl to lick it clean and stared over the rim to where Tellius pointed. The crowd of boys were clapping along by then, keeping a rhythm for Donny and then subtly increasing it in cheerful cruelty so that he could not keep up. He had folded his arms and was bouncing on his heels almost in a full crouch, each time flinging one leg and then the other out and back before he had time to overbalance. Donny was already red-faced and sweating but he was grinning all the while.

Arthur watched him, then stood once again, handing back his bowl. He bowed slightly to Tellius and walked forward through the ring of boys to where Donny had collapsed into his companions, laughing and kicking. The noise had reached a crescendo at that, but it died away at the approach of the small boy who faced them with a scratched face and flopping black hair.

Tellius blinked at the solemn little owl. Perhaps the kid was touched in the head.

'You'll welcome Arthur, lads. Seems he doesn't speak, but he understands.'

Half of those present were already beginning to turn away or talk amongst themselves. They'd seen a dozen or so arrive, most of them. Some could not settle and vanished just a while later, disappearing back to their old lives, or worse ones. Either way, the boys in that attic would not waste too much liking on a new kid, at least until he'd been there for a time.

Arthur positioned himself as Donny had done, sitting on his heels, with his arms crossed and held out in front of him. Tellius saw that and chuckled, shaking his head. He thought of stopping him, but then the lad had already had a bowl from his hand that evening, kept special and in full view of the others. He did not want them to think he had a favourite. They could be hard on those they thought were treated differently. Tellius kept his silence and waited for Arthur to fall over and be humiliated.

Afterwards, he would always remember that moment. It took him to a fine house and the love of his life – and it led to the death of some of the boys in the room that evening. In his memory, it always began with the simple Mazer step, with Arthur so well balanced, it looked as if he'd been hung from strings.

They watched him, of course, though at first they did not clap. Arthur was so much smaller than most of them, but he bounced and kicked as if his balance and his strength were just about perfect. It made old Tellius remember days he had not thought of in years, so that he forgot himself and strode through the boys, grabbing Arthur by his arm.

'*Ethou andra Mazer*? You know the Mazer steps?' he demanded.

The boy showed no fear, he remembered later. He should have known then. Fear was what was missing in Arthur, not wits. Fear and his voice. Everything else in him was like a bright torch.

Arthur shook his head and Tellius let go in exasperation.

'Micahel, will you show this lad what I mean?'

Micahel was the oldest of them all, perhaps sixteen even. Some of the lads thought he would be the one to take over when Tellius died. He'd certainly been there longer than any of the others and yet the old man hadn't pushed him out, so there could have been truth in it. Either way, Micahel had danced the Mazer steps for eight years and he had an athlete's muscles and the grace of a born killer. Only Tellius knew that was what the training was for. The patterns could not make a man run any faster, though they did not hurt his wind. The Mazer steps were to build strength into bone, memories into muscles, so that when a blade came *just so*, those who knew how could twitch or sway aside and strike back, faster and more deadly. Tellius had been a fine dancer in his day, a lifetime and thousands of miles away from that wooden dormitory over an apothecary shop.

Micahel shrugged as if it meant nothing when Tellius called. The truth was the young man was proud of his skill at the Mazer steps. He often ran through all ten sets each night before he slept, until he was dripping with sweat, looking for excellence in each stance and turn of his feet and hands. As a result, Micahel moved with a grace that had brought him through a few scrapes, swift as a thought and a threat on the street, making a name for himself. More than once, Tellius had worried someone else from the old country would see Micahel move one day, and just know. There was no hiding it from those with the eyes to see. That was a problem for another day and Tellius felt a surge of pride as the young man stood forward and bowed to Arthur with a small smile.

'The Chiung Moon,' Tellius said.

The other boys grew more focused at that, shoving each other for the best places. The Moon was the eighth of ten and the most demanding in some ways. It involved a full turn in the air, a leaping kick and a pattern of movements like a basket of snakes pushing their way out in all directions. It needed space and the boys shuffled back as far as they could, making a ring. Tellius had to tap Arthur on

31

the forehead to get his attention, the boy standing right where Micahel needed to start. Micahel took his place and Arthur stood at the side, watching him with a faint frown.

The clapping began, though it was steadier than before. They would not force Micahel to race, in part because he took the steps very seriously indeed and no one there wanted to be on his bad side. Tellius was an adult who owned where they slept, so they were afraid of his authority. Micahel, though, was more dangerous than any of the street boys or guards who chased them through the alleys when they stole. He would be a name in the city of Darien, when he was ready. That was just the truth of it, even if they did not put it into words.

'Begin,' Tellius called, watching as his best pupil slid into the first position, turning left and resting his weight in proportion on the rear leg, to raise the other in a slow kick. At that speed, it was not obviously a blow, but the requirement of controlled strength was much greater. Tellius nodded when he saw no shake in the young man's thigh muscle. Good. His grandfather would have been proud of such a student. In the few moments before he killed Tellius for granting military secrets to the subjects of an enemy nation, of course.

Arthur watched with unblinking interest as Micahel surged through fifty-eight moves, each one representing the years of Chiung Moon's life, spent marauding with the armies of the east over a thousand years before. Tellius sighed to himself. He had not taught the boys any of the histories and in truth he had not meant to pass on quite so much of his old training.

At first it had just been a way to keep them fit and occupied when they were underfoot. They all ran and did a bit of climbing and roof-running back then, but that just made for wiry men, not fighters. It had seemed a natural enough thing to start training them during idle hours. That had been almost too many years ago to remember. Tellius still worried about the results and lied to himself about the effects.

They were not just an unusually muscular group of lads, like a troupe of circus performers. By teaching them the dances, Tellius had passed on a thousand memories of his young manhood yet all the time kept back the purpose and theory behind each move. They still called it dancing, as well as 'the Mazer steps', though the movements were not a dance and never had been. At home, he remembered, they did not clap. Every strike was imagined against an opponent, every *single* block was meant to break a man's bone.

Perhaps it was because old Tellius watched Micahel leap and spin through the eyes of a new boy, but he found himself growing tense. He had not held back as much as he'd thought, he realised, licking his lips nervously.

Micahel came to an end with a knee-drive of such force that it dragged his rear foot along the floor behind him, his arms raised like a bull's horns. He gave a great shout as he did so and the boys cheered him, caught up in the performance. He stood panting before them, shining with perspiration and smiling, knowing he had done well. Tellius saw that he had come to rest in the exact spot where he had begun and he bowed to Micahel from the sidelines, proud of him.

Arthur walked to where Micahel stood, looking up. The older boy glanced down and raised an eyebrow. He stepped back and Arthur immediately took his spot, standing in the same first position Micahel had adopted before.

In amusement, Micahel walked around him, nodding at the form.

'Come now, Arthur,' Tellius called. 'The boys are raucous and I have neighbours who don't like to be kept awake so late. They'll complain to the city council and have us all thrown out on the street. To bed now, lads. That is enough.'

No one moved from where they had found places, not when they saw Arthur standing so clearly poised and ready. Tellius had hoped to leave the boy's first night on the excellence of Micahel's Moon step, but it seemed it would end with laughter instead. Very well. The city of Darien was a hard place and he had given the boy a chance.

'I see. Mazer step the eighth then, Arthur, as you remember it. Chiung Moon. Begin.'

The clapping began, then broke up and dwindled as they stared. In the space that surrounded him, Arthur began to perform the Chiung Moon. It was not simply that he kicked or punched or leaped in the pattern he had seen, he also adjusted his step and gait. He dropped his weight, then rose before a lunge almost as if he fell down onto an enemy. All the time, he flowed from one section to the next without hesitation, into patterns of attack and defence and, in the end, attack once more. His balance was superb, slow and fast, even to the final knee-strike and raised horns to strike terror into an enemy. The room was silent then as they stared, confused and somehow afraid.

As the first few moves began, Micahel had spun round on the old man, his eyes accusing. He had spent years learning the steps. How had this boy, this stranger, been given the same knowledge? All Tellius could do was open his hands in complete amazement. The lads of his dormitory of thieves looked to him in astonishment, but he had no answers for them.

Arthur had come to rest on the exact spot where he had begun, the final proof of correct lengths and accurate turns. Tellius could have told him the entire pattern formed the eighth letter of a secret name of God, but he kept his mouth shut. The boy was not of the east. His skin was marbled pale blue under the chin, so pink and sore after his scrubbing that it looked as if he'd spent his life in the sewers. Just about all his tan had been dirt, it seemed.

They still waited for Tellius to speak, while his mind clicked over like glass beads on wires. Even if the boy had been brought nine thousand miles, perhaps as a slave, he would never have been taught the eighth Mazer step. Slaves were not given the means to break chains. They were not even allowed to hold a weapon. No, the steps were for the army.

Tellius thought then of his grandfather, though he dismissed the idea as soon as it had come to him. The children of some high-ranking men were taught young, it was true. Their fathers wanted them to succeed and no law for the common folk could influence a noble father's judgement for his sons. Could the boy he called Arthur be the child of a great house? Yet the coincidence! It was impossible. If such a boy could even exist, what were the chances of him being helped off the street and presented to the one man in Darien who might recognise his training? No, the Goddess did not interfere in men's lives in such a way. Neither did the older god of his homeland, or at least Tellius did not believe he did. He shook his head, clearing it.

'How many of the steps do you know?' he asked Arthur, remembering only as the boy gazed back at him that there would be no answer. Tellius was truly disturbed by what he had seen and gathered his thoughts with difficulty. He recalled the boy's demonstration of juggling from before, the same unbroken concentration and balance, as if he could go on all day.

Tellius stretched out his hand. A small hatchet dropped from his sleeve, appearing in his grip as if by magic. A gasp went round the room, though he saw Arthur's gaze drift to his elbow. Tellius had the disconcerting sense that the boy had seen him release the leather clasp.

'Take this, boy. Throw it at the beam here – and the rest of you might want to shove back a bit further in case it spins into you.'

As he handed the blade to Arthur, the boy looked at it curiously, weighing it slightly with an up-and-down movement of his wrist. He turned and threw as Tellius gestured again, the hatchet whirring through the air and striking handle-first, making one of the boys yell as he threw himself out of its path. The rest of them laughed at that panicked reaction, but also out of relief. There was just something eerie about what they had seen before. It put the world back aright to see the new boy actually fail at something.

'Bring it to me,' Tellius called, never taking his eyes off the boy holding a weapon. The old man gripped the hilt securely as it was returned to him. He removed his shirt then, revealing his skinny frame with its mat of grey hair and faded blue tattoos in a script none of them knew.

'Watch me,' Tellius said, though Arthur's gaze had not wavered. The old man eyed a spot where he had nailed a leather strap to strop his razor in the mornings. He had not thrown a spinning axe in a lot of years, but the old action was there, the release. He rocked back and forth once and then brought his arm down sharply, sending the hatchet out to strike the centre of the strap, piercing the wood beneath.

Almost as one, the boys turned to Arthur to watch his reaction. The boy showed them nothing, though he accepted the handle once it had been wrestled out and handed over.

'Well? What are you waiting for, son? Throw,' Tellius said.

The boy threw and they all let out a held breath of wonder as the axe whirred across the room and stuck in just where the first had gone.

'By the Goddess,' Tellius whispered. 'I have never seen . . . The juggling was the same? You have not juggled before?'

Arthur shook his head slowly, looking uncomfortable.

'Extraordinary. It is more than memory. It is . . . as if you only have to see to have your muscles move in the same way, as if the skill can be stolen . . .' Tellius broke off, his eyes hooding as a thought came to him. There were skills *worth* stealing, if he had a boy who could take them.

Vic Deeds was well known in the legion camp: that was clear enough from the way the guards greeted him with grins and banter, rogues knowing their own. Even so, there was no mistaking their discipline. He and Elias were stopped in two places – first at the outer boundary with its earth ramps and ditches and again at a checkpoint inside. Elias had not dared to believe the gunfighter would keep his word, but he was witness as Deeds strode into a grey tent and whistled for a man twice his age, with a seamed, tanned face and white hair. Elias looked on, winding his hands together until the doctor began to fire a stream of questions at him. When Elias turned his head to show the sort of swollen glands his wife and daughters had, the medical man raised his eyes and half-turned to Deeds.

'You brought an *infected* man into this camp?' he said, incredulously.

'So what if I did? I've had that milk-pox syrup from you. I promised him you'd give him the same.'

'Well, you should not have promised that,' the man snapped. 'Giving someone a syrup of milk pox before they are ill is not at all the same as curing them when they are! Honestly, I'm sure I explained that to you when you were in here for the dose.'

'Either way, he's no danger, is he?' Deeds replied. 'So gentle your tone with me, meneer. Every man here has had the treatment.'

'Still,' the doctor said, pursing his mouth.

Deeds only glared at him and the man gave up his protest, pressing Elias' throat and removing his shirt to see the swellings that had become hard lumps in his armpits. Elias grunted in pain as the doctor probed at those with stiff fingers, nodding and tutting to himself.

Deeds looked up as the doctor reached into a drawer in a field desk and pulled out a bottle and a spoon.

'Did I ask you to dose him?'

'What nonsense is *this* now? Is this a game to you, Deeds? You saw the swellings. He's dead if I don't. Tomorrow or the day after.'

They spoke as if Elias wasn't there listening to them, turning back and forth to hear each man speak.

'Don't worry about it,' Deeds replied with a shrug. 'I told Meneer Post I'd send the medicine to his wife and his girls. Not him. A deal is a deal – a contract under the Goddess. If the general wants him saved, he'll make his own deal. And I think he will, when he sees what I've seen.'

The doctor looked at Elias and then back to Vic Deeds,

seeing the same brand of stubbornness in both of them. He sighed and poured from the larger bottle into a smaller one, sealed with a quick twist of his hand.

'You'll find my house in the village of Wyburn, not three miles from New Cross,' Elias said, babbling the words in his need and hope. 'On Morecombe Street, four doors from the smithy. Ask for Post. Elias Post.'

The doctor nodded and called for a young messenger to take it, repeating directions as they went.

'And that will save them?' Elias said.

'If it's in time, yes,' the doctor replied over his shoulder. 'This sickness responds very well to the ground root in the syrup. It's just a shame the muck is so very expensive, or I'd . . .'

'All right, doc. I've done what I said I would, for his women,' Deeds said. 'Now, Meneer Post. The general.'

The two men crossed a field with hundreds of soldiers moving on foot and horseback, charging and wielding weapons, roaring together in great blasts of sound, plunging pikes into invisible enemies over and over, then racing on. The Immortals had not grown fat and idle in that place, Elias could see. They sprinted up a central hill and clacked and battered staffs in pairs as if they expected a war to begin at any moment. He wondered what fool had poked the ants' nest to have them all running to and fro in such a fashion.

Elias and Deeds were stopped for the third time by the general's tent, where Elias was searched with rough thoroughness. After that, they were told to wait where they stood in the open air. Two pistol-wearing soldiers glared at them, while a third stood just on the edge of Elias' vision with a drawn knife, all but daring them to make a suspicious move.

The sun had appeared above the great earth ramps around

the camp, providing light but no particular warmth on that morning. The air smelled damp and there was a chill to it. Elias glanced at his younger companion more than once, trying to be calm. All he wanted was to go back to the widow's nag and ride home to see the golden medicine delivered. Every one of his hopes were in that small bottle.

Doubts assailed him. Had they been making sport of him? For all he knew, this was something Deeds promised every day to get whatever he wanted, then sent the doctor's boy away with a spoonful of honey in water. Elias tried to put the thought aside, though he could not see how soldiers could be somehow dosed against the plague and yet the king would let his villagers be cut down by it. Even if King Johannes was cruel, the Twelve Families needed men to tend the fields and bring crops in. They needed women to give birth to soldiers and craftsmen and farmers. Perhaps the king hadn't heard about the toll it was taking out in the villages. Perhaps someone had decided it cost too much. Worst of all was the thought that the world might be just so badly organised that a cure could exist and still not reach those who needed it.

It was at least an hour after their arrival that a voice spoke at last to summon them into the tent. A guard stationed inside threw back the flap, holding it for them. Deeds went in without a word and Elias followed, dipping his head though the tent was larger than his house and stretched at least twice his height to the crown, held up by a central post. Within were leather couches and polished wooden tables, with one very neat soldier's bunk against the outer layer of canvas. The tent smelled damp, though a brazier crackled close by the only occupant, casting its warmth and light upon his right arm.

General Justan looked up as they entered, a man with close-cropped hair and deep seams in his face from years of campaigning in all weathers. He smiled slightly to see Deeds, the expression tightening at the stranger in his company.

'I was asking about you just this morning, Meneer Deeds. I felt certain you had duties you were leaving unattended in the camp. I expect to receive orders to march before very long, after all.'

'My place is always at your side, general,' Vic Deeds replied.

Elias shot a glance at him, hearing the same irreverent tone. There was no answering gleam of humour in the general and Elias felt a spasm of panic. He was in some sort of danger and his confusion made it worse.

As Deeds and the foremost military leader of Darien exchanged a few words, Elias felt a sense of pressure building. There was *something* coming, he knew it, felt it on his skin like a wave that would send him tumbling. He looked sharply at Deeds as the man spoke about him. General Justan replied with a wave of his hand, already turning back to his maps and his plans.

'I'm afraid I have no time for games, meneer. Come and see me after lunch. I've had an accusation of corruption by the new pit boss over at Bernard's Crossing. He has imprisoned the old pit boss and awaits judgement. I have an order from the council of Darien to execute him for illegal rebellion against lawful authority. Your talents might be needed to get the mine running again.'

'Or I'll just show you,' Deeds said, as if the general had not spoken.

'No, Deeds!' Elias shouted.

The anger in his voice was enough to bring two of the guards outside running into the tent. A third stepped from invisibility behind a screen with a gun already levelled. Deeds had drawn his pistol but it was pointing away from the general. Even so, the older man turned sharply at Elias' voice and his eyes glittered in fury at what he saw.

'You *dare* to unholster a weapon in my tent, Deeds?'

'Not one that can hurt this man,' Deeds said.

He fired four times and everyone but Elias flinched from the barks of sound. Elias turned and stepped. A bullet was a very small thing. If you knew for certain where it would be, it was not so hard to move a fraction away from it. He found swords much harder to dodge, for all they were slower.

One of the guards stepped up to Deeds and put the cold barrel of his gun against the back of Deeds' neck. He froze at that touch, letting his smoking pistol dangle from his fingers.

'See?' he said. 'He cannot be shot. Take your time, general. Prove it to your own satisfaction. Tell me then if I have wasted your morning! I believe a man who cannot be killed could be of some use to you.'

General Justan stood absolutely still as he thought, his face unnaturally calm. He nodded to those of his men who had trained weapons on his cocksure gunfighter. Deeds had served him well for years, but the general wondered if he knew quite how close he'd come to being shot through for the sake of his demonstration. The men who guarded the general were men of fine judgement, the best in the army. If Deeds had even once moved the tip of his barrel in the general's direction, he would have been dead an instant later. As Justan thought it through, he discerned a wild delight still gleaming in the younger man. He knew then – that Deeds had taken the risk for the sheer joy in it.

Justan shook his head at the follies of young men who believed they could survive anything on charm alone. He gave the private signal to his guards to stand down, just a twitch of fingers behind his back. He was not hostage and Deeds had not betrayed him. The general found he was relieved at that. It would have been a shame to kill him.

With a gesture for them to follow, General Justan strode out into the morning sunshine. Elias looked to Deeds in mounting irritation, but the gunfighter just grinned at him and clapped him on the back, both men knowing he could have avoided it.

'One day of your life, I said, in exchange for the lives of your wife and daughters. That was our bargain, Elias – and a good one for us both. I think you will make another with the general.'

'I will not. As soon as I know Beth and the girls are safe, I will leave . . . this behind.' Elias Post waved his hand in irritation at the huge bustling encampment of the Immortal legion all around them, a city in a wilderness, with roads and smithies and even taverns for the officers, built and dismantled like a child's set of blocks, all to move killing men a few hundred miles safely to a border.

Elias groaned as he felt the pressure begin to build once again. In silence, the general looked into a polished wooden box presented to him, inspecting a pair of new pistols within. They were dark and deadly things, of blued metal with the snub noses of the bullets visible in the cylinder. The pressure increased as the guards spread out, each man careful not to cross a line of fire with the general or one of his companions. Elias smiled sourly at that. Easy enough to do when he was standing still.

Deeds kept his pistol in its holster, low-slung on his belt. He folded his arms instead and stood by the general.

'One day of your life, Elias,' he called. 'And I did not lie about the cure. I am a man of my word.'

Elias barely had time to snarl a curse at him, his words lost in the crash of gunfire that shattered the peace of the camp in smoke and flame.

4

Threefold

It was not a huge surprise to discover she was a thief, though it could yet be amusing. Daw watched from between slitted eyes in the dark, very aware that she had her hand in his bag. No kind of professional then, judging by the rustling. Not the sort to put a knife in his throat and take the whole pack and everything else she could remove from his person either. He'd been ready for that when she'd risen from the bed they'd shared, silent and careful, but not watchful enough to know he held a little razor, like a petal cupped in his hand. If she'd crept round to kill him, he would have surprised her, taught her a lesson. The sort of lesson that was always wasted.

Something jingled as she fumbled deeper in his knapsack. Daw tried not to smile as her shadow froze, the dark-haired girl turning sharply towards him, checking he was still asleep. That sound of coins would have brought him springing up out of the bed anywhere else, but not then. Somewhere in that drawstring pack was a trap he'd bought from his brother that very afternoon, a small and half-sentient thing that actually would teach her a lesson about stealing from sleeping men. Daw could feel himself practically shaking with the guffaw he would make when it sprang to life and sank its teeth into her flesh. Whoever reached into the bag would lose a finger, his brother James had said. Better still, the creature was not fully alive, being made of brass and animated. It needed no special care from the owner, beyond the single word Daw had learned to make it safe. After it had bitten, it would coil up wherever it was thrown, reset itself and be ready for the next time. For Daw Threefold, such a protection would surely be worth the torrent of silvers he had paid.

He opened his eyes a lot wider when Nancy pulled his coin pouch out and held it up to the starlight. He saw a flash of her teeth as she grinned and tucked it inside her blouse. Daw stared in stunned irritation as she shoved her hand back in, right to the bottom of the bag. Where was the scream? He had valuable things in there. If she didn't yelp in the next few moments, he would drag her back to that lying brother of his and demand . . . He raised his head. There was not much light in the room, but Daw could see Nancy was holding up a lizard, cast in brass. He'd seen that Goddess-cursed useless thing creeping about on the worktop in the shop earlier that day, its tiny spiked feet rattling on the glass and mahogany. Of course it had failed. His brother had a weakness for deals, for fast-talking salesmen who sold him brass and called it gold, every damned time. Threefold clenched his jaw and his fists, feeling the petal dagger's blunt side press into his palm.

With a lunge, he sprang off the bed, wrapping his arm around her throat and letting her feel the warm pressure of the knife. He found he was panting after so long controlling his breath. Daw turned it into a chuckle of relief as he tightened his grip.

'Now what sort of girl steals from her lover?' he said into her ear.

'One who has no money, usually,' Nancy answered. Her

voice was calm and matter-of-fact, as if he did not hold a razor's edge against her throat.

'You don't know how lucky you are not to be screaming at this very moment. I have a few trinkets in that bag to ward against thieves. One of them should have had your hand off. Did you know I've been watching you? I was just waiting for the lizard to bite, but it seems I was sold a fake.'

'You are the fool then,' she said. 'Magic's a game – for children and the gullible. For the mugs on the street. You're not a child. Are you one of those poor fools? Let me go and perhaps you've learned something that will change your life, Daw Threefold. Magic? It's all lies.'

He blinked at that, shaking his head. Despite his irritation, her claim was so outlandish that he wanted to prove it wrong. His uncle had told him once that people were more willing to believe big lies than small ones, but this was ridiculous.

He sat back away from her.

'You were lucky, Nancy, that's all. On any other night, you'd have lost a finger. You live in Darien, by the Goddess! We have streets of apothecaries – all with something to catch the eye in the windows. You must have seen *something* magical, some item or some spell you could not explain away.'

'You have streets of fakery – and I grew up on the other side of the city, where we don't hold with such things.' She took a deep breath, as if it hurt her to speak. 'In the rookeries along the river, all right? We don't see fine magic displays around Fiveway or Red Corners. I saw a firebreather once, but he was dribbling down his chin, so I could see it wasn't nothing magical. And I lived with a juggler for a month, though he was more a storyteller and pickpocket, if

47

I'm honest. No magic in either of them, not if you don't count the way they could separate fools from their money. I am not a fool, Daw! I am not a punter like all the fine families strolling along the ring road, taking in a show and talking about wine and . . . all that.'

He looked at Nancy then almost in concern. A slight flush had come over her as she spoke and she waved her hands. It was as if the delicate, laughing flower he'd met the previous evening had been nothing more than a creation, a part she had played.

'Look,' he began.

She shook her head.

'I don't know where you grew up, though you have that confidence that comes from always knowing you'll be fed. I don't resent it, Daw. The world *should* be like that, for everyone. But it isn't. Perhaps you think the city is a place where the law counts for all and the Twelve Families spend sleepless nights worrying about the poor folk in the rookeries.'

'You don't know where I grew up,' he said. She raised her head, waiting. He blushed slightly. 'Yew Street, by the running track.'

'How you must have suffered, Daw. I didn't realise.'

'There were gangs there, you know.'

'No, Daw. Gangs are people who terrify you and cut you. They run the streets around Fiveway – and they don't go near the fancy places. You have no idea, really.'

He frowned at her, irritated that he felt the desire to prove he'd grown up in poverty, which he hadn't. His mother and father owned their home, even if the paper was peeling and they'd seen a rat once. He suspected if he mentioned it, Nancy would counter with some awful story about eating them.

'If your rookeries are such a delight, why are you on this side of the river?' he said.

'I came over when the fever was running through the docks. Too many dead bodies and no one to clear them away. I didn't see much magic there then, with children lying in the sun, and the flies buzzing around them.' She shuddered, her gaze turning inward. 'I thought it would be cleaner in this part of the city – and I was right, too. They don't let the bodies lie for as long anyway, not around here. I work hard for Basker and he doesn't touch, which makes a change. If I see a young man I like, perhaps I'll let him buy my drinks and sweep me away for a night. I'm not complaining, Daw. You were much slower the second time.'

Daw stared at her. It seemed rude to be still brandishing his knife, so he began to clean his nails with it.

'You must have seen magic, though . . .' he went on doggedly, determined to make her admit it.

Nancy sighed.

'I don't waste my money up in the high streets, Daw. Where a sticky bun would cost me a day's wage? You'll be lucky. I save every coin and one day I'll have enough to buy a room or two somewhere, all because I did.' She clamped her mouth shut on the last words, as if she'd gone too far in revealing herself.

To his irritation, she leaned forward and rested her hand on his arm, speaking slowly as if he was the deluded party.

'Punters lose their purses every day, gaping at some street magician. It's all tricks. Tricks of the hand and eye only,' she said. 'Shall I make a coin vanish for you? I can do that. Learned it from a kid.'

As he watched, she held up a coin and moved her hands over it, finally pointing to one hand with the other and opening both. It was quite well done. She looked utterly calm and faintly pitying. Daw found he wanted to persuade her, if only to dispel what he realised was a full-blown fantasy. As a public service, perhaps, or because he really, *really* wanted her to understand, that he was right and she was wrong.

He could think of three ways without moving from that spot. Daw smiled, putting his knife in a pocket and pulling his knapsack closer. He tapped the bulge of another canvas pocket on the outside.

'I can show you magic, Nancy. If I do, I will expect an apology.'

He was about to undo the ties when he hesitated. Could this have been her game all along? To make him reveal his most powerful objects? Well, by the golden teats, that would have included the biting lizard. He'd paid his brother a fortune for it, after all. As she sat and looked at him with one eyebrow raised, he held out his hand, pointing to her blouse. She fished it out from the depths and handed it back.

Nervous at first in case it sprang to life, then with a deepening frown, Daw felt only the stillness and heft of a piece of inert metal. He rapped it sharply on the bedpost, then sat back cross-legged to drop it into the main body of his knapsack.

'Nancy, I would have turned you out with my heartfelt thanks this morning – and perhaps enough coin for a good meal. Darien can be a hard old place to make a living – and believe me, I have been down just as far and at least as often as I've been up. If you had been straight with me, I would have seen you right. Instead, you tried to rob me – and by the way, you'll return that pouch hidden in your blouse as well unless you want me to take it back. Come on. Don't make me show you the petal again.'

'Show me the magic first,' Nancy replied, patting her open blouse where the coin purse had slid down. 'And I have a knife too, Daw. You caught me by surprise before, but I'll trim your ears for you if you try it again. Still . . .' She hesitated and in the starlight Daw thought how young she looked. 'I've always wondered. I've seen the witches and apothecaries, the charms so many people carry – and they all seem to believe in it, but all the while I know it's just a lie. A great lie that perhaps no one ever challenges because if they did, the whole city would come crashing down.'

'If I show you something magic, will you give me my pouch back?' Daw asked. His mum had always said he was weak on negotiation. He felt he'd somehow lost the advantage in the conversation, but still, he had a magic item she wouldn't be able to deny, and while she stared at it, he'd have his knife back out. He hadn't enjoyed the comment about trimming his ears for him.

'I will, Daw. And I can say that, 'cause I know I won't have to. You have yourself a deal. Show me magic and get back your purse . . .'

'My pouch, Nancy. It's not a purse.'

'. . . or fail and let me keep it,' she finished, putting out her hand as if to shake on a deal.

Daw shook hands with a pained expression. Not that it would matter in the end.

'Light the lamp and run the wick high then, love. I think I have something that will expand your mind.'

The lamp was still warm and there was a steel and flint box chained to the dresser. Nancy spun the wheel with her thumb and blew on a spark in the pouch of tinder until she had a taper lit and then the oil wick, filling the room with golden light.

Daw looked up at that, sighing to himself at the slim figure she made. She sat facing him on the only chair in the room, crossing her feet at the ankles like a fine lady and leaning over them to rest her elbows on her knees. He could not help smiling at her seriousness. He even gestured, flourishing in the air, pointing to the two objects he had removed from his pack. One was just a small box, decorated in gold and onyx. The other was a sheathed dagger, no longer than his thumb, but worth more than everything else he owned put together, just about. He thought he could have bought that tavern and half a dozen homes around it for the price he would receive for that particular blade. It was the reason he had spent another small fortune on a pointless guard lizard that did absolutely nothing of use.

'Oh my dear, my darling Nancy, you have come to the right man tonight. Perhaps you look at me and see merely a dashing adventurer . . .'

'Perhaps,' Nancy murmured.

Daw stopped speaking long enough to grimace in her direction, knowing she made sport of him.

'. . . which I certainly am. Yet in these past few years since my eighteenth birthday, I have become a very connoisseur of magic. An expert in . . .'

'A "very" connoisseur?' she said, smiling. 'I don't think that is the right way to say it. You can be very brave, or very handsome . . .'

'And I am both of those – and yet impatient. Do not forget, Nancy, that I could have cried "thief" as soon as I saw you reaching into my bag. You would have lost your job here, let me tell you. Basker doesn't allow thieves in his place. Instead, I am here, doing you a favour and answering your life's great question, once and for all. If you will consider my extraordinary patience and not interrupt me every second word, you will perhaps learn something.'

The last was said in peevish style and she settled back and folded her arms at him.

'Very well, Daw, I will not interrupt again.'

'I should think not.' He picked up the box and held it before her. 'This was made by a blessing, so I was told. The magic is set into the stones and has lasted for . . . three years now. It will be about a dozen before I have to bring it in for repair.'

Nancy leaned forward, her eyes reflecting the gleam of the lamp.

'And what does it do?' she asked in a breath.

Daw found he was enjoying her complete attention and briefly wondered if the earlier part of the evening was at an end or, like the lamp, could yet be rekindled. He resolved to be pleasant, just in case.

'It is much like a compass, though it will point towards a particular man, with just a drop of his blood. I have used it many times and it has never let me down.'

'You track men, Daw?' she asked.

He shrugged, modestly.

'I do many things. And I have many ways to do them. Sometimes, those I follow are not kind enough to leave me a scrape of their blood and then I have a few other tricks. But this finder will face its quarry no matter which way I turn it. Here, give me your hand.'

Nancy held out her hand easily, though she hissed and

drew back when he touched her with a pin drawn from his lapel. Grumbling under her breath, she squeezed the fingertip until a bead showed red and bright. Daw smeared it with his own finger and flipped open the box, revealing a tiny golden disc with what looked almost like a sail in the same metal, spinning idly on some arrangement of gimbals below. Nancy looked at it in pleasure, knowing that it was a fine piece even without the lies and tales. She watched as Daw touched the tip of the sail with her blood and then held it up in something like triumph, turning the box this way and that while she watched him and wondered if she should run for the door or risk the sash window being jammed.

'Wait . . . no. Look, it is turning . . . no!' Daw fumbled with the box, opening and shutting the lid and tapping it with the side of his hand.

'Yes, I see it turning,' she said, unimpressed. 'It's a pretty thing, Daw.'

'It doesn't work! It doesn't turn the way it should!' he said, truly distressed and for the first time touched by panic. He hardly dared look at the knife he had laid out.

'Goddess, I have to know . . .' he said.

He tossed the box over his shoulder as if it was worthless, reaching for the sheath. Nancy froze as he drew the blade, curved and short and wickedly sharp. The hilt ended with an inch of polished ivory or bone. A single letter gleamed there in dark yellow resin, like an ancient ink stamp. To Nancy's astonishment, she thought she saw colours flicker along the length of the weapon, purple and gold and enough to elicit a cry of relief from Daw Threefold, before the cruel-looking blade went dark and the colours faded back to grey iron.

As she watched, he dragged the blade across the bed-clothes, leaving a crease.

'Oh Goddess, what have you *done*?' Threefold whispered to her. 'It's you, isn't it?' His eyes searched hers and she saw betrayal and true anger in them. 'How are you doing this?'

'I saw the colours, Daw,' Nancy said. She shifted position subtly, ready to leap up and run or defend herself if the wild man holding a dagger suddenly lunged at her. She had not lied about her own knife. It pressed still against the small of her back.

Daw's mouth opened and closed as he stared at the dull blade.

'The colours?' he whispered. 'They were nothing. This knife . . . it can cut through *anything*, Nancy. Or it could, before. Stone, iron, bone – anything at all, with a firm push and a bit of muscle. It has saved my life . . .' He looked up and his eyes were hard. 'It *is* you, isn't it?'

'You blame me for your fancy things breaking?' she said.

Her legs bunched on the chair and she edged forward, her left hand ready to reach behind. Daw was paler than she had ever seen him, but also colder. There was no sign of the grinning young man who had been easy with his flattery and his boasting earlier that evening. Instead, he looked at her and held the knife upright, as if he could not quite decide whether to stick her with it or throw it across the room like the compass.

When Nancy moved, it was just as he looked away. If he'd hesitated even a single heartbeat, she would have been across the room and out of the door before he could catch her. Yet he had given her the opportunity deliberately and moved to block even as she came out of the chair. She flinched away from the blade then, turning straight into a left-hand cross that crashed against the side of her head, leaving her unconscious on the wooden floor.

Daw's eyes widened as he saw she'd been knocked cold. It was not his finest moment, though he didn't care in that instant, not really. The rawness of his loss consumed him.

Slowly, he sat back down on the bed and rubbed his jaw with his bruised hand. In the other, he was still holding the knife he had stolen from a dead man's home, risking his life to get in. The old man had been a famous collector, the unmarried youngest son of House Saracen. Daw had raced across Darien to loot his home before anyone else thought of it. He'd nearly been caught even then, almost breaking his ankle getting out. He'd escaped just as guards of the Saracen estate secured the property, one of his earliest and most enjoyable adventures. They had never even reported the theft.

With a glum expression, he tried to saw the end of the bed with the Saracen blade and watched as it barely scratched the wood. The knife had been in a glass case in the very centre of a room in that old mansion. With house guards blowing whistles outside, he'd smashed the glass and grabbed for it, just hoping it would be worth his while. It had been. The mark on the hilt showed what it was: one of the twelve great treasures of Darien.

He'd never dared sharpen it, for fear of ruining whatever spell had been used in its creation. It was surprisingly blunt as he drew it back and forth. Without the magic, he might use it to slice through a loaf of bread perhaps, but not much else. He slumped. That little blade had been given pride of place for a reason. It had been Daw's secret advantage in the city.

In his world, things could go wrong in an instant. When they did, it was usually a short and violent disagreement. Men like himself sometimes had to draw a good weapon when they were threatened; that was just the price of doing business in Darien. Three times he'd been cornered over the years. Twice when he was where he should not have been, the last by a competitor. On all three occasions, he'd cut his way out, literally. The knife had saved him and he had a reverence for it. Seeing it dead and grey was like losing a good friend.

His eyes widened. What if it was a local effect? As soon as the thought registered, he was desperate to find out, his heart tripping hard in his chest. He glanced down at Nancy's unconscious form and muttered a curse. He could not let her just slip away when she woke. Whatever was going on, whatever had happened to his knife and his blood-dial – and to his lizard bag protector – it needed more measured consideration, no matter what he intended. He drew his spare bootlaces from his knapsack and tied her hands and feet with quick efficiency.

He closed the door to his room behind him as he came out. He couldn't lock it from the outside and he winced at the thought of all the other things in his pack. Darien was a great city, both a joy and a riot, at least as full of life as a leg of pork left too long in the sun. It was not a forgiving place, however, not of mistakes. There was always someone willing to leave you in the gutter, delighted to have had a better day than you. Perhaps he had grown up in Yew Street, on the nice side by the running track. Perhaps he had eaten jam and bread for tea each day and had two loving parents. It had not made him soft, he was certain.

Daw ran then, loping along the corridor and down the

steps to the main floor of the tavern, passing a dozen cramped tables jammed in to give as many punters seats as possible, then out of the door to the street while old Basker shouted about paying his bill behind him.

Every twenty or thirty paces, Daw stopped and jammed the Saracen knife against some post or along the side of a passing wagon. Even in his distress, he was not such a fool as to reveal the Family sigil of the hilt, not on a public street. He kept that hidden in his palm as he struck out with it.

Early as it was, he still drew some strange looks and left two annoyed carters shouting after him as he went on. Yet it might as well have been a spoon for all the damage it did. The effect looked permanent and hope shrivelled in his chest as he turned at last and trudged back. In that moment, he could have killed her for what she had taken from him. He wore seven charms on his person that morning. He could feel the dead weight of them as he wandered along, made cold and empty.

'Threefold! I thought you'd run off!' Basker called as he came back into the taproom, already growing crowded.

Daw always stayed in the Old Red Inn whenever he was in Darien. It was clean enough and quiet. Basker was ex-infantry and a good man in a pinch, though he didn't believe in credit and seemed to react to the idea as if he'd been asked to join a new religion. Daw shrugged at him, then paused with one hand running along the polished wood of the bar. Basker hadn't waited for his answer, having gone back to taking orders and bawling them through to his wife in the back as she sizzled eggs with small pieces of shell and burned strips of meat in the tiny kitchen. It wasn't even full light outside, but Basker's place was near the city wall and Daw knew the farmers liked to set out before the sun was up, to make the most of it. He sighed, thinking of the young woman in the room overhead who had taken so very much. A great sense of sadness and loss stole over him, like an odour of spices.

Daw Threefold had not been born to real money in Yew Street, no matter what Nancy thought. His parents hadn't had enough to pay for proper schooling, though he'd learned his letters and some history from a lodger one year. At twenty-four, Daw was not a wealthy man, but he had turned years of work and a fair skill for thieving into valuable pieces, all small enough to be carried on his person. All powerful enough to aid him in the getting of more. He had been on his way to a small fortune and a complete lack of fame when a single night of roistering with Nancy had set him back to his eighteenth birthday, just about. Without his coins, without his knife or his compass or his charms, he had very little to show for six years in the city, beyond a few scars and the tip of one finger gone. It was heartbreaking, and he looked up as the tavern clock chimed.

Daw grew still then, seeing the clock Basker had been given on his retirement. It was just a painted face that hung from a silver chain off a roof beam, perhaps the height of a man above the bar. You could see such a thing in any market, with a tiny blessing charm on the crystal behind. It kept good time and showed hands as lines of light that glowed but did not burn. Daw had glanced up at it a hundred times before, whenever Basker called last orders, though never with such complete attention as he did then. It was a magical item, admittedly cheap and tawdry, no sort of reward for a twenty-year man like Basker. Yet it swung in the same building as Nancy – and it still worked. Local effect. Had to be.

With one swift move, Daw leaped onto the bar, jumping up and snatching the swinging clock from its nail. Basker gave a great roar of confusion and rising anger as Daw scrambled down with it held to his chest and raced back across the tavern, staring at the clock hands as he went. The door to his room was perhaps some dozen paces away and a flight of stairs above.

5

Levers

Elias looked through the bars, resting his hands on the door-lock. He did not know how long he'd been asleep, though he felt better than he had in a while. The small cage that held him stood like an upright coffin on the vast camp field, just about big enough for a man, with room to sit down only if he pulled his legs up or put them through the bars. He could at least look out on the bustle and smoke of the encampment, with all the soldiers around him apparently intent on ignoring his presence.

Elias made an exasperated sound. It seemed that the commanding officer of the Immortals was a clever man. General Justan had hesitated only long enough to blink. When the sound of gunfire had died and Elias was still upright, the general had snapped an order that surprised those in the circle of Immortal soldiers almost as much as Elias himself. 'Hold hands' was not the kind of thing a Darien general usually roared at his men, but they'd done it even so. Elias had found himself at the centre of an unbroken ring.

In his heart, Elias thought he could have won free – men holding hands like children could not defend themselves. One thumb to an eye or a sharp kick at a kneecap, and the circle would have broken, enough for him to slip out. If he'd been in good health, he might have done it just to spite them, just to show they couldn't hold him. He didn't like being hemmed in and surrounded. Elias preferred the open land or the deep forest, where he could breathe.

Yet they'd made him *reach* more with their gunfire in those few moments than in a season of hunting. Elias had already been ill – and about weary enough to just lie down and die. He had let them make their circle and think they'd caught him. That much he remembered. He'd heard the general calling for the doctor, and then Elias had either fallen or fainted – he had no memory of it.

He realised his bladder was full and that he was both hungry and very thirsty. The sun was rising and he assumed he'd slept a whole night, recovering. With trembling hands, Elias touched the places on his skin where he had felt welts before. They were definitely smaller, but also different somehow, so that he sensed the poison had been drawn. The itching had certainly lessened and the lumps in his armpits felt softer, though one had burst and dribbled a foul-smelling slick down the inside of his coat. Even so, he was on the mend, he was certain of it. It was the difference between being consumed from the inside out and just being nauseous and weak. He began to hope. If they valued him enough to cure him, perhaps they'd also kept their word over Beth and the girls.

That thought brought a wave of dizziness that made him cling to the bars. He had been resigned to losing just about everything when he'd staggered from the tavern in Wyburn. Some part of him had accepted he was finished, his last card played. To find himself alive, once more with hopes, was almost too painful. He let the bars hold him up and Elias suddenly wept for his son Jack as if a wound had been pulled open. No, it was worse. A wound would not have made him weep.

A troop of soldiers crossing the field looked over at the sobbing man, but Elias did not see them. After a time, the fit of grief passed and he could breathe slowly once again, without shuddering.

The sun had risen halfway up the sky by the time he realised they were coming for him. Vic Deeds was unmistakable, even at a distance. A good hunter studied the gait and shape of everyone he met, just as Elias learned the members of a wolf pack and could identify one he knew from far off. It was strange to feel liking for the gunman in that moment of recognition. Elias shook his head at his own weakness just as soon as he understood it. Vic Deeds was the only man he knew in that vast camp, that was true. Yet the gunman was not a friend. Deeds would sell him for a penny if he needed one. For that matter, perhaps he already had.

'Good morning, meneer,' Deeds said cheerfully, stopping before the cage. 'I must admit, I thought you might not make it, you were so sick.' The gunman leaned right in and peered at him. 'The general would have had my skin if you'd died, after what we showed him.'

He gestured to the cage door. One of the soldiers put a key to the lock and Deeds raised his hand to stop him, watching Elias all the while.

'You wear your thoughts on your face, meneer, do you know that? Even with that strange thing you can do, I don't think cards are your game, not really. How can I let you out, knowing you can slip past a dozen men, eh? No, no. If we let you out, we can't stop you just walking home, can we? Even with all our guns and swords and arrows.'

'Maybe,' Elias said. 'Let's find out.'

Deeds laughed.

'A cage, though – that works well enough, doesn't it? You can't dodge bars or see which way they are going to step . . . ?' He watched carefully. Elias tried to keep his features still, though the man was reading him anyway and smiled. 'That's *it*, isn't it? The general was right then, the clever old sod. You can see a small piece of what will happen. It explains the cards – and even the bullets. But how *long* ahead? That's the key to it, isn't it? How far can you look? What if someone chooses to step the other way? Can they do that?'

Elias stared back in silence, irritated by the man and his chatter. He sensed a cruelty still in Deeds, or a coldness. He'd seen it in hunters a few times and it had served them well for the most part. There was not much room for sentiment when they were out alone. Not much room for mercy.

Deeds tapped a thick iron bar with his knuckle.

'General Justan was impressed, you know. He said, "Find a cage to hold him, Deeds." Just like that. This box won't do, though, will it? You're no good to us trapped. Ah, you don't like that idea, do you? I'm sorry then, because I had to trap you. You're just too useful. I saw it in the tavern and the general knows it now. He'll find a use for you, believe it. And he'll find the right cage as well.' For a moment, Deeds looked at his feet and Elias had the sense he was ashamed. 'I am sorry about that part.'

Elias looked around in confusion as Deeds nodded to the men with him. They took hold of the cage, tipping it up and lifting it and the man inside with grunts and curses. Deeds waited until they had it steady. Elias had clung to the bars at first, then settled down and sat in grim silence.

'Onward,' Deeds said. 'The general has a plan for this one.'

*

Tellius had fetched his best jacket and trousers to stand at the Masters' Court. It was true his widest leather belt and huge old overcoat hid holes eaten by moths. It was also true one of his boots had come away at the seam, though it was not obvious when he stood still. It had been a long time since Tellius had concerned himself with any sort of public display, and he thought he could feel the sneers of rich men and women, making him want to rub a hand over the bristles on his chin. It was ridiculous, he knew it. In his own home and his own streets, he was like a king, but in this wealthy quarter, where true noblemen brought their sons to show or be shown, he half-expected a hand on his shoulder and a boot in his rear at any moment.

The one he had named Arthur showed no sign of nervousness, of course. Another scrubbing and some old clothes from Tellius' store of 'best used' revealed a boy who might have been almost respectable. Yet Arthur had kept that peculiar stillness and watchfulness about him. Tellius smiled inside, though no trace of levity made it to his features. The boy Arthur was a mystery and he did not like those. He might also have been a gift from the Goddess, for a man who had the wit to see a chance when it came. Tellius was that man. He raised his head and applauded with the others when Master Aurelius stepped onto the rush-covered square.

'Watch him,' Tellius murmured, leaning down.

He did not need to say it. Aurelius was an arresting figure and always had been. Even at fifty, with more white than black in his hair, the man moved extraordinarily well. There were perhaps a dozen in Darien city who might have recognised the source of that grace. Three of them were students to Aurelius himself, his 'Master Pupils' as he called them. Six made up the king's personal guards, graduates of that very school. The last two were Tellius himself and his own pupil, Micahel, who was at least the match of any of the rich men's brats Aurelius had taught. Perhaps. The truth was that Aurelius taught much more than the Mazer steps, however he described them. The man truly was a master swordsman and had studied the skill like a science, reading the thoughts of others and even writing two books of his own on the subject. Tellius had bought and read both of them. In return for his service, the king had given Aurelius the property now open to the public for just one day a month, the rent paid by the performance they would witness.

Tellius watched Aurelius limber up, his movements crying out 'Mazer steps' to anyone who knew them. It brought back Tellius' past. He closed his eyes and saw the emperor's personal guard in armour of black and white enamelled iron, in balance, moving like smoke across the ancient Hall of Saints. Tellius breathed slowly as the memory grew bright before his inner eye. The columns of polished mahogany as tall as forest trees in dark red, the lines of warriors smearing shapes over a glass-polished floor. The smell of incense and wax. His people. His youth. Tellius had wanted nothing more than to be one of that elite number. His grandfather had wanted the same. It was an old ache and an entire life lost in one foolish day. He could not go back. The order paper of his execution had been issued, but never marked with his blood. Though it had been almost forty years, Tellius had no doubt there would be a dozen men setting out on the long journey to Darien if they ever heard he was still alive.

He opened his eyes at a cheer from the crowd. Hundreds of men and women had come to watch, some of them so young it made Tellius wince to feel his own age. Many years before, when Aurelius had first rented rooms above an old horse yard and advertised sword classes, he had struggled to keep his creditors from the door. With an empty purse, Aurelius had come up with the idea of a public display to drum up students, like any other tradesman showing his wares.

For an audience of just a few locals, he'd demonstrated the use of two swords and a dozen other weapons. He'd impaled beef carcasses borrowed from a slaughterhouse and climbed walls at a run. When Aurelius had trained a couple of students, they had made a regular performance of it, laughing and leaping, cutting thrown fruit in mid-air. The performance eventually became a fixture in the city calendar, until the tickets were prized and given as gifts. Royal approval had made the school the best-known in Darien.

Tellius felt his eyebrows lower. Aurelius had always been a showman, prancing about like a damned minstrel. He had sold his mastery like any other skill – like a great musician teaching chords to tin-eared children. Tellius wanted to believe the king's Master of Swords could not feel the music beyond those simple steps, but the truth was different. In every city, there will be one who is faster than the rest, just as there will be one who is slowest, or a danger only to themselves. When the skill is valued and admired, there might arise a swordsman whose balance is superb, who can make judgements of life and death in the blink of an eye, so that opponents can only hack and swish like farmers until he puts a sword through their hearts. Aurelius was that master,

Tellius admitted it. The old man knew he could never have beaten him, not even when he had been arrogant enough to confront the man after his very first demonstration bout, twenty years before.

That was a darker, more disturbing memory. Tellius tried to concentrate on the somersaults and leaps Aurelius made, moving at great speed through the equipment until he was gleaming with sweat. Tellius had still been young enough to forget his caution back then. When he'd seen the younger man perform the sixth Mazer step flawlessly, the small crowd had cheered but Tellius had been filled with soaring indignation. Who was this usurper to have stolen such knowledge? He'd barely held his anger in control until the traders had all filed out and Aurelius had come past him, laughing with one of his servants.

Tellius grimaced as he recalled what had followed. His demands, his humiliation. In his fury, he had struck the younger man. In return, the young Aurelius had held him helpless over a post and beaten his buttocks with a scabbard. Tellius felt the heat of embarrassment rise in him once more. He had not been back to the school since that day and it had taken years for Aurelius' laughter not to come to mind when he closed his eyes.

Perhaps that was why he had begun teaching his lads the Mazer steps. Age had borne him down and he'd needed to mend his wind, that was true. He could hardly have practised in the attic without the boys seeing and asking questions. Still, it had been an old ache, a scar in him to know there was another in the city who had come from the east – or been taught by one who had. Tellius had never been completely sure. It had helped ease that discomfort to walk the boys through the steps of his youth, one by one, getting faster and more sure himself as it came back to him. The years had flown and he'd hardly even known that the memory of his humiliation still hurt, until it had begun to fade.

Yet there he was, back once again. He wondered if he'd learned anything at all. Was he not there to spite the man? To bring him down a peg or two? It was a petty fantasy and Tellius knew he was not a petty man, except for this one arrogant little . . . He closed his eyes again, seeking calm.

On the open square, Aurelius had brought out his three students, two young men and a woman. As one, the crowd leaned in at the sight. There was nothing so attractive in male or female as the lithe grace and fitness of a trained killer. Tellius knew that well. It was almost like watching big cats at play as they leaped and struck and spun for the delight of the crowd.

They did not smile, he was pleased to see. They were not entertainers or circus tumblers, but warriors with blades to open someone up. Tellius looked away only once to see if Arthur was watching closely. He was, his gaze unwavering, so that Tellius allowed himself a small smile.

The king's rent required a demonstration of Darien martial skill, with at least one master coming from the school every few years. The rest was mere show for the crowd, though Tellius had certainly paid a small fortune for his chit to stand where he could see. All the talk of war in the markets had almost doubled the price. It was a good time to be teaching the skills of the swordsman, all in all. Tellius saw royal-liveried guards on the balcony above, standing back from sight but no doubt delighted at the chance to watch for free what others had to purchase.

A drum roll ended the performance and Tellius watched

69

sourly as the three students raised their arms to indicate their master, like actors calling a director onto a stage. Aurelius came out once more in stern dignity, bowing to their crackle of applause. Tellius hated him and felt himself flush again at the memory of the man's blows. He stood still as the crowd began to push out of the open doors to the courtyard and the city beyond. In that way, Tellius made himself a stone in a moving stream. He felt the flicker of Aurelius' gaze sweep over him, trained to spot threat in any form. Tellius looked up, meeting eyes he had not seen for twenty years. As if it was nothing, as if to a servant, Tellius gestured for him to come over. He looked away then, knowing it would irritate a man of Aurelius' pride to be summoned in such a way. Tellius leaned down to the boy at his side.

'Did you see all that he showed you?'

Arthur nodded. Tellius stood up straight and almost recoiled at the swordmaster suddenly standing in front of him. He had not heard Aurelius approach and he felt his face grow red.

'I know you, don't I?' Aurelius said. 'Is it you, old man? The one I put over my knee for insulting my home?'

'You did *not* put me . . .' Tellius began, mastering himself too late. Aurelius laughed at his reaction. Prods and pokes with every word, that was his style. The man was infuriating and Tellius thought he had never known a more unpleasant enemy.

'You've not aged well, old fellow,' Aurelius said. 'Eh? Can you hear me? I said you've not aged well.'

'And you have not yet learned courtesy,' Tellius said, standing as straight as he could.

'You're not the one to teach it to me, old man. So what are you here for?'

Tellius saw Aurelius' eyes flicker down to where Arthur watched with that unnerving intensity.

'I wanted my . . . pupil to see the sword used with competence, the influence of Mazer steps on your style.'

'Oh yes! That was what you said last time. "Mazer steps." Still eating you up inside, is it? Well, I'll tell you today what I said then. I don't discuss my methods with anyone.'

'Come along, Arthur. He is not the man he used to be,' Tellius said, putting his hand to the boy's shoulder.

'Your pupil, is it?' Aurelius said. He had gone pale around the lips at Tellius' words, but he smiled even so. 'Shall I judge what you've taught him? Is that what you want, lad?'

He said the last to Arthur, but Tellius answered for him, his pride making him foolish.

'Perhaps it *would* be an amusement to show you. You know, Aurelius – all this? It's very impressive. But it is not the only school in Darien.'

'Is that so? Come on then, boy,' Aurelius said to Arthur. 'Step into my parlour and show me what you've been taught.'

Arthur climbed over the low wall that ran around the square. There were still a few people lingering behind, hoping for a word with a favourite, or perhaps even the master himself. They perked up at the sight of the small boy standing on the rushes and sawdust in the centre. Aurelius tossed him a sword and at that, his three pupils stopped their quiet conversation and came over, sitting on the wall to watch. Tellius settled himself with great care, though his heart was thumping and he could smell camphor and sweat rising from his old clothes.

Aurelius took up another of the practice blades from a rack and swished the air with it as he watched the boy.

'Well, old man? What will you have him show me?'

'Arthur? If you please, show Master Aurelius what you have learned today.'

Tellius deliberately stifled a yawn when he finished speaking, though he was trembling with excitement. He watched as Arthur began to move and his heart leaped. It was like the moment in the old workshop once again, though at least he had that memory to prepare him.

A man's style with a sword is unique, though most never know it. It is created by the flex of their muscle, the strength of their bones, the range of movement in their joints. It becomes a part of them that can be recognised long before a signature move or a particular way of standing. What Aurelius saw was his own style, reflected back at him, a mirror of his grace. He had never seen it before, of course, so he did not recognise it immediately, only that it looked oddly familiar. His eyebrows rose and he narrowed his eyes as the small boy reproduced every move the master had made inside the square that day. Every turn and twitch of muscle, every leap and spinning blow.

Tellius watched Arthur for a few steps. After that, he watched Aurelius, just waiting in delight for the man to know his life's work had been stolen away from him. For all Aurelius' arrogance, for all his taunts and sneers, he truly was the most gifted Master of Swords Tellius had ever seen, up to that morning. Yet all his decades of honed skill were being reproduced on those rushes, by a whirling, leaping boy.

Tellius glanced at Arthur as the boy jumped from one foot and turned completely in the air, whipping round and landing with such perfect balance it drew every eye in envy. Tellius began to sweat, suddenly aware of the focus of each man and woman around him, all on the boy.

It was time to go. He had been given his moment and he could happily leave the school and Aurelius behind and never think of the place again except with satisfaction. He had lanced his boil, his humiliation. Yet he did not like the intensity of the expressions around him.

Tellius felt the weight of the black iron pistol under his coat and hoped they would be allowed out. There was something deeply unnerving about the concentration in both the boy Arthur, and the master watching him.

The three students were staring with their mouths open. They knew Aurelius' style better than he did himself, having witnessed it a thousand times. Tellius saw that same recognition come at last to Aurelius. The swordsman's cheeks grew pale suddenly, as if the blood had been sucked away within. Arthur spun and darted, faster and faster.

'Enough now,' Tellius called.

He saw Arthur come to a stop. The boy was panting and his eyes were bright, but otherwise Arthur faded somehow, as if a light had been turned off. The boy came to stand by Tellius, waiting patiently.

Aurelius looked up and something in his gaze made Tellius remember how easily the man had beaten him before. Age had not made Tellius any faster or stronger in the twenty years since. That was why he had brought the gun.

'What have you *done*, old man?' Aurelius said. There was no more levity or mockery in his voice. It was an ugly, threatening thing. 'Who *is* this boy?'

'Just one of my lads, Master Aurelius,' Tellius said.

He had no more appetite for their bantering conversation. He had knocked the man's confidence and salved his own. He had been a fool for his pride, that was the truth of it. All he wanted at that moment was to get out with Arthur and his own skin intact. Tellius cursed himself, wanting to clench his fists in despair at his own foolishness. All those years of being careful and he had acted like a boy, forgetting all caution! The delight he had felt at first seemed pitiful when compared to the threat he saw then in Aurelius.

'You have *stolen* from me, old man,' Aurelius said.

It was such an outrageous accusation that Tellius forgot himself for an instant.

'What? *You* are the thief! I see Mazer steps in your style, and where did you learn those if not my homeland? Who taught you, eh?'

When Aurelius spoke again, it was with slow menace, his patience gone.

'Come here, then, old man. Show me these wonderful steps. And I will spill your blood for you.'

There was so much anger in the Master of Swords that Tellius felt his own temper vanish like ice before the sun. He hesitated, but Aurelius did not, stepping forward with appalling speed and grabbing Tellius' coat in a two-handed grip, dragging him over the wall into the square.

Tellius had not been handled in such a way since the last time he had stood in that very place. He heard only a roaring in his ears and he pulled the gun and levelled it at his tormentor. One of the pupils cried out, but Aurelius turned and snatched it away from him before he could fire. Tellius could only gape as the swordmaster smashed the pistol hilt across his face, knocking him to his knees.

Tellius gasped, his vision swimming. He had become old and his legs were weak. He could not rise, even to face his enemy and die on his feet. Instead, Aurelius flourished the weapon at him, sneering.

'This coward's thing? You *dare* to point this at me? You

steal what is mine and then you bring one of these to threaten me in my own home? How did you do it, old man? Eh? How did you teach the boy my style?'

Tellius sat back on his haunches. As he slumped, one of the students cried out and a strange, almost sad expression crossed Aurelius' face. The swordmaster's cheek twitched and he wrenched himself around, revealing the sword that had been pushed up under his ribs to pierce his heart, a simple, killing blow.

Arthur stood there, looking calmly up at the man who had struck Tellius.

'*Not* boy,' Arthur said hoarsely. 'Golem.'

Tellius watched in horror as Aurelius slumped and fell dead on the rushes. Behind him, his three pupils spread out with weapons ready, not yet sure what to do.

6

Threefold

No one knew where the wasteland had come from, or why seeds and plants didn't spread across it and slowly claim it back for forest or meadow. Perhaps some old enemy of the city had sown the ground with salt, like Carthage, enough to make a desert of it; Daw had no idea. It began some twenty miles from Darien, stretching away from the city's western edge. In truth there were a few trees and thorn-bushes gripping the sand. Perhaps the return to forest simply happened so slowly, no one would ever notice until the land had healed.

He dismounted at the edge to check his supplies and gather firewood where there was still some to be had. There was no water or wood ahead of him and he knew he would need enough for two days, with a bit more for safety. He held his flasks up to his ear and repressed a shudder at old memories of thirst. It had been a long time since he'd last stood on that spot.

He could feel her gaze on the back of his head, still suspicious despite all his apologies. Nancy was a city girl at heart and they were miles from the city, with the strangeness of a desert before them. Accepting Threefold probably knew what he was doing in Darien was a little different from trusting him out there. Knocking her out had not been the best way to gain her cooperation either.

Old Basker had strolled out to the stable, of course. The owner of the inn missed very little of what went on in his home. When Threefold had appeared in the sunlight to saddle his mounts, Basker had suddenly been there, looming over his shoulder, peering down at the dazed and groaning young woman and tutting.

The big man had held Daw back with one hand planted on his chest. It had been like leaning on a wall and Daw had stopped protesting and just stood in sullen silence with his arms folded, visions of wealth and power fluttering away. Basker had helped Nancy to sit up and fetched her out into the sun to sit by the fountain there. The water ladle was a good one, on a thick chain. Basker had snapped it with a tug to get it to her lips. Threefold had raised his eyes at seeing that, though the lesson was clear enough.

When Nancy blinked her way back to full consciousness, she'd choked on the water and scrambled to her feet, staring around in confusion. Her hands had still been tied and Basker sawed her free with a tiny knife that just appeared in his right hand. Nancy seemed to know he could be trusted, though she'd glared at Threefold. The young man had wondered if she would spring at him.

'There now,' Basker had said to them both, tucking his knife away. 'I wouldn't like anyone thinking my place was one where unconscious young ladies might be spirited off. Eyes open, Nancy. Always. What have I told you? Though it's my belief that Threefold suffers more from youth than actual evil, if you follow me.'

Nancy had stood up straight and rubbed her wrists. She might have left then, Basker had noted to himself. Her shift had begun in the kitchen and the other girls would already have been wondering where she was. The big ex-soldier certainly wouldn't have allowed Threefold to stop her. Yet she'd stayed and waited for him to apologise. Basker's expression had become a fraction less stern. He'd had a cat once, too curious for her own good and always falling into the barrels. Drowned in the end, of course, when he wasn't there to save her, but still, adorable.

'You see?' he'd said to both of them. 'Civilised is better. Now, whatever was going on, it looks as if there's no reason to call the guards. Is that right, Nancy?'

She nodded, one eye narrowing at Daw.

'Good. I'll leave you two alone then. Oh, but I'll have that clock back, Master Threefold, if you don't mind . . . I don't put value in things as a rule, but that one, well, it represents twenty years of my life, do you see? I can't have young fellows like yourself just walking off with something I value so very, *very* highly.'

Basker had known right away from Threefold's dismay that his clock had been broken. The young man might perhaps have been some sort of mage, as he claimed, but he was no kind of card-player. It seemed the clock had been tossed onto the bed in the room upstairs, useless and dark. Basker had shaken his head at the wickedness of the world, gesturing meaningfully to the young man's pouches.

In the end, Basker hadn't taken quite all the coins Threefold had, though it was enough to make the lad thoroughly miserable – and enough to slip Nancy a couple of silvers while Threefold was repacking his saddlebags in a temper.

By the time Basker ambled back into his tavern, the sun had risen and the street outside had been bustling. Threefold had seen Nancy glance at the crowds and suddenly understood that she could take a few steps and just disappear. He couldn't follow her across the river, or if he did, he suspected he wouldn't make it back to safety and sunlight. He needed her, so he'd swallowed his wounded pride in one bitter gulp.

'I believe I've made mistakes with you, Nancy,' he'd said awkwardly. 'Knocking you out, obviously.'

'And tying me up,' she said.

Daw winced.

'Yes, that as well. I'd like to start again – and I have a way to make a fortune, if I'm right.' He'd taken a deep breath and Nancy saw how his eyes lit at some inner vision. 'For us *both* to be rich, Nancy. Gold or jewels, or Goddess knows what. If you are with me, I can reach it.'

Nancy had still looked at him suspiciously.

'Why me?' she'd said. 'And why did you clip me?'

Threefold had scuffed his shoes in the dirt of the stable yard. Up to a few moments before, he'd just wanted to get out of the city without a yelling bundle on his packhorse to draw attention. It had felt like a good plan till Basker had appeared and ruined it with his homespun wisdom and infuriating kindness. The old soldier had two beautiful daughters and somehow felt that gave him the right to tell other, younger fellows how they might speak or act around women. The man was a monster.

Yet Basker was also not one to cross, not even on a day when Threefold had all his usual tricks and traps and coins. In the man's own stable yard, under his glowering stare, Threefold had felt as defenceless as a babe – as defenceless as he actually had been, without so much as a sip of working magic on him.

'Some twenty miles from Darien, there is a desert,' he'd begun to explain. Nancy had folded her arms and glared at him.

Facing the black sands, he *knew* he'd been right. He could feel the excitement fizzing in his blood, making him want to dance. He still felt the glow of pride at the way his mind had leaped to it. His destination lay before him, just as it had five years before when he'd endured his sole failure as a combat mage, or thief, whichever printed card he'd been using then. Just as it had tempted a hundred other young adventurers and left them scarred, older and wiser.

The white tomb in the desert. The thought that he might be on the edge of succeeding where he had once failed was enough to make him grin and sweat. There hadn't even been a city of Darien when that tomb had been built, so they said. It was *old* – and protected. That meant something worth protecting.

The sands were as black as oil, dark and glassy, with end-less heavy crystals where the grains clustered. Each step came with a crunch and soft shoes could be cut to ribbons. Daw could almost hear the sound of his younger self, alone, stepping out on the dead earth for the first time.

'So where is it, then, this white tomb?' Nancy asked, spoiling the wistful mood of his memories.

'I can't remember for certain, though it was a day and a night from this spot – at most. Forty miles maybe, not even that. We'll stop for the night out on the sands, so that we can reach it tomorrow in one push. See these sticks? With just a few more, I'll make a fire.'

When he glanced up, it was to see Nancy had pursed her lips into a thin line.

'So you don't know exactly where it is,' she said slowly.

'It's only been five years! This is already looking familiar to me. I'll find my old path.'

'On the featureless, empty desert,' she added. 'I am beginning to think this is a fool's errand, Daw Threefold. I don't want to die of thirst out there.'

'You came this far, didn't you? Perhaps because the idea of a fortune and freedom means as much to you as it does to me. So please, no more of this reluctance and moaning, all right? You are here because deep down you sense I am one to follow.'

'You are an infuriating little man, Daw Threefold.'

'I am taller than you!' he said, stung.

Nancy shrugged at him.

'I am not a tall woman. You can be taller than me and still a short man.'

'A short mage, woman. I am a combat mage.'

'I've seen no sign of that, Daw. Blades that will not cut just need sharpening, that is all. Like your wits. So gather your sticks and let's get on.'

'I would like to go back to sullen silence now,' he said.

'Well, we do not always get what we want.'

'Why make me angry with you? Is it to test my temper? I promised Basker I would bring you back safe to his tavern, did I not? You were there? So you have nothing to fear from me.'

'You need me now, perhaps, but then you are a known thief and scoundrel.'

'When you say "thief", I can hear you mean someone who robs old ladies, or steals purses on the street. I am not that kind of man. On the rare occasions I have stolen items of power, it has been at great risk to my own safety.'

'You think because you climbed up someone's ivy or ran along a rooftop, it is somehow *not* stealing?' she said. 'It's still stealing, Daw. You are a thief, and some of us work for a living. So I would like to discuss the terms of our deal again – while you still need me.'

'All I actually *need* is your presence,' he snapped. 'Not

even awake, as far as I can tell, just this thing you do that cancels magic.'

'To enter a tomb,' she said, sarcasm thick in her voice.

'No one *knows* if it is a tomb, because no one has ever been able to get in! There are spells of protection on that place of such power that they have been proof against every young fool who tried to breach the doorway. No one even knows how old it is. Some of those who tried to get in were killed on the spot, others were so badly burned that they died as they crawled back. Their bones left clicking on the sands . . .' He shuddered. 'One or two like me were clever enough to hire servants and send them in, then retire to a safe distance to watch how the lads got on.'

'Short *and* treacherous,' Nancy muttered to herself, though he heard.

'And then I tried it myself. I tell you, that tomb is a terrible place, guarded by wards that no one alive today even understands. Not all the magicians of Darien could force their way in. No one can.' He paused. He wanted to keep his secrets to himself, to appear mysterious to a young woman who seemed less impressed with every passing hour. Yet Threefold was caught up in the excitement he had felt ever since Basker's retirement clock had stopped. 'But *I* could, if I had you standing at my side.'

Nancy looked at his wide eyes and heard the awe in his voice. She could not help feeling a tremor of excitement herself, for all her doubts. What if he was right? Her life had not been a garden of delights around Fiveway and the Red Corners. Before the plague had frightened her into running across the river, her world had been a small patch of tight-packed roads and alleys that sweltered and stank in the sun and stole away the old men and women in the winter.

Basker's place meant she had left all of that behind, but what if there could be more than just survival? What if Daw Threefold had not gone completely mad? She imagined herself owning one of the big narrow houses on a clean street, with a glossy, black-painted door and a maid or a doorman to scatter the street boys.

'I will need a half-share — and the packhorse,' she said. 'For my cooperation.'

'Last night you were ready to steal coins from a sleeping man's bags,' he said.

Nancy pursed her mouth at him.

'I wouldn't have taken it all, Daw, just a couple. Poverty is a hard mistress. Still, that doesn't matter now, does it? Today is a different day — and I find myself in possession of something you want very dearly indeed.'

'Something you did not even know existed last night.'

'Which is why I have offered you half. It is a partnership, Daw Threefold. Imagine the mountains of gold and jewels there might be inside, just waiting for us! We're here now. Would you rather I went back to Darien and asked around for someone else to take me out to the tomb in the desert? Do you think I might find someone who'll give me good terms?'

'No one you could trust,' Threefold said. 'They'd probably leave you for dead, whereas you know Basker is expecting me to bring you back. You have that man's threat as your guarantee, and that is no small thing.'

Nancy nodded.

'I think you're right. A partnership then. Half for you and half for me.'

'You know, you were not even conscious when you stopped Basker's clock, barely inside my room. Half for what? Being born with a country knack that does more harm than good? A bit of hearth magic? Your "cancelling" is a local effect – a circle around you. Imagine you are a shuttered lamp. The light . . .'

'Yes, I understand,' she said. 'Your plan is to watch for physical traps and spells, all the while keeping me close to you – Goddess knows how far into this tomb of yours. But if you stray more than a few feet from me, you believe you could be killed. That sounds . . . dangerous. Can't you see it would be easier for you to have my full-hearted, *half-share* cooperation? Why is it so hard to promise a fair part of anything we find? I am vital to you in this.' She waited for a time, but he only stared, his jaw set. 'I can't believe you won't make a gesture of goodwill. You might need me on your side before this is over, Daw Threefold. You might need a willing partner.'

Threefold tugged her reins and let her ambling packhorse catch up so they rode side by side over the black sands.

'Dear, sweet Nancy,' he said, shaking his head. 'If I tie you up, I can drag you along the ground as I go into the tomb. I will have all the benefits, with none of the cost of cutting you in.' He gave a sour smile. 'Though I may be short, I am yet strong enough for that.'

'You would be taking a risk,' Nancy grumbled, frowning. 'You don't know what's in there. What if you need both hands? I am surprised at you, Daw Threefold. You won't offer five parts of ten? Without me, you have no chance at all.'

Daw Threefold clamped his mouth on his reply, considering that a full night and day lay before him and that talking dried the throat. She would surely not continue the conversation the whole way there.

*

Tellius felt his stomach clench in fear as guard whistles sounded, first on the balcony above and then quickly echoed in the street outside. There were still small groups of shocked people milling around by the huge outer door. Even as he had the thought of pushing through them, two of Aurelius' students moved to block the only way out to sunlight and freedom. They were ready for him to try and run, he could see that much.

He bent down to speak to Arthur, keeping his voice low.

'You should go, son. Just stroll out now, nice and easy like a walk in the park, all right? If they try and stop you, run all the way back to the workshop. Ask Micahel what to do. Understand?'

Arthur looked up at him and slowly shook his head.

'Go on, boy! Before it's too late.'

Tellius glared at him until the moment had been lost and the door to the street was closed and guarded.

'Damnation,' he said softly. Tellius took a deep breath and went back to where he had stood before, settling himself on the low stone wall to wait for the guards. He adjusted his coat collar and tried very hard to look as if his heart wasn't threatening to burst through his breastbone.

He and the lads above the apothecary avoided any contact with the King's Men, because nothing good ever came of speaking to them. The guards settled no justice on those who didn't pay their wages. All they brought was fear and retribution, beatings and the cells – and in the end, the rope.

Arthur came to sit by him when Tellius patted the rail at his side. The boy stared over at the body lying on the rushes and Tellius could see strain on Arthur's face for the first time.

'Golem?' Tellius murmured, sensing Arthur look up. The

old man had heard of them, of course, though he'd never thought he might meet one. The legends described them as untiring soldiers, terrifying killers who would march right through an enemy army, obedient and merciless, with a sword in each hand. Tellius shuddered. His people had been responsible for some abominations, it was true, but nothing like this, not that he'd ever heard.

No one even knew how to make the things any more. Like all the great spells, the knowledge had been lost. Yet it did not answer the question. Who would make a golem the size and shape of a little boy? Tellius reached over and ran his thumb across Arthur's cheek, feeling the pliancy and give of flesh. The lad did not flinch or move away, though Tellius realised he could have. It was astonishing work. He would never have known.

'I thought you could not speak,' Tellius said softly, too low for Aurelius' pupils to hear.

Arthur did not respond, not even to shrug. Tellius raised his eyebrows in rebuke.

'I *heard* you, Arthur, with these ears, you see. You cannot go back to silence now.'

The boy looked afraid, he realised. From instinct, Tellius began to talk, to calm himself as well as the golem watching him.

'I suppose I should thank you, Arthur. Hmm. I imagine you have another name. Do you know it?'

The boy shrugged.

'Well, I'll call you Arthur . . . Quick, until you tell me another. You saved my life, sunshine. Master Aurelius would not have been satisfied with my humiliation, not this time. Yet I am the one to blame. I am sorry, lad. I . . . should not have let you show what you can do, not to him. I should not have come here today. I am too old to have so much pride, and so the blame for this is all on me. It was my fault and not yours. Do you understand that?'

Arthur nodded slowly, then patted him on the arm. As he did so, Tellius guessed why a golem would be made in the image of a boy, perhaps a boy who had died centuries before.

'Did you have a mother once?' Tellius asked.

Arthur looked up at him with huge eyes. After an age, he nodded again.

'Ah, lad. I am sorry.' A grieving mother of the old empire, perhaps one who cared nothing for cost. For all Tellius knew, Arthur Quick had been created to replace the lost child of a queen or some great lady. Yet golems did not age or change. Their animating force could not grow with them. To make a child! Tellius had never even heard of such a thing.

It was a great sin to have done so, he thought, however it had come about. Tellius could only close his eyes at the thought of the boy watching all those he knew age and wither. Perhaps they had looked after him at first, for a life-time even, doted on him as a beloved son. Yet after a hundred years, after two, he would have been utterly alone, forgotten by those who had made him, left to wander the world.

The captain of the king's guard paid no attention at first to the old man and the boy sitting in patched clothes on the low wall. Tellius watched as two brutish-looking fellows were sent to stand over him, while the captain removed his peaked hat to speak respectfully to the pupils of Aurelius. No doubt they were the sons and daughters of noble families, paying fortunes for their instruction. Certainly the guardsman seemed very eager to please. The captain actually bowed as they replied to him.

Tellius could feel the man's gaze flicker over in his

direction as the students described and mimed what they had seen, making sharp jabbing motions in the air and pointing to Arthur. The old man kept his gaze low as the captain strode across the yard at last, filled almost to bursting with his own importance.

'The boy was defending me,' Tellius said before the captain could manage a single word. 'This is a tragic accident, not a crime.'

'So you may desire me to believe,' the man replied with scorn. 'Now. My name is Captain D'Estaing of the King's Men. I have three witnesses who say you knew Master Aurelius and taunted him to rage – then had this boy stab him from behind.'

Tellius felt his heart beat even faster. Was it possible they had not heard Arthur's words in the scuffle and grunt of the attack? He could find a way out if they had not.

'Not boy,' Arthur said firmly. 'Golem.'

'Oh, *really*, Arthur,' Tellius snapped. 'You could not have *picked* a worse time.'

'Whoever or whatever you are, you are both under arrest for unlawful killing,' Captain D'Estaing said. 'You will be searched and taken to a cell. A legal representative will be summoned for you, if you cannot afford one. You will be brought to trial no later than one week from the date of your arrest.'

The captain spoke the words in a dulled rush, as if he had said them a thousand times before. Yet as he spoke, his eyes gleamed with fascination at the golem who looked like a young boy.

'You cannot arrest a child less than twelve years old,' Tellius said. 'He is below the age of criminal responsibility.'

'Unless he is not a child,' D'Estaing went on, peering.

Tellius waved his hand.

'It is just a game, sir. Arthur is my son, I will vouch for him.' He sensed the boy looking over at him, but Tellius kept his gaze on the captain, willing him to agree.

D'Estaing shook his head.

'Whatever he is, three upstanding subjects say he stabbed Master Aurelius and killed him. I do not think I will let him go, no. I suspect my superiors will want to see this boy.' The captain lost his wondering stare, his manner suddenly brisk. 'Come along, meneer. Make this easy on us all. Master Aurelius lies dead, Goddess take his soul. The city will be in mourning and I suspect I would have to take you into custody to protect you from the mobs. Do not make this difficult for me, especially in front of . . . your son.'

Tellius made a slight bow and the guards swept in around him as he walked out to the street. The news was spreading quickly and hundreds of eyes turned to see. Tellius felt Arthur reach for his hand and he almost pulled away, but then took it. Together, he and Arthur left the Masters' Court behind, without looking back at the man they had killed.

7

Elias

Elias put his feet down again as the cage was upended, so that he stood upright, on a floor of thick matting. He recognised the general's command tent from the few moments he had spent in it before. The soldiers trooped out and only Deeds remained, looking at him through the bars.

'I promised you a single day,' Elias said. 'And yet here I am, still a prisoner.'

To his surprise, Deeds looked away, flushing slightly.

'That does not sit well with me, meneer. I prefer to keep my word. You know there are times when it is impossible. I am sorry, as I said.'

'What news of my wife and daughters? Can you at least tell me that much? Did the doctor get out to them? Come on, Mr Deeds. You must owe me that.'

Deeds clenched his fists in a brief spasm, though whether it was in anger or embarrassment, Elias couldn't tell. The gunfighter was not an easy man to read. Deeds stepped closer and Elias thought he might have said something more if not for the sound of others approaching the far side of the tent, some forty feet away across the damp interior. Instead, Deeds stood back, his expression blank.

Elias forgot everything else when he recognised the voice of his youngest, Alice, six years old and busy explaining an endless story to the general walking at her side. The small group came to a halt some dozen paces from the cage. His two daughters were gazing up at General Justan and he was listening to them, fully aware of Elias watching.

Elias put his hand through the bars, helplessly. He could hear a roar in his ears that drowned all other sounds. His oldest daughter looked up and her eyes widened.

'Daddy!' Jenny said in surprise. She rushed up to the bars, the general forgotten. Elias took hold of the hand she put in his, enclosing it completely. It broke his heart to feel how small it was. 'What are you doing in there, Dad? Are you a prisoner?'

'Well, perhaps General Justan can tell us,' Elias said. His voice was as light as he could make it. He forced a smile so as not to alarm his girls, though it was not a kind expression. He had been a hunter all his life and the gaze he turned on General Justan held a promise of bloodshed. The general nodded as he watched, as if he had finally confirmed something he had doubted before.

'Jenny, dear. Come back and stand with little Alice, would you? Your father and I are playing a game. He has to guess what I want him to do – and I can't let him out until he does. That's it, dear. Stand with your sister. Goodness, what charming girls you both are.'

'Where is my . . .' Elias began. He broke off as General Justan shook his head sharply, almost as a conspirator. To Elias' astonishment, the general raised a finger to his lips.

'She is back at home, Meneer Post. My doctor was able to treat these dear girls, bringing them to the hospital in camp while they recovered. They left your wife asleep. I will . . . send word when she wakes.'

His expression was dark and Elias knew then that his wife had been dead when the doctor reached her. He gripped the bars, wanting to roar or weep or strike someone. First Jenny, then Alice sensed the rage and grief in him, for all he tried to hide it and beam at them through tears. Jenny began to sob and would have rushed to him, but the general took her by the arm. She struggled wildly to pull away then, like a cat finding its paw caught. General Justan swore as she scratched him. The youngest, Alice, began to wail in fear, standing alone and making a noise to fill the entire tent.

Elias felt his grief burn off in the heat of his anger. The rage was more immediate and he had to struggle not to fight the bars. He knew he was helpless. He was just feet from his own daughters but could do nothing to save them. That was what the general wanted him to know.

Elias understood Deeds had been right that a bargain would be made. His service, for the lives of his girls. He realised then why Deeds had looked so ashamed of himself.

'Come now, Jenny, Alice. Settle down,' Elias called over the noise of his weeping girls. 'We are guests here. Anyway, I think I can guess the answer now.'

General Justan clapped his hands, startling both of the girls to silence. Alice stared red-eyed at him, still on the edge of sobbing.

'How clever your father is!' the general said, though his eyes glittered. 'I should open the cage door then, of course!'

The two girls began to smile and snivel once more. Alice held out chubby hands to her father. Still babyish, she wanted to be picked up. The sight of it made Elias hollow with pain.

'Come on, Daddy. Say it!' Jenny called to her father. The general no longer held her arm and she looked from one to the other in confused suspicion, trying to understand.

'I'm afraid it is a secret, girls,' General Justan said. 'Run along now. Mr Deeds here will show you the camp kitchen and find something for you to eat. Why, you must be starving! Your father will see you later on, when we have finished our game, of course.'

'No!' Jenny ran to the bars. Alice would have followed her if Deeds hadn't swept her up. She bawled in his arms, shrieking and struggling, going red. The gunfighter winced at the high sound close to his ear.

'It's all right, girls!' Elias said. 'Settle down. I'll be along in a while. Honestly, what would your mother say if she could hear you? Come on now. No more caterwauling.'

'You'll come later? You promise?' Jenny asked him.

He nodded, though he could feel Deeds watching.

'Of course, love. I promise. I'll come for you.'

Deeds cleared his throat and ushered her away, though Alice clawed the air over his shoulder, her screaming like a saw blade in green wood. Still, they went and silence returned.

General Justan approached the bars.

'I am sorry about that – and sorry about your wife, meneer. You must know I would have saved her if I could, if only to have her look after the girls. As it is, one of the women in camp will have to be a nurse to them.'

'What do you want from me?' Elias Post said. 'What could ever justify threatening my daughters?'

'I did not intend them to become distressed, meneer. They have no sense of being in danger, I promise you. They will not be threatened. I just wanted you to see that I had them. You do not know all the orders I have given. Perhaps you would not want to. Yet when I let you out of this cage, you will know you can't kill me – and you can't run. Do you understand that? My intention was to find a way to hold you still, a man who can step aside from anything. Iron bars have their uses, but you are not much good to me in a cage, do you see?

93

I need you to be able to move, to travel. Wherever I send you, your daughters are your bars, your guarantee.'

'I am not a fool, general. I understood that much when you brought them in. Open the door, then.'

The general stood with one hand across his chest and the other elbow balanced on it, a comfortable position for him that raised a hand to his mouth. He stroked his upper lip with thumb and forefinger in thought, as if he'd once had a moustache. It was a nervous action and Elias showed his teeth in the cage.

'I will set you free, in a moment, but I have seen what you can do, Elias Post. I am very, *very* keen to have you understand your position completely. You might think to kill me here and race across my camp after the girls. Perhaps you believe you could spirit them away from the heart of my Immortals. I wonder if you could? With every hand raised against you, with an army of pikes and swords, I truly wonder. But either way, you will not try, because I have given an order to kill them if you are sighted. Please understand. I have children of my own. It was not an order I wanted to give, nor one I would ever like to see carried out. Yet I did so, because I would bind you to my service. We are at war, sir, or we will be, any day now. Do not test my resolve in this.'

'Unlock the door,' Elias said softly.

The general hesitated even then, so that Elias knew the man had been shaken to his core by the display under gunfire. Damn Deeds and his sharp eyes. Damn the plague and his lost wife, cold in her bed and never there again to hold him in her arms. His eyes were dry and very pale as General Justan clicked the key in the lock and stood back.

Elias stepped out and stretched, disdain written in the twist of his mouth. The general's response to fear had been to seek to bind him, to take his daughters. A man who would steal the cubs of a wolf, it seemed. General Justan was a risk-taker, a gambler for the highest stakes. Perhaps it was why he understood a man like Deeds. Elias considered then how satisfying it would be to beat a general to death in his own tent. The older man seemed to sense the colourful scenes playing out behind Elias' eyes and he blanched, looking away.

'I am a hunter, General Justan,' Elias said, 'not a soldier. What use can I possibly be to you? What must I do to have my daughters returned to me?'

The general settled himself, controlling the appalling sense of helplessness he felt under Elias' gaze. The hunter looked like any other prisoner, with hollowed cheeks and banked rage in his eyes.

'You have shown you can walk through armed men with no more than the smell of gun smoke on your jacket. That means you could get to *anyone*. You could walk right through a camp or a palace guard – and cut the throat of a man in his bed. No one could stop you, not as I understand it. By the Goddess, Meneer Post, you are the deadliest man alive.'

'Such a man might react badly to having his daughters stolen,' Elias said softly.

Once more the general paled a shade before he swallowed and went on.

'A man who might understand that wars can be won with a single bloody act, in a single night.'

Elias shrugged. His health was still returning. The furnace that had been building in his chest had gone as if a door had been shut on its heat. He knew he was clean of the plague. On its own, that felt like waking to a new morning.

He had not expected to live. Yet instead of that chill and

calm resignation, he had a life and the lives of his daughters to consider. He could not dwell on the loss of his wife, any more than he could the loss of his son. Those were doors jammed shut in his mind. He dared not open them.

'One task, then. You would have me kill the satrap? I don't know where he lays his head, even. I'll need maps, horses . . .'

General Justan chuckled.

'The Satrap of Astan is a weakling, Meneer Post, a man inbred by generations of his fathers marrying their own sisters. If his armies ever get round to invading us, I will destroy his precious legions of red and yellow in the field. No, meneer! The man I have in mind is our own king, in Darien.'

'What? What madness is this?' Elias snorted. 'Do you think I'll commit treason for you? You have lost your mind.'

'No, meneer. I have not. Our King Johannes sits in his fine palace, surrounded by his swordmasters, fearful of his life. He sends no orders to me and has not for sixteen months now. He keeps me in the field, while he and his Twelve Families enjoy the theatre and the wine and the . . . *whorehouses* of Darien!'

The general had grown pink-cheeked with his rising anger, Elias noted. The last few words had been drawn out in stutters of indignation. The man despised those he claimed to serve, it seemed.

General Justan waved a hand as if at a biting fly.

'And while they clink their glasses together and grow fat and soft, the satrap's forces march up and down our border, more and more arrogant when they are not challenged. It is a state of war without any fighting, meneer! Yet my men must eat. They must replace whatever wears out, piece by piece. The costs! You have no idea what it takes to keep these men at a fine pitch of readiness. I have a dozen creditors who need to be paid, who will not deliver any more supplies unless they have their old bills settled. Can you imagine, meneer? The elite legion of Darien made paupers, made *beggars* by those fools in the city. If I were free to act, I could end it all in a season. That is what you would bring about.'

He stepped closer to Elias and the hunter could see sweat had broken out along the man's hairline, running down his cheek unnoticed. There was an intensity to the general that was disturbing.

'I do not fear the enemy, Meneer Post. I fear another year in this camp, with the latrines all overflowing and uniforms patched and good men going to rust and sloth in their inaction! That is what I would change – and that is what you could bring to an end with just a knife thrust!' The general's eyes were wide and terrible, far from the urbane mask he had worn before. Elias sensed it was the truth, though the idea still appalled him.

He had never even seen the city, never mind the king's palace. The idea of murdering a stranger in his bed filled him with sick frustration, but he pressed it away behind another door. There was no question of refusing – he would not fail his girls. When it was done, when he had them safe, Elias told himself he would come back one night in snow and darkness – and leave the general's head on a stake by his tent. Deeds too, or the man might seek his kin in turn. When he was free to act, Elias would have a dark and bloody vengeance on them all.

He nodded.

'Very well, general. I do not have to say that you hold a knife to your own neck with my daughters. If they are harmed in any way, I will visit destruction upon you. If you understand that, I will do as you say and return here.'

General Justan cleared his throat, though his voice was hoarse as he spoke.

'I understand,' he said.

'Good. Have Mr Deeds brought to me. Give him a free hand, anything I need. Beyond that, stay out of my way.'

Tellius did not like D'Estaing. The king's captain of guards paced up and down the small room as he rattled off a stream of accusations, each worse than the last. Murder, assassination, treason. The man was lithe and the sword at his waist looked worn and well used, but there was a goodly difference between a Mazer-trained swordsman and one who was merely talented. Tellius would have liked an opportunity to demonstrate the difference to the man. Taking on a master like Aurelius had been one thing. Humiliating an arrogant guard captain should still have been possible, even with the warm hand of old age on his shoulder.

Tellius shook his head at himself, catching the captain's attention so that he paused, with his eyebrows climbing to his hairline. The old man was trying hard to be on his best behaviour. He did not know if it would help him. He did not know yet how he would even get out of that interrogation room.

'Nothing else to say, meneer?' D'Estaing said. 'You disappoint me. I had the pleasure of seeing Master Aurelius demonstrate his skills to the king just last month. Whatever you may have intended, whatever the exact truth of how it happened, you and your . . . accomplice are responsible for his death in a grubby brawl, with a knife literally in his back! That is no way for a gentleman to die! Stabbed from behind, while his attention was on some bony foreign beggar.'

The captain leaned close enough for Tellius to feel the pressure of his breath on his cheek.

'I know all about you, Androvanus Tellius. Your lads too, in that workshop on Dial Street. We've had complaints before and I could kick myself now, but we didn't act on them. There aren't enough guards in Darien to go after every purse-cutter or pickpocket! Some part of the blame will doubtless fall on my shoulders because I did not act. Yet who would teach people to be careful if my men and I went around mopping up after them, eh? Are we king's guards or street-sweepers? If I gave back every stolen pouch or wallet, the people of this city would be dropping them in every gutter! *Stupid*.'

It was clear a part of D'Estaing's anger and grief was directed at himself or his own career, with the rest focused on Tellius. The old man had no sympathy for the red-faced captain. He had his own problems. Tellius' arms had been manacled to the floor on a short chain and he fidgeted, making the links clank.

'But this?' D'Estaing went on. 'Murder does come to my attention, Meneer Tellius! The murder of one of the king's favourites even more so. Master Aurelius was like an uncle to the king, a man much loved and admired at court. You've no idea, have you? There must be punishment. There must be retribution. Do you understand?'

'The boy was defending me, that's all.'

'The "boy", is it? The lad who steps up to a master swords-man without fear and slips a knife right up, under the ribs, into the man's heart, easy as that. Most *boys* might have stabbed down, you know? In their panic, they would have raked the blade along the ribs and Aurelius would still be alive with a nasty gash. But not this one. No. This one steps in and out like a damned *assassin*.'

'Where is Arthur now?' Tellius asked, though he did not think he would be told.

'There are a few people having a look at him, old man. To see if it's true what he says, or if he's just another street rat with a knife and a touch of madness. Who ever heard of a golem that size anyway? What would be the point?'

Tellius almost replied with his theory about a mother losing a son and trying to replace him, but D'Estaing's angry words had put a nastier thought in his mind. A golem who looked like a small child would be the perfect killer. What man or woman would even see the threat before it was too late? Tellius shuddered at the thought and hoped it was not true. He liked Arthur Quick. He did not want to be afraid of him.

The door to the interrogation room came open after a brief warning knock, giving D'Estaing barely enough time to stand to attention. Tellius looked up to see King Johannes de Generes enter. He tried to stand in open-mouthed surprise, but his chains pulled him up short and left him hunched over in a half bow.

The king was a slender man of thirty, with a narrow chin that came to a point of wispy beard, and long slim fingers that were never still. King Johannes looked nervous as he stood there, glancing around the tiny room in distaste as if he could hardly believe such a horrid place existed.

'Remove those chains, would you, captain?' the king said, waving a hand.

D'Estaing didn't hesitate and had the locks clicking open in moments before returning to the same spot and bowing his head. Tellius stood up slowly to his full height, then bowed as deeply as he could manage.

'I am at your service, Your Royal Highness. And may I say that I am sorry for the appalling accident at the training ground this morning.'

'This boy of yours,' the king said, ignoring his words. 'How long have you known him?'

Tellius guessed then that Arthur had not spoken to them. He wondered whether it affected his chances of avoiding the hangman's dance that afternoon.

'A few days, Your Highness.'

'He seems very attached to you,' the king said.

Tellius could only frown. He felt like a card-player who had bet too much on a weak hand. All he could do was lay each card down slowly – and hope.

'I was being attacked, Your Highness. I am an old man and I do not believe I could have stopped Master Aurelius from killing me. The boy came to my rescue and it should not . . .'

'I don't mean that,' the king interrupted.

Tellius broke off immediately. He knew very well that he was helpless in that place. Only the goodwill of the man he faced could save him and he strained every nerve and channel of his brain to see the right way forward.

'I have had him examined,' King Johannes went on. 'It seems he truly is one of these "golems", though his likeness to a living child is . . . extraordinary. He does not bleed, did you know that? He has a sort of clear ichor in his limbs. It dribbles out when he is cut, though he seals up fast enough.'

Tellius felt his expression grow cold. Despite himself, he could not keep his anger from his voice.

'You had your men *cut* him? And he let you, I suppose. And now he will not cooperate with you. I wonder why that might be?'

The king waved a hand, blowing air out in a puff.

'I have been advised that golems are machines, meneer. Animated by magic – in this case with extraordinary artistry.

I am assured they do *not* feel. He showed no distress, if that is your concern. But I want him! If he was properly obedient to me, I would give him a place amongst my personal guard. The students of poor Aurelius said he possessed the skill of the master. If that is true . . .' The king shook his head in awe. 'No more poor copies for me in the men and women Aurelius trained. I would have the golden source itself – better! *Unchanging* and eternal, a guard loyal to me, to watch over me and keep me safe.'

His eyes were bright and Tellius saw the young man was trembling with excitement.

'I asked him to show me, Tellius. He made no reply, though I know he spoke to you before. He feels no pain, so I cannot torture him. I am at an impasse. Tell me, do you have some word of command, some charmed object to make him do what you want? Did he give you anything that seemed insignificant at the time? I will fill your pockets with gold for it if you have.'

Tellius looked at the arrogant young man standing before him. Compared to that clear and certain gaze, Tellius felt all his years and all his poverty sitting heavy on his shoulders. He saw a way out then, though it shamed him like acid creeping in his veins. On any other day, the killing of a noble son would have had him burned and torn, then swinging at the end of a rope, no matter the rights and wrongs of it. The Twelve Families of Darien did not take well to losing one of their own to a common man.

While the king waited for an answer, Tellius tried to think it through, realising what he had not quite dared to see before. There was no going back from that point. Even if a miracle occurred and the king freed him, he would almost certainly be dead before the week's end. It was true he and

Micahel might surprise the first assassin they sent against him, but that would only make the Twelve Families more determined and more ruthless. Instead of that fate, he was being offered a chance, a nettle he might grasp, if he could get the grip just right.

The sun was setting outside the interrogation room, sending a bar of golden light across them all. At last, Tellius nodded.

'I would like to speak with the golem, Your Highness. He forms a great bond of loyalty and I will need to reassure him I have not been harmed, before anything else. After that, for the right price, and my freedom, I might be able to help you.'

8

Desert

Threefold had slept badly. The black sand was actually quite pleasant to lie on at first, as it could be shaped and moulded around him. Yet it did not give way when he turned over and he woke up a dozen times in the darkness, increasingly stiff and sore. On top of that, the desert was not as dead as he had believed. Things called and hooted to one another through the night and more than once something had scuttled right over his sleeping form, startling him awake and gasping. His small fire had burned itself out and of course there was no more wood to build it back up. He'd spent some of the dark hours staring up at the stars, seeing them more clearly than he ever had in Darien. In all honesty, the wonder of that wore off fairly quickly. They were always there, after all. He had more pressing concerns.

The temperature had dropped alarmingly and he was stiff and grimy, though it was nothing he hadn't known a thousand nights before. He could hear Nancy wandering off to dig a hole to relieve herself and hoped vaguely that she would disturb something unpleasant. He could hardly believe he'd considered her a worthy bedmate back at the tavern, though she'd played up to him then, complimenting him and making herself all frail and feminine. She seemed rather less attractive after a dozen hours of persuasive bargaining. If it wasn't for the damned tomb, he'd have ridden off in a temper, he was certain. Let her find her own way back to Darien!

Only the possibility that she might actually do so and find someone else to lead her to the tomb held his temper in check. It did not matter if she mocked his magic, or that he could never show her that she was wrong, though that stung his pride. All that mattered was that her presence might cancel out the wards on the tomb.

As he lay there, it was hard not to fantasise about the wonders that might lie within. He still remembered the white entrance, half-hidden in a drift of sand. He felt a pang of worry that it might have been covered and he would have to search for days, running low on water and food, all the while enduring Nancy's acid commentary. No, the Goddess loved a brash young man; everyone said that. She would guide his steps and his memories. He'd find it again, he promised himself. His mother had told him once that if he truly wanted something, he should imagine it happening. The Goddess might adjust the world, if he found her in the right mood.

'The sun is almost up,' Nancy said by his ear, making him start. The woman moved like a spider, making no sound at all.

'Don't creep up like that! I can see the sun is rising, can't I? Goddess, you gave me a shock then.' He saw she had taken off her boots and was flexing her bare toes in the black sand. He considered warning her about scorpions and decided not to.

'I want to get started, Daw. Today is the day, unless you've been lying to me.'

Daw stood and dusted off the sand clinging to him, taking the time to fold his sleeping blanket and let his heart return to a slower pace before he trusted himself to respond.

'I will do my best, Nancy, as I said last night. I've offered you half of what we find – which is more than fair. I've also offered you my packhorse to take your share. Unless you actually want my coat and boots as well, you've been treated honourably. So how about a bit of quiet for the final few miles, eh?'

Nancy shrugged, then appeared to mime something. When he only stared at her, she went to the packhorse and tossed him a packet of dried meat and onions. Honestly, she was infuriating.

'I know what I'm going to do with my share,' she said.

Daw raised his eyes to heaven.

'How long was that? Enough to draw breath? Why must we spoil this lovely dawn with your constant nattering?' As he spoke, he picked up his saddle and approached his horse, the animal chewing away on a nosebag of grain.

'I'm going to hire hard men,' she said, behind him. 'Like Basker.'

There was no trace of humour in her voice and Threefold looked back as he began to tie the belly strap.

'You'll get yourself killed if you do,' he said. 'Men like Basker are retired. You couldn't buy his service for a fortune. Or did you mean the gangs where you grew up? They'll steal all you have and leave you dead in a gutter – or get themselves caught and have you and them kicking at the end of a rope. I'd stay clear of anything like that. That's just my advice; you don't have to take it.'

'I don't intend to,' she said, pertly. 'Though I could ask Basker to find me reliable sorts. If he'd vouch for them, I'd take his word.'

Threefold sighed.

'All right, princess, I'll ask. Why would you take this *one* chance to have enough wealth to live a life of comfort and ease, this one opportunity to drag yourself out of whoring or thieving or whatever it is you do – and waste it on murderers for hire?'

'I don't whore myself out,' she said. 'I didn't ask you for money, did I?'

'You were searching my pack.'

'Taking is not the same. Forget it, though; you don't understand. What will you do with yours?'

'No, I won't forget it. If you want to hire soldiers, it's not to dig your garden, is it? You must have someone in mind. Your father? An old lover? Who?'

For a long moment, Nancy just stared at him. His horse nibbled its way onto the iron bit and Threefold tossed the reins over and tied them in a knot on his saddle horn.

'The chief magistrate,' she said. 'Don't laugh at me.'

Threefold sighed, shaking his head.

'I really wasn't. I've felt the same way once or twice. I've seen him, when I went to watch three men hanged in Sallet Square. Lord Albus was primping and preening to his people, all waiting for him to call the sentence. The hangman was beaming away like it was a festival. And all the while, three young men stood there and kept their silence because they still hoped to be pardoned. None of them were. I do understand, Nancy. Those damned families, riding over us all like we're nothing. You never see one of them hanged, do you? Have you noticed that? It's always thieves.' He fell silent for a moment, lost in some grim recollection. 'They wouldn't even have to steal if not for all the taxes, so a man can't hardly earn a decent amount without some king's bastard holding out his hand for half.'

Nancy nodded. She was reassured by his anger, so that words poured out of her.

'If you *can't* pay, like my dad couldn't, they throw you out and sell your house for the debt. But not for what it might have made. They auction it off with a dozen others and one of their friends buys it for almost nothing, though there are other bidders all waving away.'

For an instant, they looked at each other with more common feeling than either liked to admit.

'What happened to your dad?' Threefold asked.

Nancy shrugged, but her eyes were bright as she turned to the packhorse.

'He tried to get to Lord Albus, to ask for more time. He put a hand on the man's shoulder. One of the guards beat him. He took a fever and died.' She breathed slowly, in and out before going on. 'He tried his best, I know that. After he was gone, life got a lot harder. So if I find a fortune today, Daw Threefold, I actually might just use it to put a knife in Lord bleeding Albus, the king's judge. Just to please my dad's memory and let him rest.'

Threefold mounted up, treating the idea seriously. The tomb was still some way ahead and it was better than enduring her bargaining.

'This kind of thing – it's not your world, Nancy, do you realise?'

'More mine than yours! You grew up in, where was it? Yew Street. Trees and that, all in a line. You don't know what my world even looks like.'

'I know that violent men who might kill for gold would be more than happy to steal it. It's easier than what you're suggesting and they won't risk themselves if there's an easier way.' He shook his head, wanting to dissuade her, or at least stop her from getting her throat cut. 'Listen. The Twelve Families have swordsmen marching around their houses all day and night, did you know that? Not some cut-purse bullies from the gangs, but real, trained men, with years in the legion under their belt. They would be your problem. Lord Albus is the king's uncle – and he knows he's not loved. He never steps onto the street without his own private army. He goes from his house to the royal court each afternoon, or the palace for festivals, to stand on the balcony and wave at all those who hate him. You think you can just hire a few hard bastards for that sort of work? They'd run a mile. No, you'd be better off seeking out the lord who bought your father's house. There! That's a better idea, Nancy. Have whoever it was beaten up one night. You are welcome!'

He looked over as she rode alongside. Nancy was not smiling and his own expression became solemn.

'It's just a dream, Daw,' she said. 'You and me – people like us – don't get justice. We don't get revenge, not ever. That's for the noble families who do whatever they want. If we raise a hand to them, they hang us in front of our friends and families and take everything we own. That's just the way it is. I know I can't get near Albus and, honestly, I know I could hire a hundred murderers and they'd just take everything I had. I am not a fool, Daw Threefold. The world is a hard, cold place, without much kindness in it. You know it and I know it. All right? So if I want to daydream about hiring my own army and whipping fat Lord Albus through the streets before stringing him up, I'll do it.'

'Naked through the streets,' Threefold said in a murmur.

'Of course naked! The point is to humiliate him. Otherwise, I'd just wish he died in his sleep.'

Threefold laughed in genuine pleasure and looked over to see she was grinning at him. For the first time since leaving the city, he found her slightly less than irritating.

Tellius saw Arthur Quick sitting on a marble bench in a training yard within the palace complex. It was of the same dimensions as Master Aurelius' school, but roofed over and lit by lamps all along the walls, so that it was almost as bright as day inside.

The king and D'Estaing had agreed not to interfere, allowing Tellius to approach Arthur alone. It was to his advantage that none of them knew how a golem needed to be handled. Tellius understood that was his best card to play – that they could be bluffed, if he just found the right way to do it.

Either way, it was not as if he and the boy could have run off, not from that place. The training yard was surrounded by guards and they'd taken so many twists and turns to get there, he wasn't even sure he could find his way out on his own.

As he approached, Tellius heard his steps echo back from the empty balcony that stretched all the way around. The king was a famous lover of swordplay and Tellius assumed the balconies were crowded with members of the Families on some days, with lesser masters than Aurelius showing off their skills. He sniffed to himself. Stolen knowledge, he was sure of it. He only wished a true master of the Mazer steps could travel the nine thousand miles west and show them what a swordsman could actually do. He smiled at the image, staring up at the balconies as he imagined it. They could only be clumsy and slow next to one of the teachers of his youth. Even the best of them would be like men trapped in honey.

Arthur looked up as Tellius stopped in front of him. Once more the old man marvelled that the boy was not just another street urchin of Darien. As Tellius sat down, Arthur wiped his nose on the sleeve of his jacket, leaving a trail of silver. He must have cost the wealth of an empire to make, Tellius thought in wonder. Yet mere gold could not buy the artistry of him, not in this century. That mastery of magic was lost, with even the word 'golem' slipping into legend. The child . . . the creature, was magnificent.

Tellius sighed, grunting as he stretched a back made stiff by too many hours chained. He stared across the yard.

'So, Arthur. I imagine you know better than me that life can be harsh and cruel. Good men do not usually get what they deserve. Wicked men often live long and happy lives, to die surrounded by their loved ones and loyal servants. You, though, you go on. I can hardly conceive all you must have seen. Do you even know how old you are?'

Arthur shook his head and Tellius blew air in disappointment. Darien had been a city in the Empire of Salt, two hundred years before. He'd wondered if the boy had been around then, though of course he could have been born, no, made, anywhere.

'Do you remember the old empire, Arthur? The royal house of Salt? When being a king meant something more than ruling a city or two?'

'Yes,' Arthur said. His voice was a croak, a tool long unused. It sounded like the grave and Tellius was hard-pressed not to shudder.

'Ah, what a thing. To have lived so long. I don't know whether it would be a blessing or a curse, I truly don't.' He let all his breath out, his chest shrinking and his shoulders growing hunched. 'Arthur, they held me in a room in this place, on one of the floors below.' Tellius gave a slight shudder at the thought. 'Before I came out here, I was certain they were going to hurt me and then kill me, just for my part in the death of Master Aurelius.'

He felt the boy turn to watch him and Tellius wrestled with shame.

'I thought to myself, "Tellius, you have maybe a dozen years left to live." Which makes them precious, d'you understand? I thought about you, Arthur, and how I've come to think of you as a son. And how, perhaps, you think of me as a father – I don't know. You see, the thing is, you can save me.' He leaned closer and dropped his voice very low. 'This king is a coward who dreams of assassins. His father was killed by one, when Johannes was just a boy. The man he became . . . well, he is afraid of every shadow. As a result, he surrounds himself with swordsmen.'

Tellius stopped as Arthur rubbed at a spot on his upper arm, his eyes clouding.

'And he is a fool and a tyrant, Arthur, yes. I imagine you have known a few of those as well, in your time. He won't hurt you again, son; I think I can make certain of that. If you show him what you can do – all of it – he will take you into his guard and he will let me go. He believes you have no will of your own, do you see? That if he tells you some word or phrase, you will be bound to obey him. Is that true?'

Arthur went very still, so that for the first time Tellius saw an absence that was not completely natural. After an age, the boy shook his head.

'I thought not, Arthur. I didn't know how you were . . . created, so I wasn't sure, but you seemed to have your own will, before. Good, that's as it should be. No man should be a slave. No boy, either. So it comes to this. If you wish to save me, we'll make up a phrase to whisper to the king. I'll tell him you'll obey as long as he never hurts you again. Oh, you may have to fight a few of his masters and scratch your name on an oath. Can you really not read and write?'

Arthur rolled his eyes and Tellius recalled how easily he learned.

'Of course you can, son. After that, you can either stay here, which will not be a bad life at all. Or you can just leave one night, when no one is watching you.'

'To . . . you?' Arthur said.

Tellius shook his head.

'I'm sorry, Arthur, but no. I was involved in the death of an Aurelius, one of the Twelve Families. I am a marked man and if I escape this palace with my hide intact, I will leave the city immediately and lose myself in some village too far away for them to ever find me again. I have some savings buried in a few places, don't you worry. I will see a few good years yet, with a bit of luck. I'll send a message to Micahel and Donny and the lads as well. The deed to the workshop is behind a stone on the mantel. They can have it, or sell it, to give themselves a stake. I'm for retirement.'

He paused then as the word sank in, shaking his head in amazement.

'Retirement! Well, why not? Why should I work till I drop just to keep you buggers off the streets, eh?' There was a brittle quality to his smile. 'It's always been my aim to get my lads fine apprenticeships, after all. I haven't had one of my boys join the king's personal guard before. This could be the making of you!'

Tellius spoke cheerfully, but there was pain in his eyes. He did not want to abandon Arthur to the company of hard-faced strangers. Once again, he told himself he had no choice. If a path led to torture and death, always choose another way. It was only sense, though he could not shake the sense of guilt that gripped him. He looked up as Arthur spoke again.

'Very . . . well. I will show them. I will . . . swear. Goodbye.'

To Tellius' astonishment, Arthur reached over and hugged him. For all Tellius told himself it was the embrace of a construct, centuries old and without a drop of living blood, it still felt surprisingly like a hug from a nervous child. The old man's eyes filled with tears and he wiped them away hurriedly as he stood.

'Good lad. Look, here they come, son. Follow my lead.'

King Johannes entered the yard with a clatter of his guards. The king had taken the time to change his clothes to green and gold, with a robe sweeping out behind him. Tellius saw the young man wore an ornate sword and wondered if he had ever drawn it in anger, or if it was as useless as any other bauble.

Around the king, four men and two women spread out as they approached, showing, to Tellius' eye, complete trust in one another. A man of his training read a great deal from their stances and how they overlapped, from the way each one left a space for another to fill and didn't creep over to fill it themselves. Master Aurelius had trained them well, that was clear enough. The six of them would make a formidable force.

For just an instant, Tellius wondered if Arthur would fail. The Mazer steps trained the muscles and the mind, but they were usually learned over a dozen years of hard work and endless repetition. Tellius was not certain Arthur's trick of instant learning would have the same result. A swordsman had to think as well as move. He had to make a hundred decisions very, *very* quickly. Is my opponent's left shoulder unprotected? Should I lunge a fraction too far and tempt him in? Will he see it coming? Can I taunt him into carelessness? It was more art than science and the best masters had no sense of conscious thought at all, but considered themselves empty of all distraction. In the east, anyway. Tellius had no idea what Master Aurelius had done with his mongrel version of those stolen skills. The king's guards offended him with their very existence and he only hoped Arthur would make them all look like fools.

The king's steward had entered with him, standing ready. When he clapped his hands, servants ran out with chairs. King Johannes took his seat in the yard itself, his protectors around him in a phalanx, hands on their swords and eyes always moving. Tellius sighed to himself.

'Arthur, I have not said thank you,' he murmured. 'I am only sorry we did not have longer together. I will say that when I saw what you can do, it was . . . perfect. I have never seen better and, believe me, that is a greater claim than you know. Perhaps one day you will head east, about nine thousand miles or thereabouts, to the city of Shian, where I was born. They would welcome you there.'

Tellius smiled at the boy's earnest expression.

'Now, if you fight the women, you'll find they lunge further than most. The muscles in their thighs stretch faster and further than those of most men. Watch for that. Oh, and try not to kill any of them, unless you have no choice.'

He patted Arthur awkwardly on the shoulder. As small as he was, it was impossible to escape the sense of leaving a child to be torn apart by wolves.

Tellius felt only bitterness as he approached the king. The masters all bristled as he came close, of course, like fools. Tellius moved one way, then another, making them all react so that behind him Arthur could see how they shifted balance. None of the six understood what he was doing, but by the time he came within arm's reach of the king, they were all frowning and irritated, sensing some threat but unable to say exactly what it was. Tellius shook his head, pleased anew that Master Aurelius was dead. He had not trained them well enough.

'Your Highness,' Tellius said. 'If you wish to retain control over the child, I must whisper the words of command in your ear. Once the bond is made, he will obey only you – until you cause him pain.'

'Until I cause him pain?' the king repeated, confused.

Tellius nodded sternly. He did not want it to be forgotten.

'The words create a bond in him, Your Highness, as I understand it. I was lucky enough to be able to read the paper he had with him when he came to me. Yet if he is injured by you, or even at your order, he will be unbound and cannot be bound to you again. Your Highness, this is the moment you will feel safe for the rest of your life. Arthur Quick is unique in the world – his service is not a small thing.'

King Johannes flickered a glance left and right to his guards, warning them to be ready. Tellius almost laughed at that. If he'd wanted, he could have killed the king with one sharp blow to his throat. The guards would have cut him to pieces, of course, but what good would that have been to Johannes de Generes? In such a circumstance, Tellius thought a king should be breezily confident. If an outcome cannot be controlled, you are left only with style.

He bent down and cupped his hand to cover the king's trembling ear, feeling the man's shameful cowardice in every shudder of his breath.

'The phrase is said only once, Your Highness. Say it clearly and be careful not to make a mistake. It is this: "When we are all gone, there you will be. Remember us with kindness then."'

The king blinked, committing the words to his memory. As Tellius stood back, Johannes rose and walked stiffly to where Arthur waited, bending very low to whisper them into Arthur's ear in turn.

When the king straightened up, it was with an air of expectation. Arthur showed no change of expression, but he knew the words were from Tellius and, for an instant, his gaze turned to the old man watching him intently. Then Arthur went down on one knee to the king and the sense of tension left some of those watching.

'I accept your service,' the king said in visible relief. 'Now, I would like to see you spar. Fetch him a sword. Let me see this wonder I have found.'

Tellius caught the eye of a servant in the cloisters, standing by a large chair. The young man came out with the seat in his arms, red-faced and struggling under its weight. As Arthur was given a weapon, Tellius settled himself with small grunts and noisy throat-clearing. The king's guards made no objection. Like the king, they were intrigued by the small boy standing with a sword. Those six had devoted their entire lives to the study of movement and attack. They had heard they were in the presence of something new and they were fascinated.

Tellius wondered how long it would be before the king's elite guards wore guns instead of swords. He shuddered at the idea. For all he knew, the foul things were already being used. He'd seen a pistol fired at the spring fair and known even then it was the end of an era. Men did not value what came too easily. They never had.

That thought brought him back to Arthur, standing motionless as two of the king's guards bowed to him formally and drew swords, the men taking up positions at a third and two-thirds of the circle. Tellius nodded to the king as Johannes returned to his own seat, looking surprised to find the old man comfortably there alongside him.

'My knees, Your Highness,' Tellius said apologetically. In fact, he was keen not to be dismissed before he saw Arthur spar, and also to share a few words with the king, to have the man think of him as a colleague rather than a criminal.

'Begin!' King Johannes called out, leaning forward in interest. At the first clash of swords, he stood once more, unable to remain still any longer.

Tellius leaned back, though his awe was, if anything, greater. Arthur moved like Aurelius; that was obvious from the first moments. Once again, the master's style was there in every flourish and step. It lasted a dozen heartbeats, just long enough to be recognised – and then the shadow of the master vanished. Aurelius' muscles had retained a certain limit that Arthur could exceed. Tellius felt his mouth open, gaping in wonder at what he had created. The Mazer steps were beautiful because all predators move well – and there is a part of men that will always thrill to see a hawk stoop or a hunting dog leap a stile. The steps were designed to turn a body into a weapon and Arthur was the perfect host. He moved with such economy, he made the two swordmasters look slow in the first instant, then like children waving wooden swords. The boy spun and ducked and swept their legs away. He rested his sword length on their necks like a kiss, just long enough for them to know they had been helpless, that all their skill and all their training had not been enough to save them. It was the brutal reality of the sword, as Tellius knew as well as anyone. If you could not defend yourself, you owned nothing, not even your life.

Most men spent their days pretending this simple truth had no place in their existence. They denied it, seeking instead the strength of laws and cities. Yet the personal guards of King Johannes de Generes had devoted their lives to mastery. They knew very well what it meant to face another who would take everything you loved from you. To be defeated so easily robbed them of the confidence they actually needed to step up to a line and fight. Tellius wondered if either of them would be of any worth again after that day. He imagined they might bluff and bluster, as men must who depended on their position for a wage. Yet if it came to it, if they faced another master, he thought Arthur Quick had probably broken them for good, as a knife would be ruined without its sharpest edge.

When the king called a halt, his face was shining and flushed. Johannes de Generes shook his head in astonishment and congratulated both Arthur and his two sour men for their skills and the extraordinary display. No one smiled in return, not Arthur and certainly not the two humiliated swordmasters who could not even defeat a child. The other four had lost their sulky expressions at not being chosen. They looked instead both thoughtful and hawkish, convinced they would have done better.

Tellius rose to his feet and glanced back only once to see Arthur watching him. The old man nodded and Arthur dipped his head in what might have been a bow. He was not out of breath, though the two swordsmen ran with sweat and panted like bellows.

Tellius found himself walking along a dark corridor of stone, leading away from the yard. The king had come behind him, with both of his female guards, leaving the other four behind. Tellius hoped that did not mean he would be killed. Women could be cold creatures in his experience. Perhaps because they created life within them, they seemed to have no special remorse about ending it.

9

Tomb

Threefold found the tomb somewhere around noon, judging by the sun. He'd begun to experience a sense of familiarity, until every stunted bush seemed to bring back memories of five years before. Yet when he finally saw the door, he breathed in relief. It lay exactly as it had before, slightly raised from the horizontal like a brewer's delivery hatch, looking almost like a white mouth made of scrolled stone in the black sand all around it. Without the wards, he did not doubt any normal door would have been covered over by drifts centuries before. Yet there was something in the protection that had sand skimming right across the open surface. He remembered that, from when he had gone as close as he could bear, when the pain had been like flames licking his skin. There had been sand on the door then, like dust on a sheet of glass, but trembling, always moving away.

'There,' he said, pointing.

Nancy shaded her eyes.

'I see it. Looks like a hole with . . . white columns. Like teeth, sort of. What now?'

Threefold swallowed.

'The last time I was here, I felt a prickling on my skin, beginning when I was a couple of dozen paces away from it. It wasn't too bad at first, but it doubled with every step, just about. It felt like I was on fire, to the point where I thought I could smell fat burning.'

He closed his eyes in memory and Nancy looked at him with interest.

'How close did you get?'

'My servants ran away,' he said. 'Left on my own, I went up and laid my hand on it.' He shuddered. 'I couldn't see any blisters or marks and so I told myself it was only pain, that I could bear pain for a while, no matter how bad it got. I was wrong. It had been bad before, but it went away if I backed off. When I touched it . . . it stayed bad. It . . . was too much. There is a reason I haven't been back. No one ever comes here twice, so they say. I ran a long way and I almost died of thirst before I found a road with travellers heading to the city. They gave me water and a place in the shade on their cart. And that's it – my story from five years ago. I know now that I was luckier than most. Some have endured for longer than I did, by using shields and barrier wards. They usually die at the door, trying to push through. There are bones there, in tiny white pieces. Some of them get blown away, but the door traps a few that spin . . . slowly. I've had nightmares about those.'

'You really believe all this, don't you?' Nancy said.

His expression changed on the instant to intense annoyance.

'I am not discussing this again! I understand you don't believe in magic, and if you have a knack that cancels it out, I suppose that makes some sort of sense. But I know what I know – what the whole city knows, the whole world apart from you! Just trust me on this. We'll walk up to it together, staying very close. If I feel the prickling begin, we can either back away or see if it stays bearable. I won't risk my life or yours if the wards are still working, all right? For all I know, your little talent only works on small things. Remember that no one has been able to get into this place. Every king or mage of Darien has come out here sooner or later, with the best people they can bring with them. They've all failed.'

Nancy rolled her eyes, sensing he wanted her to show some sort of caution or awe. The truth was, she did feel nervous at what they were going to do. Any sane person would have, with a door that looked like bleached teeth in black sand waiting for them. She felt goosebumps sweep across her bare arms, despite the noon sun.

Threefold dismounted and hobbled his horse with a length of rope around its front legs, doing the same with hers. The animals seemed unhappy, their ears flicking back and forth. To Nancy's eye, Daw looked a bit pale as he took tools and weapons from his packbags, tying on a thick belt with loops. The last piece of kit was a full flask of blood-warm water. He blew air out of puffed cheeks and wiped perspiration.

'Ready?'

'We are not the only ones here, Daw,' Nancy said, pointing.

He spun round, cursing aloud at the sight of two men approaching. One of them was dragging the tip of a sword in the sand as he came. He looked large and fit and Daw Three-fold didn't want him anywhere near. They were a long way from any sense of safety or the rule of law. The other man wore a simple brown robe that revealed his arms to the elbow as he raised his hands.

'Thieves,' Threefold hissed.

'What do we do?' Nancy replied, without taking her eyes off the pair of strangers.

Threefold had his hand halfway into his pocket before he

remembered he had no magical weapons worth the name, not any longer. Before they'd left the city, he'd had an edge ground onto his knife, but it was no sharper than any other. His throwing coins were just bits of metal. He looked again at the swordsman sweeping a line in the sand. It was theatrical somehow and Daw began to grow angry. He had endured a great deal to get to that place. Men like this pair always took the easier path – and never saw how it destroyed them. Daw detested them, with their sly grins and slippery gaze.

'Steady there. No need for alarm,' the swordsman called as they came within a dozen paces. Both of the men halted, though Threefold noted the one in the robe kept his hands high.

'Oh no, Nancy, look! A mage!' Threefold said, pointing at the man. Nancy shot him a glance, but the strangers looked pleased.

'We don't want to hurt either of you,' the swordsman said. 'But I will if I have to. You won't get into the tomb. No one does. So instead you'll hand over the food and tools and weapons you brought for the task and go back to the city, with a nice adventure to tell your fancy friends. Though we might borrow the girl for a while.' He let his gaze linger on Nancy and she scowled at him, trying not to show fear.

'I don't think you let anyone go,' Threefold said to him. 'I think you couldn't get into the tomb, so now you just rob and murder those who come out to try in turn. I think if you ever let them walk away I'd have heard of you by now. The city would have sent guards out here to hang you. So, *damn* you for making me do the king's work.'

He took a sudden step forward and the robed man spat words at him, extending one arm as if throwing a blade. Something passed through the air, like a heat shimmer.

Daw screamed and pressed both hands to his head. He staggered forward, giving out a sound of horror and pain that echoed back from the bare sands around them. The robed man looked puzzled and opened his mouth to call a warning, but Threefold had reached them by then and the swordsman was not as sharp as his companion. The man was grinning at the sounds of agony and did not see the stone until Threefold swung it to crunch against his brow. Without a sound, the swordsman folded onto the sand, face down.

Threefold stopped his screaming and turned slowly to face the sorcerer, now gaping in confusion. The man was pale with fear and for a few heartbeats he twitched and spasmed and called strange-sounding words as he tried a dozen different things that had no effect whatsoever with Nancy standing behind him. Threefold turned away from his antics to bring his stone down once again on the swordsman's head. That man would not be getting up and that was fine with Daw Threefold. The world was a hard place, at least the part of it that was Darien.

As Threefold made sure of his companion, the robed man suddenly hitched up his robe like a woman's skirts and ran, his pale legs flashing as he put distance between them. Daw watched him go, raising an eyebrow at his turn of speed. He wondered idly if the man would recover some of his magic once he was well away from Nancy and the tomb. That would have been an interesting thing to know.

Daw was disappointed the man had escaped. Perhaps he disliked those who robbed travellers so much because it was always what awaited him, when all other plans had failed. Roadmen were the lowest kind of vagabond. Daw Threefold, on the other hand, was about to be a grave robber, which was at least one rung above. For this tomb, perhaps even two or three rungs.

Nancy was watching his expression with interest.

'Did you kill that one?' she asked.

Daw looked down to see and then shrugged.

'I think so. There is no law beyond the city walls. Oh, there could be, if the king and your friend Lord Albus wanted to enforce it, but instead we have men like these two. Every trade caravan has to have armed guards – and there are gangs of men living like filthy animals in every deep wood.'

He saw her surprise at his anger and waved his hand, embarrassed.

'I don't enjoy having my dignity stripped from me any more than you do. I am just a little bit weary of what goes on in Darien every single day. I don't like having to bow my head to every nobleman, or that they can strike us and we daren't even look up. Darien has all the work and all the wealth, but perhaps the price is a touch high at times. For people like us.'

'What did you mean then, about gangs of rebels in the woods?'

He gave a snort at that.

'Oh, they'd love to hear you call them rebels, they really would. The truth is they are what the king's courts say they are. Thieves and murderers and rapists, some of them. Driven to run, then free as birds to starve and root in the ground. It's no life for anyone.'

She did not say anything and Threefold shook his head, annoyed with himself. When he'd run away from home, some hard years had followed. It wasn't something he wanted to discuss with Nancy, or anyone.

'Now, will you come on? All you've done so far is cost me

a fortune in broken things and the silver to repair Basker's ugly clock. I would like to see what lies in this tomb, after all the trouble I've taken to get here.'

Deeds looked over at Elias in the firelight, listening to the night around them.

'We're camped too close to the road,' Elias said.

'I'm a king's man,' Deeds said in a low voice. 'I don't hide myself in the hills or keep a cold camp. No, I sit out in the open. If anyone has a quarrel or feels an injustice, they are welcome to come and lay it at my feet.'

Elias shook his head.

'Whatever else you are, Deeds, you're not a king's man. Not when you're with me . . . for what we're doing.'

'You don't have to lower your voice, meneer. Or do you? Even in the dark, you can tell if anyone is creeping up on us, can't you? Just by looking ahead. Is that what makes you a good hunter?'

'What makes me a good hunter is knowing when to keep my tongue still,' Elias replied.

Deeds chuckled.

'Well, I'm not a hunter, meneer. Not of deer and hares, anyway. And you know the thing about deer and hares? They don't fight back, do they? They don't lay traps and ambushes. They don't come at you in a rush.'

'Wolves do, if you're fool enough to give them no way out,' Elias said softly, rubbing one arm.

Deeds sat up, his attention sharp.

'That an old scar, is it?'

Elias nodded and the gunman made a tutting sound.

'So you *can* be hurt, then. You can be overwhelmed. All I'm saying is that there's a difference between what you do in the deep woods and what General Justan wants you to do in the city. It's just good sense to test yourself against men, to sharpen those skills a touch.'

Elias looked straight at him as Deeds removed one of his pistols from its holster. Deeds rolled his eyes.

'You need to trust me, Meneer Post. I'm the general's man and so are you for the moment. You're no good to me dead. So . . . think, as I do this.'

Slowly, Deeds raised his gun, not wanting to startle the hunter watching him so hawkishly. Coming up onto one knee, Deeds stretched out his arm until the tip of the barrel was almost touching Elias' head. Deeds looked past it to the eyes glaring back at him.

'This is astonishing, really,' Deeds said. 'There's no fear in you, is there, even when a gun is that close? Because you can see if I'll shoot. Even if I decide earlier to do it with no warning, you'll still see it coming.'

'Yes. I am not a mind-reader. Now go to sleep, Mr Deeds. I have no interest in helping you learn my weaknesses.'

'You think that's what I'm doing?' Deeds said, then chuckled. 'Well, perhaps a little. You have an interesting knack, meneer. Yet I'm going to risk my life in Darien with you. I would quite like to walk in and then walk *out* of that place alive. I have no interest in getting myself killed at your side. So you'll excuse me if I look for your limits.'

'You put me in a cage,' Elias said. 'That worked well enough for you.'

'I don't want to trap you again!' Deeds replied. 'But if I'm going to face guns and swords at your side, I'll want to know a few things first.'

Elias scowled and then shrugged, putting a few more pieces of firewood on. The stars were very clear and he thought there would be frost that night. He hated waking in the open when there was frost.

'Ask, then,' he said.

'How far can you see ahead? That's the heart of it, isn't it?'

Elias made a pursed-lip expression like a stubborn dog, then gave a quick nod.

'A few moments, a shade more if I can remain still and concentrate.'

'Not much chance of that when someone is swinging a blade at your face. So you see something coming and step out of the way. But what if one choice looks bad but will lead you out – say through a burning room to freedom – while the other path looks safe but leads to disaster? What would you do then?'

'I imagine I would put water on the fire, or wait for it to die down,' Elias said irritably. 'Or die, perhaps, who knows? Unless I let you put a bullet in my head first rather than listen to you.'

Deeds said nothing and Elias flushed with anger, knowing that the man was deliberately not mentioning his daughters. That threat did not need to be repeated. Deeds knew he knew and that was the end of it. Elias clenched his fist around a piece of dry stick. He was a slave until this was over. Like the doors of his grief, it was something he kept closed, intent on one task at a time.

'If the king's guards knew I was coming, they might prepare traps of the sort you described,' Elias said grudgingly. 'With one choice after another, so quick it would lead to disaster before I could see it was going wrong. But they don't, do they? My best chance, *our* best chance, if you truly insist on coming with me, is to go in fast, kill . . . the king and then run like rabbits for the hills. It won't be smooth or pretty, but if I can get into the king's presence, I can do it.'

'You *think* you can,' Deeds said quietly. He'd heard the scrape of a boot on stone nearby and his voice dropped once more to a whisper in the darkness. 'It's my belief you need to practise first. Men ain't wolves.'

Elias looked up suddenly with a curse. He scrambled to his feet and an arrow buzzed through the air where he had been sitting, appearing as a white blur through the firelight.

'What *is* this?' Elias snapped.

Both men stepped instinctively away from the fire into the darkness. Deeds could hear stealthy movement by then. He held both pistols ready as his eyes adjusted.

'This stretch of road has a very bad reputation, meneer. Scavengers and monsters murder travellers around here, so they say.'

He spoke loudly and clearly and some of the shadows chuckled nastily, certain they held the upper hand.

'General Justan Aldan Aeris asked if I could stop here on my way to Darien, to show them the error of their ways. My name is Vic Deeds and I said I would be *delighted* to teach the lesson.'

The sound of their jeering rose in volume, like the howling of wolves. Elias put out his arm and pulled Deeds a step to the side, so that an arrow hissed past his face. In the noisy darkness, he still heard the gunman's expression of surprise.

'Here is your practice, Elias,' Deeds said. 'They will certainly kill us both unless you act. Or if these simple road rats are too much for you, I will at least know better than to walk into the presence of actual swordmasters and offer them my throat!'

At that moment, the mewling, howling shadows attacked, the darkness erupting in chaos and fear. Where Deeds stood was revealed as his guns fired, pressed against a man's side. Sensing that the flashes of light made him a target, he immediately altered his style, firing shots in close pairs to help him aim, then moving away to another spot.

In the midst of them, Elias drew a knife from a stiff new scabbard, as long as his hand and sharp enough to shave with. He closed his eyes. He did not need to see to move and the sudden flares and cracks of sound from Deeds' pistols were distracting.

The howling still went on at the outskirts of the struggle, though only from those who had not yet come against the two men. Not many of those would have heard of the new guns, nor seen them used, unless it was at a country fair. They carried swords and bows, or hunting knives older than they were themselves. No doubt they'd intended to rob and murder the pair of fools as they sat and talked by their fire. It would have been a single moment of savagery in a cold and uncaring place. In the early morning, perhaps other travellers would have seen the ashes of the fire or a few scattered pieces of their kit. They'd have hurried past and given thanks it hadn't been them.

Elias breathed slowly, just as he did when he approached a deer. His knack didn't help him get close to his prey. That took woodcraft and patience, though when he was in arm's reach, he could hold even a great stag, binding it with rope for the kill as it struggled and heaved against a grip it could not shake.

He had not told Deeds he had never killed a man. It was not something he was comfortable discussing with a gunman whose job it was to bring the roughest sort of criminal to justice or at least administer some sort of vengeance. No doubt Deeds had killed dozens in his young life, but Elias had not, until that evening and that first moment when he swung the heavy blade at neck height and swept the life right out of a man whose face he never saw.

Elias hesitated then, growing angry with the attackers for making him kill them, though it made no special sense to feel that way. He was surrounded and he could feel his knack splintering as every choice revealed another weapon arcing in at him. The Goddess only knew how they could see so well in the dark. Perhaps the firelight had blinded Elias a little. He had not known to expect an attack and he hadn't kept his gaze away from the light.

Deeds continued to shoot and Elias stepped across his line of fire between shots to plunge a knife into the chest of a man wielding some sort of axe or cleaver. Elias opened his eyes and saw only chaos and moving shadows, so he closed them again and peace returned.

There was a way out when every choice led to danger. The answer that occurred to him in the darkness by the road was to kill them all. He felt astonishment that he could, but by then he was almost lost to it, spattered in their blood as he gashed and stabbed and swung until his arms were leaden and his chest burned. He'd thought he had a hunter's fitness, but he'd never found anything as exhausting as those few moments, or hours, however long it took. His world had become a simple place and then Deeds stopped firing at last and Elias opened his eyes once again.

They stood, not quite back to back, some thirty yards away from the firelight. There were bodies all around them and the rest were racing away through the trees and the night, terrified at the savagery. Both men were panting and Elias felt suddenly enraged. As Deeds began to say something, he grabbed the gunfighter and almost lifted him up by his shirt, forcing him a step back.

'Is that enough for you? Am I ready, Mr Deeds?'

'Just about,' Deeds said calmly. 'Though I will need a third pistol, or some way of loading them faster. Or a sword. When I ran out of bullets, I thought I was done. So, thank you. You saved me more than once.'

Elias set him down and stalked back to the fire. As Deeds watched, the older man used a rag and his water bottle to wipe blood from his skin, grimacing all the while. Deeds came and sat on a log, reloading slowly and watching the hunter.

'It was not my idea to take your daughters,' Deeds said. 'Just so you know. I had nothing to do with that.'

Elias turned slowly to him as he wiped the red cloth over the back of his neck, now sodden and dripping like a piece of beef.

'I've answered your questions – and I've killed. So answer this for me, now. What if I die in the city? What if I just can't get through? What if you and the general are wrong about me? If I catch a bullet, or break my neck, what happens then to my daughters?'

Deeds held his gaze.

'General Justan Aldan Aeris is a man of honour. He does not make war on children. You have my word they would be sent back to your village and given to the care of someone there. If you fail, the general will want nothing around him to link him to you, believe me.'

'You and he would be wise to walk carefully around my girls, Mr Deeds. Around me.'

For an instant, the two men stared at each other. It had been a long time since anyone had dared to threaten Vic Deeds, as his reputation spread. He looked away as Elias turned back to his wiping and wringing-out. The man looked like a painted devil and Deeds found himself shuddering in reaction. He had expected a few roadmen or rogues, not dozens of the howling bastards coming at him in the dark. No wonder the general had been getting complaints of murders and robberies on that road.

Yet even so many had not been enough. Deeds shook his head, wondering just what he and Justan Aldan Aeris had unleashed on the world. He looked at the older man cleaning himself, seeing how the bristles on Elias' chin were coming in white. When the king was dead, perhaps it would be an idea for Deeds to take ship for somewhere else for a time. He did not want to stand between Elias Post and his daughters, nor have such a man consider him an enemy.

Jenny took Alice by the hand as they sat at the wooden bench and waited to be served. The woman bossing the camp kitchen was huge to them, pink and sweating through her apron from the heat of bubbling stews. Mrs Dalton oversaw the vast quantities of carrots and potatoes, spices, carcasses, fowl and fish that had to come through the camp to keep five thousand active soldiers alive. There were constant sittings throughout the day and forty young men helped her to chop, prepare and serve the food to those who lined up for it, ladling it out into bowls and mugs. It was thin stuff, but there was never any left when the horns sounded for the change of watch.

The two young girls were given the same as any of the

Immortals. It was rare for either of them to finish, so instead they sat and dragged their spoons through a glutinous mass, while hungry men passed by with polished bowls and stared. Only Mrs Dalton spoke to Elias' daughters, when she dropped the bowls and picked them up, always tutting at how little they ate.

'You're like sparrows!' she said, shaking her head. 'You'll waste away if you don't eat a bit more, you know that? You'll just be shadows, sitting in those dresses, all miserable. What will the general say then, eh? He'll have my ears. Here, put this in a pocket for later.' She placed an apple on the table between them.

Jenny sensed no malice in Mrs Dalton, but she didn't trust her either. It was easier to have Alice ask the questions they wanted answered. The younger girl looked like a chubby blonde angel and people saw no guile in her, as they sometimes did in Jenny. As her sister was still fiddling with a bit of grey gristle, Jenny nudged Alice, making her look up with a start.

'Oh! Um . . . Mrs Dalton?'

'Yes, dear?'

'Why are all the lads packing up their tents? Are we going home?'

The big woman reached out with a hand and pinched her cheek.

'Aren't you *adorable*! No, dear. Not home, not yet. The general says "up sticks" and off we go. It's a soldier's life, love. We just go where we're told.'

'Will there be fighting, Mama Dalton?' Alice asked.

The 'Mama' was a nice touch, Jenny thought, glancing sideways at her, though she kept her own head down. The lady in question grew pinker at hearing it.

'I think there might be, yes dear, but not for us, never for us, don't you worry about that. We'll be far behind the soldiers, with the camp followers, do you see? With the pots and pans and the dogs and menders and the smiths. The soldiers march about in all their fine metal and colours, but they wouldn't get far without us, would they, love? They wouldn't get far without food, or without horseshoes! I should say not!'

Mrs Dalton chuckled at the very idea, then collected up the bowls and bustled off, pausing only to ruffle the little girl's hair. Jenny smiled after her in thanks, though she knew she lacked the easy touch with people that her sister had. It was different for her, somehow. At ten, Jenny felt she had not yet met enough strangers to feel comfortable with any of them.

'If they're moving, how will Dad know where to find us?' Jenny said softly.

Her sister looked up, eyes wide and immediately close to tears.

'He's coming back for us. He said he would.'

'Of course he is. I just think we might . . . go and find him on our own, that's all. If we could sneak away, you know, without being seen.'

The two girls looked around them, at five thousand Immortals bustling to clear a permanent camp and transfer it all onto horse and mule and cart. Units of clattering horsemen cantered across the open ground. Horns sounded, bells rang and men roared orders in ceaseless cacophony. The legion swarmed and, as they worked, parts of the camp simply collapsed and vanished into bricks or spars and cloth. The very walls and gates were knocked apart, unbolted and piled ready to be loaded on. It was frightening, somehow, to see the solid world taken down, as if there was nothing real to any of it.

Jenny looked behind, to where a young subaltern assigned to them still stood. Peter Jay had been polite and pleasant to them both, but he took the general's orders seriously and he was never far away. Jenny groaned in frustration as she realised he'd seen her glance over. He came to the table.

'All finished, are we? Good. General Aeris has asked for you to ride with him as we break camp. Won't that be a treat for you? He has his own cart, so you'll ride like princesses.'

The two girls exchanged a look of despair. The Immortal legion was forming in huge squares on the field, thousands of men in mail waiting patiently as others finished their errands. It had been astonishingly quick. Even as the girls stood and looked around, someone came and swept away their table, bearing it off to the line of carts alongside the marching squares.

'Where are we going, Peter?' Alice asked, her voice high and babyish.

There was no one else around. The young officer bent down.

'We're going to the city, girls! You'd like that, wouldn't you? We're going to Darien.'

10

Bones

Threefold watched the young woman at his side as they walked slowly forward across the black sand. Nancy seemed to share his nervousness. Her eyes moved sharply and yet he felt no sense of pressure as they approached the tomb, no prickle of pain beginning on his skin. His heart beat so hard it made his head throb, but Daw allowed his hopes to rise with each step.

Nancy paused, almost stumbling. She looked up as if she was scenting something.

'What is it?' Threefold whispered to her. There was no breeze and under the sun the air was completely still. It felt like they were being watched.

'I don't . . . know. Something odd.' She shook herself and blinked, looking determined. 'Let's keep moving.'

The white mouth of the tomb was no more than half a dozen paces away. Threefold was almost certain he had felt pain at that distance, but it had been years before and the memory itself was of agony, with details blurred. Step by step, the pair of them came closer to the raised white columns, sticking out of the black sand like a fallen gravestone. Threefold's mouth was dry, but he could no longer deny he was close enough. He stood within arm's reach and he could remember the sensation of agony from the last time, making him sweat.

'Anything?' he hissed at her.

'A headache, no, a feeling of pressure perhaps . . . not pain, but I don't like it.'

'It's working, Nancy. Just hold on. I'm going to touch the doorway.'

He put out his hand and saw that it was trembling. He glanced at Nancy for the last time, finding her staring back at him and looking just as pale and nervous as he felt. He braced every muscle as his fingertips touched the clear surface of the tomb mouth.

There was a rattle as sand and tiny pieces of whitened bone fell away. Nancy blinked and straightened, opening and closing her mouth and working one finger into her ear, then holding her nose and snorting.

'Oh!' she said. 'That felt . . . awful. Wrong somehow.'

'Are you still all right?' Threefold asked. He could hardly contain his excitement at the sight of the dark opening before him. He did not doubt the wards had fallen. It was almost as if a hum was missing from the air. He watched as Nancy shook her head, blinking one eye and then the other.

'I think so. I feel odd, but it's nothing like pain.'

'All right, then,' Threefold said. He took a deep breath and held it, then stepped down through the entrance, still wincing in expectation of agony or death. He took her hand tightly as he went, so that she came after him, leaving the desert and the sunlight behind.

It was instantly cooler below the level of the outside ground, as if the warm days never penetrated. Threefold sniffed the air, though there was no odour of rot or damp. Whatever the wards were that had protected the tomb, they'd kept out all living things. The walls were of dry, grey stone and there were no mouse droppings, or even lichen or moss. The tomb was cool and dusty, but not unpleasant. Threefold used a spinning flint and iron striker to light a lamp. He could hardly breathe for tension and it helped to concentrate on nursing the flame until he could close the lantern sides and hold it up.

A tunnel descended before them, sloping down as far as the dim light would reach.

'We should go slowly,' he whispered. 'Yours is a local effect, but it seems to be permanent. Yet these wards are old magic. They might return, they might not. If they do, the moment we move away from this door, we'll be completely cut off.' He knew he was babbling in relief, but he could not stop himself. 'So there's no rush now, Nancy. Let's just go, shall we? Step by step, slow and careful. You tell me if anything changes, or if you feel ill, anything like that at all. All right? I don't want your knack to burn out or give up at the wrong moment.'

He reached for her hand again and, rather shyly, Nancy held it out. She was as excited as he was. She nodded to him, her eyes glittering.

'Can you still feel the pressure?' he said softly.

Goosebumps appeared along her arm.

'Not as bad here, I think,' she said.

'Let me know if it gets worse,' he said, raising his lamp once more. Together, they walked slowly down into the earth.

The tunnel went on for a long time, until Threefold began to worry he would not have enough oil in the little lamp to take them back out before it guttered and died. He'd seen no other paths off to the sides though, so even if the light failed, he thought they could hardly get lost. The idea was not particularly reassuring, so far from sunshine and the surface. Yet his imagination could almost have lit the way, bright with pictures of what might lie ahead.

They had no warning of the room at the bottom of the shaft. The light of the lamp reached only a few steps ahead, so they were at the entrance before they knew it was anything more than just another stretch of dusty passage.

There was no door to prevent them looking into the room beyond. Threefold waved his lamp around as if he could cast the light further out, peering for anything that looked as if it might be dangerous. The doorway appeared to be lined in a different material to the walls, as bone-white as the stone mouth far above them. He eyed it warily, seeing nothing more threatening than a pale thread set into the stone. It was unbroken, on both sides and across the entrance, forming a threshold.

'Can you see inside?' Nancy whispered.

It seemed only right to keep their voices low. There was the sense of millions of tons of rock around them, of being more alone than any other man and woman alive. If the wards had returned, no one could even enter to save them. Only the small lamp and their own voices kept the darkness and silence from flooding back.

'There's *something* in there. Too far from the door to make out. I don't like the look of that threshold, though. I just wish I had a plank or something to lay across it.'

'What about your knife?' Nancy asked.

Threefold nodded and went down on one knee, carefully placing the lamp on the ground. He took out the blade that had once been the most valuable thing he owned. He knew by then that it couldn't be restored, but he knew he'd never throw it away or sell it for a silver or two. Hope sprang eternal, that was the problem. With two fingers on the hilt, he eased the dagger over the grey stone until it touched the white line.

Threefold thought he could feel pressure increasing, building between his eyes as if a migraine was coming on. Behind him, Nancy gave a gasp and suddenly her hand was gone from his arm.

'It . . . hurts, Daw. By the Goddess, I can't . . . !'

Threefold turned his head, about as slowly as a man facing his death.

'*Please* don't run, Nan. I'm done for if you do. I might not even be able to get out on my own.'

With enormous care, he stood up and turned round. Nancy was standing with both palms pressed into her eye sockets. When he put out his hand to take her fingers in his, he almost recoiled from the heat in them.

'Is it plague, Nancy? Have you met someone with it in the last few days?'

As he spoke, he peered at her skin, looking for the raised welts he'd been told were one of the first symptoms. It had burned out in Darien, but he'd heard it was still causing havoc in the villages around it. Yet there were no signs of swellings on her bare skin. After a time, she gasped as if she'd been holding her breath, then removed one hand from her eyes, peering at him.

'It's passing, I think. Goddess! I thought the top of my head was coming off. Yes, it's getting less . . .' She groaned again. 'I haven't seen anyone with plague, Daw. Not recently.'

'You're hot, though, almost too hot to touch,' he said.

He looked back at the room beyond, still protected by the white line that seemed to gleam in malevolence, somehow.

'Can you go on a bit further, Nancy? I think this is a barrier, like the one outside. If I'm right, the discomfort will pass when we go through.'

To his immense relief, Nancy nodded immediately.

'I'm not going back with nothing, Daw. No matter what. Hold my hand again. Pull me into the room if you have to.'

He picked up the lamp with one hand and put the other around her waist. Holding his breath, he took one great stride over the threshold, yanking her across. He felt something change, reminding him of when he would climb hills as a boy and sometimes feel his ears pop on the way down. He had not really understood the vastness of the pressure bearing down on them until it had gone.

'Are you all right?' he hissed at her.

Nancy shook her head, her eyes still closed. When she opened them, they were fever-bright in the lamplight, but she nodded at him, rubbing her temples with both hands.

Daw raised the lamp once more to see the room they had entered. It was not much larger than he'd been able to see from the doorway, with just one stone block set back against the far wall. In that first instant, he knew the thing resting on it was a sarcophagus of some kind, plain and polished. His heart sank as he looked around in vain for anything like gems or gold. To have come so far and risked so much, just to find a bare room and a coffin! He wanted to throw the lamp in rage, though sense prevailed and he rested it carefully on the lip of the stone block and checked the oil. Half-full still, thank the Goddess.

Dust had settled on the lid of the sarcophagus and Daw brushed it away with his hands, revealing a fine black stone. There was no name or inscription cut into it, though he supposed that made a sort of sense. The wards protecting that tomb were the most powerful anyone had ever known. Visitors had never been part of the plan when the occupant of the coffin was laid to rest there. Daw shuddered at the thought of that thick silence, without even insects or mice to disturb it, for how long? Certainly centuries. There were some who said the tomb was older than the desert, though Daw could not see how that could be so. Deserts grew; they were not created in a flash of light.

He gathered his thoughts as Nancy came to stand at his shoulder. He had been daydreaming in his disappointment, trying not to think about the complete lack of gold and jewels in that room.

'There's only one place left to look,' he said softly.

He could feel heat coming off Nancy still, as if she was burning up or had run miles. Yet her skin was dry and she breathed slowly as she nodded to him.

The lid was not particularly heavy. As soon as he pushed at the curved surface, it moved to reveal a dark space below.

'Take the other end, would you? It doesn't seem right to let it smash on the floor.'

He felt foolish as he said it. The owner of that tomb would care far more that they had broken the wards and entered in the first place. Yet still it seemed simple courtesy not to destroy something that could be saved.

He and Nancy lifted the lid away and laid it down, then straightened at the same time to gaze on the face of the occupant lying within.

'Ah,' Threefold said, a smile spreading across his face. 'Now, that is more like it.'

A gleaming face gazed back up at them, blue eyes painted on the surface of a metal that could only be gold. The mask covered the entire head of whoever lay beneath it, stretching down the chest in an enamelled spike. Threefold grinned in awe and delight and a little fear still. Those unblinking eyes had stared in darkness for Goddess knew how long before he, Daw Threefold, had brought light into that tomb once more.

Without breaking his gaze, he reached out for his lamp. His fingers touched the top and fumbled against the iron ring there, knocking it off the tomb and plunging them both into absolute darkness, so thick it was like velvet suddenly pressed against a face.

Nancy shrieked and Daw froze. He hated the dark. He could hear his breathing tightening up, so that it felt as if he was choking. His heart beat faster and he struggled with the desire just to leave everything and run like a rabbit up the tunnel to the outside.

'It's all right, Nancy. I still have the spinning flint. I can light it again.'

'Do it, then!' she hissed at him.

Unable to see his own hands, he might as well have been blind. He edged around the sarcophagus and went down onto his knees, sweeping the ground with his hands. He'd thought he had a picture in his mind of how the room looked, but he still couldn't put his fingers on the lamp.

'Did you pick the lamp up?' he asked. 'I can't find it.'

'No. Daw? Listen to me. If you don't light it right now, I will run.'

He heard her voice shake and faced the worse horror of being left alone. He felt sick at the thought of being trapped in there, all the wards springing back after she passed them. His knife had never recovered, but who knew what would happen with such old magic? He would die in the dark and never see the light again, or burn as he pushed his way up to the outer door. When he spoke, his voice was quiet and firm.

'Nancy? Please don't run. Let me find the lamp and we'll have a rummage in the coffin for anything valuable, and then we'll walk out, easy as a stroll, all right?'

'No, it's not all right!' she snapped from a new position.

'Light the lamp or come right now. There's something wrong and I'm going.'

Goddess, had she found her way to the door? He could hear complete panic in her voice and he spun round, his own fear swelling like a live thing uncoiling in his stomach.

'Fine. Wait for me, please.'

His hand brushed the stone sarcophagus and he swallowed drily. If she ran, he'd be left there to go mad in the silence and dark, to claw at the walls until his nails were torn out. He reached into the stone coffin and felt for the gold mask, hooking his fingers under the edge. With a great wrench, he ripped it away.

Light crackled from some source he could not see, like fireworks sputtering and burning out. Nancy gave a cry of pain or terror, he did not know which. Daw had been looking into the coffin and in that moment he saw a moving face and eyes that turned to see him. A smell of acid and fire filled the air and then the light was gone again.

'Nancy?' Daw said.

There was no reply and he heard footsteps racing away from him. He crossed the room to where he'd seen the doorway, feeling for it, then stumbling through and sprinting for his life. He had no idea if the wards above would still work, but he was mindless with fear then, just running faster than he ever had before.

The path stretched up and up, much further than it had seemed when they were walking in, full of excitement. He saw a dim patch of light ahead and knew it was the outside air and the blessed sunlight to warm his skin. He hungered for it, feeling as if he was climbing out of his own tomb, back to the living world.

Ahead, he saw a shadow cross the brightness. He knew

then that Nancy had gone out without him and he sobbed in fear as he raced faster, muttering, 'Please, please let it be open,' as he went. If the wards had come back, he told himself he would rather crash through and burn like the sun for a few moments than remain in the darkness of that place.

Nancy wondered if she had gone mad as she staggered the last few steps onto black sand. She and Daw had surely not been down there for the best part of a day. It didn't seem possible, and yet the sun had passed noon and sat low and red in the western sky.

She was panting like a dog from running so fast and for so long. Worse than that, guilt consumed her for having abandoned Daw in the tomb. All she had wanted was to get out of the dark for a while, just to catch her breath and get her bearings once more.

Whatever she had planned fell to pieces as she looked out on six men facing the doorway at a safe distance. Two of them carried drawn bows, with the arrows aimed right at her. She thought the wards on the tomb would have stopped a shaft, at least before she and Daw had gone in. Yet she'd felt no pressure bursting as she'd come through the second time, not like she had when the thing in the tomb had moved. She did not know if the wards would return when she moved away. With a sinking feeling, she realised she could not let them take her while Daw was still down the tunnel. Until he came out, she was stuck by the door.

Nancy shook her head, trying to clear it of flashing lights as her eyes adjusted. She recognised the robed man who had gone racing off across the sand that morning, an age ago. He had summoned friends, it seemed, perhaps after he'd crept back and seen the two of them pass alive through the entrance in the sand. The others were all strangers and Nancy could feel their gaze like tongues on her skin.

'Come away from the door now, miss,' one of the men called. 'We'll be having whatever you brought out of the tomb.'

Nancy turned to face the speaker.

'There's nothing down there. Just an old corpse in a box. Look! You can see I don't have anything.'

She held her arms out wide and one of the archers side-stepped, adjusting his aim.

'Easy there,' Nancy said to him.

'Not many women out here, miss,' the robed man called. 'And you are a beauty, aren't you? You can be useful, don't worry. Where's the cocky one, though? Your mate?'

As he spoke, Nancy could hear running footsteps getting closer.

'He's coming now,' she shouted back, hoping Daw would hear. 'We didn't find anything!'

Out of the tomb, Daw came skidding, falling onto his knees on the sand. Nancy looked down and recoiled from the golden face staring up at her. Goddess alone knew how much the thing weighed, but rather than abandon it, he'd carried it all the way to the surface. It gleamed in sunlight for the first time in centuries and the lips seemed to smile.

The men ringed around the tomb entrance nodded and grinned to one another at the sight of it. They knew gold when it rested on black sand. Their eyes were drawn to it, bright and greedy, already considering shares and what they might do with such a king's treasure.

Nancy watched as Daw wiped tears and sweat from his eyes and stood, gathering up the mask into the crook of his elbow, as if he held a child. She blinked at him, feeling suddenly ill, as if a plague fever was spiking higher. She saw Threefold was looking at her in astonishment and she shook her head, seeing flashing lights crackle across her vision.

The robed man pointed at her. He froze in that position as she looked up. Nancy thought she would vomit, her stomach surging. Around her, the roadmen began to edge away and a burning sensation seared through her hand. She raised it up, to see.

The bones glowed through the skin that covered them, sparking with light as the corpse in its box had done. Nancy could still see its eyes turning, flesh forming around them and then dissolving into ashes or dust once again. She felt *full*, as if water had been poured into her, to the very brim, so that it sat quivering, ready to spill over.

All the magic in that place had not been made null by her presence, she realised. Her knack was not to cancel. It was to soak up. Daw Threefold had brought her to the most potent source of power in Darien and, for all his caution, he'd almost drowned her in it. The outer door, the strange threshold, all of it. Even the final smell of fire and chemicals had been some spell, at least as potent as the others. It had been meant to animate the corpse, perhaps even to bring the owner back from the dead long enough to destroy his tomb's robbers.

Instead, she had drunk it all and she was so full it would surely consume her.

'Your eyes, Nancy,' Threefold whispered at her side, breaking into her sense of wonder. 'How are you doing that? They're glowing.'

'I'm not surprised,' Nancy said.

She looked up at the strangers gaping at her. Without thought, she raised her hand again and poured out some of what roiled and surged within. A stream of heat and light crackled, turning the robed thief into a screaming pillar of flame in an instant.

Daw turned as if from a blow. The rest of the men froze, some of them in mid-step. Their eyes were wide as their companion choked and died. Even when he fell, the flames still burned.

Nancy looked up at the blue sky. She put out her tongue to scratch her nail across the pink surface.

'Strange. It itches,' she said to Daw Threefold, still watching her in astonishment and rigid fear. 'It itches, Daw. Did you know that?'

'What does?' he whispered.

'Magic.'

She lifted her second hand and threads of flame leaped from her fingers, striking each of the thieves gathered around the tomb entrance. One of the archers got a shot off as he blistered, but the arrow burned in the air, vanishing into reddish ash before it could reach them. In moments there were six burning piles on the sand, collapsing in on themselves. The only sound then was the flutter of flames and the crackle of spitting fat.

Nancy turned to see Threefold watching her, much as a mouse might watch a tiger. She nodded to him and her gaze snagged on the golden mask in his hand.

'We'll have to go back to Darien to sell that,' she said. 'Half shares, remember.'

Without turning his head, Threefold's eyes swivelled to gaze at the streamers of black smoke coming off the burning bodies on the sand.

'My brother knows some people who might help,' he said weakly.

Nancy smiled at him. She was brighter somehow, certainly

more beautiful. She seemed to glow still, though at least the horrible gold and red had dimmed in her eyes.

'Good. That's good, Daw. We'll have to walk, though. All the horses are gone.'

'They ran away,' he said slowly.

'Yes. Come on, then. It's a long walk to the city and I'm already thirsty.'

Daw hadn't been thirsty before, but her saying the word seemed to remind his body and his throat suddenly felt papery and dry. He swallowed with difficulty, hefting the gold mask in his hand, then taking a grip on the long chin-piece so he could balance the rest on his shoulder. It was heavy and he was surprised he hadn't noticed the weight when he was sprinting up towards the light.

The black desert stretched before them. Nancy set off at a stroll and he followed her, looking back only once at the tomb entrance and the smoking corpses left behind on the sand.

11

Darien

King Johannes de Generes clapped his hands in pleasure as Arthur came out. This time, his little golem sword-master was dressed in loose trousers, felt boots and a tunic of gold and black. Arthur approached the throne and its occupant, halting in exactly the same spot as he had three times before that morning. The king tapped his lips with one hand as he looked over the latest addition to his personal guard.

'Yes, that is much better than the red or the grey. Black and gold. Oh, you are like a wasp! And your sword is your sting!'

An appreciative chuckle sounded from some of the courtiers gathered around. Lord Albus was asleep in his chair after a heavy lunch, but two junior members of the Twelve Families inclined their heads and smirked. Lady Win Sallet ignored the king completely, though she continued to watch the golem from the corner of her eye.

Word had spread amongst the families of Darien that their idiot representative Johannes had stumbled across something of true value. In any normal month, the king would have had only his own people in that audience chamber. As a rule, the nobles of Darien preferred to leave him to design new gardens, or whatever grand project or foolishness he indulged in to pass the time.

Lady Sallet knew better than most that Johannes was merely a figurehead or a lightning rod for the Twelve Families. His father had striven for a more serious role, she recalled with some sadness. A man of great energy, he had paid an unpleasant price for that ambition. Lady Sallet remembered the assassin had made a point of killing the father in front of the boy. The lesson had not been lost. Instead of being an actual leader, who might have interfered in the running of the city, Johannes had his parties and his lovers and his delight in art and glass. He had his guards as his companions, for those days when he dressed as a mercenary and walked with a swagger amongst them. The business of the city, the trade and threats and bargains – the true power – all went on without his hands anywhere near.

Lady Sallet showed no sign of the irritation she felt. The little boy, the golem, was the most interesting thing to have come to her attention in Darien that year, she was certain. Only the Goddess would have known the value of such a creature in gold and gems – so much that no one could ever have bought him, perhaps. An actual relic of the old Empire of Salt, from which her own surname had its origin – and somehow it had fallen into Johannes' childlike hands! It was infuriating. Her own spies had brought her the news, of course, including the existence of a secret phrase to control the creature. How she had longed then for this 'Arthur Quick' to be hers. Unsleeping, eternal and loyal. He would be a magnificent ornament to her household, if she could . . .

'Lady Sallet,' the king called to her, interrupting. 'What do you think of Arthur in black and gold? Is my wasp not very fine?'

Lady Sallet bowed her head in response. She stepped

153

down from the raised chair at the side of the hall and walked slowly to the throne, her long green dress swishing against polished stone. She knew she was a striking figure, hair tied tight to reveal her neck, taller than most women, gliding towards the king. The floor had such a high sheen, she could see the apexes of the ceiling above as she passed over them, like beads on a chain.

None of her spies had suggested Johannes was lonely. It was odd to have him use the creature's name with such familiarity, as if the golem was his companion, or even a friend. It was rather pitiful, if that was the way his mind was going. The little killer looked like a ten-year-old. One of her spies had reported the king walking his gardens only that morning, talking and gesturing to the golem all the while. Lady Sallet had dismissed it as idle gossip at first, but in his loneliness, perhaps Johannes was confiding in the magical thing. By the *Goddess*, he was a weakling.

Lady Sallet came to the foot of the throne and curtsied, sinking into the thick folds of her dress. She looked sideways then at Arthur as she rose once more. The king's aunt had remained slim over her sixty years, with fine posture and a physical confidence born on horseback. It came quite naturally to her to pat the golem's head, as she might have done to a hound.

Arthur swayed away from her touch, just enough to frustrate her, so that her long fingers patted the air a hair's breadth from his face. She tried three times to touch him before she gave it up. It irritated her to hear Johannes laugh, but she allowed him to see only amusement as she faced him and bowed again.

The golem showed no expression at all, though she thought she sensed something even so, as if he saw more of her than his master. Impossible, surely. Once again Lady Sallet wondered how old the golem was, how many people it had known over its centuries of life.

The thought brought conflicting emotions surging in her. Against all reason, she suddenly wanted to see the thing destroyed, burned or cut into pieces so that it was no longer a mockery of life and a child. If she could not bring that about, she would make it her own servant, obedient to her and no one else. Perhaps she would make Arthur Quick walk into a furnace then, or perhaps not.

There was no third choice, to leave the creature in the clumsy care of her nephew, Johannes. Her spies had not heard the words of command and yet there might still be a way. Only two men in all the world were said to know the phrase – her nephew, of course, but also the old man, Tellius. She had a dozen trackers out looking for him in the city at that very moment. If he tried to pass through one of the main gates, or was foolish enough to return to his workshop above the apothecary, she would have him.

'Your Majesty, this creature is a wonder of the age,' she said, then chuckled. 'Or of a previous age, perhaps. It is a great ornament to your court. Like the words on the old coins, Johannes! "Decus et Tutamen" – an ornament *and* a shield.'

Her nephew did not smile in response and Lady Sallet wondered what she had said to cause his simple face to frown so.

'Aunt Win, his name is Arthur Quick. I'll thank you not to call him a "creature" in my court chamber. *He* is a part of my personal guard. I must ask you to treat him with the same courtesy you would give any other member of my staff.'

Lady Sallet bowed her head as if chastened, though she allowed herself a brief roll of the eyes, hidden from the rather pompous young king her sister had produced. Lord Albus chose that moment to begin snoring, his open mouth hidden by the napkin he had placed over his entire face. Honestly, at times it was almost as if Johannes believed he was more than just the image for stamps and coins in Darien! She clenched her jaw, thinking again of the old man and the string of words he knew. Tellius. He was the key, if she had to send men out looking for a hundred miles around Darien. He could not simply vanish.

Elias had said very little for two days after the ambush. Each evening, he and Deeds took their horses away from the road to find some hollow of land where a fire would not be seen. The hunter would vanish into the woods and return with whatever he could forage: onions and mushrooms, as well as a hare and even a thick-bodied snake on the second night.

Deeds had tried to begin a few conversations, but the hunter was used to silence and seemed almost to sink into it, so that it became his natural state. By the second day, Deeds too would have found it odd to speak and he no longer felt any particular resentment. There was a task ahead and he suspected Elias Post was the man to do it, just as he could wring the neck of a hare or hack off a snake's head without hesitation. The hunter would do the job they'd given him and then he'd take his daughters back. Deeds wondered how the general would handle that particular transaction, but he could think of one or two ways. The daughters could be left somewhere far off – on a hilltop, say, or the far shore of a lake. The general's servants would shout the location and then gallop clear. Elias' knack didn't make him fast enough to catch a horse, thank the Goddess. Deeds had spent a long time thinking about how he might survive the anger of the hunter he and the general had blackmailed. He felt Elias watching him sometimes. The expression on the man's face was not a kind one.

On the afternoon of the third day, they saw Darien city far ahead, the enclosing wall making a dark line across the horizon. From high ground, the view stretched all the way to a range of mountains behind the city and even a glimpse of blue coast in the far haze. Yet Darien sat close before them, ancient and fortified, clustered around a river that twisted through its heart like the snake Elias had roasted on a spit the night before.

Deeds watched Elias as they approached, enjoying the man's changing expression as he compared the size and scale of the city with anything he had known before. The wall itself was centuries old and thick enough for Elias to make out crowds walking back and forth on its crown, some of them wearing bright colours as if they strolled in a park. Seeing people up there in their hundreds made the hunter realise how wide the wall must be. Elias whistled softly, making Deeds grin at his back and speak for the first time in days.

'Impressive, isn't it? When those gates are closed, the city is a fortress. Perhaps four or five hundred thousand people live within those walls, meneer! A dozen parks lie inside and each one is larger than your Wyburn. A hundred theatres! Entire streets of apothecaries and markets and schools. Can you imagine so many? I don't think I can – and I have lived in Darien for some years.'

Elias looked back at him and shrugged. His voice was rusty from lack of use.

'I have come to kill only one. What do I care for talk of walls and parks? Do you know the way to the palace or not?'

Deeds forgot himself and stretched out a hand to take Elias by the arm. It infuriated him when the hunter moved away without even looking at him. Deeds was a man of his hands and it hurt his confidence in the strangest way to be physically helpless in the presence of another. He knew by then that he could not stop the hunter killing him if Elias chose to. It was a frightening thought and the gunman detested being afraid.

'Oh, damn your cold shoulder, Elias! I have apologised for making you kill those roadmen, haven't I? I had to know you could. No, *you* had to know. I should not even apologise, in fact! You have never been to a city before, never mind Darien. If you think you can just walk past a thousand soldiers into the king's bedroom, you are mistaken. They would cut us down and *overwhelm* you by sheer numbers. What would your daughters do then?'

Elias turned so sharply at his words that Deeds raised both hands in reflex, lowering them in a mixture of anger and shame as the hunter glared at him.

'You keep mentioning them. According to you, they would be taken back to Wyburn and left in peace. Are you saying that was a lie, Deeds? Be careful how you answer.'

'I meant how would they get by without *you*, that's all,' Deeds replied, flushing. 'And I gain nothing by lying to you. Look, tonight we'll find a tavern and we'll sleep in comfortable beds. I will purchase some more bullets and perhaps a third pistol. I have a letter of credit from the general that should get us whatever we need. You look exhausted, meneer. Will you at least accept I know a little more about this city than you do?'

Elias nodded, grudgingly.

'You're so sure we need to wait for this festival, this harvest?'

'I am. Reapers' Eve is the key to all of this. The rules relax a little tomorrow night – and all the general's plans come into play. We'll hide ourselves in the festival crowds and they'll never see us coming.'

'All right, then,' Elias said, some of the tension going out of him.

Deeds blew out air.

'Thank the Goddess for common sense.'

'You don't understand, Deeds. Every day, every *hour* I waste on this is one more where my daughters are alone,' Elias said softly. 'If you had children of your own, or any kindness in that little soul, perhaps you would understand that.'

'I understand you well enough – and your daughters are safe in the camp while you do the general's bidding, believe me. Yet this is no small thing, what lies ahead of us. If you intend to survive it and return to see those girls grow to be young women, you will settle down and trust me. Understand? I want this to work, meneer. Have you considered what will happen when the king is dead and the city is in chaos, twisting up on itself like that snake you killed?'

Elias looked at him and shook his head. He truly had not thought further than what he had been forced to contemplate. He cared very little for what came after, as long as he got out and back to his girls. They'd already lost a brother and a mother. He would give anything just to be left in peace to raise them.

'The general will bring the Immortals into Darien,' Deeds

said. 'He's planned it all, down to the last step. He'll turn out the Twelve Families and their courtiers and their guards. He'll settle some old scores and banish the rest from the city – and he'll rule instead of them. And then we'll go to war. He thinks I don't know all he intends, but I see his frustration when he talks of them. It's why he'll do anything to keep you on his side, Elias. Anything. He couldn't cut off the head before. He couldn't get a man to King Johannes, not with all his tasters and his master swordsmen. You, though – you change everything. The Twelve Families unite behind the king. That's his entire purpose. While he is alive, there is still order. The people know it, the Twelve Families can rally around it. If he dies though, they'll eat each other alive – and while they do, the Immortals will take the city from them.'

Their horses had ambled along the whole time they'd been talking, bringing the wall closer. Elias looked up and up, leaning back in his saddle to see the distant figures he knew were walking the road high above. The gate stood open before them and there were armed guards in leather and mail to check carts and strangers. Deeds fell silent now they were within earshot. He gestured for Elias to follow him and angled his mount into a queue heading into Darien.

'Chin up now,' Deeds said. 'It doesn't hurt to show the world a nice smile, especially before you kick its teeth in.'

Tellius knew very well he shouldn't have been there. He'd given the damned workshop away anyhow, so it wasn't even his, not really. It was strange to look at a place he'd called home for so long and yet to be almost certain there was danger there instead of safety. He'd known threats and bad nights once or twice over the years, when one of his lads crossed the wrong river gang or nobleman and they all had to lie low for a while. Tellius preferred the parents and grandparents to the current crop, though. The old-fashioned ones seemed not to hold a grudge half as long. Oh, they'd demanded respect and terror from the men and women of the street, no doubt about that. They'd been just as likely back then to send a couple of footmen to administer a reminder as well. It just wasn't done in *malice*.

He sighed. It was probably some trick of the memory, his belief that even his enemies could wink and be gentlemen. Perhaps the nobles of the Twelve Families liked a bit of brash talk and swagger in the young men of the city, but would not abide it in the old – there was no way to know.

Tellius blinked, aware that he had been off in another world for a time, just when he needed to be sharp. Old age took so very much from a man. It was why keeping something back from the hands of the taxmen and managing to retire to somewhere peaceful was so very important. You just didn't have the wits or the concentration to stay ahead of the bastards for ever, not after sixty anyway. He couldn't play the odds any more and he couldn't duck fast enough.

Instead, there he was, staring out of an abandoned workshop across the road to his old home, just because he had a little bag of personals in the space under a floorboard by the hearthstone. The boys would not have found it, he was reasonably sure. Micahel would have kept it safe if he had, anyway. If they'd already sold his workshop and split the shares, some new owner would be levering the thing up any day and then telling all his friends how lucky he'd been.

It was a risk, a really stupid risk to come back, Tellius knew that. Or of course it was no risk at all. He had the purse of gold King Johannes had given him, all legal and above board, signed out of the palace treasury by some wet-nosed clerk, sniffing all the while as he'd counted over a fortune. It was enough too, except for the fact that Tellius knew he would never sleep soundly again for thinking about the things he'd left behind. What if he wasn't even being hunted yet? It had only been a few days since Master Aurelius had met his end. The Twelve Families were no doubt preparing for the Harvest Festival, when the whole city dressed as reapers and farm girls and drank themselves insensible. Would the Aurelius family or their allies take the time to watch an old man's workshop when everyone knew he'd run with gold in his pockets? Tellius scowled through a tiny circle he'd wiped in the glass, just big enough for him to press his eye to and peer across the street. He couldn't know for sure.

The moon was up, he saw, the sky clear. Though the moon wouldn't be completely full for another day, it was still light enough to reveal him if he stepped out onto the cobbled street below. Yet it was so quiet! If the boys had all gone, he knew he could be in and out in moments, though he'd fear then that someone was waiting for him inside. That's where he would be, he thought, if he were the one waiting. Right in the workshop itself.

If the boys were still there, he knew he'd have to take a little time to explain things to them. They'd understand, though, better than most. Sometimes you have to run. Other times, you have to get your medals and your gold rings and *then* you have to run.

He made up his mind. There was no sign of a threat and

he would not spend the rest of his life wondering if he'd lost his most treasured memories by being a coward. Old men should be cowards, he remembered his grandfather saying, from an age before. He shook his head. Too late: his mind was made up.

He crept back down the stairs and closed the locked door he'd picked hours before, while the sun was still setting. The road wasn't completely empty, with a barrow man trundling along with a full load, taking the ordure of the city away while it was quiet. No bodies lay sprawled between the long shafts, Tellius noted, thanking the Goddess in a murmured prayer.

The plague toll must have been a few thousand that year, a nasty one. There had been some anxious months, with all meetings and gatherings forbidden and the streets empty. Yet it had dwindled after that, as it always had before. It seemed the fever had burned itself out for the year – and the barrow men were back to their usual trade. No one wanted to see them during daylight hours, so it was lonely work that began in the evenings and went on all night. Tellius waited until the fellow passed, mumbling to himself, then stepped out, quick as a thought, darting across.

The moment he moved, he knew they were there. Young men who practically danced across the cobbles towards him, in silent felt boots. They had not moved or talked in all the hours he'd waited and watched – just stood there with the sort of physical control he could barely remember, not since everything had started to creak and he farted every time he stood up.

He did not try to fight them as they took him by the arms. Rough hands searched his pockets, removing a knife and the fat purse he had not dared leave behind.

'The king himself let me go, you know,' Tellius said, sadly.

'He doesn't want you back, neither,' one of the men said with a hard laugh. 'Lady Sallet desires your presence, Meneer Tellius. Now come on, you old bastard. You have kept her waiting long enough.'

12

Nancy

She didn't seem to feel thirst as much as he did, Daw noted. As it happened, they'd found the horses with three others not too far from the tomb. The hobble ropes were long gone, but none of the horses had gone far into the black desert once their nerves had settled. Even so, he'd had the impression Nancy hadn't been worried.

The little herd of animals had spooked again as Nancy strode over the sands to them, so that it was Daw who actually had to approach them and gather the reins. They seemed none the worse for their experiences, though the new horses were unkempt and skinny beasts. He'd taken those too, of course. The thieves were certainly not coming back for them.

As he'd eased into the saddle and slumped, Daw had offered a silent prayer of thanks to the Goddess for watching over him. It looked almost as if Nancy could have run back to Darien, but appearances could be misleading. Either way, the desert stretched to the horizon as they'd headed back across it. Even on horseback, Daw found himself growing listless, his head bobbing along as he went. He was also relieved not to have to return to Basker's tavern without the man's horses. The old soldier took a dim view of people who treated animals cruelly. Daw was pleased he would not have to find out what

Basker did to those who just left them to die in the black desert.

Nancy's horse calmed down when she was back in the saddle. Their bags had been emptied, no doubt while they were in the tomb and the thieves had gathered to ambush them. The only item they had between them was the golden mask with the blue eyes painted on the surface. At least that was a thing of beauty, Daw thought with some pride. When he'd come awake from dozing in the saddle, he kept wanting to take it out again and examine it, just to run his hands over the cool slickness of the metal. He resisted because of the memory of the corpse in the sarcophagus, trying to turn and see them, straining to return to life while Nancy drank the magic right out of him. Whoever the old sorcerer had been, he hadn't expected that.

Daw reached down and patted the bag where the mask lay. His brother James knew people in Darien. They'd have it examined by someone well away from Nancy's influence, just in case there was anything more to it than great age and a nice weight in gold. After that, Daw thought he'd probably have it melted down. It was a shame to ruin something of that kind of beauty, but men in his line of work tended to get imprisoned by the noble houses when they approached museums. A poor man's claim that he had inherited some valuable item was almost never believed, and the prices the museums offered were no better than scrap weight anyway. The best thing was to have it stamped into gold coins. Daw knew a couple of counterfeit shops with good presses. For a tenth of the value as a fee, they'd make him a bag of gold that would still be more money than he'd ever seen, certainly more than Nancy had ever seen. He'd decided to play fair with her on the shares. It was only reasonable, after watching her destroy six healthy men fool enough to stand in her way.

'Do you want to talk about what happened yet, back at the tomb?' he asked.

She looked across at him, her eyes shadowed by her hair as it fell loose. Those eyes no longer seemed to gleam red and yellow, he was thankful to note. They were brighter, though, and he thought she had grown more beautiful, more arresting to the eye. Perhaps it was simply that she gleamed with health, like a racehorse.

She said nothing for a time and the horses ambled on together. The animals needed water as much as or more than those who rode them. Luckily, both of their horses knew they'd find it in Darien, at Basker's stable. It was hardly even necessary to hold the reins. The weary beasts were content just to make their own way home.

'I told you I was right about magic,' he said.

Nancy's head turned sharply at that and Threefold flinched, almost sliding sideways off his saddle.

'Oh, calm down, Daw, I'm not going to hurt you. I knew you'd say that, sooner or later. Yes, you were right. Happy?'

'I thought it needed saying, that's all. I think you draw it in, somehow. You've probably been doing it for years without even knowing.'

He shook his head at the thought of how many displays or magical items Nancy had almost certainly ruined, just by living in Darien. He'd heard of things failing before, of course. Making a spell wasn't like building a wall at the best of times, so his brother James said.

Threefold was not yet ready to admit that his own knowledge of magic was not even enough to start a small fire. His brother was the one who usually made his coins and traps and toys, though the Darien traders moved stock amongst themselves each day. All the worst pieces seemed to find their way to the Threefold shop. In turn, Daw was the main consumer of those items, usually for cost or a family rate. With that small advantage over his competitors, Daw had won or bought or occasionally stolen others – and had been on the verge of a decent living. In return, Daw paid his brother well and kept their relationship secret from prying eyes.

'I could feel it at the tomb,' Nancy said softly. 'I could *feel* it, Daw, pouring into me, filling me up like oil, just waiting for a spark to set it on fire.'

'Those wards were powerful enough to hold for centuries,' he said. 'If you soaked those up, I'm surprised it didn't kill you. The threshold of the room below must have been the same. I thought you were going to pass out then.'

'I couldn't understand what was going on, as if I had a fever and my mind had gone. It was . . . horrible. I could feel myself heating up, almost. No, not heating up . . . It is hard to put it into words. I had it under control, I think, just about, like standing on a cliff with a hurricane roaring around me – and then you took hold of the mask.'

'The last of the wards. Meant to bring him back, or something like him, to slaughter whoever had made it so far. Instead, you drew the magic into yourself. Honestly, Nancy, we're both lucky to be alive. What you did to those men at the tomb entrance – *no one* has that kind of . . . raw power. Do you realise that? There isn't a combat mage to touch you at the moment, not in Darien, perhaps not anywhere. Is it still there in you? Is there . . . anything left?'

He watched in astonishment and awe as she raised her hand, staring at the fingers. For an instant, fire seemed to lick along the tips of them. She let her hand fall once more.

'Oh yes, Daw. It's like an ocean. But when it's gone, it's gone. I can feel it even now, that there's slightly less of a storm in me than there was when I came out into the sun and saw all those men standing there. Not much less, Daw. I feel like a leaf thrown around by so much . . . force I can barely keep . . . *talking* to you, like I'm just watching someone else.'

'I suppose you could burn it off,' he said, worried both for her and for himself. He had no desire to be turned into a pile of charred clothes and bones if she lost control of whatever surged within her. He could not imagine how powerful the wards must have been. His brother would know a little more, at least.

'Burn it off?' she hissed at him. 'Waste it, you mean? I don't think I'll be doing that, Daw. For the first time in my life, I have been given something of an advantage. Now, perhaps it won't last long . . .'

'Perhaps it will kill you or drive you mad – have you thought of that?' Daw interrupted.

She turned her head and her eyes gleamed yellow and red like raw flame through her hair. He looked away.

'Or perhaps it will last just long enough, Daw Threefold. I haven't told you all my reasons. Some of them are not for telling, not ever. Do you remember I said before that I might use my share of any treasure to hire hard men?'

'I'll have the mask melted down and made into coins, Nancy, don't worry . . .' he babbled at her, disturbed by the fierce gaze crackling at him.

Nancy laughed.

'I have something a little more direct in mind, Daw. It's my thought that the city of Darien needs a cleansing flame this harvest. To burn the stubble in the fields. Lord Albus is the king's uncle. At the Harvest Festival, the chief magistrate will be standing with King Johannes, waving at all those who hate them but can't do anything about it. Perhaps if someone burned the palace down with Lord Albus in it, the city might become a touch less vicious. Perhaps there might even be justice for those who deserve it, then, for a while.'

Daw blinked at hearing that. He did not want to argue with a woman brimming over with flames she did not seem to feel. He could see them gleaming along her fingers as she gripped the reins, making them smoke.

'I don't think you change anything by killing one man,' he ventured after a time.

'Well, that's settled, then,' she said. 'I might just have to kill all of them.'

He could see she was being brash, that for all her power, she was as afraid as he was, perhaps more so at what had happened and was still happening to her. Grand claims of vengeance did not refill their water bottles, unfortunately.

'Before you do that,' he said, 'I would take it as a favour if you'd drop in on my brother James. He lives in the Street of Apothecaries and . . . he has a wife and two daughters and a young son.'

She heard his worry and snorted.

'I have not gone insane, Daw. Nor will I run mad the instant I enter the city. If you think your brother might be some help, fine, I will go to him. But after that, I think I will walk into the palace and I will find Lord Albus and I will know he won't have the faintest idea who I am as I burn the place down. I will make a torch with everything I have inside me – and when it's gone, I'll take my half of our gold mask and I'll live a quiet, forgotten life. But they'll remember that they could not stop me.' She thought for a moment and a look of panic crossed her face. 'Isn't it the harvest soon? We haven't missed that?'

'No, Nancy, it's tomorrow, though it starts tonight, really. Darien will be full of innocent people by sunset, all celebrating the harvest coming in.'

'With alcohol and lamps and sheaves of wheat,' she said, grinning evilly at him. 'Which should burn nicely.'

'You said you hadn't gone insane, Nancy, didn't you? My brother's family lives in Darien, remember? Good people who have never hurt you?'

She shook her head as if dazed.

'Yes, all right. If you could only *feel* it, Daw. It's a little like being drunk, but with just a glass or two fizzing away inside you, without sickness. Do you understand? My whole life I've had to bow my head when the king's guards walk by, knowing that if they chose to hurt me, like they did my father, no one would ever come and stop them. No one.'

She fell into silence again and Daw shuddered, wondering what particular memory put that expression on her face. He would not want to be Lord Albus, not that day.

Her horse whinnied suddenly, tossing its head at some odour of the city or water on the breeze. Darien was still a few miles east of them, already full of life and preparation for the great feast of the year, when the streets ran with the blood of slaughtered animals turning on spits and every table groaned under ripe fruit and fresh bread and steaming cauldrons of meat. Into that city, into the revel, he and Nancy would ride, like a knife to the heart.

Elias carried a wheatsheaf in the crook of his arm, part of a growing number in the crowd who had already begun their celebrations ahead of the Reapers' Eve. Some wore painted skull masks, to remind observers of their own reaping. It did not seem to dull their enjoyment as the crowds swelled. The Harvest Eve had once been a staid and formal affair, when farmers brought their produce to the markets of the city. Some of them had gone a little wild with the coins in their pockets. Over the decades, it had become a celebration of the Goddess, eclipsing all others, with garish costumes and all manner of excess, lasting from the night before to the following sunset. There would be a number of children born nine months or so after that day, so many that the month in question was known as Birther's. There would be a few bodies in the gutters the following morning as well, drunk or dead. It was just the rise and fall of life in Darien, and respectable people could avoid it simply by staying in their homes or their rooms. If they were on the street by midnight, they were signalling their willingness to drink, laugh, sing, fight, howl and risk their lives.

Elias could hardly believe so many people existed in the world. He was breathing too hard in his discomfort, making himself dizzy. Deeds smiled widely and pointed at his own grin in the hope that Elias would copy him and lose his perpetual glower. The hunter swayed aside from a group of young men running bare-chested down the street, sending oblivious drunks spinning out of their way as they charged past. One of them saw Elias move and tried to reach out and snag him. Elias slapped the hand and the man was carried on by his mates, struggling and swearing. It was still early, with half the crowd hurrying home to change into costume. The gangs of men already out had not yet drunk enough to pick fights with strangers or push young women up against a wall. All that would come later, as the city erupted and threw off all the bounds of civilised behaviour.

If it had not been for their serious purpose, Deeds would have been enjoying it. As things stood, he found the noise and distractions irritating. Dancing, drunken men and women were nowhere near as much fun to one who was sober as a stone. He clutched his own wheatsheaf and waved it in the air, all the while staring at the gates of the royal palace, not twenty yards away along the road.

'Nothing you can do will get you through a locked gatehouse door, will it, meneer?' Deeds said over the clamour of singers marching arm in arm. One of them tried to gather them in but failed and was swept on.

Elias shrugged as he looked up. He could count guards easily enough, but however many he might see on the outside, there would surely be many more inside – and that was without encountering the king's famous swordmasters.

'Don't just stand and stare at the gatehouse,' Deeds hissed. 'The guards look for breaks in the pattern, meneer! They look for anything out of place – and they are not stupid. Turn on the spot every now and then, wave your arms or dance with someone. Do *something* apart from standing and scowling at them like you're the Day of Judgement!'

Elias turned his glare on Vic Deeds. In response, the gunman took his hands. Elias was so surprised, he let it happen and allowed himself to be dragged around. Deeds leaped in a circle, throwing his head back and howling.

'We are a dozen paces from men watching for anyone showing too much interest in this gate, Elias!' Deeds said, laughing loudly. 'Perhaps you could play up to it a little so that they don't believe thieves are planning something. Would you prefer to have them double the guard? Aroooo!'

Elias pulled his hands away, anger growing. He suspected Deeds was poking fun at him, and not for the first time he thought the gunman was too wild, too delighted with himself, to be a sound and useful companion.

Elias knew Deeds was following as he slid again through the crowd, away from the massive stone gatehouse that led into the palace. Elias thought hard as he walked, moving like a fish through a stream as clutching hands failed to touch him.

Behind, Deeds had a much harder time keeping up, so that he arrived back at Basker's tavern flushed and with his collar torn, yet grinning from ear to ear. It was quieter in that area, a mile away from the palace. The revelry had not yet spread to that part of Darien and respectable families were still hurrying home on the street outside, dragging their children along with them.

'*Goddess*, I love this city,' Deeds said, breathless and laughing.

The little courtyard was empty as Elias pulled up a seat. Deeds flopped down beside him, looking round to be sure they could not be overheard. It was hard to be too careful in a place like Darien, so he believed.

'It gets a lot wilder later on, then begins again tomorrow, after they've slept it off.'

'I don't care how wild they get. We'll go tonight. If you're right about the palace gates being opened.'

'Of course I'm right. I've seen four Reaper festivals in Darien. At midnight, the people of the city are allowed past the gatehouse, down an avenue of torches into the inner courtyard, to roar up their adoration and love for His Splendid August Majesty at his window. King Johannes lets them call and plead for a while, then gathers a few of his courtiers together, or his latest lover, leads them out onto the balcony and waves. He'll have his guards close to him, of course, but I don't think you'll have much trouble with those. I'll be there with you, for anything unexpected.'

'You'll get yourself killed,' Elias said grimly. 'And if you do, how will I know the general won't hurt my daughters in return?'

'Because he made a deal with you, meneer,' Deeds said seriously. 'The general keeps his word – you can take that as truth because it is, just like the sun will come up tomorrow, no matter what happens tonight. Even if you and I aren't here to see it, still it will rise.'

Elias looked at the young man before him, at the feral excitement in his eyes.

'This is not a game, son,' Elias said. 'Not for these stakes, not to me. Do you understand that?'

''Course I do,' Deeds said.

The coldness had returned to his eyes, though Elias found he was relieved to see it. The sight of the fortress palace with its host of guards had daunted him. Going in with Deeds practically drunk on the revels of the city would have pushed it over a line into impossible.

'Those guns of yours that you wear,' Elias said suddenly. 'Are you any good with them? I saw you shoot straight in the darkness when we were attacked, but are you better than other gunmen? Or gunfighters, or whatever you call yourselves?'

'You should know General Justan would not employ a poor shot as his right-hand man,' Deeds said. 'I take your point, though. I still need to buy that third gun and it must be soon, before all the good people close their shutters and the party starts. Come on, the gunsmith I have in mind has a range at the back of his shop. I'll show you there.' He put his hand in his pocket and drew out a letter of credit from the general, with gold lettering gleaming on a white card. 'Perhaps I'll get you a gun as well, eh, meneer? Would you like that?'

Elias stood up, his expression stern.

'No. Look, I'm ready now, if you are. We can't go back to the palace till the gates are opened at midnight. I confess I would like to see if your high opinion of yourself is even half-justified.'

Deeds looked a little wounded as he too rose to his feet. He wore his pistols on his hips and he tapped both of them in the holsters, as if for luck.

'All right,' he said.

'All right,' Elias replied. 'Lead the way, then.'

The streets there were still full of workers making their way home, some of them laughing and calling to one another in anticipation of the evening ahead. Deeds seemed to have been offended by Elias' doubt in him and he stalked through the walkers at stiff-legged speed. No one snatched at his coat then and Elias slipped through the crowds behind, keeping him in sight as he passed a street of apothecaries.

A woman of surpassing beauty stood on one side of it, apparently in argument with a young man. Elias could see the man gesturing to the line of shops and shaking his head as he passed. Elias wondered what he was refusing to buy for her. Because he was watching the beauty, Elias stumbled on the kerb and almost fell into the road. Smiling with embarrassment, he silently wished the young fellow luck.

Ahead of him, Deeds darted down a side alley with such a turn of speed it almost looked as if he wanted to make Elias sweat at losing him. The hunter sighed to himself. There would not be many gunsmiths in the area. The foul things were still so new and expensive, he doubted there were more than one or two shops in the whole city. It was not hard for a hunter to follow the smell of oil and gunpowder to the door of the establishment, with a little bell still ringing its note as Elias pushed it open.

'I would like another to match these two,' Deeds was saying. 'And a few dozen shots in your range with it. My friend here has mentioned a desire to see me shoot.'

The gunsmith was a short, rotund man of around Elias' own age, wearing spectacles on his nose that seemed to help his sight when he peered at the guns before him. He might have been a bookkeeper or a butcher, but when he picked up the pistols, his hands moved with utter familiarity. Elias watched as first one, then the other became part of the fellow's hand, fitting snugly. He and Deeds were equally enamoured of the things; their expressions made that obvious.

'I have a new pair of an improved design, meneer. Very accurate and my best work – made in my own workshop to my own standard. I couldn't break up a pair, meneer.'

'And you won't have to,' Deeds said, placing the general's letter of credit on the glass counter. The owner of the shop smiled with genuine pleasure as he read the words in gold.

'Very *good*, meneer.'

He handed over a pair of pistols and Deeds took an age to examine them and slide pieces out and back in. Elias could see no difference between those and the ones he already wore on his belt.

The owner of the shop passed over a box of bullets and left his thick fingers on it as Deeds went to pick it up. The man's other hand had dropped back to rest on a single pistol on his waist in a holster there. The shopkeeper's face had grown very serious.

'I don't usually let customers load in the shop, meneer. Before you do, I want you to know that I am armed – and if you turn towards me, if you even *begin* to point a loaded gun at me, I will shoot you dead without hesitation. You have my word on that. Is that understood?'

'It is,' Deeds said, with no trace of his usual arrogance.

The shopkeeper took his hand away and Elias watched as Deeds loaded all four pistols, carrying the thick belt with the new ones in his right hand. As he had promised, the shopkeeper watched him very carefully, his hand always on his gun.

'Lead the way, meneer,' the man said.

Deeds didn't argue, but walked ahead of him through the shop to the back, where they passed through into a long, echoing room with sandbags piled to the ceiling at the far end. When the door closed, the noise of the city seemed to vanish, so that Elias felt like holding his nose and blowing to remove the sudden pressure.

'The targets are at twenty yards,' the owner said. He seemed to sense disappointment in Deeds, or imagined he did. 'No pistols are accurate further than that, meneer. Beyond that, well, you can always try bottles and cans out in the black desert. Land's too pricy in this city to get a longer range, more's the pity. As it is, I turn down offers for this place once a week, just about.'

Deeds nodded, unconcerned. He handed one belt and its pistols to Elias, then stood, relaxed, looking down the range. Elias *reached* and watched what would happen before it began. It wasn't any less surprising, despite the warning he had.

Both guns seemed to leap out of the holsters into Deeds' hands, just appearing there as he poured fire into the targets. Each of the pistols fired six shots and they were empty instants after one long barrage of sound that left Elias' ears ringing. Stunned, he passed over the second set. Deeds strolled down the range to replace the targets. The ones he handed to Elias had lost the central ring, like an eye cut in the middle.

Deeds shot the second pair with more care. They were guns he did not know and he slowed right down and took his time. The result was the same, with a central eye appearing in both of the sheets.

'It must be a little harder when someone is shooting back at you,' Elias said.

Deeds shook his head.

'No, it's not. It's really not.'

Elias noted the awe in the shopkeeper. It seemed Deeds was almost as good as he thought he was. Perhaps they might even live through the evening ahead.

Threefold held up his hands to block her once more, though if Nancy pressed forward he'd be holding her breasts and he thought he'd back away before he took that kind of liberty with her again.

179

'My brother deals in magical items, Nancy, please! You know what you can do now, don't you? So there's no excuse for taking a man's livelihood, the way you destroyed the things in my pack back at Basker's. You nearly ruined me, Nan. Please don't ruin my brother.'

He didn't think he would have had to argue with the young woman he'd met at Basker's a few nights before. Goddess, had it been almost a week? Since the tomb, Nancy had been harder somehow, less open to persuasion. He could see she was on the point of just shrugging and striding into his brother's little shop, sucking the value out of a dozen things inside. Threefold could see it almost like hunger in her and he wondered if she needed it the way some people needed a drink.

Her eyes followed a passer-by crossing the street, the whole area already growing busy as the evening came. Daw risked a glance over, seeing just another swaggering young bravo, though this one had low-slung guns, which made him a rarity. They were so valuable, a man had to be truly dangerous to show them on a public street, for fear someone would take them from him.

An older man loped lightly across behind the first, his gaze snagging on Nancy as she stood there, still undecided. She noticed his gaze like a predator, assessing a threat and then choosing to ignore it.

Daw tried again.

'Please, Nancy. Just let me fetch James out to you. Leave him his living, would you? He's all I have – and he's all his wife has as well.'

Some of the hunger and irritation seemed to fade from her eyes and she shrugged.

'Go on, then,' she said. 'I've nothing better to do till

midnight. After that, I'm going to pay old friends a visit. Perhaps I'll top up my reserves along this street before I go – yes, with the exception of your brother's shop. I am not a monster, Daw.'

'No, Nancy. I know you're not,' he said firmly.

He held his palms up to her as he backed away, though she just rolled her eyes at him. Some men whistled as they passed, calling out lewd suggestions for her evening. The smile she turned on them made theirs fade away and they hurried off without another word.

The two little girls watched nervously as huge squares of marching men tramped away down the road, in neat white ranks as if on parade. Scouts galloped around them to confirm no contact with an enemy force, but they expected none. The Immortals were in their own territory, barely a dozen miles from Darien. If some farmer saw them on the march, he'd just have a proud tale to tell his mates.

It had not been completely unpleasant travelling to that place on the general's carriage. It was by far the largest vehicle Jenny or little Alice had ever seen. On a different occasion, it might have been fascinating to see the world trundle by from the height of the hedges, even when the great flatbed went into a ditch half a dozen times and had to be levered out by cursing, sweating men. The girls had learned soldiers were at least as good as oxen for that sort of work – better, really. Yet General Aeris had chafed and bristled at every delay, his temper shortening as they approached the final valley his scouts had marked for the last camp.

They had marched thirty miles in one long push the

previous night, hardening the Immortals further. Those men hid their weariness, but they had welcomed the chance to drink fresh water, eat and then sleep as best they could through the afternoon of the Harvest Eve. Now the sun was setting and they were up and rested, restored once more.

Alice gave a little shriek of happiness when Mrs Dalton appeared at the edge of the general's cart. It was over a mile from the rear of the column and the cook was perspiring and dusty. Mrs Dalton was nervous, Jenny noted. The big woman curtsied elaborately, dipping low, and waited to be noticed.

General Justan was striding about the flatbed with his hands clasped behind his back, snapping commands, adjusting formations or tactics, then despatching men to carry his new orders. He made himself the heart of the legion, so that everything had to pass through him. Jenny wondered why he didn't trust the men to solve their own problems, but it seemed that was not his way.

No one asked the fat, sweating cook why she was bobbing along at the cart's edge, so at last she spoke up.

'General? I should feed these two girls now. I have wrapped some sandwiches for them in wax paper, if that's all right. They can't have eaten since this morning.'

General Justan raised a hand to interrupt two men reporting to him and turned slowly. He strode over the planking to look down on Mrs Dalton.

'Well, we can't have that, can we?' he said. 'That's thoughtful, Mrs Dalton, thank you.' He appeared to consider the conversation at an end and raised his eyebrows as she spoke before he could turn back.

'I thought . . . meneer, I thought I might see if they needed

182

another trip to the bushes, if you understand me, sir. If that's all right with yourself.'

Alice looked up instantly, but Jenny put a hand on her arm. General Justan had often watched them as the cart rolled along, his Immortals marching stolidly alongside. He'd never said exactly what he'd been thinking, but he'd devoted hours to his silent contemplation. Though he was polite enough, Jenny had formed an opinion of him by then that did not include him as a friend of her father. He seemed to have more care for his horses and his men than the two girls he insisted on having in sight at all times.

'Very well, Mrs Dalton,' the general replied at last. 'I should have remembered.'

'You've been busy, meneer. Thank you. I'll bring them back sharpish, don't worry. Shall I take them?'

The general looked down at the red-faced woman, clearly troubled.

'I have . . . I want you to know they are important to me, Mrs Dalton. In a way you do not understand. We are not far from the city now, so you'll forgive me if I am cautious. Girls? Come here. Now, please.'

Nervously, Jenny and Alice rose from the long wooden box that had been their seat and tottered over on stiff legs. They watched in confusion as the general opened a trunk fastened to the floor of his cart with iron straps. He took out twin sets of manacles that clinked and shone gold. The two girls had never seen such things before, but whatever colour they were, no matter how they gleamed, chains were still chains.

'I don't want to . . .' Alice said, backing away.

The general chuckled.

'Now, dear, you don't want me to be angry at you, do you? Or at Mrs Dalton? They are to keep you safe by my side. I can't trust you if you don't wear them, do you see?'

Alice was close to tears, so Jenny stood forward bravely and put out her hands, wincing as the manacles were shut on them. They pinched her skin a little and she saw a spot of blood fall, but she didn't react in case it scared Alice further.

Alice was snivelling as she held her hands out, then wailed as they clicked. Jenny saw Mrs Dalton had paled and that her eyes glittered with anger. The general, however, seemed to relax.

'There. That will do for the moment.' He indicated an iron ring in the floor of the cart. 'I have another chain to keep you both secure there when you come back. I wouldn't want you getting lost or separated, do you see? It's for your own good, girls, so no more crying, please. Mrs Dalton, take them to the bushes, whatever you need to do. Return them to me immediately. I must be at the city walls at the right time. Is that clear, Mrs Dalton?'

'You won't be thinking of taking such young children into the city with you?' the woman said in astonishment.

General Justan bent down to a crouch to reply.

'You overstep yourself, Mrs Dalton. Be careful. You don't know what they are to me. I would not harm a hair on their heads. But if I choose to, it is not any business of yours!' The last was said as a crescendo, with the final words bitten off at her. 'Captain Diggs! Accompany Mrs Dalton and make sure she does not lose sight of these two girls.'

The officer touched his hand to his brow and dismounted.

Mrs Dalton grew pinched and even paler, but also afraid. There was no doubt which of them had the power in that place. Jenny looked from one to the other and saw defeat in every line of the cook.

The general sensed it too, so that he smiled tightly.

'There now, I should not have raised my voice in front of the girls. Captain Diggs will look after you. I have a long night ahead of me, Mrs Dalton. I must have everything just so. As I have said, then – go about your business.'

Mrs Dalton curtsied once again and helped the two girls down when they would have fallen. Alice pushed mutely at the woman's hand with her smaller one until it opened and then tottered along off-balance at her side, the chains making both girls clumsy. The harvest sun was gone, though the sky still held streamers of mauve and golden red, shading into night. Around them, five thousand Immortal soldiers marched in silent ranks.

When they had finished, the two girls were returned to the general. Mrs Dalton embraced them both and was dismissed. The young captain helped them up onto the flatbed when the chains made them clumsy. Torches had been lit by then and they found the general's cart had been draped with purple cloth so that it resembled an actors' stage. Yet the iron loop was still there, with a new length of gold chain spilled across the cloth like a snake. General Justan himself closed a lock on their manacles, so that they had only a few feet between them and could not step down to the ground again. Alice went to lean over the edge to look at the turning wheels and was brought up short, so that she sat down hard and sobbed quietly.

From the darkness, one of the men from the cook tents ran alongside with cushions for the girls, tossing them up one by one. He grinned at them and they took comfort from the kindness of Mrs Dalton, though it was all she could do for them. General Justan saw, but said nothing as the fellow fell behind once more.

The moon appeared on the horizon and the road stretched palely ahead of them. Jenny cradled Alice in her arms and stroked her hair, trying not to be afraid.

13

Harvest

Getting hold of costumes on the one night of the year when half of Darien would wear them was no easy challenge. Finding costumes that would allow them to carry hidden weapons was even harder. Deeds wore the long purple coat and tall hat of a bishop, with his guns strapped on beneath. After much grumbling, Elias had accepted the black robe of a sorcerer, which concealed the short sword and dagger he wore. He had refused to take a pistol, though the shiny metal things had appealed mutely to his hand. Yet the skill wasn't there and his knack would not make him any more accurate over distance. Their best chance was to stick to the tried and tested that evening. Once again, the general's letter of credit took a beating, with initials marked and another section of the card torn away. Deeds and Elias sank into a thickening crowd, trying to blend into the laughter and song.

They made their way back to the palace with some time still to wait before midnight. Deeds at least had seen a Reapers' Eve celebration before and he didn't want to be stuck out in the street when King Johannes and his courtiers were ready to come to the balcony. He and Elias staggered drunkenly to a good spot by the gatehouse around ten o'clock, still solidly shut. Glowering guards stared down at the crowds, though one or two of the young ones called remarks to passing women, who yelled and hooted back at them, either in outrage or amusement.

Deeds and Elias bought a bottle of something sticky and strong and sat on the kerb across the road, where they would be hidden from view. Deeds made a point of waving the bottle around and laughing, but Elias kept his head low, saying he'd rather look like an ill man than a fool. They were accosted twice by women demanding a kiss from Deeds, though no one asked the same from Elias. He stretched out his legs to ease stiff knees and found himself in the centre of an angry group of young men as one of them tripped and went sprawling on the cobbles. Deeds calmed them down when he poked the largest one in the stomach, winding him. It had been done with such casual confidence that the rest took the warning and left, still calling names and threats as they went. Deeds watched them go, his eyebrows raised.

'Not drunk enough yet,' he tutted to himself. 'When I was their age, Elias, I'd have sunk a pint of hard liquor before setting off, even. If someone had poked me in the gut then, I'd have laid him out.'

'You like to fight,' Elias muttered. 'Perhaps they don't.'

'I do like to fight,' Deeds said, 'but only the winning part. No one likes to lose. Be sure we win tonight. You'll get . . . what you want. I'll be the golden boy and right-hand man to our friend. Our friend will get his own reward.'

'I thought you said you already were his right-hand man,' Elias said.

'I may have overstated it.'

'I see. Do you think he will try to have me killed afterwards?' Elias asked.

Deeds looked at him and judged him to be serious. He shook his head.

'I've said he is a man of his word, Elias. He made an arrangement with you, for one task. Trust me in this, as one who knows him. He won't break it, not ever. He might try to use you again after . . .'

He stopped himself going on, but Elias had heard enough to understand. When it was all over, if he lived still, he would take his daughters somewhere the general couldn't possibly find them. He'd lost too much that year, with two dark doors he still didn't dare open. At night, when he was trying to get to sleep, he thought he could feel them coming loose. His son, Jack. His wife, Beth. He could not drown himself in grief while his girls needed him. He could not lose himself in rage either, not then. It would come, though.

The crowd was thickening and Deeds nodded to the men and women gathering before the gatehouse. It was impossible to see the stars or the moon through the lights of the festival hanging from every house and corner, but midnight could not have been far off by then. As the two men stood, the gates slid smoothly back and there was a sudden rush forward as those in front decided to run for the best places. Deeds and Elias found themselves caught in the flow of people, beyond even Elias' ability to navigate in such a press. It made the hunter uncomfortable, but he could do nothing as they were swept along an avenue of torches and tall trees, all trimmed and plucked to ovals, like old-fashioned sword blades.

At the end of the drive, the palace itself seemed to grow out of the ground, with two huge wings enclosing a central yard. It was by far the single biggest building Elias had ever seen. He counted forty windows across the upper floor, with three floors below it. Deeds was inclining his head, calling him over to the side, so Elias jogged across while there was still room. A glance back at the avenue revealed it thick with people coming in. The individual groups and parties would become one solid mass in just moments and Deeds was determined to get to an edge, while most favoured the centre by the balcony. Elias went with him, moving free of outstretched hands and stumbling drunks as they crossed his path. The air was warm and filled with the sweet breath of drinkers and sweat.

At the edge of the western wing, there were half a dozen entrances to the building itself, all blocked by uniformed guards standing in pairs. Deeds began a story of some sexual conquest that he told with relish and delight, gesturing wildly and then hanging on to Elias as he laughed, as if his legs would no longer hold him.

'You should have been an actor,' Elias hissed, trying to look as if he was enjoying himself.

'We need to wait for the crowd to thicken, I think. When they're so packed in they can hardly move, they won't be able to raise an alarm.'

'You think so?' Elias said.

It was happening even as they stood there. Thousands had poured in from the city streets outside, taking up every space in the vast palace yard, so that each open spot that remained was winking out. The crowd was so dense in places that it became a dangerous force in its own right, with currents and pressures that had no care for the lives of those within. For Elias, it was a nightmare. He shuddered at the thought of losing himself in a sea of people, wanting only to run back the way they had come. He crushed the fear as best he could, presenting a cold expression to the man watching him so closely. Elias leaned in.

'We know the king is inside, Deeds. Now, either this will work or we will be killed. There is no good time, much better than any other. Not any more. We go in – and if you and the general were right about me, we'll survive long enough to kill an innocent man. If not, we'll be cut to pieces. So one way or the other, we don't have to worry about tomorrow or what happens next.'

With every passing moment, the crowd grew more solid, so that both men were buffeted and made to feel helpless. Revellers were leaping and dancing and singing all around and Deeds could feel Elias' distress.

'Come on, then,' he said. 'I'm ready if you are.'

On the other side of the yard, so far across a roaring mass of men and women that it seemed impossibly distant, there was a flare of light, shortly followed by a crump of sound on its heels. The ground trembled underfoot, though it was hard to be sure with so many stamping and jumping. Deeds craned his head, but he could hardly see anything over those around him. More light flashed, reflecting back from the walls of the palace. Deeds heard a sound that could have been screaming, but he wasn't sure. He shook his head, irritated that he had been distracted.

'Let's go. Push through to the door.'

Elias moved quickly, using his knack to take a path where Deeds had to shove and even punch one fool. They arrived at the entrance with two guards staring straight at them, having watched the last part of their progress. One of them held up a palm and shook his head.

'Sorry, but I *must* use a privy,' Deeds said, slurring his words and blinking slowly.

There was no tension in the guards at the sight of a drunken bishop and sorcerer. As Deeds came close, he leaned against the palace wall and began to fumble with his buttoned cassock. One of the guards grunted in anger and took hold of him, pulling him away. Elias watched as Deeds allowed himself to swing round and fall within the arch of the entrance, scrambling up in apparent confusion. The man really should have been an actor, he thought. He heard the guard give a gasp of surprise as Deeds jammed a knife into the side of his neck.

As the second guard turned to see what was happening, Elias stepped in and pushed a long dagger up under his ribs from behind. It was unpleasant, feeling the life slip out, but it was not as if there was an alternative. Elias had come to kill a king that night. There would be many others standing in their way who had to die first. He had always considered himself a man of sense, not too given to emotion. If he'd been asked how many men he would kill to save his daughters, he would not have put a limit on it.

He and Deeds bundled the two dead guards further in, holding them up as if they were engaged in conversation. Elias had no idea if the little scene had fooled anyone, but at least no cry of outrage or alarm sounded from the crowd behind. They left the corpses slumped against an inner wall and he and Deeds straightened up together.

They stood in deep shadow, letting their eyes adjust to the gloom after the better-lit palace yard. Bars of moonlight came and went and they looked up to see stars overhead, finding themselves in a roofless inner yard, surrounded by high windows. Facing them were dark doors, reminding Elias of the things he could not consider until it was all done, not if he wanted to finish and survive.

There was no sign of anyone watching. Deeds removed his robe and dropped the squashed hat, revealing his long coat, worn trousers and a white cotton shirt, as well as both sets of guns. He threw his bloodied knife down onto the discarded robe, drawing his pistols. The pockets of his coat jingled with bullets and he made a show of checking all his guns one last time.

'I'll back you,' Deeds said, utterly focused. 'Understand? You go in and just keep moving. I'll pick off anyone you can't get to.'

He saw Elias was looking grimly at him and he shrugged.

'There are limits to your knack, Elias. You know it and so do I. If they come at you too quickly, you can be brought down. So that's my job tonight. To thin the defenders. To keep you moving until we get to the king's rooms. Now, the balcony is three floors up, in the middle of the house. We'll need to find stairs. It might be an idea to get to the king before he actually comes out to wave to the crowd, but I'll take my chances as they come – and I don't mind either way. Let's just get this done and go home, all right?'

'All right,' Elias said.

He pulled his sorcerer's robe over his head and drew his sword and dagger, one for each hand. He was trembling, Deeds saw. For all his peculiar talent, for all his experience with hunting, Elias Post was afraid. Deeds grinned at him, his own reaction to fear being a kind of wild excitement. He opened the door, holding it for his companion.

'After you, meneer,' he said, bowing as deeply as any courtier.

Daw followed in Nancy's wake, pushing through with the crowds as the palace gate opened and the people surged in. It was odd how those around them gave Nancy a wide berth, as if they sensed peril and moved aside from it with nervous glances, without really understanding what they were doing. Even the drunk ones stayed clear, and so Daw just walked behind her.

The mistake he'd made, Daw thought, was thinking he had any influence over Nancy after the experience in the tomb. Power was a dangerously seductive thing, he knew that well enough. His brother James had more than a few tales of men and women destroying themselves in the pursuit of some bauble – all to lord it over other people. He'd understood by then that Nancy had been helpless and hurt at some point, that she'd felt the sting of injustice. Well, who hadn't? It was always a fantasy to seek vengeance, though a satisfying one, perhaps even part of the healing. What was unusual was a young woman suddenly finding herself with the ability to punish those who had wronged her before.

Daw wasn't even completely sure what he was doing there. He had the sense that Nancy wasn't truly in her right mind, that the power she had taken from the tomb had driven out her sense and caution for a time. He'd watched in dismay as she'd strolled down the Street of Apothecaries, the finest street in the city just about, with great sheets of clear glass held in oak surrounds. The houses near there were the grandest in all Darien, and though his brother owned a flat in one of them, Daw still felt out of place, half-expecting a hand on his shoulder the whole time. Nancy had risen even further than he had, but she seemed to enjoy walking along the wide, quiet street with its bronze statues and trees. Fearing a shout at any moment, Threefold had watched her press her face up against display windows, getting as close as she could to whatever lay within. She'd strolled back with heat almost smoking off her skin and her pupils once again dark gold with red flashes. She'd ruined a few businesses that night, but she had spared his brother's place, which was something. It showed Nancy was not completely lost, or at least he hoped it did.

From winning dishonest bets with his first trinkets, to all the paraphernalia of the combat mage he claimed to have become, Threefold had used his brother's skills and finds to turn a few useful effects into a living. Without his tools, he could not escape the fear that he was of no more use to Nancy than any other young man might have been. At least he had the weight of a proper knife on his hip, a steel spine that felt a lot stronger than his own at that moment.

She hadn't asked him to come with her, but on the other hand, she hadn't turned him away either. He looked ahead to where she strode through people, the crowd parting for her step. He'd be there if she needed him. That was only fair. She'd never have gone into the tomb if he hadn't asked her to. Whatever happened that night was, in some small way, his fault.

Threefold swallowed as the crowd thickened around them. It was all he could do to stay on Nancy's heels as she headed through the press of people to one of the arches in the main facade. Threefold rubbed the back of his neck as he went, feeling sweat trickle. He did not like to think what she would do when they tried to stop her. He suspected it would be extremely unpleasant. He shook his head and bulled on through the mob, uncaring. He owed her that much.

Nancy reached the shadow of a small archway on the right of the palace yard. The crowd swirled and heaved, but their gazes were on the central building of the palace, where King Johannes and his ministers would come out onto a small balcony and accept the devotion and love of his people. Nancy set her jaw at the thought. She glanced back to see Daw was still with her, his loyalty quite touching in its way.

The archway was guarded by two broad-shouldered men in mail, with swords showing on their hips. One of them was looking at her in something like admiration, while the other stared open-mouthed. She smiled at them both and raised her hands like pistols, with the thumbs raised and a single finger pointing out. They chuckled at the sight of a beautiful woman laughing along with them – and then she dropped her thumbs and thin lines of white fire punched right through them both.

Inside the arch, perhaps a dozen other guards were off-watch, grabbing a bite to eat before they went back to keeping order in the vast crowd. They sprang to their feet, drawing weapons as Nancy strolled on past the two dying men. Screams sounded from the crowd behind as she raised her hands again, pouring thick, smoking threads into the guards in cracks of sound that lit and echoed across the palace yard. They fell, pierced and burned, still twitching as Threefold padded through after her, murmuring prayers and apologies.

A door lay beyond, leading to steps she could see through

a panel of glass. Nancy smiled, feeling the power surge in her. It was intoxicating, more than she could explain to poor Daw, following in her steps, Goddess bless him. With a sweep of her hand, she blasted the door to smoking pieces and swept through, breaking into a run as she reached the stairs.

'Stay with me now, Daw,' she called.

He nodded, determined not to let her down. He tried not to think about the bodies in the archway. They had been men like Basker, but unlike him, they would never know a quiet retirement. As he ran, Threefold felt a little sick come into his mouth and winced as he swallowed it.

Elias and Deeds faced a group of six astonished guards. Two of them wore pistols much like the ones Deeds carried. The gunman punched those two from their feet with snap-shots even as they were reaching for the holstered weapons. He had been ready and they were just too slow to realise they were actually under attack.

The rest of them shouted and charged. The men wore swords and held shields they hadn't truly thought they would need as they investigated the sounds of gunfire. Deeds shot one of them in the foot so that he howled, but the final three rushed in and Deeds stepped clear at last to let Elias work.

The hunter was so brutally quick that Deeds was left staring. Elias used only his knife in three quick thrusts, stepping aside from blows as if the soldiers were acting out a scene, while he was the only one trying to kill. They fell with confused expressions, already glassy-eyed before they struck the thick carpet with very little noise at all. The last of them had gone down onto one knee to hold his shot foot. Elias sliced his dagger through the side of the guard's neck and turned from the spray.

As Deeds watched, Elias sheathed his sword, not feeling he needed it. He already understood he was more deadly with the knife, darting in and out. He nodded to Deeds, panting lightly and speckled with blood. The gunshots had been very loud in that space. Shouts and running footsteps sounded in the room beyond.

'That worked well enough,' Elias said. 'If you can drop the ones with pistols at a distance, I'll get the rest. If you can't hit them all, just go for cover and stay out of sight until I'm through. Ready?'

Deeds nodded, his mouth tight with irritation. He truly did not enjoy being the least capable of the two of them.

'Look for stairs leading up,' he said.

Elias nodded, then swayed aside as two new gunmen reached the doorway, shooting blindly around the door into the room. Deeds was dropping as soon as Elias shifted, knowing how he worked. The bullets passed overhead and by then Deeds was lying prostrate and resting on his elbows, able to aim and place his shots perfectly. The two men howled as bullets slammed into them. Elias went through the doorway in two quick gestures, leaving them holding their sides and crumpling.

It was a slaughter and Deeds wondered once more what he and General Justan had unleashed – and how they could possibly control him now that they had. The general couldn't hold the man's daughters for ever. They'd told themselves it would be a problem worth considering on another day, when the king had been killed and the Twelve Families had been thrown into chaos. Watching Elias go through armed men made it a little more urgent to Deeds' mind.

They went forward into a long room decorated with paintings and plaster of cream and pale blue. A rug that would have cost as much as any house Elias had ever owned lay across black oak boards. Gun smoke drifted oddly inside the room and Deeds and Elias shared a glance.

'There are stairs at the end there,' Deeds said, pointing. 'Servant stairs, I think. Easier for them to defend than the main ones.'

'They are the closest,' Elias said with a shrug, turning towards them. He cursed suddenly and Deeds readied his guns on the door at the far end before it opened. He was already shooting as men came rushing into the room, so that two of them fell before they even saw the threat.

Behind them more and more came in. Deeds swore under his breath, walking forward with shot after shot, closing one eye against the sting of gritty smoke but smashing men from their feet and covering for Elias as he strolled up. They assumed the gunman was the most pressing danger and focused on him. They were wrong. Elias went through the crowd like a butcher, calmly chopping men from life as he passed, never still, always turning, killing with each strike.

When there was silence again, Deeds found he could not swallow, his mouth had dried to such a point. Every shot he had fired had been from some way off, while Elias had gone in close enough to stab and slash. It meant the hunter had begun to resemble some mad, demonic thing, with eyes bright against a mask of blood. His knife and sleeves dripped with gore and Deeds had to look away from that calm gaze.

'The stairs,' Elias said, turning back to them.

Deeds nodded, reloading as he went, so that he left a stream of spent brass cases on the carpet behind.

14

Nancy

Nancy frowned as she passed a smoking heap that had been one of the king's guards. She'd had no idea the royal palace would have quite so many people willing to draw a sword and rush at her the first moment they saw she was there. King Johannes was quite the employer in Darien, it seemed.

Behind her, Daw stopped to be sick again, though there was surely nothing left by then. Nancy waited for him. It was the oddest thing. She knew Daw was next to no use in that place, but still his presence, or even just his familiarity, was comforting. She may have carried great powers within her, but it had not changed who she was, or at least she hoped it had not. She was walking through rooms of such extraordinary, ornate wealth that they took her breath away. It was pleasant to go with a friend, though she left corpses littered behind and scorch marks on all the walls.

She felt a twinge of fear as a new group appeared and raced towards her. She had not expected guns, nor really understood how effective they could be. They were still too new to be well known in Darien and her only response had been to step up and widen the level of flame she vomited out at them. The first pair of gunmen had been left almost as ash and bone after that great blast, their weapons twisted from heat so intense it had left the walls flickering. That had pleased her, though she did not want the palace to burn until she was sure she'd brought down Lord Albus himself. She had only seen the man once, when he swept by her fallen father, not even looking down. She thought she would know him again, though. She had been given a chance to be the Goddess for an evening – and she would not waste it. Once Albus was a streak of spitting fat, then and only then would she make a vast funeral pyre of the palace of Darien. Let them explain that away in the daylight. Let them all fear.

Nancy dropped to one knee and raised her hands, sweeping the room with a line of flame so hot it ripped the air right out of those coming against her. She felt something tug at her sleeve and she looked in wonder at bright red blood, smearing it between her fingers. She'd used so much of the furnace within against the gunmen that she worried there would not be enough left. She could not bear the thought of getting so far and having no power left to finish what she had started, but there was no way to judge. All she could do was react and hope she and Daw would survive. She could hardly fault him for bravery, after coming in with her. Whenever she looked, there he was, pale and appalled, but still gesturing for her to go on.

She rested for a time, knowing that the king's rooms had to be somewhere ahead. A glance out of the windows onto the palace yard showed she had made her way to the middle of the main building. The crowd was still out there, of course, dark as the sea, pushing and pointing. She could hear them chanting and they would have seen the yellow flashes of her flames in the windows. No doubt they had cheered them in their drunken excitement, like a firework display. The

thought made her smile, so that Daw looked at her in puzzle-
ment and fear. He thought she had gone insane, Nancy was
well aware. She felt the power from the tomb buzzing in
her stomach and womb. She was controlling an ocean of
bees as they beat and pulsed and flew within her. It was
intoxicating.

A door opened to reveal a group of four men and two
women. Nancy lifted her hands and all six raised long tear-
drop shields, protecting their faces. They drew swords and
Nancy saw on the instant how well they moved. The king's
champions, his swordmasters. Or were two of them sword-
mistresses? She felt her fingertips tingle with heat when,
without warning, the woman brought up a pistol from
behind her shield and fired.

Nancy closed her eyes and *poured* flame along the room,
burning the air and hoping only to spoil the aim or melt the
bullets coming at her. She left them no space to leap aside.
They moved like spiders in a furnace, she saw that much,
impossibly fast but unable to escape, so that sudden spastic
movement became still the next instant. Their armour
melted, their swords gleamed red, too hot to hold, even for
dead hands.

When Nancy sagged, she could feel nothing left inside
her, no trace of the roaring sea she had brought into Darien
from the desert sands. It was a terrifying emptiness, and as
fear blossomed, she heard a weak cursing behind. She spun
to see Daw lying on his back, blinking up at the painted ceiling. A red patch was spreading on his shirt. At first, it looked
like a poppy worn on his breast, though it opened, blooming
as she stared.

Nancy ran to him with a cry of distress, never more helpless than at that moment. Of *course* they'd shot him, the

handsome young man, discounting her as a threat. Well, they'd paid for that.

Daw smiled as he saw her.

'I thought it would hurt,' he said. 'Why doesn't it hurt?'

He began to laugh, showing bloody teeth as she looked at him in confusion.

'Ah, the magic makes you so beautiful,' he said. 'Did you know?'

She nodded, rubbing tears away as her vision blurred.

'The magic has all gone, Daw,' she said.

He reached up to her and smiled.

'No,' he said. 'It can't have.'

Nancy took his hand in hers and held it tight, feeling his strength and pride. He looked away as if something had caught his eye, turning his head. He took a huge breath then and she knew the pain had found him.

He held that breath as long as he could, shuddering sips of air in and out until his strength failed in a great rush. She knew he was dead as he let it out and out.

No one intruded upon them. Nancy knelt at his side, waiting until she saw his eyes lose their sheen. Gently, she laid his hand across the other, then bent further to touch her cheek to his. She realised she had planned a life with him, unspoken between them, but perhaps understood.

'I'm sorry, Daw,' she whispered. 'I thought we had more time.'

Nancy stood up, pale and terrible, turning to face the blackened flesh and metal that had been the king's sword-masters. Curtains and carpets still flickered with flame along that banqueting room, taking hold, finding new paths. As she stalked forward once more, she saw one of their swords had been flung half the length of the room. It lay deep in the carpet, its shape burned into the fibres. She pulled it free, wincing as the heat stung her palms. She frowned at it, thinking that the flames inside her had never burned her skin. Yet the magic had gone and she suspected she would not leave that place. In that moment, with Daw cooling on the carpet behind her, she did not much care. Perhaps she'd done enough. She was almost too weary to hold the sword at all.

Behind the charred bodies, at the far end of the room, the blackened door was pulled open once more. This time, a small boy stepped out, closing it carefully behind him before he turned to face her.

Nancy's despair and rage turned instantly to dismay. Was there a prince? She had never heard of one. The idea sickened her, forcing her to examine her vengeance in a new light.

'I do not want to hurt a child,' she called to him. 'Please, kid, just, just go away from here. Run before I burn it all down.'

'Not a child,' Arthur said firmly. 'Golem.' He drew a sword of his own and Nancy raised her blade and advanced on him, her eyes filling once again with red and gold.

She felt it as he stumbled, this boy who seemed to glide across the carpet, showing the same unnatural grace she had witnessed in the swordmasters. Even as she slowed down and realised in awe what was happening, the little boy came to a halt.

Arthur looked at her in astonishment, his head moving from side to side as if he was trying to forbid her from entering even then. Yet he slowed down and down, becoming still with his head turned and his throat exposed. He stood, utterly vulnerable, and even so, Nancy did not strike. She could not cut the throat of a little boy and her attention was instead on the new ocean pouring into her.

This time, she understood, but still looked in confusion for the source. Only the perfect statue of a child she had seen move and talk went some way to explaining it. She did not know what the boy claimed to be, had never even heard the word 'golem' before, but the power that had animated him sank into her as water into a dry well. She felt the heat come back to her hands and her skin begin to smoke.

A man opened the door ahead of her and stood aghast at the scene of death and destruction. Nancy smiled at him and the man blanched and slammed the door shut as she rushed towards it. As she burst through, she was in time to see the man pulling double doors shut on her left hand. They were panelled in glass and she could see through them to the royal balcony. Two guards stood gaping at her. They had drawn their swords but seemed reluctant to do anything more to a woman who had come into the room in an explosion of splinters and flame.

'Run away, lads, would you?' she said to them.

One of them raised his sword and died for it. The other set off like a man determined to survive.

Nancy smiled as she peered through the glass to the balcony. The wound in her arm was beginning to throb and she knew she was in danger still. Yet she could see a blurred group of figures trapped outside that double glass door, just waiting like chickens to see if the fox would find them.

Nancy opened the doors and stepped through, pulling them shut behind her. She recognised Lord Albus easily enough, the enormous chief magistrate staring at her in horror. There were six others in fine uniforms or coloured silk. None of them looked like the coins that carried the head of King Johannes, which was a pity. Still, she smiled at Lord Albus and saw how he was sweating.

'I'd like a word with the judge here,' Nancy said. 'He's mine. The rest of you . . . go away.'

One of them cleared his throat.

'May we . . . go past you?'

'What?' Nancy said, turning towards him. 'No. Jump. Or die, I don't care which.'

The man took a terrified glance over the balcony. They were three floors up and the chances of survival were slim.

Nancy waited only a moment and then new flames sprang up from her hands. Her eyes smouldered and her hair coiled.

They jumped, leaving only the chief magistrate of Darien to face her. Lord Albus raised his hands, each one adorned in gold rings.

'You don't know you had me put out onto the street when I was just a girl,' Nancy said. 'You sold our house to one of your friends and when my father protested and tried to beg for more time, one of your guards beat him so badly he never recovered.'

'I see,' he said. 'And how many have you killed tonight to stand where you are now? How many families will weep for the loss of fathers tonight because of . . .'

He vanished in flame that bloomed and spread like a vast flower, yellow-white across the faces of the crowd below, knocking them back with heat and sound and brightness. Against the night, they were flash-blind for a time, or they would have seen the blackened balcony and the lone young woman standing there.

'*Lawyers*,' Nancy said.

She was exhausted and leaned over with her hands on her knees for a time. She knew she should get going before more guards found her there. The ocean within had dwindled again and she was so tired she could hardly stand, so full of grief that she could easily have stepped off the balcony herself just to end it all. As she stood there, she heard the low voices of men in the corridor. Rather than face or kill another, she took a step to one side and put her back to the wall, so that she was invisible to anyone passing. The stone was cool on her neck and she just stood there and breathed.

The doors remained closed, though she thought she could sense someone looking through them. Nancy felt tears come for Daw Threefold and all those she had killed. It had been a kind of madness.

Elias and Deeds stared at the strangest figure they had seen that evening. Arthur Quick stood frozen before them, as still as if he'd been made of stone, but carved and painted to some semblance of life.

'What . . . *is* that?' Elias whispered in awe.

Deeds shook his head in answer. Gingerly, he tapped the barrel of his gun on the thing's forehead. There was no answering movement.

'I don't know,' Deeds said. 'Perhaps some magical defence that failed? There's fire ahead of us as well – see that flickering? Something else is going on here and I don't know what it is. No, I don't care. The balcony is through there – those glass doors. There's no sign of the king, but this is the grandest part of the palace. He has to be close, unless he's run off or his guards have taken him away. We came through so fast,

I thought . . .' He trailed off as he looked at a polished oak door on the other side of the corridor, facing the balcony. Elias fell silent as Deeds put a finger to his lips, sensing someone close by.

The gunman took a step to the balcony doors and looked through the glass, frowning at the soot-blackened stone he could see out there.

'No one. Still, he has to be here somewhere.'

Elias blinked suddenly. Without a word, he went to the door across the corridor and knocked hard. Two shots sounded on the instant, smashing splinters from the wood but not quite going through. Deeds looked pleased.

Elias grimaced at him, then kicked the door open, rushing in. Deeds knew him well enough not to follow too closely and waited for another shot to whine past before he put his head around the door.

King Johannes de Generes was lying on his back, his hands raised in fear. He'd arranged a table to protect himself, but Elias had walked up and yanked it away, taking the man's pistol from him.

'Quickly now,' Deeds said, looking back. 'There'll be more guards coming; you can bet your life on that. Do it.'

Elias sighed, looking down at a terrified young man, close to tears but trying to be brave.

'Please!' King Johannes said. 'You don't have to.' He was trembling.

Elias shook his head, raising a knife and then letting his hand fall.

'I can't,' he said. He winced then as Deeds strode into the room, emptying his pistols into the king until all life had fled from him, then standing coldly and reloading from his pocket.

'There, it's done even so,' Deeds snapped, his relief making him curt. 'The general won't care how it happened, you can be sure. Only that it did happen. Tonight's the night, Meneer Post. Darien will have a new order by the morning, a new king and perhaps a new head of the army, standing before you.'

Deeds turned away and Elias went with him. Neither of them looked back at the dead king, now that they could not change his fate. Yet they were both grim with all they had done and there was no sense of triumph in the way they glared.

In the room beyond, Deeds caught a twitch of movement and began to react with his usual speed, bringing a pistol from its holster so smoothly it seemed to grow from his palm. Elias knocked it up and a shot went into the ceiling.

The still figure of a boy holding a sword was moving, slowly, like an old man almost.

'I've had about enough of killing, Deeds,' Elias said. 'It's finished now. You won't shoot him as well.'

Arthur Quick had not been stilled for as long as he had known. He felt life returning to him and when his eyes could focus, he looked first for the young woman who had been coming towards him. He could not understand it. He'd been defending the king, just as Tellius had asked him to. He'd drawn his sword and challenged her, but . . . His memory faltered and he found himself flexing his hands and turning his head back and forth, hearing it creak. That had not been pleasant and he could still not quite understand it. Had he somehow been knocked out? It had never happened before but he knew a good blow could put a boy down for a while, or for ever, if it was hard enough.

There were two strange men watching him, arguing in

angry whispers. Arthur blinked at their presence as well. From his point of view, they had appeared from nowhere. He saw one was covered in blood, just drenched in it from hand to foot. Arthur had a sense of having failed then.

'The . . . king?' he croaked at them.

'Dead. I'm sorry,' Elias replied. He watched the little boy, or whatever he was, slump in disappointment.

'Elias, we have to go!' Deeds said, trying and failing to snatch at his blood-soaked sleeve. 'There are ten or twenty thousand outside who will tear us apart if they catch us, do you understand? Even you can't go through them all.'

'Do you have a mother, boy?' Elias asked, ignoring the man. 'No? No family to look after you?'

Arthur shook his head and Elias frowned at the gunman, hopping from foot to foot in his impatience.

'Not boy,' Arthur murmured. He paused then, considering. 'Arthur.'

Saying the word seemed to upset him and tears shone in his eyes. Elias felt some of the hardness he had cultivated over the previous days crumble away. The boy looked nothing like his son, but that was not the point.

'Well, I have two daughters, Arthur, two girls who lost a little brother recently. If you want, you can come with me for a while. If you want to, all right?'

Arthur nodded and took a step towards him, looking back at the king's room.

'Have you lost your mind?' Deeds said.

'This place is on fire, Mr Deeds, if you hadn't noticed. I'm not leaving a stunned child here while the palace burns down around him.'

Elias set off with Arthur walking stiffly at his side. Deeds followed them, his expression dark.

They left behind them rooms filled with gun smoke. Flames licked up the curtains and were already taking a grip, leaping from chair to chair of ancient wood, spreading along the floors until the walls themselves were scorching brown and creaking with all the heat that lay within.

The crowd was milling in something close to madness by the time Elias and Deeds brought Arthur down to the palace yard once more. The people who had come to see the king had instead witnessed lords and ladies who fell fifty feet from the balcony, breaking legs and ankles and yelling for guards despite the pain. They had all watched the massive figure of Lord Albus turn to face someone, his back to the yard, then the great gout of white flame that had poured across the night sky, like a ship's sail unfurling.

By then, all the revellers could see flames lighting the upper floor and even showing in patches through the tiles of the roof. There would be no saving the palace, and the people of Darien were caught between the desire to get away to safety and the fascination of fire and destruction, the chance to say they had been there on that Reapers' Eve when the palace had burned down.

It was wearisome getting through so many. Stepping past thousands of gaping men and women was tiring work, whether asking to be let through or just shoving those who would not move. Grim-faced, Deeds and Elias sheltered Arthur as best they could, winding their way through the crowd until they found their way past the outer gate and into the city proper. The numbers had been heavy there before. Now that the sky was lit by flame from the palace, the whole city seemed to have been drawn to the western quarter.

Deeds saw two soldiers appear on a street corner nearby. They wore the white tunics of General Justan's Immortals. He inclined his head, pointing them out to Elias.

'There it is, starting.'

'The legion is coming in tonight?' Elias said.

'When did you think? Of *course* tonight. You and I are the excuse for it, Elias! The king is dead. Oh, we didn't plan for the palace to be set on fire, but General Justan had more faith in you than even I did. His legion broke camp days ago, moving into range of the city. They force-marched the last few miles at sunset. They are outside the wall right now, waiting for his order – and there's no danger of them being kept out, either. The general has his best men holding the gates open – and more moving onto street corners in the city. I don't doubt it will be a rough night, but by morning there'll be a new king in Darien. This is our time, Elias. You'll see.'

'I don't want to see anything, Deeds. I just want my daughters back.'

For some reason, it irritated Deeds to have Arthur Quick turning his head back and forth as the two men spoke over his head.

'I've said a dozen times you'll get them back and that the general's word was good. You will. I don't think it will be tonight, any more than it would have been tonight if General Justan was still in the camp where you met him, understand? So don't go claiming I have broken my deal with you. I haven't. You should just come back to the tavern with me to throw yourself in the horse trough. You're that covered in blood. It's only because it looks like a costume that all these people aren't running away in terror.'

As he spoke, screams did sound, though they were not

aimed at Elias. A man and a woman had stumbled into one of the Immortals. In response, the soldier had plunged his sword into the man's stomach, in two quick blows. There was a moment of stunned silence in the crowd around them, then the woman flew at the soldier, trying to claw his eyes out. Red lines appeared down the soldier's face and he reacted savagely, bringing his sword across her neck. She sprawled next to her companion in the street, her blood pouring blackly. Passers-by began to screech in panic and an angry roar went up from those who had seen.

'This could get ugly,' Deeds said.

'It is *already* ugly,' Elias snapped. 'Since when do soldiers attack unarmed men and women? Is that the plan you're so proud of? These people don't want a military leader, Deeds, do you realise? Once they understand what's happening, they'll fight.'

'You'd make a poor shepherd, meneer,' Deeds said. 'There will be some examples made, yes. I might wish for it not to be so, but we both know some people won't be cowed. After that, though – when the natural leaders are gone, the rest will fall in line. There are thousands of soldiers streaming into this city, Elias. There will be fear and chaos for a few hours, of course – and there'll be blood spilled. Yet when they see General Justan Aldan Aeris has arrived to restore order, I imagine they will be delighted. It's just a shame that the palace is on fire. I dare say he'll take some other building for his base.'

'I never was a shepherd,' Elias said wearily.

The crowd was rushing by the pair of soldiers then, stealing glances at the bodies and keeping their gaze on the cobbled street. Elias had seen more death that evening than in his entire life. He saw the same frightened glances when people passed him. He knew he was daubed in blood – he could feel it itching on his skin, as if it was still sinking in. The idea sickened him. He had killed a lot of men and he was just bone-tired. He wanted the night to end, but instead it seemed he would be witness to an invasion.

PART TWO

15

Choices

Lady Sallet kept all trace of kindness from her face as she observed the man sitting across from her. He was an adversary and she suspected he knew that as well as she did. Yet for all that, she found herself liking him, which was an odd and inexplicable sensation, like a smell of childhood roses drifting into the room.

Tellius looked steadily at her, wondering how this would play out. He had no cards left that he could think of, so his only option was to wait and watch. He did not like his chances, not now they had him in the cells. He imagined the Sallet estate was probably magnificent when seen in daylight, though of course he'd been taken there in the evening. He'd seen nothing grander than the inside of a cloth bag and had his heels bumped down a few flights of stone steps. Beyond that, he could have been anywhere in the city, just about.

The cell had one little table, bolted to the floor, with loops of iron welded to the top. A length of chain had been threaded through the hoops, then shackled to each of his hands. He could not stand up, nor do much of anything, so he was trying his best to look relaxed – and not at all like a frightened and exhausted old man, near the end of his resources.

Lady Sallet was a handsome woman, at least. Broad-shouldered and clear-skinned, with eyes of very dark blue.

There were worse sights in Darien, certainly worse cells. Tellius gave a tiny shake of his head to stop that thought, causing her to frown in interest. He knew he mustn't under-estimate the woman. Lady Sallet was one of a very small number of family heads and powerbrokers in the city, so far above the grubby exchanges of the street that Tellius had never so much as glimpsed her before, in all his years in Darien. There were some who said the king himself was no more than her pawn, though Tellius thought that an exag-geration. No law could be passed without Johannes adding his personal seal. Surely that gave the king the power to refuse, even if he never actually used it.

She seated herself across from him, folding and smoothing the lines of her dress in movements that were so controlled they seemed like ritual. At last she was still and she raised her head to fix him with those dark eyes. Tellius felt goosebumps rise along his arms.

'Under . . . all this,' Lady Sallet said, waving her hand to indicate his general state of decrepitude and ingrained dirt, 'you seem a civilised man. You made a deal with my nephew for gold, so you have no particular attachment to the . . . golem child. All I ask is to be told the phrase that binds his obedience, only that. In return, I will double what you were given before and you may leave the city this very night.'

She laid one hand on the other in her lap and sat back from the table, waiting for his response. Tellius looked down at his chains, cursing his own stupidity. He should not have gone back to the shop. What did his old medals and rings matter compared to his life? Yet the woman did not want to kill him, or he'd already be dead. His one advantage was that only he and Arthur knew there was no special phrase, no magical order to make the boy obey. Arthur would obey if he chose to, or not at all.

It wasn't much to make a bargain for a life, but perhaps, Tellius thought, perhaps it could be made to be enough.

'The problem, Lady Sallet, is that you can see each of the choices that lie ahead of me, just as I can. After all, if I tell you how to wrest control from your nephew, what is to prevent me telling another how to wrest control from you?'

'My nephew let you go with a purse of gold, meneer,' Lady Sallet said coldly.

Tellius inclined his head, almost apologetically. He thought best when he was talking and always had.

'With respect, my lady, you are not your nephew. I was not certain he would let me live. I am certain you would not.'

'Am I said to be so cruel, meneer?' she asked.

'You are said to be practical, my lady. You would not have let me go.'

Lady Sallet raised and lowered her shoulders just the tiniest of fractions, acknowledging the truth of it. She lifted one hand and tapped his chains, reminding him.

'And yet we are here, in a room so deep in the earth that no sound can reach through these walls. Even on Reapers' Eve, the stillness in here . . . You might as well have been buried alive.'

Tellius chuckled.

'I am too valuable for that, my lady, at least for tonight. Your nephew has not shared the phrase with you, or I would not be here. That much is obvious. Nor will he, which is more interesting. He does not trust you completely, then. Though who can blame him, when it comes to his own safety? He has always been afraid, ever since his father's murder.'

'Be careful not to . . . overvalue your life, meneer. This golem is not an army, after all. No matter how obedient or how skilful it appears to be, it is still one sword. I do not imagine it can stand against crossbows or gunmen.'

'Oh, dear lady, you truly have no idea,' Tellius said, his eyes bright. His value depended on how she saw Arthur, so he took the opportunity to praise him, knowing all the time that the woman could probably read his motivations as well as he read hers.

'The boy is faster than any swordsman or gunfighter alive, my lady. He feels pain, but can ignore it. On a battlefield, he might be overwhelmed, perhaps. As you say, he is but one. Yet in the right place – as a protector, no man alive could stop him.'

'Too valuable, then, for my nephew to control,' Lady Sallet said firmly. 'Now, I do not wish to have you burned and blinded and all the horrors my men can inflict. I would rather you told me what I need to hear. I would rather you took a bag of thick gold coins from me and simply vanished from Darien, never to cross our wall again.'

'But you will kill me, dear lady, the moment I tell you the words you need,' Tellius said, almost sadly. 'You know it and I know it. As things stand at this moment, my life is worth the breath it takes to speak the words – and no more than that.'

Lady Sallet frowned at him and he thought again what a fine, statuesque woman she was.

'If you wrote these words down, meneer, could you give them to a trusted friend? In a sealed box or letter, perhaps. A friend who would not read them but would only hold them for me?'

Tellius shook his head.

'My lady, I admire your mind, but I suspect you would still kill any friend I had named.'

'You believe I am so ruthless?' she said, indignantly.

'To rule the Sallets in Darien? Oh yes, my lady, of course,' he replied.

Lady Sallet inclined her head, giving him the point as he went on.

'My lady, even if I found such a one to hold a sealed box, you would still keep me captive, in case I had given you the wrong phrase. When you were satisfied, I do not doubt you would whisper an order – and there, that would be the end of an old man who trusted too much and deserved better.' He tried to spread his hands, making the chains rattle. 'I'm sorry. I do not want to lessen my chances of walking out of here, but for that to happen there must be no lies, no confusions. It is better that I bring it up now.'

Lady Sallet stared at this strange man who seemed to understand every part of the challenge she faced at least as well as she did. Trust was the difficulty, that was the problem. Yet a fair part of Darien was made of banking houses, some of them wealthier than the king himself. Her own family owned one of the oldest banks in the city and she had some experience with hostile trades. Surely more than an old man running urchins and thieves from rooms above a shop.

'Your desire is to remain alive, Meneer Tellius, to leave Darien, with or without a fortune in gold. Mine is to know the words to control the golem – and for him to be loyal only to me. Once he is mine, I cannot allow my nephew to take him back, do you understand?'

Tellius nodded, watching and listening with total concentration. She was very impressive, he thought. Her beauty was distracting and at that moment likely to get him killed. Really, it was quite an unfair advantage.

'If you make it too difficult for me, meneer,' she said, 'I will have to call an end to this negotiation. Do you understand? A circle cannot be a square. Some things cannot be resolved. If I decide there is *no* path through, I will rise and leave. The next person to enter this room will be the last you ever see. Do you appreciate the stakes?'

'I believe I do, my lady,' he said.

'Then let us find the path,' she replied. On impulse, she reached out and took his hand. Tellius blushed, astonished at the familiarity.

'Your difficulty lies in my knowledge,' he said quickly. 'You have thought to yourself that if you could have me captured and forced to speak, so could another, one who could take the golem from you. The *only* answer then is my death. After all, King Johannes trusted me – and yet here we are. This very meeting is the example of what can go wrong.'

'Go on,' she said.

He took a deep breath, feeling younger than he had in years, as if his mind was giving off sparks.

'I had the chance to question the creature, my lady, though he would not speak at first. Yet he came to trust me. He showed me a piece of parchment with the words of his maker, centuries old, but in a script I knew from my youth. I translated them into Modern and as I spoke them aloud, I bound him to me, all unknowing.'

'How fascinating. Do you have the paper still?' she asked, clutching his hand tighter.

Tellius shook his head.

'I understood its value – and so I threw the paper on the fire in my hearth, my lady.' He tapped the side of his head.

'Yet the words survive. I sold them to King Johannes. I can sell them again to you. And when you have bound the golem to your service, you will think it too great a risk to leave me alive, so . . .'

He made a peculiar sound to indicate his own death, like a goose being strangled. Yet he looked at her in triumph then, shaking his head.

'But you did not read the warning on the paper, my lady. You do not know that if you kill the one who passes on control, the golem is freed for ever from all masters and mistresses. It is as old as the magic itself, my lady. They were made for kings and queens, but even empires come to dust. Without such a safeguard, there could never be a successful change of owner.'

Lady Sallet removed her hand from his, delicately, unfolding her fingers where they left whiter marks. She looked thoughtfully at the old man.

'Interesting. I think you are lying, meneer. To save your skin.'

'Can you take that risk?' he asked quietly.

She stared at him for a long time. There were ancient stories of golems in her library, but no one alive had ever seen one. Their mechanism, their driving energies, were unknown. Here was a man of the east who claimed to know how to control one – and yet he could not be killed to protect the secret. A thought occurred to her and he nodded as her pupils dilated.

'There, my lady! You are thinking that you can merely give the order and someone else will kill me. The golem will not know – how could he? Would you be my guardian, forced to keep me alive? That is madness! Clearly, I can die a natural death, of course, and perhaps one not so natural – and then

225

you would have the golem *and* the command words to yourself. Was that your thought?' He smiled at her, shaking his head. 'My lady, no. The magic is more subtle than that. I am an old man and I will not live so many years now. Yet if you are involved in any way in my death – in a breath shared with my killer or an order whispered into an empty room, or even by sharpening a knife that kills me – the golem will be freed for ever.'

To her surprise, he suddenly gripped her hand, just as she had taken his.

'You must trust that I will keep my mouth shut for the years I have left. I tell you, my lady, I was content with what I had. Double that purse and set me free and I will tell you what you need to know.'

She stared into his eyes, seeing confidence and faith in her. It was a little unnerving and she welcomed the sound of footsteps that allowed her to pull back her hand once more and rise from her seat. She felt as if she had woken from a daze and glared at the old man, wondering.

The captain who entered was pale and shaking. Tellius became very still as his gaze drifted to him, taking in every aspect in one glance. It would not be good news, that was clear.

'My lady Sallet, the king has been murdered,' the captain said breathlessly.

He surely expected a gasp or a cry of horror from his mistress. Instead, there was silence. Lady Sallet sighed.

'I see. Did I promote you for your looks, captain? Was that it?'

He shook his head in confusion, unable to understand her reaction.

'My lady?' he said. 'King Johannes, your nephew . . .'

'Yes, I understood. News of such import might have been delivered more privately. Off you go, captain. Wake the Sallet soldiers. There will be unrest in the city. I will be up in a moment.'

The captain bowed, his confusion deepening. He left at a run and Lady Sallet turned to find Tellius watching her, his face carefully, completely blank.

'Yes,' she said. 'Of all the people in Darien this evening, you and I might see some benefit in this tragedy.'

'You do not seem . . . upset, my lady. Was he not a favourite nephew?'

Lady Sallet closed her eyes for a moment.

'I grieve, meneer. I just choose not to show it. Johannes was a fool, but . . . a kind fool. A harmless fool. He deserved better than to be murdered like his father before him. But, of course, it does mean your golem has no master. The value of the creature has surely dropped now that he let Johannes be killed. Or perhaps the creature has been destroyed. Here in this small room, in this silence, we cannot know – and yet you must decide even so. Perhaps the golem lies broken at this moment – and you have no value to me at all. In my anger, would I show you spite or kindness?'

Tellius swallowed uncomfortably at the glitter in her eyes.

'Tell me the phrase of command,' she said. 'Take the purse of gold we confiscated from you and leave Darien tonight. That is my offer to you. Or I will have you killed here, in this room. What need have I of a protector who cannot protect?'

'It would take an army to get past that boy,' Tellius said, with such certainty that it made her blink.

'*Choose*, Meneer Tellius. I am out of time. I offer you your life and your own purse. Or your death and nothing.'

He gestured with the chains and she tossed a small key onto the table, holding it under her fingertip, her eyebrows raised in question. He sighed.

'Say these words, my lady: "The juggler asks this of you." Just that and no more. He will obey from that moment, unless you hurt him, or me.'

'If you are lying, Meneer Tellius, in *any* way, I will make you regret your games,' she said.

'Of course, my lady,' he replied.

Tellius twitched and the shackles snapped open. Lady Sallet looked down to where she'd thought she still held the key under her fingertip, but found it was gone.

'Come along then, meneer,' she said. 'Until I have found your golem and spoken the words, you are my prisoner still. Put on your mourning face, or perhaps one of anger. The king is dead, on Reapers' Eve of all nights. There must be justice. More important still, there must be punishment.'

Nancy waited until the sound of voices had been gone for some time before opening the balcony doors once more, instantly cringing back from an inferno. The strange boy-statue had disappeared, which was a relief as the thing had unnerved her. Her eyes stung with thick smoke and she began coughing, remembering that it was the lack of air that killed before the actual flames, so they said. She looked back at the blackened balcony, then at flames pouring up the walls and over the ceiling, almost like a liquid. The fire made a sound like breathing or rustling pages as she gaped at it. The heat crisped her long hair and she could feel it sucking moisture from her mouth as she gasped and heaved for breath. The magic had been drawn out and it felt like the last stage of a fever, as if a drunken night had finally ended and she was going to stagger home through the quiet dawn. If she could get out.

A new wave of stinging heat washed across her, making her skin prickle and dragging her thoughts back to the living world. There was no escape the way she had come. The fire had become a wall down there, impossible to pass.

The smoke was so thick she could hardly see anything, but she could make out the open door across the corridor, with no sign yet of flames flickering beyond. It was just a few paces to be taken at a run, but the heat made the air too thick and hot to breathe, so that she could feel her lips cracking. She raised one hand to protect her eyes as she backed away onto the balcony again, leaving the doors open. Heat licked after her and smoke poured out so thickly there was no clean air anywhere. Instead she breathed through a sleeve, filling her lungs then holding her breath, darting across. She felt the passage as an intense flash of heat and then she was through, shoving the door closed against the furnace. Her clothes were smouldering from that brief exposure and she missed the power over flames she'd had before.

When she went further in, she saw the body of King Johannes de Generes, dead and already bluish with great dark holes in his chest and forehead. It seemed the face on the coins and stamps had been just a man, a little like Daw Threefold, smaller and made pitiful in death. She had seen that change before, she realised, when the guard had beaten her father. Though he'd been a strong man, something had been broken in him by the guard's boots. He'd slowly filled with blood until his entire chest sloshed with it.

Her father had died a few days after that, lost in fever dreams and crying out. No one had ever been made to answer for it, not until that night. Nancy thought of the huge, charred corpse of the chief magistrate on the balcony. She grinned through her tears, wiping them hard enough to leave a mark.

She blinked in the roaring silence, trying to focus. That had been a long time ago. She imagined Daw had already been consumed in the inferno she had made. No doubt she would be as well, when the flames burned through the doors. She looked up from the body of the king, knowing that she was dazed and needed to move faster. Her arm still seeped blood and she wanted very much to curl up and go to sleep. There were windows all along one wall, where it made no sense for them to be. An internal square of some kind, overlooked by the king's apartments.

She began tearing sheets off the bed to knot them together. She found she was weeping and heaving for breath after just a few moments of frantic activity. The pain in her arm was like a burning brand held to her skin. No. She would not panic. She would get down.

It was strange to feel no trace of magic left inside her, no sea of flame. It had happened so quickly the first time that she'd hardly had a moment to mourn the loss. Before she even understood it was the end, the child had stepped out into the corridor and magic had poured into her once more. It had been . . . a really strange night. As she sat and twisted sheets into ropes, staining them with her blood, the emptiness was like the absence of an itch after days of scratching, a blessed relief and at the same time a gap, a loss. She rubbed her eyes as she thought about it, then scraped one fingernail across the surface of her tongue.

The door to the king's room was of thick, polished mahogany. As she stared, it started to smoke, filling the room with a pungent, almost sweet haze. Nancy realised she had been looking off into nothing again and sprang back into motion, knotting and yanking the sheets, knowing her life would depend on them not slipping apart under her weight. She went to the windows and pushed one open, staring out at the silent training yard below. She did not have to get all the way down, she thought blurrily to herself. The smoke was making her sleepy and she put her head out of the window to breathe. It helped a little but the whole room was misting into haze and getting hotter. Fire rose, she remembered. The floors below should still be clear.

She felt a bit stronger as she picked up a chair and smashed it on the floor. She took two pieces from the wreckage and tied one mahogany leg across the window frame, shoving another through her belt. There would be guards on the floor below, of course. There was still every chance she would be killed or captured. She thought of Daw as well, who had come to that place because of her. He had been kind, which was about all you could ever say of someone. She would not let him down. She remembered too that he had left the golden mask with his brother in the street of apothecaries. It had not seemed so important earlier on, but if she survived, she'd have to find a way to make her claim on that. It was all she had in the world at that moment.

Gripping the thick rope of twisted sheet, she edged out over the window ledge. The heat in the room increased as the fire burned growing holes in the door, like fireworks blooming in slow circles. She touched the braced wooden chair leg for luck and eased her weight onto her shaking hands. The pain grew in her wounded arm until she wanted to scream. It could not hold her, but she could not climb past the knots with just one. For a moment, she hung there, helpless and despairing.

Her head was clearing now that she was out of the smoke. With a grunt, she wound the rope around her aching wrist. It would hurt and she would lose skin, but the twist aided her grip enough to slide. She could do it. Nancy began to skid and swear and sob, all at the same time, stopping at each knot to adjust, then continuing, jerking down the wall of the palace as fast as she could go.

16

House Sallet

On the busy street, Elias did not have to shake off Deeds' hand as he walked away. He just turned and left the man angrily grasping thin air. The boy Arthur went with him, gliding along with a peculiar grace that made him look almost like a swordsman. Elias shook his head. The child wore a blade on his hip but he was too small to threaten anyone. Yet he was also a responsibility, now that Elias had brought him out of the palace. When Elias glanced down, he found Arthur was watching him and he sighed.

'I'm going to try and find my girls, Arthur. The two daughters I mentioned? I said I would do some . . . well, some horrible things to keep them safe and they're done now. The thing is, I don't know if the general will just give my girls back to me and let me go. Do you understand any of this? Look, I thought I wanted vengeance, for using me, for forcing me to be a killer of men. At the moment, I just want to go home, to my little place, to visit the graves and to settle back into my life. Men like the general want much more than that – and I will not put you in danger. If I tell you to go, you must walk away, understand? Make your way east to the village of Wyburn and someone will tell you where my old place is. Just nod, would you, boy? I won't be responsible for you being killed as well.'

Arthur nodded slowly and Elias felt a weight lift from him

as he pushed on through the crowds. The nearest city gate was barely a quarter-mile from the palace behind them, some four hundred paces. There was already a change in the noise coming from that part of the city, a note of fear and anger in the air. Half the people of Darien were still in shock at the sight of flames lighting the horizon. Very few were even looking the right way, to see the greater threat of the Immortals marching towards the city.

Elias set his jaw as he strode through the crowds, not caring whether Deeds still accompanied him or not. It was an odd aspect of his talent that he knew the gunman was there even so, following in his wake. All Elias had to do was imagine stopping and there Deeds would be, once again at his shoulder.

He understood after a time that he did not have to concern himself with Arthur as he might have with one of his daughters in a crowd. A drunken, frightened city was a dangerous place for children who might not even be seen before they were trampled, yet Arthur seemed to step away and around the revellers almost as well as Elias did himself.

The hunter pressed on, not knowing for certain what he would do when he got to the western gate. Many thousands had gathered on those streets for the festival. Yet some sort of order was being imposed, he realised, his fists clenching on their own.

As Elias came to a halt and watched, the crowd parted ahead of him like a wave against a boat's prow, men and women pushed to the edge of the road by lines of Immortal soldiers in polished mail and surcoats of white. They used spear poles and the flats of their swords to press people back, but the message was clear enough and there were already one or two bodies sprawled on the ground. Many of the crowd were red-faced and yelling, too bawling drunk to go peacefully. They chose to scuffle when they were pushed and the soldiers responded with casual, cheerful violence, grinning all the while.

Elias stared through the open city gates at the sight of the great marching column coming to enter Darien. General Justan Aldan Aeris was certainly not trying to hide his approach. Trumpets began to sound in a great blare. Torches dragged trails of orange sparks through the warm night and at the heart of what must have been thousands of men and horses, huge white banners swung and rippled in the breeze.

The Immortal legion had come to Darien. The general himself was still too far off for Elias to see his face or to know if he had the girls with him. That and the presence of Arthur at his side was what stayed the hunter's hand, though he wanted to lash out. Elias had seen so much blood that night that he knew he could run mad, intoxicated with violence. He grimaced in bitter memory of some of the things he had done. It was not enough for him to say he'd had no choice, though that was true. It was why he had insisted on taking the boy to safety – one small act to try to offset the rest. He sensed he could not balance those scales no matter what he did, perhaps never again.

The king himself was dead, the hunter's awful task completed, even if it had been Deeds who fired the final shots. Elias could turn his gaze without embarrassment on the general who had brought it about. He could demand what he was owed. He did not know yet how he would deny that man his triumph, but if there was a way, he would take it. He had not lied to Arthur about his desire to go home, but that did not mean he wanted General Justan Aldan Aeris to achieve his desires. Some men did not deserve to win. Some men did not deserve to live.

With an arm around the boy, Elias moved aside with the crowd, though he remained right at the front, pressing against the line of soldiers, making them work for every step. Those citizens who tried to push past him found themselves grasping at air, subtly pressed aside. When one man lashed out in spite, he found his wrist gripped hard enough to hurt, the pain piercing through his drunken fog. The man backed away, rubbing where Elias had held him, sensing more threat in that one red-smeared fellow watching him than all the soldiers in their mail with their swords drawn.

Elias stood with the flat of a soldier's blade resting across his stomach, disdaining the threat of it. He had been a hunter long enough to know the danger of what he was experiencing. Stillness and care were the keys to his craft, above all else. Deeds was right to point out that Elias could not catch a horse or a deer by running after it. He succeeded as a hunter because he could see the best spot to wait, blending into the land until his prey came unsuspecting through the gloom. Patience had always been a part of him, deep in the bone for as long as he could remember.

Something had changed and he could not find the inner calm he needed any longer. Perhaps it had been the killing in the palace. There was something shining in his blood, to have walked through so many dangerous men with nothing more than a knife and his knack. He feared the wildness of it, but felt it still: a desire to win, to rule, to *crush*. No doubt the general would have recognised the emotion, he thought. Elias shook his head, trying to focus on the great column of elite soldiers marching into the city. Immortals. Deeds had said they claimed that name because their deeds lived on beyond their lives. Of course, that would be just as true for evil as for good.

Elias could sense Arthur watching him. He could feel the danger in the air all around, but he could not leave that place, not then. He had to see if the general had brought his daughters into Darien.

Elias turned to Deeds as the gunman came up behind him, panting hard.

'Here,' Deeds said, passing him a sopping wet cloth. 'There's a horse trough over by the gate. You're still a sight. You should clean your face with it. Your hands too, maybe.'

It was unexpectedly thoughtful and Elias took the cloth without a word. It was true that the mood was changing around them, the light laughter and revels of Reapers' Eve altered by flames on the horizon and the march of sandalled feet. The city was growling and some looked at the red man standing amongst them with anger and hatred and fear. No one laughed and assumed Elias was in costume there, not when marching ranks were coming in and every whisper was of murder and invasion.

Grimly, Elias wiped his face and hands as best he could. He needed to wring out the cloth and wash properly, but the general's armoured horsemen were still riding through the gate, his heralds blowing trumpets of brass so highly polished they looked like gold. Elias nodded his thanks to Deeds. He did not give back the fouled cloth, considering what had changed its colour, but a thought struck him as he faced the younger man.

'Don't interfere now, Deeds. I will kill you if you do.'

'I can't let you do anything . . . foolish, Elias.'

Elias snorted.

'You can't *stop* me. You know that. Better than anyone else alive.'

'No, meneer. Better than anyone else – except the general. And no, I can't stop you. Not on my own. But then, I am no longer on my own.'

Deeds seemed tense as he took a pace away and whistled, with a hand to his lips. The Immortal knights turned their heads to the sound and orders cracked out along the lines, halting the entire marching column in three steps. They had been ready for that signal, Elias realised in shock. He turned his back to Deeds, seeking out the figure of the general in the centre of the column. He could . . . no. As he *reached* to see himself step forward, his advance was met by dozens, surrounding him instantly, hundreds, all focused on killing him above every other priority.

Elias shook his head. It seemed the general had given some thought to the threat he might face from his own rogue assassin. Without moving a step, Elias saw how the man's guards would bring all their force to bear, more than he could evade or dodge. As he strained to see further, he found his future selves blocked again and again by a sheer wall of struggling, armoured men. He would kill dozens, but his small knife would not win him a path through. His knack would not take him to the general.

The road had fallen oddly silent as the legion crashed to a halt. Banners moved in the breeze and torches fluttered and huffed. Even the sound of jeering from the citizens of Darien dwindled to nothing. The Immortals were still as they glared into the swirling mob. They had been told to wait for the whistle signal and the order to halt, that much was clear. There was no confusion in their expressions, only purpose and the surly promise of violence. Behind the wall of swords and armoured horsemen, people milled nervously.

Elias watched a stone arc over from beyond the torch-light, catching his eye like the flight of a bird. It was a large one and it cracked onto the visor of one of the Immortal knights, making him reel and spit blood. Some in the crowd cheered, though that mood changed quickly as one of the officers gave a nod. A dozen of the man's companions dismounted and they approached the edge of the crowd with blades drawn. Screams and shouts of warning sounded from people, unable to get away as they struggled and shoved.

Elias had time to grab Arthur's hand and then found himself pushed back by a moving tide of frightened men and women. His knack was of little help to him without room to move and he felt fresh frustration at the limits of it, even as he snarled and heaved, desperate not to lose the boy whose grip was so tight on his.

Elias was still close enough to see Immortals cutting into the crowd like true reapers, killing with savage, sweeping blows. Hands scrabbled at their mail, but the people of the city were dressed for a festival and the soldiers were armoured for war. Elias swore under his breath, sick of all of it and yet helpless, carried along in mindless, shoving terror. He and Arthur were forced a dozen paces closer to the gate in one great surge and he saw General Justan there, at last, seated in armour on a great wheeled cart drawn by oxen.

Elias *reached* and held the spot, using his knack and all his strength to protect Arthur from the buffeting of the crowd, as he would have done with his own son. The boy stared at him the whole time and Elias smiled down at him, wanting him to stay calm. When he looked up again, the world seemed to recede and he simply stood, transfixed and gaping.

General Justan had decided on a show, it seemed. His ambition was there to be seen, in every part of the display. The cart itself was sheathed in purple cloth. An awning swayed on poles of gold above his head, no doubt to protect him from archers on the roofs. Lamps gleamed by the general as he sat on a bench, with two girls in white dresses kneeling at his feet. Elias swallowed at the sight of chains running from the general's grip to their little hands. The chains seemed to be of gold, but it did not make them any less a demonstration of his power.

In the roar of panic and rage from the crowd, Elias felt his own fear grow. General Justan had brought Jenny and Alice to Darien to secure his own safety, that was obvious. Yet the city was dry wood on that festival evening. The whole place could go up in flames, like the palace and the dead king within. Elias could feel it. As he stared and saw the general rub at a line of sweat along his neck, he thought Justan too was beginning to understand.

He saw the general's head turning, searching the packed faces for him. Elias gave up his plans, his thoughts of vengeance. His little girls were looking wide-eyed and afraid, of the mob, of the soldiers, of the man who held them chained like dogs at his feet. Elias could hardly speak for rage, but he turned to Arthur.

'Time for you to go, son. Yes? As I said before. Just slip through the crowd to the gate. Head south a few miles, then east to Wyburn with the sun ahead of you as it rises for two or three days. Ask for the house of Elias Post and say you're a cousin, all right? The key is in a slim iron box under the doorstep. Just lift it up. They won't stop you and you'll be safe there. I'll bring my girls to see you, as soon as I can.'

He gave Arthur a little push and waited until the boy had vanished between the mass of legs and heaving men and women. Elias raised his hand then and called out.

'Here, general. Elias Post! General Justan, I am here!'

He saw the general's hawkish gaze snap round to him and a look of honest relief cross the man's face. Once again, Elias felt Deeds come to stand at his back and he did not trouble to turn round as he spoke.

'Well, Deeds, it seems you have planned this between you. You chose to follow a man who would put chains on little girls. Perhaps you should tell me what you want.'

He heard Deeds clear his throat uncomfortably.

'That was not my idea, Elias. We just want to survive. There is not much point winning the city if you lose your head in the process, is there?'

Elias showed his teeth as the general called an order and the first ranks parted before him, accepting him into their midst. He stepped forward and could not help meeting the eyes of his daughters as they stared. Jenny looked angry, while Alice sat and quivered, close to tears. Elias could only imagine what a horror he must look. Despite his rough wiping, he was still smeared with blood, his clothes torn and half-burned. He imagined he looked more like a nightmare come to life than their father as he stepped out of that crowd. He smiled to his girls even so and raised a hand to wave at them.

'It won't be long now, Jen, Alice,' he said, as cheerfully as he could. 'Be brave for me, girls.'

He kept coming and *reached* with every step until his hands were trembling with the effort. The general stood above him on the cart and every pace Elias took was ringed with gun-men and swordsmen who stepped in so close he knew he would never be able to dodge them all. He grimaced at the lengths they had taken to control him. When he considered lunging forward and looked ahead to watch the outcome, he saw bright bullet trails criss-crossing the space where he stood. In the first instant, there wasn't room enough for a man between them. The general must be truly afraid.

Elias came to a halt and he knew Deeds had drawn two pistols and levelled them at his back. He ignored the threat. He was straining his knack all the time then, as far as he could go. He would see it coming.

'I have done what you wanted, general,' he said, preferring not to say aloud what his task had been, not in front of that crowd and his daughters.

'I can see that, though setting the palace on fire was never my intention,' General Justan replied.

It felt obscene to Elias' eye that the general still held the golden chains, stretching in a loop to the outstretched hands of his daughters. They were dressed in finer clothes than they had ever known before, Elias saw. Yet silks and satins could not hide their fear, for themselves and for him. It seemed the general was a monster, more so than Elias had understood at their first meeting.

'Why the chains?' Elias said, keeping his voice light, though his eyes were red-rimmed and terrible.

The general chuckled.

'This city is a frightening place for little ones, don't you think? I did not want them to slip away in the confusion as I entered. I certainly did not want their father to come hunt-ing me. I had a tiger by its tail, meneer. I could not let it go without it turning on me.'

Elias blanched as he saw gunfire erupting in the moments ahead. He knew what the general would say, *reaching* further than he had ever done before in his agony.

'Yet a tiger . . . can be killed . . .' the general began.

Elias froze, futures crashing. The general was looking off over the crowd, his mouth opening and shutting in surprise. He did not give the order Elias had seen coming. On the edge of the crowd, something like fire or lightning cracked out in a series of huge explosions, lighting the entire street as bright as day.

Tellius could feel his age as he breathed once more in the open air. He sniffed deeply as he approached the inner gates of the Sallet estate, with the anthill of the city proper beyond. Inside those walls, the estate was an oasis of calm and quiet order. Outside was chaos and danger. Yet even those high, ivy-covered walls could not keep it all away. There was a taint of smoke on the air and Tellius could hear a different tone in the beat of the Reapers' Eve. Something was off, as if a bell had cracked and was still sounding. No doubt the death of the king was part of it. He sidled closer to Lady Sallet as she spoke to her advisers and guard captains, sending them away with cool efficiency as her understanding grew. Messengers came and went like bees to a queen, helping her to build a picture of the events in Darien over the previous few hours.

Lady Sallet glanced up at the old man watching her and frowned, considering Tellius as a problem that intruded on more serious business. In the face of an assault on the city, the little matter of her nephew's golem had become one she was happy to leave to another day. Tellius could almost sense the moment she decided to have him thrown in a cell once again until it was all over.

'The golem has no master at this moment, my lady,' he called. 'If he is on the streets, he will surely be a target. Can you imagine what a drunken crowd would do to him?'

'Are you trying to appeal to my pity?' Lady Sallet asked in genuine surprise. 'The creature has survived long enough. I imagine it can fend for itself for an evening, wherever it has gone. I don't need you at all.'

Tellius knew he was but a single order from being sent back to the cells.

'Let me remain at your side, my lady,' he said. 'I was a swordsman – and I can command the golem. Better to have me with you and not need me, than need me and not have me with you, eh?'

Lady Sallet raised her eyes to the heavens, amused by him. She suspected she would have to kill him in the end, of course, just to tie up the loose threads of the business with the golem. Until then, there was no reason not to enjoy the man's company.

Two of her guard captains were already waiting for her orders, standing to attention. She looked them over, biting her lower lip in thought.

'Oh very well, meneer,' she said. 'Stay close to me and pray you are more help than hindrance.'

Tellius bowed as deeply as he could manage, delighted at the chance to leave the Sallet estate with his hide intact.

He heard a grating sound and watched as doors opened in the lower floor of the house, each much wider than a man. Six figures in green armour came bounding out and Tellius gaped at them when he saw how large they were, looking up in awe and actually taking a step back.

The six figures wore the same panels as any knight, though they gleamed in a way that was more like smoked glass than metal. From the vast shoulder-plates to the gauntlets and spiked feet, every part was marked in darker sigils, a flowing script of numbers and letters that Tellius vaguely recognised. He swallowed.

They stood eight feet tall, and yet when they moved, it was with the lightness and speed of masters. Tellius could only shake his head in astonishment as he turned to Lady Sallet. He saw she was pleased at his reaction and wondered if perhaps he had been allowed to remain just so he could see the famous Sallet Greens, her true protectors. They were every bit as astonishing as legend claimed they would be.

'You said you were a swordsman, Meneer Tellius? These are my guards. Are they not very fine?'

'My lady, I have never seen anything like them. Are they . . . golems?' He could see no sign of human intelligence in the green helmets, just a glassy and insectile gaze, weighing him and dismissing him in an instant.

'Beneath the armour, they are men, the best and strongest of all those I command. Warriors who train their entire lives for the privilege of defending House Sallet. Greens in formation! Protect me.'

The six huge figures clashed their arms on their breastplates, so that the panels hummed and rang. They moved to make a diamond shape around Lady Sallet and one of the massive legs almost knocked Tellius from his feet. There was a crackle of energy there and Tellius wondered what magic was employed to make such a huge weight of metal so light and yet strong. That the suits were magic he did not doubt. House Sallet was one of the wealthiest in Darien, in the whole west coast. Whatever could be made, though it took fortunes and lifetimes and the labour of entire cities, they would have.

Lady Sallet saw he had been buffeted and tutted, looking up at the green figures looming over her like a daughter admonishing her parents.

'This man is my guest. Keep him from harm – unless by so doing you might fail to save me, or fail to keep me from danger.'

The six warriors bowed their heads in response. Tellius realised he had not yet heard them speak and once more he recalled Arthur. He hoped the lad was holed up somewhere safe, not least because Lady Sallet had not passed over his purse of gold in her hurry. He did not think it was the right time to ask, but convenient forgetfulness was typical of such people. They ended up holding the gold because no one else had found the right time to ask for it to be returned.

'Whatever happened at the palace will wait,' Lady Sallet said in a voice used to command. 'King Johannes cannot be brought back to life and I do not doubt his own guards will collect what evidence there is and track the assassins. For House Sallet, there are other threats to the city. I am told there is an attack on the western gate, that General Justan is marching his Immortal legion into Darien. If that turns out to be the case, he must be punished for his insolence, his forces scattered.'

Behind the six green warriors, the personal guard of the Sallet family marched out of their barracks, rank after rank in formation. Tellius counted three hundred of them, a huge number for one family to support and equip, no matter how wealthy. Yet it would not be enough to hold back an entire legion. Tellius looked askance at Lady Sallet. She would need allies if they were to hold the walls that night.

The ranks of men in mail and steel armour formed up in silence, becoming almost as still as the Greens. Tellius shook his head in awe. The gates of the Sallet estate were already being winched apart to reveal the street outside. He could hardly believe how fast the night was changing around him. Just moments before he had been in chains in a cell, awaiting an uncertain fate. Now the estate gates were opening and a swirling mass of drunken citizens was rushing past outside, all exclaiming at the sight of the green-armoured warriors and the woman they protected.

'West, then,' Lady Sallet ordered. 'To the city gate.'

Tellius looked for horses or even a litter to carry the mistress of the house, but there was no sign of one. To his surprise, Lady Sallet took his arm in hers. The green warriors straightened up from their murderous-looking hunch, their heads jerking back and forth to seek out the slightest threat.

Lady Sallet's order was repeated at high volume, echoing back from the high walls around that yard. She walked forward and both Tellius and the six green guards kept in step as they cowed the crowds into stillness and awe. The forces of House Sallet were out in Darien.

17

The Gate

All Nancy wanted was to get away from the palace. Until she did, it was only too easy to imagine someone pointing her out and shouting 'There she is!' She'd skinned the palms of her hands on the knotted sheets climbing down to a balcony on the floor below. As she'd staggered inside, she'd almost been caught by one young guard who was fast on the straights but not the turns. She'd stayed ahead of him until he'd been gasping and wheezing, falling behind with every step. Luck or the Goddess had been with her then as she raced down stairs and out into the night, already lit by flames stretching to the sky above her. Her hands still throbbed and stung. The entire royal yard was bathed in yellow and shadows by the fire she had started. Thousands were streaming away from a building they thought likely to fall on them, while others stood and prayed or even sang in a dreamy stupor as if at a campfire, delighted by it all.

Nancy slipped in with the more sober groups heading back down the long drive and away from the palace. As the upper floors became an inferno, flames poured out of windows like thick tongues exploring the walls outside. Gleaming embers drifted through the air overhead as another silent hazard, beautiful in their own way, but still burning, like seeds carrying the fire further on the breeze.

More and more of the royal guards appeared in the grounds,

ordering people away, sometimes at the point of a sword if they refused to go. They were panicked: confused and angry at the lack of information. The entire palace was going up and the chain of command had been snapped, so that on one side of the yard there were men trying to keep the crowds from leaving, while on the other someone had given an order to clear the grounds. Hundreds froze where they were when the royal balcony gave way and crashed down, echoing back from the enclosing wings like cannon fire.

In that chaos, Nancy walked down the long drive, lost in a mass of people, unutterably weary and yet thrilled to be alive. There was dried blood on her arm and she could still feel where she'd been shot, like a pulsing ember. She knew nothing about bullet wounds but suspected she would have to find a doctor to look at it before it went septic. Yet despite her wounds, despite all she had seen and done, she was out – and walking away from horror and violence with a feeling of relief so intense it was almost euphoric. It was another chance to live her life and she was only sorry Daw Threefold would not be there to share any part of it.

There had been something unfinished between them, now left as raw and weeping as all her scrapes and cuts and burns. In just a few days, she'd grown used to him always being somewhere near, so that she could turn and see him. She frowned at that thought. They had shared the desert and experienced together the soaring emotions of the tomb and its sparking occupant. It did not seem possible that she would not see him again, that she would not hear his complaints or feel his arm around her.

The gold mask still awaited her in his brother's shop, which had the benefit of being some way clear of the palace. Nancy kept her head well down as she walked back to the city road, still half-expecting to be stopped or accused at any moment. Daw's brother's shop was full of magical things, Daw had been quite clear about that. Just walking into it would give her enough power to make him hand over the mask, if he chose to be difficult. It was not a pleasant thought, but she would not allow a stranger to cheat her of the only valuable thing she owned. She had earned her share of it, no one could deny that.

Around her on the great drive, Nancy could hear a dozen worried conversations. Men and women moved from group to group, passing on what they knew and gathering more. It might have been amusing for her to hear rumours of a dozen assassins sent into the palace by one of the Twelve Families, but she had killed men that night and it was not. She had not killed King Johannes at least. That part was a mystery, though she thought it had to have been the men she'd heard while she hid on the balcony.

She felt no especial guilt about the death of Lord Albus, which surprised her. The expression of disdain on his face had helped to burn away any last chance of forgiveness. That was something she clung to, now that the magic had all been used, leaving her hollowed. She had gone a little ragged for a time, it was true. Yet she'd found the man she wanted to see punished and she had ended his life. Perhaps it changed nothing. Perhaps there would even be remorse later on, she couldn't know. For the moment, it felt good that she had made her own justice.

As Nancy came closer to the road outside the royal estate, she heard other snatches of gossip: that the western gate had been taken, that the Twelve Families were out in force, that Darien itself was under attack. It made sense, when added to her knowledge that the king had been murdered. Something big was happening in the city. She found herself hoping that others would sort it out, a child's desire, dismissed as soon as she recognised it. She would walk and see, with all the others doing the same.

Nancy made her plans as she passed guards lining the great drive, watching everyone with suspicion and bare blades ready in their hands. She had been a part of something that night, right at the beating heart of it. Yet someone else had shot the king. Until she knew more, she was not quite ready to slip away to Basker's or Daw's brother.

As she came to the royal gates, she knew she was walking clumsily, like someone who had temporarily forgotten how to be natural. It was still dark, and of course she was lit from behind by the burning palace, but surely they would see the scorch marks on her clothes, the blood drops in her hair? She waited for the yell and the clatter of feet, but they did not come.

She slipped out into the city, turning west into the flow of people like a fish plopping back into a river. As she walked, she still kept her head low, though she wanted to run and breathe hard and fling her arms wide. She was alive and she had escaped.

She felt tears come suddenly for Daw then, and for those she had killed, an erupting sense of grief and sickness. Faces flashed at her and without warning, without pausing even to bend at the waist, she felt vomit rising. She pressed a hand to her lips in horror and watched as a thinner stream poured through her clenched fingers, spattering down the coat of a man in front so that he recoiled with a cry of outrage and disgust.

She was drifting to one side of the road with her hand still over her mouth when she saw the Sallet estate doors pulled open. The great enamelled family crest broke along its length and the two gates creaked apart to reveal what looked like an army led by monsters in dark green glass. Nancy choked slightly and then coughed until she was red in the face, hanging limply from a post on the Sallet wall. On any other night, she would have been told to move on.

Ahead of her, Lady Sallet came out with an old man at her side, surrounded by the huge figures in green armour, like beetles. They stopped the crowd with the sheer size and threat of them, so that a bottleneck was created right back down the road. Behind that spearhead marched rank after rank of house soldiers, following their mistress out into the city.

'What is happening?' Nancy called to the people around her.

Many of them were coming back from the city gate. They pointed behind them as they walked or ran, shouting warnings in answer to her question, shaking their heads in fear. She saw some were wounded, with one young man cradling his wife with an arm that ran with blood and stained her white dress.

Nancy had no idea who General Justan was, nor the Immortal legion. She had lived in Darien all her life but stayed away from soldiers, just as her mother had always warned her to. The legion hadn't saved her father from the king's guard. She probed the source of her anger and found it had been drained. She had boiled enough blood that night to repay that old pain – and it was all gone anyway, the sea, the ocean of power that had filled her up and made her able to take or spare lives at a whim. It was not pleasant to feel so vulnerable once more.

She looked down the street to the west, where the green

glow of the Sallet ranks could still be seen, dwindling as they marched away. Nancy smiled, showing sharp teeth. Perhaps it was worth a look. If she chose to, she would act. She just wanted to see what could possibly bring Sallet Greens out onto the streets. She'd thought they were a legend, not real.

Nancy understood as well that she wanted to remain at the heart, rather than to sleep and hear about it all over breakfast. Her city was alive around her, the crowds like blood moving faster and faster in its veins. She made her decision, setting out after the Sallet forces. Dawn was still a long way off, after all.

Tellius was fascinated at the insight into the way the Twelve Families worked in Darien. Lady Sallet must have been sixty, but she ruled there, with the guards and Sallet Greens about her. Like a spear thrust, she and her ranks of soldiers marched along the western road. It was no more than a quarter of a mile to the great wall, and yet in that time he saw three messengers in different house liveries come to her. None of them were allowed to approach close enough to raise a knife. Instead, they fell in with Sallet guard officers, bowing as they walked and handing over sealed boxes. Those were broken open and tossed back, with the guards checking for poison and running a polished stone over the papers within. Tellius assumed the thing would glow or chime at the presence of hostile magic, but he could only guess. The process took no more than a dozen paces to complete and then the message was passed to Lady Sallet. She read each one without expression, then tucked them away in a pocket in her skirts as Tellius watched. He knew his gaze could be affecting and he kept it on her with raised eyebrows until the trace of a smile appeared on her lips.

'The other houses are sending men, Meneer Tellius. All over the city. Is that what you wanted to hear?'

'I am relieved, my lady, if the legion of Immortals has breached the city wall.'

'With the help of traitors, I do not doubt. If that gate had stayed shut, they could have howled for an age and never gained entrance. Yet my nephew was murdered and the gate was held open.' Tellius watched with interest as she waved her hand across her face, almost as if wiping the past away. 'Well, here we are. I suppose he is after the great pieces – like my Sallet Greens. There is a *reason* we are jealous of our magic, meneer – a reason why they are held in the city except in time of war. It is for this, to defend Darien. General Justan will not find it as easy as he thinks.'

'I hope that is true,' Tellius said. 'Though, my lady, if I were planning such an assault on this city . . .'

'Yes?' she asked, tilting her head.

For a moment, he had her entire attention, though another messenger had arrived to go through his ritual.

'My lady, if I had thought far enough ahead to have men keep the gate open, as you said, perhaps I would also have placed men inside the city. You should keep an eye to the rear, my lady. General Justan is not a fool, as I've heard it.'

'The Twelve Families can match his legion in force,' she said sternly, though Tellius could hear the crack in her confidence, just as she could.

'Acting together, perhaps, if you can guarantee they will do so,' Tellius said gently. 'If they understand the threat is absolute and implacable, that their survival is truly threatened. If they do not understand it quickly, if they remain in splintered groups, acting alone, a ruthless enemy could take them one at a time.'

He saw her mouth tighten, refusing to accept it.

'Even so. He cannot match artefacts like my Greens. Each one is worth a hundred soldiers, more.'

'Oh, I do not doubt that, my lady,' Tellius said.

One of them was looking down at him as it . . . as he marched. Tellius had grown used to the sheer size of them, but the thought of one of those massive warriors plunging into a battle line was almost obscene. They carried swords, he saw, green blades made on such a scale that no ordinary soldier could have swung the weight. Tellius shuddered at the thought of seeing them used.

'Do the other great families command similar . . . artefacts then, my lady?'

'Never you mind, meneer! Though I will say there are things in this city that could destroy a dozen Immortal legions and their general.'

The road narrowed ahead and for the first time Tellius could see the great western gate itself, standing open and lit by torches. He heard Lady Sallet gasp at what awaited them. General Justan was there, barely inside the city and yet halted. His men had come a little further so that armed and stationary ranks blocked the road.

Tellius looked at Lady Sallet and she smiled at him, acknowledging his interest and welcoming it. She did not halt her men, nor hesitate.

'Destroy the invading force,' she snapped out. 'Execute all traitors — *anyone* in Immortal armour or bearing their sur-coats. Make a path through to close that gate.'

Her Greens bounded ahead, almost blurring to Tellius' eyes, so that he could only gape at their speed. Around Lady

Sallet, the ranks of her traditional guards surged. She was able to halt with her hand on Tellius' arm, letting her soldiers flow past to do their duty.

The first of the giant green warriors struck the ranks of Immortals as if they were scything grass. They had drawn the greatswords and swung them with such speed and power that they swept through three men at a time. Each kick and blow from those green figures slammed soldiers into the air or crushed them underfoot. It lasted a dozen heartbeats and the carnage was terrible.

None of them had seen the young woman in scorched and torn clothing standing at the side of the road, her back to the houses there. When Nancy darted forward, it was to run straight at the Sallet Greens, slapping her hands against the flanks of two of them as she passed.

The green gleam filling the street winked out, leaving them grey and sagging, all signs of life snatched away. In moments, all six of the huge armoured warriors had frozen and were still. One had been off-balance as Nancy passed him, so fell slowly, crushing screaming Immortals under his weight. From inside the rest, the confused cries of living men sounded, deep within each frozen carapace. They were alive but trapped in their armour, as unable to move as if they were held in a coffin.

The young woman left them behind as she went to defend her city – and her eyes were filled with red and gold.

Nancy felt clammy and overbrimmed with the raw power she had slapped out of the green warriors. She could hardly hold it in and she felt physical sparks fly from her as she rejoiced at its return. This was better than being an observer. The city was her home. For all its faults, she had no other.

She was a citizen of Darien and perhaps on that night, it meant something.

She would be *damned* before she'd let an invading army into the streets. King Johannes may have represented everything she had hated about her city, but he'd been *their* king even so, not some bastard military usurper. She had seen Johannes dead, that most intimate of meetings. She had seen him when he could not turn from her gaze, when all his royal dignity was in her hands. The king had looked innocent then, just a young man who would never grow any older. He deserved better.

She showed her teeth as she stood there. The closest ranks of Immortals were cringing away, a ring developing around her as they sensed the raw heat coming off the woman grinning at them.

Nancy laughed, suspecting she was risking madness again even as it overwhelmed her. Perhaps one person wasn't meant to hold so much. Daw had been hinting at something like that back in the desert, she recalled. She raised her hands and, though they were empty, the closest Immortals flinched. They were right to.

It took no effort at all. She did not need to point or clench her jaw, or even twirl and leap. Nancy simply *let go* of the fires raging in her – and the street went white with a great crack of sound and heat. When she blinked and could see once more, she had made a fused mass of entire ranks a dozen deep. The general was on his litter, jabbing the air in her direction. Was he too far off? She aimed a thread at him and found that it burned the air in a line that would not reach. Her lips tightened, an expression of rage. If this was madness, it was a good kind, she thought.

Behind her, she heard the tramp of marching men. Nancy

moved quickly aside then, having seen too much of guns and spears and every other sort of weapon. Her best chance was to keep moving, she remembered, so they could not aim as well.

She stepped through the burned ranks of invaders, men who would have stormed across her city but had been reduced to smoking, flickering figures, their flesh made char. If she touched them, they broke into ash and twisted pieces of metal, while ahead, still-living men cowered from her approach. Further off, Immortal officers roared orders to take her down.

Shots sounded and arrows flew, so that she was in the middle of hornets and flies, all whining past her ears. Nancy frowned at that, recalling how much it had hurt the last time. She concentrated, raising the temperature around her until the air itself crackled with heat in a sphere. She did not know if it would protect her from bullets and shafts, but she exulted at it even so. As she moved forward, soldiers threw themselves aside or burned where they stood in columns of flame. She had been filled with a deep well of power, the six grey statues her testament. The air ignited white hot around her and yet she felt no discomfort, beyond the slightest of breezes. She walked through Immortal ranks as if through the street on a spring day, leaving them twisting and dark behind.

Elias saw the patterns change around him. Bright lines began to shift, small gaps appearing amongst the golden strings only he could see. The men aiming guns and swords at him were disciplined, but not inhuman. From over on his right came a huge crack of light and sound, then a slowly building wave of heat that dried the air and rolled over everyone by the gate. Elias did not turn his head. He stood, waiting.

In that unnatural stillness, he did not look like a threat. He certainly did not look like a man more dangerous than anything else on that part of the street. As Elias waited, time seemed to slow. He saw the general's gaze shift from him over to the road into the city. In that moment of inattention by their commander, some of the men assigned to kill Elias also allowed their focus to falter, just a fraction. One of them lifted his pistol to resettle his aim, no doubt exactly as he had been trained to do.

Elias had not stopped *reaching* since he'd first drawn the general's attention. He saw the passage of bullets as lines or threads, criss-crossing the air in front of him if he made a sharp move. He could not duck or dodge past a single one, they were too fast for that. All he could do was not be there as they passed. The pictures flickered and blurred, constantly shifting.

He pushed his knack to the limits – and the limits began to crumble. Elias could see blurring futures spreading out from every soldier there, as if they had grown new dark arms and shadow selves. It was frightening in its complexity. As he watched, a larger gap opened in the moments ahead, just large enough for him to stand in it. Almost. He winced, knowing that it would hurt, then closed his eyes. He moved, stepping into a barrage of gunfire.

He was deaf after the first moment and he kept his eyes shut, relying only on his knack to see where he had to turn and step and pause to stay alive. All the time he dreaded the lines closing, so that the general would have his way and every step, every possible outcome, would lead only to death.

*

259

On the great ox-drawn flatbed, General Justan jerked back as he saw Elias close his eyes and walk forward, twisting and turning as he went so that somehow the bullets missed him. The gunmen poured in fire and a number of them fell, shot through by their own. General Justan saw a bullet rip a stripe in the hunter's side, revealing white skin that was quickly stained red. Yet the hunter still moved, wreathed in smoke and smiling, though his eyes were closed.

General Justan felt himself tremble. From the moment Deeds had brought him into the field tent, Justan had seen the terrible potential in such a man, such a weapon. There was no one else alive who could walk through bullets and bolts and swordmasters virtually unscathed – and General Justan had taken the man's *children* to make him obey. He had not exaggerated before about holding a tiger's tail.

Justan had risked it all to send the hunter against King Johannes, then his own legion against the open gates. The king may have been just a figurehead for the Twelve Families, but that was why it would work – a figurehead could be cut off and when the smoke cleared, when the streets were quiet once more, there he would be as the new ruler of Darien. Life would go on as if it had never happened. The Families needed order and peace. In a year or two, it would not matter if one of the Aeris sons ruled Darien instead of the Sallets. They would be forced to accept what they could not change.

Justan had planned it like the conquest of any foreign city, and even though plans failed and had to be remade on the hoof, it had gone about as smoothly as he had hoped. The king was dead, the city was in chaos – and only he had the strength of will and ruthlessness to snatch up the reins as they fell loose. Justan had been delighted with the evening to that point, right up to the moment he sighted his own assassin staring up at him through the ranks of marching soldiers.

He'd watched Elias take in the golden chains and shackles he had clasped around the girls' wrists. They were not to keep them safe in the city, but to prevent his hostages being snatched from his grasp. The extent of Elias' knack still terrified him, as one who preferred to see the world in solid terms. All men could be bound in iron. All men could be cut or shot. All men could be killed. All men but one.

Justan looked up as the sound of thunder continued to batter the air. The Sallet Greens facing his men had somehow been drained of colour and movement. In their place, a new threat was walking closer, one Justan had not seen before. Whatever it was, it gave off cracks of sound and light like massed cannon firing at close quarters. He could hardly peer to the core, so bright was it. Some dark figure stood at the centre of a sun, a sphere of threads, filling the street with light and heat that seared life right out of his men, welding one to another as they struggled to get away. All this, General Justan took in with a glance. When he looked back, Elias was gripping the purple cloth of the flatbed and was trying to pull himself up.

The general backed away from the edge. The two girls were staring at their father, the youngest holding out her hands to him. Justan gave a savage jerk on the chains and Jenny took Alice protectively in her arms before she fell, staggering with her across the wide cart. The golden leash was short and, with the girls in tow, Justan strode right across to the other side. Where Elias tried to climb, gunfire bloomed, so that a cloud of smoke obscured that part of the street. More of the Immortals fell, shot by those around them in blind panic.

Justan did not wait to see if Elias would survive the killing ground he had made. The hunter was no faster or stronger than any other man. One defence against him had always been simply distance. Justan tried to yank the little girls along, but once again they were almost underfoot and the loose chain just whipped through the air. White warhorses had been brought alongside and his officers were there to take both girls onto one huge mare, running the chains through saddle loops so they could not fall or escape. It took just moments and Justan could hear his blessed captains roaring for an attack further down the street. Darien had sorcerers, it was known, though he had never heard of one who could burn the air or massacre a century of his vanguard. Even so, he had more men.

'Advance!' General Justan bellowed, to give his soldiers heart. 'Spread out. Secure these streets!'

He had to get further into the city, he realised. It had been a child's mistake to halt just inside the gate, with so much of his vital force still outside the walls. Yet the sight of the hunter Elias had unnerved him, the man part of his nightmares for a week. To see him there in the flesh had overcome every other concern. Justan cursed to himself as he took the reins of his own destrier as well as those of the mare, glancing back across the flatbed for any sign of Elias Post coming after him. It had been close, in the end. If not for the distraction of that unnatural fire, he thought his gunmen would have closed the trap and brought the hunter down. It was the exquisite frustration of the man's knack: that he was utterly vulnerable. Elias Post would fall to a single shot or cut – if they could hit him.

General Justan tried to show confidence as his legion soldiers forced their way into the ring street of Darien, clear of the first defenders. Behind him, flashes of light clicked and reflected back from the walls of houses on either side. The roads around the gate were narrow, some old rule of defence that would not save Darien that night. Yet they doubled in width just a hundred yards from the wall and his men were almost there on the main road and the ring street. Most importantly of all, every step they made into the city brought more of his Immortals through the gate, fresh and ready.

One family, one witch, no matter how powerful, could not hold back his Immortals, Justan was certain. He'd feared the Sallet Greens more, but they had failed like the shoddy toys they were, legends of the city reduced to useless grey pillars. He tugged the reins of the horse behind him, angling the two little girls into the stream of his elite soldiers. He thought he might have the Greens mounted on the gates of the city as a warning to others, when he was king and this night was over.

18

Golem

Captain Galen of the Sallet guards was an impressive-looking fellow, Tellius thought a little grudgingly. Tall and broad-chested, the man moved well in armour, though of course natural gifts were no substitute for proper training. The soldier had chosen to ignore the old man walking arm in arm with Lady Sallet. Captain Galen showed no sign of finding such familiarity irritating, but it may have played a part in the angle from which he approached. A different old man might have been shocked at his sudden appearance, perhaps. He might even have let out an unmanly squawk. Captain Galen had not actually opened his mouth before he found himself pressed back by Tellius' arm, held off with such force that he had to take a pace or fall.

'Ah, captain, you startled me,' Tellius said.

He made a point of easing back to a ready position, in balance the whole way, one foot trailing in a half-moon, barely in contact with the ground. The captain smothered his surprise, allowing himself only a glare, though Tellius was certain Lady Sallet had seen every part of the exchange. Men were rather childish sometimes, Tellius thought, in the presence of a woman. He stepped aside and gestured for the captain to go on, as if giving permission. Lady Sallet's mouth moved a little at that, but the situation was too serious and her patience was thin. All around them, the street was going to hell.

'My lady, with the Greens down, we are too exposed. I cannot protect you in the open.' Galen pointed to where threads of white fire spat and sparkled, not twenty yards away. 'That . . . witch woman seems to be attacking the Immortal soldiers, but I do not know her, nor whether she will turn on us as well. With your permission, I would have you escorted out of the area, perhaps back to the estate itself, which is defensible.'

'Not the estate,' Lady Sallet said quickly. 'I will not wait for news. I wish to remain, to give what orders need to be given. Goddess knows, there are enough fools out tonight.'

'A house then, at the side of the road?' Captain Galen asked. He gestured with an outstretched arm almost in mimicry of Tellius just before.

Tellius could not help glancing along the line and it was his turn to be surprised. A door stood open there, with men in Sallet green and gold standing as guards and within. The captain had known the offer to return to the estate would be refused. Perhaps a good part of his role was pre-empting the whims of Lady Sallet, but it was still impressive.

Tellius was surprised at the words that came from Lady Sallet then, so much so that he re-evaluated his view of her and found more to like than he had recognised before.

'Where are the owners?' she said. Did she glance at Tellius then for his reaction? He hoped he could believe it.

'We are the owners, my lady,' Galen said. 'As of a moment past. I offered them three times the value of the house and sealed my ring to it.'

'Excellent,' Lady Sallet said.

That time, Tellius was sure she had looked at him as she lowered her gaze. Goddess, was the woman interested in him? He looked again at her upright carriage and fine, clear skin. For the first time that day, Tellius felt grubby and unkempt. He ran a hand through his hair, pushing strands of it back behind his ears.

'This way, my lady,' Galen said, turning so that he half-blocked Tellius from her sight.

'Will you go in with me, Meneer Tellius?' Lady Sallet said clearly.

Captain Galen was left with no choice but to step aside to let him answer, though he looked fairly constipated in his irritation.

'My lady, I would like nothing more than to continue in your company,' Tellius said with a dip of his head. 'However, I would prefer to be useful, if I can be. If you don't mind asking one of your men to give me a sword, I promise I will join you when it is over. I would not feel . . . able to leave the city without seeing you once more.'

'And, of course, I still have your gold,' she said coolly. 'And a golem to find.'

'Ah, yes. There is also that,' he said, half-bowing.

Lady Sallet nodded to the closest of her men. He took his second sword from a sheath across his back, passing it over with enormous reluctance.

'Can you . . . use such a weapon, meneer?' Lady Sallet said. Tellius smiled.

'I believe I can, my lady. It has been a long time, but I believe so.'

Lady Sallet nodded to him, then turned away, crossing the part of the street held open for her by her men, though battle raged all around them. It was the oddest and most artificial moment Tellius could remember, all to keep the mistress of a great family safe. When the door to the house closed behind her, he turned to Captain Galen.

'A *formidable* lady,' he said.

Galen glowered down at him.

'Worth a dozen of you,' he said. He was halfway through presenting his back to Tellius when he relented and faced him once again. 'But she seems to like you, so try not to get yourself killed. Better still, stay close to me and I will do my best to keep you alive.'

Tellius ran his thumb across the edge of the blade and smiled. He had taught the Mazer steps to every one of his lads over the years, taking hours each day to insist on perfection. Though he was perhaps the oldest man in that street, he chuckled.

'Thank you, Captain Galen,' he said.

Galen looked at the way the old man was standing. Despite the patched cloth of his coat and trousers, despite the white bristles of one who shaved rarely if at all, there was still an odd confidence in the man's stance. Captain Galen jerked his head to the men around him.

'That witch, or whatever she is. It looks like she's on our side, but if she turns on us, I want her down and out. I'll give her a chance to come into the ranks. If she doesn't take it, she's the target, understood? Hit the greatest force first – rule number one, gentlemen. So – gunmen to the front rank, loaded, drawn and ready. And I want a team looking at those Greens and dragging them back into that stable yard, understood? Well, find ropes! Fourth company! That is your task. At least discover if we can get our men out alive. Clear? Now, the rest of you: Lady Sallet is safe. This road is ours to defend. *Steady* now. Advance, Sallet!'

Captain Galen fell into step as the front rank came abreast of him, looking left and right as he went. Tellius took position on his shoulder and some part of him rejoiced, though it had been over thirty years since he'd stood in a line with warriors, bearing sharp iron and with an enemy ahead. He could not help the smile of satisfaction that crossed his face, just at feeling young again. A moment later, his aching knees reminded him of his age and he scowled. Still, Darien was his adopted city and Johannes had been his king. He didn't believe for a moment that the murder and the invasion were unrelated. The traitors spreading out from the gate were responsible for bringing fear and chaos into his home. Tellius only hoped Arthur had not been destroyed trying to save the king.

The old man swished his new sword back and forth in patterns ahead of him, getting the feel of its weight. His throat grew dry at the thought of using such a blade in anger once again, though whether it was in fear or anticipation was hard to say. It had been a long time, it really had.

Nancy felt fear begin as a twist in her stomach, like the puckering of a mouth filled with vinegar. The power she had taken from the green warriors was draining away at a frightening rate. She had no true sense of how much was left in her, beyond a mental image of a sea vanishing to reveal a desert. Yet with every thread of white fire, she felt a sucking sensation in her chest and stomach, as if the great torrent was being reduced to a trickle, a dry teat after a waterfall. It made her want to weep for its loss, but the more pressing fear was that Immortal soldiers still blocked the road in front of her.

They had brought up shields, she saw, great boards of wood and hide to protect them from gunfire or crossbow bolts. Those things burned very well, but men still cowered behind them, preferring a heat they knew and could withstand to the one that tore air from their lungs and made their skin crisp. For a while, Nancy exulted in the destruction she could cause, but her threads were growing thin and she knew she could not be far from going dark and seeing them rush her. Already, there were soldiers in Immortal surcoats creeping around on either side. She picked them off, but they were fanatical. Even as they died, more and more pressed in, until she was snarling at them and forced to use all she had taken.

When the lines of fire were no thicker than hairs, she heard a voice close behind her.

'My lady, please fall back,' a man called. 'You are growing weary. We are ready.'

Nancy risked a glance over her shoulder at the speaker, seeing a tall soldier in silver armour and a green surcoat. Bullets whined around her as she did so, thumping into the shields of the men at her back. Sallets, she realised. She hoped they would not blame her for taking the power from their famous green warriors.

She felt something snag her wounded arm then and hissed at an agony so great she thought she might faint. Nancy cupped one hand in the other and Captain Galen flicked his fingers at two of his men so that they put shields around her and gathered her in, falling back through the ranks.

'Take her to Lady Sallet and keep her safe,' Galen said. He

stared after her for a moment longer than he should have done, thinking how very beautiful she had been, with hair like flames in red and gold.

Tellius watched the young woman half-carried back to at least the semblance of safety. In all his years he had never seen anything like her for sheer violence. He was not sure yet of the source, nor why she had run dry. He was cynical enough to suspect that Lady Sallet would be very interested in such a powerful witch, or whatever she was. Still, he had other concerns at that moment.

'Shields! Keep your damned shields up!' Galen called to his men.

Bullets thumped into them and Tellius shook his head in disgust. Was this the face of warfare for the new generation? He hated the idea. In his youth, it had been about champions and skill and the Mazer steps that honed the body and the mind to make a living weapon out of them. This fusillade of shots was madness – and also terrifying. He had no desire to be cut down by some sweating soldier with a trembling gun-hand. He hoped to see Lady Sallet again, for a start.

Sallet gunmen poured their own fire into the Immortal ranks. The army pressing in from the western gate had begun to spread the news that the witch had fallen back and more ordinary soldiers awaited them. Their response was a great surge forward, closing the gap between the two forces so that the street filled with murder and snarling, two wolf packs released into one another.

Tellius raised his sword, and killed with it the next moment. He had faced an armoured warrior hardly able to believe his luck in coming across an old man. Yet Tellius had guided the soldier's blade in a safer arc with a hand pressing against a shoulder, then jabbed his own sword under the man's neck-plate, finding a spot where the point just slipped in. He jerked his hand and blood sheeted across the silver metal, making the Immortal's eyes widen.

'Sorry, son,' Tellius said. 'Go to the Goddess now.'

He hoped Galen had some sense of how the battle was going as Tellius found his world filled with the savagery he could suddenly recall only too well from his youth. It was ugly and exhilarating at the same time, with the stakes as high as they could possibly be. Yet he felt his own worm of doubt as his age began to tell almost immediately. Every man he cut down was a professional soldier in his twenties or thirties. They had stamina and strength he could not possibly match. He moved well enough against the first three men, leaving them to fall and twitch as they died, but the fourth almost had him – would have done if Galen hadn't spotted the man gripping Tellius' throat and bearing him backward, raising his sword like a cleaver. Galen had cut down the Immortal and Tellius had been left heaving for breath and holding his bruised neck, nodding his thanks.

Galen was a gifted fighter, Tellius could see. The captain of the Sallet forces kept a sense of space around him that few men managed. Anyone who crossed into range of his sword was engaged and sent reeling in two or three strokes at most, a nicely economical style that would mean Galen kept fighting long after the rest were exhausted. Lady Sallet had chosen her commander well, it seemed. Yet there were five thousand in the Immortal legion. If they were prepared to die to take the city in their madness, Tellius did not see how the forces of Darien could hold them off.

He had not yet seen any sign of the Twelve Families beyond Sallet. With the Greens down, the few hundred estate soldiers could not hold back an actual legion, not even with the advantage of the narrow streets by the gates. Tellius didn't doubt the Immortals were already spreading around from the western gate, taking other routes into the city. The ordinary citizens of Darien might throw a few tiles or bricks, but they would not fight, he thought, perhaps because their lives would not really change. Places like his own workshop and his lads would go on, or something very like them, if General Justan Aldan Aeris took over. They would merely be exchanging one set of masters for another. The Twelve Families had a much greater stake in whoever ruled. They faced their own destruction, so it was up to them to defend Darien, if they had the sense and the will. Tellius only wished he could have seen some sign of it that evening. The Sallet force was already being pushed back and he could see no reinforcements coming.

Arthur Quick climbed higher and higher on the tiles, determined to watch the fighting. He'd been unhappy when the hunter Elias had sent him away, though he understood it was meant to protect him. The man had mentioned a home in a village and two daughters. It had been an age since Arthur had known anything like that and he was grateful for the image of it, even if it did not come about.

Arthur had always been good at climbing. He went hand over hand to the peak of the roof, lying prone on the ridge beam and staring down in fascination as the fighting began in fire and explosions. The golem had frowned when he'd recognised the woman from the king's apartments. He did not want to face her again, not the one who could somehow drag life right out of him. For the first time in all his years, he thought he understood what it meant to come to an end.

It was a revelation, and as he stared down in the darkness at the armies heaving back and forth below, he could only wonder at the short lives of men and the way they were willing to risk them.

Arthur lay as still as any gargoyle until the witch woman's threads of light began to fade and die out. He saw her twitch as if she'd been hurt and leaned right over the ridge beam to watch as she was taken into the ranks of the Sallets, wounded but alive.

Arthur's gaze sharpened further as he saw Tellius standing in the ranks of those soldiers. The old man went forward in smooth movements, almost gliding where others plodded. Arthur smiled in recognition, but from the height of the pitched roof, he could see how few the Sallets were, how shallow their line – and how many they faced. The witch woman had smashed the front ranks of the Immortals, but they were still pushing into the city. Beyond the wall, Arthur caught glimpses of a column of torches flickering like stars, all marching into Darien.

He sat up, looking over to the gate. To decide was to act and he did not hesitate or ponder, as another might have. He skittered down the roof and along to the dipped section over a doorway where he had come up. From there, he jumped down to a balcony, swung over the edge of it and hung-dropped to the street below, coming up at a sprint.

The massive western gateway lay ahead of him, just a hundred yards from where he was. He had lived a long, long time and he had a good idea how such things worked, how they were opened and how they could be closed once again. The Immortal legion would react quickly, he thought, as he dodged and weaved past shouting drunks and marching soldiers. They would know as soon as the gate moved, and wherever he stood would become the hottest part of Darien in a few moments. He would be killed, certainly, but he would close the gate, or at least draw vital soldiers from the attack. Either way, both Tellius and Elias were in that bloodied, savage press. Whether they ever knew or not, Arthur could not watch those men cut down and just do nothing.

When the crush of soldiers was too great even for one of his size to slip through, he yanked open a door into a tavern packed with terrified citizens, all watching him in astonished silence as Arthur ran across the benches and tables and out the other side.

Ahead of him, huge stone steps rose to the winching mechanism: ancient cogs of oiled iron and black lignum vitae wood set against the inner wall. It was all on a grand scale, as befitted one of the main gates of a city like Darien. It was also the first spot the Immortals had secured, using men already in the city. Every one of the great steps was guarded by soldiers wearing white surcoats and silver mail.

They were watching the heave and ebb of the battle inside the walls, enjoying a duty that gave them a perfect view and yet forced them to remain clear of the fighting. They did not see him at first. As he walked up, Arthur drew the sword King Johannes had given him and felt the weight of it, flicking his thumb across the edge. Johannes had been kind to him and Arthur had failed to repay that kindness.

He had lived for centuries and he could feel the weight of those years. Arthur had never truly been able to imagine death before. Yet the witch woman had given him a glimpse and it no longer frightened him, not really. Like sleep, there was no sense of loss, no wrongness. It was just darkness, with no regrets. He felt a twinge of sorrow that he had not seen the Goddess the people of Darien mentioned. Perhaps she was not for things like him.

The first group of Immortals looked away from the bloody street battle at last as he approached. The sight of a child with a sword did not unnerve them, though one of them made a comment to another and both men laughed. Arthur did not smile. Such men had trained to fight others of their own size; Tellius had told him that. It was a most extraordinary advantage. Everyone Arthur faced was taller, so that he had to bring them down with one cut, then finish them off. He had learned the style as easily as anything else. The men on the first step were facing one of his size for the first time – and they did not get long enough to adjust for it. On that Reapers' Eve, he went through them like wheat.

He leaped up onto the step to land amongst the soldiers. One of them instinctively tried to kick him off and cried out as the sword gashed his thigh, falling to one knee as the leg folded. He was dispatched and the crowded soldiers panicked at the glimpsed child in their midst, stabbing and gashing, leaving blood splashed across their white surcoats. They struck each other as they lunged for him. He never stopped moving as he cleared each step and hacked at the ankles of those above. They stabbed down at him, trying to pin the vicious creature to the ground and then yelping and cursing as his sword found their flesh. They had trained for years to fight men. A golem the size of a ten-year-old boy was a whirlwind coming through them.

Arthur was on the fourth step of twelve, with bodies littered behind him, when a shot stabbed a burning finger through his chest. He looked up in astonishment at the line of gunmen facing him. He raised his hand to the hole and saw a smear of clear fluid dribbling from it. It hurt. He never showed it, but it really did.

He gave a cat-growl and rushed them, gashing the gunman's pistol hand with his sword so that he pulled it back, spoiling the aim of the next one along – and by then, Arthur was in amongst them, stabbing and cutting. Those above could not see him to aid the ones below, so he could continue to fight his way up until he was too wounded to go on, or too tired. He had been cut and shot and he felt weariness in his arms that would only grow.

The secret of the Mazer steps was to remain utterly calm, a calm that it took most men a lifetime to learn. Arthur had sensed the rightness of it from the moment he saw Micahel demonstrate the movements back at the workshop. Physical control and strength for balance – yes, of course, but the peace came from a prepared mind. So he did not panic as another gunshot clutched at him. He had not expected to live, though he had to remind himself of that when he grew afraid.

He continued to climb and leap and kill, but there were too many of them. He saw the last few steps filled with Immortals in white coats, emptying their pistols in smoke and thunder. He felt impossibly tired and he could hear a roaring in his ears, like the sea. He hoped it was not his life's blood spattering on the stone steps, but he thought it probably was.

'Arthur!' he heard behind him. 'It *is* you! We have this.'

He turned, still ducking and moving so that they would not cut him down. Arthur blinked as Micahel, Donny and the older boys from the workshop raced past him. They had collected pistols and shields as they came and they were holding them up. No, Micahel held only his sword and he raised it in salute as he went past. None of them hesitated and the Immortals threw empty guns at them and drew the swords they actually knew how to use.

Arthur sat on the steps and wondered at the pool of sticky fluid all around him. He had to crane his neck to see, which hurt him, though he would not have missed it. He watched Micael sweep through the remaining soldiers with an economy of movement Arthur knew very well, that would have made Tellius weep with joy to see once more. The others were not quite as perfect, but Micael wove a storm with his blade, an archangel on the stair.

Arthur found he was panting. The air would not come properly, though he had never really thought about breathing before. It had always just been part of him, for centuries of nights and days. He had learned so many things.

He looked up once more as his sword fell with a clatter from his hand. The boys were spinning the massive gear wheel into a blur and they were answered by a confusion of sounds Arthur could not understand as his senses began to fade. Above all was a roar of metal and stone as the gate began to close, incredibly slowly, but with inexorable force. New cries of anger and panic sounded both before and behind it, as the Immortals understood what was happening. Frantic orders were shouted for those already inside the gate to get up the steps and hold it open.

Arthur watched as the boys from the workshop came over to stand on the walkway at the top, Micael with them. Donny spun and spun the gate wheel, laughing at the speed of it. Another held a long shield over them both as bullets from below began to rattle against it. The rest made a line, with shields and swords and even pistols held ready as they looked down on the struggle going on around the gate. Not all of them had reached the top. Yet those who had conquered the mountain were triumphant and howling. They had faced grown men and somehow lived.

Arthur smiled at his friends and slumped against the step. For an instant, he saw light gleam around him and he heard a voice he knew, the mother who had created him, or the Goddess herself, he could not be sure.

'Come to me, my son,' she said, and he was gone.

19

Blue Border, Blue Border

Lord Gandis Hart had never ridden at speed through the city streets before. If he had known how the people of Darien would fling themselves aside at the sight of cantering horses, he thought perhaps he might have. On a normal night, it would have taken him an hour to make his way from the Hart estate on the eastern wall right around two quarters of the city. Yet he and his men had put their heads down and pelted round the ring street as if it was a racetrack.

He could still hardly believe what was happening. Festival Eve was usually his favourite night of the year, a celebration, but also a release of pressure, with its edge of danger and chaos. The Harts were the sixth eldest of the Twelve Families and had various traditions of their own for that evening, including drinking from the huge silver wassail cup in the estate hall, one after the other as midnight came.

That moment of family contentment was now a memory, the city fragmenting in panic and violence, with screams sounding alongside the clatter of metal and running soldiers. At that point, Gandis longed for dawn as he'd rarely longed for anything in his entire life. The king had been murdered. The royal palace and half the beautiful art in Darien had been burned to the ground. That was bad enough, a loss of such a magnitude that he dared not think of it. To hear General Justan's Immortals had launched an attack on Darien and actually forced their way in was news to eat at the foundations of his faith.

The Harts were comfortable in their mid-ranking in Darien. They had a vote in council, though in fairness it was usually bought and paid for by the time the count was called. They had a few fine houses and businesses in the city, as well as an estate inside the wall. The Hart holdings were smaller than most, but the estate had its lake and copse of trees and the building was a triumph of light design compared with some of them. Next to the Sallet or Regis hall, it was small, but to the rest of the city, the Harts were on a level of wealth beyond dreams of avarice.

In the darkness, Gandis Hart reined his mount down to a trot, surrounded by thirty men ahorse and allowing another thirty on foot to keep up, their swords already drawn. He would not like to meet such men in a dark place, yet he could not congratulate himself, not that evening. It was too late to wish he'd armed his servants with the new pistols flooding into the city. That trade was controlled by the Regis family and, frankly, the price of outfitting sixty men had been a little too rich for Hart coffers in time of peace.

He cursed himself then for his lack of foresight. It would be different when they next met as a council, or perhaps he would invest in his own smiths and workshops. Yes, that was better still, to compete with the Regis gunmakers. Hart pistols. He'd have his steward look into poaching one of their lads, offering him a fortune to set up a new line.

Lord Hart and his men had cut around the edge of Darien, closing fast on the western gate, though they left yells and terrified citizens in their wake. Gandis was enjoying himself; he could not help it. For all the desperation of Lady Sallet's plea, he had never seen the city rush past at such a speed. Back at a trot, his responsibilities and duties caught up once more, making him frown. Even then, he fought to remember every moment of that wild ride, knowing instinctively that he would never have such a chance again. Unless he organised a race around the city, he thought suddenly. It was a Hart curse, to see opportunities in the middle of chaos, or because of it.

From the height of his saddle, Gandis thought he could see the glow of the burning palace in the western sky. The thought sickened him, but even that destruction, that appalling treason, could not be his concern. The box message from Lady Sallet had been clear. Her house needed his family's most famous treasure, to help contain the Immortals. He swallowed at the thought of thousands of whitecoat soldiers loose in the city to murder and run wild. The Immortals were the primary armed force of Darien, turned against her. It was hard even to think of them as an enemy. By the Goddess, they had paraded through the city only months before, with the king's subjects all throwing white flowers. Had their general been scouting his attack even then? It seemed a possibility. Gandis knew he had to consider the man as he might a foreign invader, as terrifying and as ruthless. There could be no mercy or attempt to negotiate with him. Yet the Immortal general had advantages no steppes clan or foreign prince ever would – Justan Aldan Aeris knew Darien, and all her strengths and weaknesses. As Gandis had the thought, he wondered how many of the city would welcome the coup. He felt himself pale at the thought of traitors. Who amongst them had betrayed the Twelve Families? Who might already have been bought? Not the Sallets, at least, if they still sought to break the general's pincer grip.

In the frenzy of his tumbling thoughts, Gandis might

have wondered too how Lady Sallet knew how the Hart Blue Border actually worked, though that was a trifling concern. With all her family's money, he assumed she had spies in his house. As long as they did no harm, Gandis couldn't care less whom she paid in his household. In fact, he suspected Sallet money would provide rather better servants than he might have found for himself. After all, to be good spies, they had to remain in place and be excellent at their jobs.

The joy of leading the Harts was that the family was too small to be a threat to anyone else. As a result, men like Gandis, his brothers, his sister, his wife and children merely lived and married and grew old in comfort. Darien was a pleasant home for the eighty or so cousins under Hart banners of blue and gold. Gandis could not bear the thought of losing it all, not to some mad soldier like General Justan, marching his men around at all hours and murdering innocents.

He remembered Justan from school. Damned Aeris family. Definitely close to the bottom of the Twelve, if not the least of them. No decent bloodline or money, but they had military experience and took pride in that. Too much pride, as it turned out. The boy had been a favourite of the masters in school, but with no trace of kindness or humour in him. No, it would not be borne. The Blue Border lay across the saddles of two of Gandis Hart's most loyal men. He could not do much, but he could certainly use his family's treasures in defence of the city he loved. It would not hurt to have Lady Win Sallet owing him a favour in council either.

'Immortals ahead!' one of his men shouted.

Gandis drew his mount to a halt, looking around for a good place. He swallowed as he saw wavering torchlight playing along the buildings on either side. There was time, if he did not hesitate. The street curved around to the western gate and there wasn't a side road nearby. He could hear the sound of soldiers marching in step and he gripped the reins harder to stop his hands from trembling.

'I think this looks a likely spot, don't you? Here, then. Sergeant Owen? Hold this street until the Border is deployed.'

Gandis remained in the saddle, though his horse sensed the tension and skittered back and forth, getting in the way as he reined in tight and turned the animal in a complete circle. The sound of tramping feet and clashing iron was growing so loud he thought he would surely see them at any moment. He wiped sweat from his face as a dozen of his horsemen moved to block the road, raising lances and spears. Hard-panting foot soldiers mingled amongst them with axes and swords in their hands. He knew them all, of course. Some of the officers were men who had dandled him on their knees when he'd been a boy, while others fulfilled another role as servant or cook or stable master while they were not training. The Harts could never have afforded to keep a standing army ready at all times. The cost in wages alone would have given his mother the vapours.

As Gandis looked over the soldiers in their blue surcoats and oiled mail, he recognised them all and saw them as men. The prospect of seeing them face the famous Immortals was not a pleasant one, not at all. In silence, he prayed to the Goddess to let them live through the night.

The last dozen of his followers raced to assemble the four pieces of the relic he had only seen used at family celebrations. The Goddess alone knew how old the Blue Border was, or how it worked. When he'd been a boy, Gandis had been a little disappointed with the ancient Hart treasure. The Regis family had their famous red shields, the Sallets their green warriors. The Harts had the Border. Yet on this night, Lady Sallet herself had called for it. Gandis Hart felt a touch of pride at that.

He swung his gaze from the street ahead to the men erecting what looked like a pair of massive candlesticks in bronze on either side of the road. The base of each one had feet cast as claws and toes, like the huge paws of a lion. Even on the mud, they were planted solidly.

'Come on, no dawdling!' Gandis called.

One pillar had slotted neatly together, while the other team seemed to have jammed something and were cursing.

'Sergeant Owen, have your men move back behind the Border now, if you would.'

One of the few old soldiers on his staff roared orders at all the others, as if they had not heard every word Lord Hart had said. They turned their mounts and came back to stand on the far side of the bronze posts. All eyes turned to the men still struggling with one of them.

'Ready?' Gandis called.

One of the men shook his head as he grunted and heaved, bright with sweat. They were out of time. In desperation, Gandis gave the warning shout he'd heard every year since he'd been a boy.

'Blue Border, Blue Border! *Ready!*'

He looked up when a roar sounded ahead of him.

General Justan of the Immortals was not particularly dismayed by the setbacks he had suffered to that point. He had not expected his men to sustain quite as many losses, especially not by fire. Yet they had been trained for battle and he had worked hard to ensure their first loyalty was to him, not the king, or the Twelve Families, or even the city of Darien. They were *his* men, like a legion dedicated to a Caesar. He had raised them up and hardened them like spearpoints in a fire. He had been a father to them and punished them and so made them stronger. In return, they endured still, despite everything the city of Darien had thrown at them.

Men died when there was fighting. That was expected. The only thing that mattered was the core strength – being able to continue on as your enemies slipped below that point and became a routed mob. The Immortals understood that. They trusted him not to waste their lives, that was all. They gave their honour and their obedience into his hands, but they understood some would fall away. They put the legion above themselves, he thought proudly. It made them . . . magnificent.

The general stiffened his jaw as he rode, the only sign of his frustration being the sharp tug he gave on the reins of the horse behind. He had hoped to see Elias killed by then. The little girls were an irrelevance, but then his men had missed their best chance to end that threat – and so General Justan still needed his hostages. The man had become his obsession, but still he could not put him down. Setback after setback had plagued General Justan Aldan Aeris. Yet he was not some callow fool given too easily to panic. *Every* strategy had to be rethought on actual contact with the enemy. What was it that old boxer had once said? 'Everyone has a plan, until they are punched in the face.' What mattered was what you did when there was blood on your teeth and lips, not what you did to reach that point.

He'd missed the shot on Elias. Far more of a blow was failing to hold the western gate open. Justan shook his head in anger, recalling the madness of seeing his best men fall on the steps, wreathed in their own gun smoke, yet cut down by children wearing rags. He'd stared in shock over his shoulder, the scene dwindling behind him as he moved away from the hunter still snarling and straining to reach him. The huge doors of the western gate had closed on ranks of screaming Immortals, crushed and broken as they threw their weight against scarred wood and iron, trying desperately to hold them open. Yet the gearing was a masterpiece of invention, so that the doors moved slowly but could not possibly be stopped by men.

Justan clenched his fist on the reins. He had been rocked back, yes. He had been punched in the face, but by then almost three of his five thousand had made it into the city. If he'd lost a few hundred against the Sallets and their witch, at least his legion was still in Darien. More, his men were not the soft-bellied house guards of the estates, but professional soldiers, the elite of the west coast. The Immortal legion weeded out those who grew slow or too old for the demands placed on them. They were kept young and strong by forced marches and dismissing the weakest tenth of them every second year. Those who remained were obedient – and made of iron. He would bet on his men over any force the city of Darien could possibly muster. Let them have the damned gate for now! He was in, was he not? Bloodied, but unbowed. He recalled the words of a poem his mother used to say to him when he had wept in her arms, unwilling to go back to the school where they had beaten him so cruelly.

'It matters not how strait the gate, How charged with punishments the scroll – I am the master of my fate: I am the captain of my soul.' The words still brought him comfort. He felt them ease some tension within him, some sense that he had overreached. Justan lived for war and for tactics, like all the Aeris men. He had not *failed* merely because his first objectives had been missed.

The general glanced behind him as he and six hundred of his elite guard rode away from the great west gate, securing one arm of a pincer around the city. He had more men working their way up from the centre, having just strolled in the day before. They would ambush anyone who dared to stand against him. That was the entire point of tactics and reserves – to turn a loss into a victory. All that mattered was who still stood at the end.

He nodded, pleased with his foresight, building his own confidence back. There was no king to rally the city. The council of the Twelve Families could not meet while they were under attack. All Justan had to do was hold the streets till morning! His men had slept and eaten well the day before, resting themselves for the forced march and this night. When the sun rose, when they were in control, they would spend the following day imposing a curfew and raiding the estates of the Twelve Families one by one. He looked forward to that part. He had the numbers still, even with the gate shut behind him. Even if he could not get it open once more.

Like a twitch, he suddenly looked back the way he had come, finally admitting to himself what he feared to see there. He dreaded the sight of Elias coming for him. The man was a hunter, after all. Yet the neat ranks of Justan's cloaked horsemen stretched right round the city curve, the battlefield at the western gate now hidden from view. There was no sign of the man who frightened him. Perhaps Elias had fallen, crushed by a trampling crowd even he could not dodge. The general closed his eyes and touched his hands to a relic at his throat. Let it be so, Goddess. He did not look at the man's daughters, watching him like sullen kittens on the horse behind. He could feel their gaze on his back, accusing him.

'Soldiers ahead, general!' came a cry from his front rank.

Justan rode his horse in the third row, the command position that could not easily be brought down by crossbow or gun ambush. He craned in the saddle and swore aloud when he recognised surcoats of blue and gold across the road. Gandis Hart. Fat Gandis.

Justan recalled the man from school, but in a flash he remembered more than that. He took in the scene as he came round the corner: huge bronze pillars placed far apart, each as tall as a mounted soldier. Two men were still heaving desperately at one of them, rocking it back and forth. Every other Hart man stood behind those columns. Justan's eyes widened as he understood.

'Attack! Quick now! Advance against them! Cut them down!'

He kept bawling orders even as he dug in his heels. The horse on the long rein behind him almost brought him up short, so that his men raced ahead, but he did not let go of the golden chains wrapped around his hand, even in that moment of panic. The Hart family could be discounted, but they had one relic of old times, one piece of such power that Justan could not allow them to use it against him on the streets of Darien.

Gandis Hart could feel sweat trickling down his back as a line of white Immortal cavalry suddenly roared and lunged at him. He saw his own death in their swords, and the sight of his own horsemen and foot soldiers readying themselves in defence was no comfort at all. He looked at the team still wrestling with the Border. One side was finished and the men there were yelling wildly at the others. Gandis didn't know what had gone wrong. He saw only the wall of armoured horsemen coming at him, their cloaks flying out as they accelerated. Goddess, this was going to *hurt*. He was only sorry he would not see another day. It was a shabby thing to die in the darkness, he thought. He offered up his soul for the Goddess to pick over and felt the tension leave him as the noise grew.

'That's it!' the team yelled. 'Blue Border, Blue Border! Clear!'

Gandis turned sharply to see the other pillar had been twisted properly into place. In the teeth of the Immortals, his soldiers stepped back without fuss, or any sign that a charging line loomed just paces away. Gandis took a deep breath. If the thing failed, they were all dead. He looked feverishly past the bronze posts, past the clawed bronze feet solid on the street beneath. There was a lever on each one, shaped almost like a raptor's beak. Gandis breathed out as both of them were pulled down together and a filmy screen sprang up across the road.

It was too late to halt the Immortal charge, even if they had tried. Whether those men understood what they faced or not, Gandis had no idea. The Border looked no stronger than a soap bubble stretched across the air. His own men flinched back from instinct as they stood just feet from pounding hooves and half-tons of horse and iron and man going at over thirty miles an hour.

The crash was horrific, as if the Immortals had run their horses at full gallop into the side of a house. Gandis felt his mouth drop open like a child as he saw the Border used in earnest for the first time in his life. It seemed a more malevolent thing somehow, now that he'd seen men smash against it.

Perhaps forty men and horses were broken and crippled in those first terrifying instants, each rank crunching into the one ahead. Gandis felt he could have reached out and touched a man's leg as it tumbled before him, striking the Border more than once but always to bounce back from it.

The damage done was simply astonishing and Gandis knew he would never see his family's treasure in quite the same way again. He remembered once, when he was a boy, knocking into a porch post and giving himself a broken nose and black eye, though he'd only been walking at a stroll. The Immortals had been racing to attack the men swarming beyond the bronze posts, going at full speed in armour.

Gandis shuddered. He would never forget the horrors of that particular moment, not as long as he lived. Legs bending the wrong way, men *crushed* against the clear surface, with every instant of their torment visible to the horrified soldiers within arm's length of them. No one reached out. The Immortal cavalrymen spun and died as if behind glass.

General Justan watched his men pile up against an invisible barrier. It worked rather better than a tripwire at throat height. As far as he could recall, the Hart Blue Border could not be passed. Any thought of putting men in to smash at it with hammers faded. If an armoured knight at full speed could not break through, no mere axe or hammer could do more. Justan cursed under his breath as he looked around. The Blue Border was a trinket, useless in almost every situation. If it had not been, a family like the Harts would never have been allowed to keep it. Yet, and yet and *yet*! He gave a roar of anger, unable to hold in his frustration. In the right place, it had blocked his path, his advance into the city, completely. There were no side roads on that section of the ring street. He'd have to backtrack almost to the western gate, then cut across. He'd lost only a few against the damned barrier. He had the rest, still fresh, still willing to ride anywhere at his order. It might have daunted him with a force on foot, but horsemen could swing back and in, like a spear thrust through the centre.

He peered past the Blue Border film, seeing it ripple almost, as if the breeze could make it move. Gandis Hart was gaping at him there, overweight and red-faced, but unmistakably triumphant. Justan looked beyond for some sight of his reserves coming up that street, but there was no sign of them. They were further south, deeper into the city, not wasting their strength on the one part he was meant to be holding himself.

Unable to go forward, Justan turned in the saddle to look behind him – and blanched at what he saw.

20

The Sallet Stone

Nancy came to with a start, finding herself in a quiet parlour, with a fire in one corner and clothes hanging on a line that steamed and filled the air with a smell of damp cloth. A stranger was tending her latest wound, wrapping her arm in clean bandages and breathing through his nose as he did so. He smelled a little like her father, she thought blurrily. Had she passed out for a moment? She sat up straighter and folded her hands in her lap, in unconscious mimicry of Lady Sallet, who sat across from her, looking as out of place in that home as a swan in a chicken coop.

Nancy drew air sharply as the stranger tightened the knot on a bandage around her arm. The man was one of the Sallet soldiers but wore a blood-red armband to show he had been trained as a surgeon. She smiled at him and nodded her thanks. The pain had dimmed a little, no longer making her want to actually scream. His hands had trembled, she remembered, probing her torn forearm for fragments of metal or bone. Bullet wounds were still new in Darien, presenting different problems to those caused by a blade. Nancy had understood that much of his explanation to his mistress, though she hadn't cared much by then. In the warm kitchen, exhaustion had hit her like a weighted truncheon. Whether it was the lack of sleep or loss of blood, she'd lolled in the chair, slipping across the edge of consciousness and back, over and over. Every time she opened her eyes, she found Lady Sallet watching her, straight-backed and stern, resplendent in the wide-skirted dress she wore. Had she passed out again for a moment? Nancy hoped not.

There was fighting still going on outside, that much she could tell, whenever she was aware enough to focus on it. The noise and clash of arms was like a storm beyond that snug little room, while they sheltered inside, safe from the violence. The sting of Nancy's wound being cleaned had woken her up, but she felt dazed, almost hung-over. She had just lived through so many events that she needed a few quiet hours to put them all into their place. In the meantime, Nancy wanted desperately to sleep.

One of the Sallet soldiers cleared his throat and pinched her cheek. She opened eyes that were red-rimmed from nothing stranger than weariness. She tried to grab his hand, but was too slow and could only glare at the man as he stood back.

'I must ask you again, once more,' Lady Sallet said. 'Who are you, dear? How did you ruin my green warriors? Are you a danger to me?'

'I just want to sleep,' Nancy mumbled.

'When this is over,' Lady Sallet replied. 'Shall I have one of my men slap you to wakefulness? Meneer Jacques has tended your wound and you are in no danger now of bleeding to death. So wake *up*.'

Nancy blinked, then groaned as she sat forward on her chair. She sensed the surgeon and the Sallet soldier draw back, though Lady Sallet leaned a fraction towards her, as if refusing to be afraid. Nancy found herself admiring the older woman. It was just a shame that the ocean had run dry within her, sunk back into the black desert. She did not think she could have lit a candle, and that made her completely helpless. She did not like to be helpless under the dark blue gaze of Lady Sallet.

'The six Greens you damaged were worth . . . oh, I can hardly put it in terms you would understand. They were beyond price, centuries old and the greatest treasures of my house. I am told they *cannot* be made again. They cannot be replaced.'

Nancy bit the inside of her lip to keep herself alert. She understood the lady was angry, though the only sign was in the clipped way Lady Sallet was speaking. Nancy sensed she'd never seen anyone quite as angry as that woman at that moment. A little oil was needed, she realised.

'I am sorry, my lady,' she said as humbly as she could. 'My name is Nancy Cupertino.'

'There is a Cupertino Street in the southern quarter, is there not?' Lady Sallet said.

Nancy nodded, surprised.

'You must know the city very well, my lady. Yes, I was born there, at the corner of Fiveway by the river.'

She looked at her feet, ashamed to admit a poverty that would have been a different world to the woman facing her. Nancy was only too aware at that moment of her complete lack of power. What had seemed a refuge and a comfortable little room had a soldier standing between her and the door. She tasted blood in her mouth and swallowed, thinking hard as Lady Sallet went on.

'So, Nancy. I'm told you touched each of my green warriors as you passed them. Is that something you must do . . . to take the magic into yourself?'

Nancy looked up to see Lady Sallet watching her like a

hawk, the woman's eyes almost black in the firelight. She shook her head, feeling as if she was confessing to a teacher.

'I just need to be close, my lady.'

'I see. You did *incalculable* damage, do you realise?' As Nancy began to speak again, Lady Sallet held up a palm. 'Yet I have a different problem now that must be solved. I cannot just go back and *back* over all the things I have seen go wrong this evening, do you understand? My nephew lies murdered and his palace burns, but I cannot attend to that because the city itself is under attack. I cannot take the time I need to explore your . . . ability, not with the effort and expertise it demands, because I am informed that I have loyal men *strangling* in my suits of green armour!'

Nancy felt herself grow pale as she understood. Lady Sallet nodded to her as if they had agreed something in that instant, though Nancy could not think what it had been.

'So, my dear, you will forgive me if I am impatient. My green suits contained a vast store of magic, each one, in such complex forms we cannot possibly recreate them. They have never been . . . drained of power before and so we can only guess how long the men within can survive.'

'My lady, I don't know how I can be of help . . .' Nancy said softly. She could not bear to think of this woman depending on her to save men when she had not the slightest idea how to do it. One thing was for certain, Nancy had no knowledge of how the suits worked, nor the powers that drove them. Her knack allowed her to visualise magic like a liquid, not to know how it functioned when bound to objects as extraordinary as the Sallet Greens.

'I wonder . . . could you put back a little of what you took?' Lady Sallet said. She too was describing concepts she did not understand and she spoke hesitatingly, feeling her way.

'Enough just to allow them to remove the suits, perhaps? The weight of the metal is too much, as I understand it. There is air, but they cannot take full breaths. It will be a cruel ending for those men if we cannot get them out.'

Nancy could only shake her head, though she knew the woman she faced could order her death at any moment. The Sallets were famous in Darien, the royal house of the Twelve Families, at least as it had been before that night. Nancy clenched her eyes shut for an instant, trying not to picture the woman's nephew lying with bluish holes in him.

'My lady, I used it all,' she whispered. 'Even if I knew how to force magic back into them, I have none left.' As she said the words, Nancy realised she was admitting to being completely defenceless. She was out of her depth with this woman who seemed to see into her.

'Yet you would help if you could?' Lady Sallet asked.

'Of course, my lady. I didn't know what would happen when I . . . when I touched them. I mean, I *did*, but I didn't think of the men inside. I'm sorry. I saw the soldiers coming in and I was angry. I just didn't want to see the city invaded, any more than you do.'

'Good. From the little I saw before, I noticed you were . . . profligate with what you took from my Greens.' She saw Nancy frown and raised her eyebrows. 'Do you know that word, dear? It means you wasted your power. You could have achieved far more damage if you'd worn armour of your own, or had shield teams walking ahead, to keep you safe from bullets.'

Nancy blinked in surprise at the comment, but Lady Sallet turned away, taking a slim wooden box from a pocket in her skirts. It was lustrous in its polished grain, but not even thick enough to conceal a pack of cards. Nancy stared at it with unease, feeling a prickle of something uncomfortable as it came into the firelight.

'I sent a runner back to my estate for this,' Lady Sallet said. She smiled as she held the box up for Nancy to see. 'I used to play with it when I was a child, oh, a very long time ago. See, here, how it slides open.'

The box came apart, lengthening with pressure from Lady Sallet's hand to reveal a lining of pale grey metal and a long oval of polished green stone, like pale jade. Nancy gasped as the box opened, feeling as if she breathed in flame. Like the armoured Greens, the stone was marked with tiny sigils, carved into the surface with extraordinary precision.

Lady Sallet was watching her, she knew, but Nancy could not have hidden her reaction. Her exhaustion fell away and she felt the magic enter her like a torrent, making her hair move as if it might reach out on its own.

'How interesting,' Lady Sallet said. 'The box shielded the stone in some way, it seems. No mere ornament then, but not magic in itself, or you would have drawn it in.'

Lady Sallet spoke with dry fascination, as if she was watching an experiment. Nancy found herself breathing harder and she could see sparks running along her skin like threads.

'Enough. Please, my lady . . . please close it.'

Lady Sallet snapped the box shut before Nancy had finished asking. The air crackled in the room then at what they had brought into it. Nancy could not help but stare at the box as Lady Sallet held it up in the firelight.

'The Sallet Stone, my dear, the very heart of my family, in the nature of a hearthstone. Yet it had no use we were ever able to discern. Goddess knows how many centuries or thousands of years old it is, but all it would do is glow dark green. I believe it is the reason for the colours of my house. I am just pleased it was not a toy, after all this time.'

Lady Sallet was uncomfortable with the changes in the young woman sitting before her. Nancy was flexing her hands as if she had never seen them before. Her hair seemed to writhe and it had changed colour, becoming a dark red that was almost the shade of liquid blood. The balance in that little room had altered and Lady Sallet understood that she had become a supplicant in that moment, rather than a mistress. The power the witch had shown on the street was proof enough of that, though Lady Sallet reminded herself the young woman had no defence against a gunshot to her head.

Behind Nancy, the surgeon stood with a pistol held against his leg, ready for the slightest attack on his mistress. He was a healer, it was true, but he would not hesitate to kill if the witch went berserk with the power she had been given.

'I have trusted you with something of great value, Nancy,' Lady Sallet went on, smoothing the folds of her dress with the wooden box. 'Will you come with me now and save the young men of my house?'

'If I can, of course I will,' Nancy said, rising to her feet with no trace of her previous weariness. 'But, my lady, I do not know how to do what you ask. My knack is to heat the air. I do not know if there is a way . . .' She stopped her prattle as Lady Sallet rose and put a hand on her unwounded arm.

'My dear girl, there are farmers with knacks for knowing where to plant their grain, or how to call their dog to them from far away. What you do is of a different order completely. At the very least, you can take power to yourself – and release it as heat. That is two strands of power, or even more. I do not believe there is another to match you for a thousand miles. No matter what happens tonight, you must be kept safe, do you understand? It is my hope, my desperate hope, that you can bring back the Sallet Greens, but if you cannot, you are still more precious than you know, to me and to Darien.'

Nancy could only stare at her. She sensed her eyes fill with tears and she could not have said exactly why, though it reached some cold and blackened part of her to be valued and treated kindly. She might have been embarrassed to have been touched quite so easily by a few words and a hand on her arm, but it had been a long day and she had lost a good friend. She gave silent thanks to the Goddess that she had not been the one to kill the king.

Lady Sallet indicated the back room of the house and Nancy went through before her.

'They are in the stable yard outside,' Lady Sallet said behind her.

Nancy clenched her jaw, suddenly afraid that she would have to watch six men choke to death and know that she was responsible for yet more suffering and fear. The tears in her eyes blurred into a wisp of steam as she reached the open air.

The armoured figures lay on their backs like dead insects, grey as statues and still with the ropes lashed around them that had allowed them to be dragged off the street. Sallet soldiers crouched at their side, trying to tip cups of water to reach the mouths of the trapped warriors without choking them. Those Sallet men looked up as Nancy came out into the small yard. As one, they recognised her from the street. Every man there blanched and reached for weapons, guns or knives, tossing down the cups as their hands scrabbled for something to defend themselves. They had not been told she was within the building, that much was clear.

'Stand down, all of you,' Lady Sallet said as she came out behind Nancy. 'The lady is an ally, not an enemy. Give her any assistance she might need.'

She felt Nancy look over to her and returned the gaze calmly.

'My dear, I ask only that you try. I will not pretend my motives are all pure, of course. As much as I would wish my most loyal men saved from a slow death, I also want to see at least some of my Sallet Greens rise up once more. They are – they were – a vital pillar to the prestige of my house – and through us to peace in the city. No other family would risk civil war while my Greens could be brought out against them, do you see? Their existence has meant peace for . . . a very long time. Please. You did not know what you did when you drained them. It is only common justice for you to restore them now.'

Nancy closed her bad hand into a fist, feeling the ache of the bullet wound flare so it shook. She had been given a great deal, though most of it she had taken without asking anyone's permission. She stood very still for a moment, with the eyes of a dozen men on her, all waiting expectantly for her to do as she had been asked. Yet she did not move. If the Sallet Greens were the threat that kept order, should she play a part in trying to save them? Perhaps that state of peace and order was a kind of death, in a city where only twelve families could rule half a million of the less fortunate. Where men like her father had no recourse to law.

'Nancy? Can you hear them?' Lady Sallet said suddenly.

Beyond the gated wall of that stable yard, there was still a running battle going on, with shrieks and cries and clash of metal to drown out smaller sounds. Yet in the lulls, Nancy thought she could hear weak voices, calls that were failing, men who could only sip at air and drown under a weight of metal that made her shudder just to think of it. It would be a horrible death and she found she could not stand by if there was a chance to save them.

Nancy nodded sharply, her decision made. She did not see the way Lady Sallet sagged in relief, nor how the medic holstered his pistol once more as she strode forward to the closest grey beetle lying on its back. Two men stepped aside, glaring at her but held by their habit of obedience. Nancy went down on one knee and laid her hands on the polished curve of a glassy chest, closing her eyes. She could indeed hear the man within. She heard the way he wheezed and choked and her heart went out to him as he called for help with every breath, every whisper.

'I will try,' she said.

The sea of power flowed and surged in her as she spoke. It seemed to run in liquid fire to her fingertips and she jerked back as she felt the heat rise. No. She had drawn it out of the Sallet Green warriors. It had been unconscious then, as it had always been before, as when she'd ruined the tricks of travelling conjurors come to her street to perform, so that they were sent on their way with kicks and rotten fruit. She'd laughed with the other children, about fools and fakers. Magic wasn't real, she'd known. Until it had filled her to the edges and poured back out. She saw it like liquid running down her arms and pooling in her hands like molten gold as she pressed them against the armour. She heard a grunt and slowly opened her eyes.

A smell of burned meat came hissing from between the

green plates. One of the men standing around her suddenly vomited and the other swore and turned away. Her hands had melted their own outlines into the armour, leaving dark prints as she pulled them back. The smell made her gag in turn as soon as she realised what it was. The man within no longer cried out or whispered for her help. She had seared him within his armour, killing rather than saving. She slumped, head down, appalled and ashamed.

'Again, dear,' Lady Sallet said by her shoulder.

'I'll kill them all,' Nancy murmured.

'Perhaps you will. Yet he was the weakest of them, the first of those you touched back on the street. The others have a little more strength. Perhaps they can guide you. Please. I do not have the tools to get them out of the armour tonight. Either you find a way or we lose them all. Do you understand? It is a cold thing, but there is no other choice. They all die without you – or *perhaps* they all die with you. I gave you the Sallet Stone to win them a chance.'

'And to see your precious Sallet Greens restored,' Nancy snapped.

Lady Sallet nodded without embarrassment.

'I have not lied to you, Nancy. Of course I wish to see them rise again. This city was built by my ancestors, with eleven other families in a different age. It is not perfect . . .' Nancy snorted wearily. 'Very well. It is far from perfect, but there are more savage places, Nancy, believe me. Darien is the worst of all societies – except for all the others we have tried.'

Nancy tightened her mouth and stood, walking briskly to the next of the massive figures, lying at the end of a trench in the dirt where it had been dragged in. She knelt again, and when she rose another man was dead and smoke or steam

302

issued from the cracks and plates in the armour. Without a word, Nancy took three steps and knelt by the third.

One of the nearby soldiers cried out in anger to Lady Sallet, but went unanswered as she stood and watched, caught between fear and fascination. Lady Sallet did not know if the young woman was trying to save her men, or to destroy them for ever. For those few moments, Nancy held the balance of power in Darien under her hands.

Lady Sallet felt the gaze of her surgeon and turned to see his hand resting once more on his pistol, his eyes holding a question. She shook her head, holding up a palm for him to wait as, one by one, vast irreplaceable fortunes were ruined in front of them all.

Nancy made some sort of misstep with the third. Without knowing exactly what she was doing, it felt like a moment of panic, close to the fear of being shot she had felt back in the palace. The magic roared out of her and the armour cracked open with the sudden rush of heat, pouring in like liquid iron. The chest-plate broke into two pieces, but the shaking, blackened thing within had no sense of freedom as it shrieked and perished. Nancy stood, her chest heaving with emotion. She moved to the fourth, her feet dragging.

The man inside heard her steps. Perhaps he had some sense of the fate of his companions before him, or he could smell the burned meat that lay so strongly on the air. He too was sucking hard at every breath, trying not to panic in a jointed coffin that was killing him. As Nancy knelt at his side, he whispered in the darkness that was all he could see.

'Good luck,' he said to her, his will crumbling as he struggled with choking madness.

No one in the armour was troubled by small spaces, not on a normal day. The Sallet Greens were no more constricting than any other set of plate. Yet the fourth man to feel heat from Nancy's fingers lance across his flesh and sting felt something like relief at the thought of death, before he became a gibbering, twitching thing that could not even find the breath to scream.

Nancy was engrossed in her task, lost in concentration with her eyes closed. She didn't see the bloom of green spreading from her hands to the armour. The man within reacted with violent force as soon as he felt the first give in the coffin that held him. He lurched up to a sitting position, sending Nancy spinning across the yard. She scrambled to her feet with wide eyes as the man pulled his helmet free and opened part of the chest to reveal a warrior, dark with sweat and red-eyed with terror. He did not stop there, touching levers and buttons inside so that the entire carapace peeled and allowed him to fall forward onto his elbows and knees, panting and laughing and sucking in lungful after lungful of air, as pure and sweet as vengeance.

'You see how it is,' Lady Sallet said at Nancy's shoulder.

The warrior was young and extraordinarily fit, which was perhaps why he recovered enough to stand to attention after just a few moments. Nancy saw how he swayed even so.

'Will you try again?' Lady Sallet asked.

Nancy nodded. She did not know if restoring the Sallet Greens to power would mean the city was kept waiting for justice. She could not imagine the horror of being slowly crushed – and she could not allow two more men to die in that way when she might have saved them.

She walked forward to the last two, waiting with the stillness of death to burn or to be saved. Outside, the battle for the city still roared and clashed. Perhaps the Sallet Greens could play a part yet, if Nancy could bring them back. She did not know.

She knelt at the fifth and heard the terrified whispered prayers of the man trapped inside.

'Be calm. I will try to help you,' she said to him.

21

Hunter

General Justan watched a man walk slowly around the bend of the road towards him. At his side, the two girls whispered 'Daddy!' excitedly to each other. He did not turn to them, not while he was so close to the enemy he feared most. The Blue Border blocked his retreat, with Gandis Hart and all his men clustered behind it like the pitiful cowards they were. He could not retreat from that position. Yet General Justan raised his eyebrows at the state of the man who challenged him still.

Elias stumbled as he sighted the general, his feet dragging. He had not fared well in the crush of the mob back at the gate. All the advantage of being able to use his knack had not saved him when the massed gunshots had sounded, setting off a wild panic in the crowds. Elias had gained one leg and one clutching arm onto the general's cart, then had his grip torn away, falling into them as hundreds battered past. He'd taken a shot across his stomach and he could feel the sear of that and blood dripping down his leg from some oozing cut. He had not explored the wounds, as he could not have done much about them. Instead, he'd been working to avoid the trampling feet of citizens and soldiers, all rushing and killing in a scene of utter savagery.

The man General Justan feared looked more like a home-less beggar than a hunter. Elias' coat collar was ripped, so that it hung loose, with the stitches showing like teeth. He was filthy, to say the least, with a combination of dried blood and road dust that made him look like a walking corpse. It was hard to tell what was dirt and what was bruises, though one eye had swollen almost shut from some blow he had not been able to dodge.

It raised the general's spirits to know he could be hit. A man who could be hit could be killed. As his initial spasm of panic faded, General Justan smiled to see his enemy so exhausted. Elias was not a god or some great killer of men. He was just a tired father, following in the wake of an invading army. No commander enjoyed having a line of retreat cut off, but there were almost six hundred horses and men in that unit of Immortal guards. Justan put aside his previous fears. He had wrapped himself in his terrors, when the truth was he faced only a man. A man who could be surrounded, who could be overwhelmed – and brought down.

The two girls broke into wails behind him. Justan made a sound of frustration. He looked at the three captains reined in around him, waiting for orders.

'Kill that man for me, would you?' he said. 'A purse of gold to the one who brings me his heart.'

Elias looked up as thunder sounded. He knew he had taken a blow to the head back at the gate, a bad one by the feel of it. He'd ducked away from a sword and in doing so been clipped by a piece of wood spinning through the air. The world had lost colour for a time and yet he had staggered on, bleeding and battered. The experience of the mob had been one of the worst of his life. For a man who preferred days where he would not hear a single human voice, it had been almost like drowning, like being lost in the animal sounds and flashing teeth of his own kind. It had been an ugly thing and yet he had *reached* and gone through them as best he could, accepting some knocks to avoid others, then entering a moment where there was no good space to stand. He had swayed aside from gunfire, he recalled, but then been knocked onto his back by a shield boss thumped into his ribs. He was getting slow, he realised. Weariness played its part. Even when he could see threats coming, he had to be fast enough to duck. He could not remember when he had last eaten or slept and he was no longer young. He was no longer fast.

He spat a dribble of his own blood onto the street, seeing the way it lay in a pattern across the cobbles. It was a pretty thing, he thought, a good bright colour. The noise was growing louder and some part of him knew it and was roaring away in a little room, desperate and angry. He saw the road ahead of him filling with Immortal horsemen in their white surcoats and cloaks. Goddess, the sight of them! Elias squinted his damaged eye and found it helped the other one to focus. They . . . all seemed to be moving, coming at him. He could see a host of swords and he thought for an instant he could hear his daughters crying out. The high sound sharpened his wits and he *reached* all around him, deeper than he ever had before.

The horsemen coming at him sprang into writhing shadows of themselves, each one a nest of choices that were born and died every instant. Elias shook his head, trying to focus. There were so many and the noise was terrifying as they pounded down the road at him. He could see swords glinting almost as shields as his knack showed every place they could be made to move. It was too much and he felt exhaustion hit him, driving out hope.

He closed his eyes, though every other sense screamed out

against it. There were few more frightening things in the world than standing before a line of charging cavalry. To do it blind was against all the animal instincts that wanted him to scurry and dive away from the threat and the noise. Yet his daughters were on the other side and he cared more for them than his own life. Far more than his own life. At that moment, he would have thrown all his futures away in an instant to save his girls. All he could do was stay alive. There was no other plan, though he could feel a dark wall on that road with the horsemen, a wall he could not see beyond, no matter how he strained.

He had no time to consider other choices. He drew his little knife and offered up his soul and walked in amongst the horsemen trying to kill him.

The last of the six Sallet Greens was dead by the time Nancy knelt at his side. She sensed it immediately and bowed her head, sending the man's soul on with a prayer. She did not know them, any of them, but it was a hard way to die and she had been responsible.

Nancy did not lay her hands on the last suit then, though she felt the pressure to do so from the lady at her back. It was a test, of a sort. Nancy straightened and faced the older woman, so stern and regal in her fine silks. She knew Lady Sallet well enough by then to understand no words were needed as they stared at each other. The head of House Sallet had argued for her to save the lives of young men with the power she had been lent for the task. She had revived two of the Sallet Greens – and burned another three, with one cracked right open. Nancy shuddered at the memory of that, refusing to look over the yard at the shrivelled corpse inside.

No doubt Lady Sallet would point out the debt she owed

to that house, that family. Nancy had drained the suits in the first place, hardly knowing what she was doing, but blundering through in her desire to be a weapon. As Nancy stood there with the smell of burned men thick in the air like steam, she felt a weight of guilt settle on her shoulders. She nodded to Lady Sallet then and knelt once again at the last suit.

There was still every danger she would fry the Sallet Green armour, or crack it open. The process was like connecting threads together in such a way that colours could flow from one to another, then thickening the weave until it was raw cloth. She felt the sigils on the armoured plates drink up the power she put into them, holding it steady like a dye, or like liquid metal pouring into a mould.

Pulling back was harder, almost a tearing as the suit suddenly blushed green over grey. Nancy stood, uncoupling her senses from the inanimate thing. She shuddered at the intimate awareness she still shared of the cooling body inside.

'You have three of your creatures restored,' she said. 'I have done all I can and I would like to leave now.'

Nancy glanced to where the two surviving occupants of the Greens were standing, looking shaky. As fit as they were, they would recover quickly and she frowned at the armoured Greens waiting for them.

'You would do well to keep those things away from me, my lady. I would not want to make them grey once again. Will you try and stop me if I leave?'

'No,' Lady Sallet said. 'Though I hope you will come to see me in a few days, when we have restored order and peace in Darien.'

Nancy looked into her eyes and saw no doubts there at all. Perhaps that was why House Sallet ruled the city, she thought. They had no misgivings about their right to do so. It was a rare trait – and a frightening one. Nancy found herself nodding and she had to resist the urge to bow. Instead, she turned on her heel and walked to the gate, stepping through it and standing with her back to the wall outside as she looked for anyone following her out or any new threats to her.

In the yard, Lady Sallet watched the gate close and shook her head.

'Impressive girl,' she said. Whatever else General Justan and his Immortal legion had done, he had been part of the awakening of an extraordinary new force in Darien.

Lady Sallet walked closer to the two men who stood before her, shining in sweat that made their hair into wild spikes.

'I do not want to ask you to get back in, either of you . . .' She saw them tense, knowing that she would ask even so. There were times when ruling a noble house meant using those who had pledged their loyalty, even to the dregs. It did not make her proud. 'I do not want to, but I must. Gentlemen, please. Climb in and make yourselves ready. The city needs you.'

They were trembling as they saluted, she saw, though they still turned to the gently glowing suits, stepping inside and losing themselves in the rituals that brought them back to full life. She saw the fear in the two young men as the visors closed once more over their faces, but she did not stop them. She called for a volunteer for the last set and watched as a young officer received his first instruction in its use, his pride and nervousness showing in equal measure. They were the greatest weapon of her family and they were all needed then.

On the other side of the wall, Nancy realised the mood of the city had changed in the time she'd spent with the Sallet faction. Where before the festival crowds had seemed stunned and indignant, they were now angry – and armed. Half the people rushing past were carrying some sort of weapon, from swords and axes to stones or roof tiles to throw. The fighting had moved on from that spot, but it was still going on nearby. Nancy flexed her fingers, pushed off the wall and vanished into the packed streets of Darien.

It was hard to see the Immortal soldiers as men, Elias thought. The general's guards clustered around him like ghosts and shadows, every move they might make appearing and vanishing each instant. He had been kicked twice in the face and had a dagger jammed under his collarbone in a long slice. He had not tried to count how many he had killed in reply. On foot, he could not see high enough to stab horsemen above their waists, but he had hunted deer and elk before and he knew where to cut. There was a vein along the inside of the thigh, protected by all the muscle and fat of the upper leg. It carried the life's blood of a man, and if it was severed, it would pour it all out in a great slick. His father had said the old legions trained their men to aim for it when they fought.

Some of those who fell did not even know they had been cut. Elias went through them, stabbing up with a knife made jagged as it caught on chain mail or skidded across armour. Yet he did not miss often. Almost every thrust brought more gouting blood and he found he could not escape the spatter as well as the blows, so that he was soon a gleaming red figure, ducking and capering amongst enraged soldiers as they slashed and hacked and could not find his head.

He was slowing, badly winded as two horses came together with him between them and all the air was driven out of his chest. He groaned at that, his ribs creaking, though even then his hand stabbed out and another man grunted in disbelief, seeing his thigh pumping blood. They wore iron armour but sat on wide saddles with gaps opening between the plates. Elias cut again and heard an exhalation of pain and anger above. One of the horses kicked out, but Elias had *reached* past it and he was not touched.

He could sense the black wall coming and he could not see anything beyond that point. It was death then, and the hand of failure clutching at him. He did not feel too much in the way of regret as he spun and staggered on and killed and killed. His arms were leaden and he could taste a stranger's blood in his mouth. He had done all he could and it had not been enough in the end. He could not regret failing on those terms, though he did anyway.

Behind him, Vic Deeds walked around the bend of the road. He too had suffered in the tumult they'd left behind and his gait hitched as blood filled his boot, so that it squelched with every step and left a print. He had not been able to dodge and weave like Elias, to stand at the centre of gunfire and turn, just so, to make bullets and blades miss. Deeds had come through a storm and he had emptied his guns at those who might have brought him down. As he walked, he reloaded each pistol yet again, throwing spent casings into the mud behind him. He was dark with blood and filth and his teeth showed white as he snarled.

Ahead of him he saw Elias Post vanish into a line of horsemen that would have smacked down any other living thing. Deeds cursed as he saw them rein in, instantly confused and turning to strike the red man dodging and stabbing in their midst. The general sat his fine white mount some way back, his hands tight on golden chains. Deeds wondered at Justan Aldan Aeris just frozen there, watching. The damned city gate had been shut on the legion, leaving half of them outside. The witch woman and the Sallets had done for hundreds more, but the shock had been the crowds themselves, arming up and fighting back. On an open field, they would have been cut to pieces, but in the crush, in streets they knew, the people of Darien had created carnage.

Deeds looked up at that thought, fearing another sight of mobs along the rooftops, lobbing down stones and tiles. They were not there yet, but he had seen enough to know how much damage they could do. Goddess, the last thing he and the general had wanted was for the city to rally. The entire operation had been to kill the king, hold the gate open and secure the city before the Twelve Families could properly organise and respond. Instead, the citizens had picked up clubs and swords from fallen soldiers, or torn them from walls in taverns and private homes. They'd come out and every side road and alley brought new attacks on the Immortal lines.

Deeds glanced over his shoulder as he followed Elias in. The sound of the mob was getting closer and he froze at the sight of the road behind him packed with men and women, holding torches and sharp blades aloft. They gave a roar at the sight of the general's white horsemen and Deeds made a quick choice to survive.

'Onward!' he yelled, turning with them and firing at the Immortals still struggling to kill the twisting, bloody figure at their heart.

The sound of the crowd made the soldiers look up, but they were experienced cavalry and they reacted as they had been trained. In good order, the Immortal guards lowered swords over their horses' ears and kicked the trained mounts into a canter. This was battle as they knew it, not the madness of trying to pin a single man who would not be pinned. The lines had a moment to form before they struck the first of the mob, cracking bones and slapping roaring men and women down onto their backs.

Deeds slipped past on the edge, trying to judge which side he was on. The general would not forgive him a betrayal, but he didn't want to see a trapdoor beneath him with a rope tightened about his neck either. Deeds wanted to survive, of course, but he also wanted to be amongst the victors, if he could just pick it early enough. General Justan had no idea yet how many they had lost around the western gate. The Immortals with him could surely cut their way through screaming mobs all day and night. They were doing so at that very moment, Deeds saw, slaughtering citizens who thought they could just charge at a line of armoured cavalry and not pay for it with their lives. It was butchery and the roaring crowd was already pressing to get away, desperate just to survive. Deeds knew how they felt. He thought he could see the light of dawn coming over the rooftops and he blessed it. He had been trampled and kicked and battered in darkness for too long. It was time to stand up.

Lord Gandis Hart watched wide-eyed as the Immortal horsemen charged a single man, milling around him like wasps, yet without any sign that they were able to cut him down. The Blue Border was a window across the street and Gandis was able to observe the action with perfect clarity, protected from it all. He saw a lone gunman come around the corner after the first, then the extraordinary vision of the ring street filling with a true mob. Gandis swallowed as he saw General Justan roar an order and the lines of horsemen crash into the citizens of Darien. He turned away, then glanced up to see his men were all looking at him as well as the events beyond the Blue Border. Gandis could see their mood and he nodded to them in pride. It matched his own.

'You know, lads,' he said, 'there is a good chance we'll all be killed on this bit of road – and we won't be remembered for it if we are. Yet I have seen these soldiers attacking the people of my city and I have a mind to go out and make them pay for that.'

They grinned at him and for once in his life Gandis felt like a leader, rather than just the lord of a house. Perhaps the secret was finding the way they wanted to go, he thought in surprise.

'There are but sixty of us,' he said, 'many more of them. But you'll notice General Justan is not far from where the Blue Border blocks the road. I think we might reach him, if you are all willing.'

The last was a question and he looked around at men he had known all his life, the staff of the Hart estate. In twos and threes they dipped their heads and he had to knuckle brightness from his eyes.

'Thank you,' he said, wishing his father could have lived to see such a moment. 'Turn off the Border, gentlemen – and guard it well. It is my greatest treasure – after you men here.'

Two of his foot soldiers walked to the bronze pillars and reached for the levers together. They met each other's gaze and flipped them at the same instant. The filmy barrier vanished with no sound or drama, as if it had never been.

Gandis looked up to the backs of General Justan's Immortal horsemen. The head of House Hart drew his cavalry sword and dug in his heels, making his horse spring forward. His men roared a challenge, crashing across the line with him.

*

On the streets by the western gate, Captain Galen and his small Sallet force had been whittled down, though they had fought for every step. Not half of the original three hundred had survived the murderous attack of General Justan's first ranks in, his Immortal shock troops. Only the narrowness of the street had prevented a complete rout, as the Immortals could not bring a wider line or surround them. Numbers counted for less when the road could be blocked and held. It was all that had saved them.

They gave a great cheer as the three Sallet Greens returned to reinforce their position, each one surrounded by a widening space as no one on the street wanted to come too close. The armoured figures seemed to straighten as they sighted the enemy. All three took huge blades from sheaths on their backs and pointed them at Immortals struggling and hacking at Sallet lines. It was both a challenge and a promise and Captain Galen's men roared louder, in relief and pride at the power they represented.

The sound spread, bringing back hundreds of the citizens who had fled that part of the city. They came to see the Immortals destroyed and when they glimpsed the white lines still heaving and chopping, they picked up fallen swords, or just shards of glass and wheel spokes from broken carts. Dozens of them kicked in doors and raced up to the roofs overhanging the Immortal positions, beginning a rain of tiles that knocked men cold or smashed into razors on the cobbles so that they howled and fell. There were no reinforcements for them, not with the gate shut.

Captain Galen looked back and found goosebumps rising on his skin at the rage he saw all around him. The Immortals had forced their way into the city. They were now locked in with its citizens and Darien was a hard place.

The butchers and builders and carpenters and smiths brought out the tools of their trade and hefted or threw them, standing in line with Sallet soldiers and accepting Galen's orders. They went forward and bright new blood was flung from every crash and swing. A battle could turn on a single man. They had thousands wanting to strike a blow, just longing to bring down one or two of those bastards who had dared to enter Darien.

The Immortals were not afraid of violence or losses. They might have fought to the last man if it had not been for the three jade figures whirling amongst them, breaking their lines with appalling violence. Tiles and stones smashed down from above and none of the Immortals knew when they would die. They staggered back in disarray and the people of Darien roared at them, an endless sea of fury, pushing them into smaller and smaller islands while they nibbled at the red edges and trampled those who fell.

22

Witch

Nancy walked through a street she could not recognise as the one she had known mere hours before. Flames flickered still in places, though there were groups of local homeowners rushing about with buckets of water, desperate to prevent any fires from spreading. Every road battered by the fighting, every shop and home in Darien, had someone willing to defend it, ready to repair the one thing they owned. They did not try to stop her, perhaps seeing little to fear in the bandaged young woman, walking dazed like so many others.

There were a lot of dead, with a vast number in white surcoats. Horses lay alive but with broken legs, unable to stand, raising their heads and peering in pain at anyone passing by. Nancy felt their brown eyes on her and shuddered. Butchers would come and break their heads with hammers. It was a quick end, which was something. Wounded men would not get as much compassion, she thought, not if they wore the colours of an enemy. She saw one or two Immortals scrabbling in the mud of the road, trying to hide themselves as broken bones made them useless and afraid. There were already gangs of street children seeking them out, hooting their presence to men still willing to kill. They came rushing over to cut throats while the children laughed and jeered. There was no mercy to be had there, as the sun rose. There was enough anger on that street alone to drown a city.

Nancy felt no sense of danger as she walked amongst the dying and the dead. There were other women there, standing in small groups or tending the fallen. Even if there had not been, she had not given all she'd received from the stone to restore the Sallet Greens.

She shuddered at the memory of them coming out to fight a second time. She had not fully understood how brutally effective the things had been. It made her blush to think of her own white threads and the small damage she had done compared to those vaulting green figures, leaping and smashing through Immortal ranks. It did not suit her pride to know they were worth far more to the city's defence than her destruction had been. The mobs had seen them and returned to the fray, armed with anything they could pick up, from broken bottles to legion swords and shields. That pride still shone in the faces of the people as they stood and turned their faces in relief to the rising sun. They had played a part and risked their lives against the invaders. They had saved themselves. For just an hour or two, some of the great families of Darien had fought alongside the meanest of the citizens – with a common enemy to unite them.

Nancy shook her head as she walked around a smashed cart draped with bodies. She had made mistakes, but it had been a long, long night. The sky was turning gold over to the east and she ached for the light, to grow and restore, to heal and remake.

She found she had wandered right to the base of the western gate, the source of the invasion. Huge steps led up to the wall and at the top there was a ragged group, bullied into line by one young man who moved unusually well, catching her eye as a leaping cat would have done, just for the sheer marvel of it.

Nancy spent a moment thinking of Daw Threefold and regret. He had set her on a path and yet not lived to see her walk it. As she lowered her gaze once again, she saw the body of a child on the steps, a boy she recognised. Nancy's eyes widened at that, as shocked as if she'd come across a childhood doll somehow held in the hands of a stranger. She had seen him last in the corridors of the palace itself, now so distant an event that it felt like something that had happened to someone else, someone consumed by rage and a desire for vengeance that was now ashes. It had all cost too much. Perhaps it always did.

Nancy sat by the broken figure, looking down on his stilled face. She opened his shirt just a little and winced at the sight of holes there, dust settling on drifts of clear liquid. She shuddered, thinking. There was fighting still in the streets nearby. She could hear it, but she knew she would not be a part of it. There were limits to what any one person could do and, by the Goddess, she had reached hers. The power within her was little more than a trickle, but she sensed it moving like sand drifting across her skin, summoned to her fingertips without her even being aware of it.

The boy swung his legs as he balanced on the branch. One hand found a higher grip and, for sheer pleasure, he dangled from it, so that the sinews in his wrist stood out like double wires. His mother smiled to hear his voice.

'Watch me, Mum! Look!'

'I can see, Oryx, I can see.'

The garden was a lovely place, he thought, breathing in the sweet air.

There were trees and flowers and soft green hills around them. Best of all was the mother he remembered as vividly as the first day they had met. He could not forget anything he had known. He had not been made to.

Oryx let go of his branch and dropped to the grass, enjoying the smell of mown lawns that meant summer to him. He came to sit at the table, where she had laid out plates of sticky things he remembered from a long time ago, with tea and spreads. A fine white cloth covered the table and the cutlery was all of polished silver. He knew this garden from his first years and he remembered only happiness there.

The thought brought a small frown to his face. There were other memories, he was certain, though he could not quite bring them to mind. His mother had grown old, had she not? Surely she had. Yet she was young and clear-eyed once again, with strong hands and her hair tied with a ribbon. He was confused, but she seemed to understand. Gently, she touched the underside of his chin, so that he raised his head and looked her in the eye.

'I have missed you, Oryx, my sweet,' she said. 'It has been such a long time. Were you very lonely after I was gone?'

He tilted his head, confused.

'When were you gone?' he said. 'I . . . remember . . . did you grow old?'

'Oh, it does not matter now,' she said, reaching out to embrace him. He sank into her arms, at peace.

'Who is Arthur?' she said, after a time. He opened his eyes and found her looking down at him. 'You were murmuring the name, Oryx, while you slept in the sun. Was he a friend of yours?'

'No. I am . . . Arthur,' he said, his voice no more than a whisper. 'And Oryx. I am a golem.'

'That is not a word we use, Oryx. You are my son,' she said firmly. 'You were made to be my son.'

Arthur felt something change. Gently, he removed her arms from *around him. He looked up at the woman who had beggared a nation to have him made in the likeness of her lost boy.*

'I am more,' he said.

She touched a hand to her mouth and he felt tears come to his eyes. There was a tugging, deep inside him, pulling him away from her.

'I love you,' she said. 'I always will.'

'I know, Mother,' he replied. 'I love you too. I miss you. I'll see you again.'

'Do you have to leave?' she said. 'Did you see? I made the garden just as it was. I made it for you.'

He could hardly see her for tears as the light changed.

Nancy sat back, empty. She'd caught the edge of some sadness she could not begin to understand, or perhaps it was the thought of losing Daw that had undone her, she didn't know. Yet she began to sob, until it choked her and her nose ran.

Arthur gasped as he opened his eyes. He looked up to a pale dawn sky and he felt at peace. For an instant, he could remember the garden he had known when he had first been made, but it faded even as he sat up. He could not hold the memory, though he tried, clutching it like grains that would not stick to his fingers.

The young woman at his side scrambled away from him in panic as she saw him move. Arthur held up his hands and saw the bullet holes had closed, leaving paler discs on his skin.

'I won't hurt you,' he said.

The woman shook her head, her eyes wide. He knew her from the palace then. The woman of fire.

'It's not that,' she said, her voice hoarse and strained. 'I don't want to take back what . . . It is a little complicated.' She hesitated even as she spoke, realising that she had not drained the Sallet Greens a second time. If it was not a conscious control, at least it could be unconscious.

She took a moment to tell herself so, dreading the sight of the child becoming still and frozen once more. He was looking at her in confusion, but she kept a safe distance, glancing up only when the tall young man from the wall came bounding down at the sight of Arthur standing again. The stranger was as striking up close as he had promised on the heights above, Nancy could not help noticing.

'Did you . . . heal him?' Micahel said in awe.

He was still suspicious of her, she saw, standing slightly across the step in defence of the boy. Nancy shook her head.

'Not exactly, no. I returned something I had taken, that's all.'

She was backing away as she spoke and she saw Micahel twitch as he considered and rejected the idea of trying to stop her.

'Goodbye, kid,' she said to Arthur.

To her surprise, she saw his eyes gleam suddenly with tears, though he shrugged and wiped at them in embarrassment.

Lord Hart's charge crashed into the rear of the Immortals, cutting down a dozen of them before they even knew they were under attack from behind. They had been so focused on the road beyond, and so certain the Blue Border could not be crossed, that not a single pair of eyes had been placed to call out a warning.

General Justan turned in time to block a blow aimed at his neck, though it rocked him. In fury, he dropped the golden chains he held and scrabbled for his sword. Already his

Immortals were recovering. They were not house guards and boot-polishers, pressed into itching uniforms and called soldiers. They *were* soldiers. The shock of an attack from the rear wore off quickly and Gandis Hart saw men he had known all his life cut down. He had gone straight for the general and he found himself locked in clashing combat with a man who might have been his age but seemed utterly tireless, grunting with every blow as he guided his warhorse with knees alone.

Gandis had brought sixty men with him across the Blue Border. He saw half a dozen killed as the general rallied – and more and more of the Immortals were turning his way. Sweat was already stinging his eyes and he could only defend against the blows, feeling his strength fade. It had been close, he thought. His right hand was going numb under the battering impacts and he knew he would lose his grip on his family's sword at any moment. He tried to pray, but the damned general would not allow him enough of a respite to find the right words.

Step by step, the Immortals pressed their attackers back along the road, exactly as they had been trained to do. The Hart men fought like lions, but sheer pride and will could not overcome Immortal fitness and years of training. They fell underfoot to be trampled, crying out in anger and fear as they felt their strength failing. Pace by pace, the rest of them were made to retreat, losing every step they had gained, passing the bronze pillars standing in the mud once more.

Gandis had seen some of his men clustering at the pillars, though he had not dared to look over under the ferocious assault. Only when the Blue Border sprang once again into life did he breathe more deeply and risk a triumphant smile at the enemy who had forced himself over the crucial few yards of space.

The Blue Border was back up and General Justan was on the wrong side of it. Beyond, his Immortals recoiled from the barrier, shocked by the pieces of men and one horse caught between the pillars as the Blue Border came back. They littered the ground, four of them, cut by a razor so thin they barely even bled.

Six Immortals had come with the general in their counter-attack. They were cut down with sword and axe in moments, surrounded by thirty or forty and overwhelmed while their companions howled and hacked at the Blue Border pillars behind them, unable even to make a scratch.

General Justan turned and roared his frustration. As he did so, Gandis Hart jammed a dagger up under his back-plate, wrenching it side to side as the general went stiff and mouthed silent words at the lightening sky. He fell from his horse and Gandis sat still, panting wildly.

'Form on me,' he called to his men, so that they made a rank in order on that road. He faced the Immortals milling in chaos beyond and prepared to call for their surrender.

Elias searched for his girls. He had left the mob behind and he walked in the midst of the Immortals, with eyes that stung and glittered. He was all but drowned in blood and he still hacked at anyone who came past him, though his speed and strength had gone, leaving him to spin and caper in murder and madness. He had thought the wall across the road was his own death, but then it had vanished and Hart guards had come rushing through it.

He saw the two little girls running through the feet of soldiers ahead of him, trailing golden chains. Elias watched as one of the Immortals snatched instinctively, grabbing at the golden length as it came past him. Something in the gaze of the father standing close by registered with the man. His hand remained open as the links slid across his palm.

'Daddy!' they cried, weeping and laughing at the same time as they rushed to Elias' embrace. He was too weary to do anything but hold them, though he tried to stand, suddenly afraid that the soldiers would cut them down at the very moment he had them back in his arms. He did not have the strength to lift them. His muscles had torn and he had half a dozen wounds.

He stood, even so, with the girls clinging to his shoulders. They were heavier than he remembered, but it was not too much. He could hear voices demanding the Immortals surrender to Lord Gandis Hart. Elias ignored them, walking back towards the western gate with his daughters nestling against his throat on either side.

'Mum's dead,' Jenny said suddenly. 'The general told me.'

'I know, love. I am sorry,' her father replied. He could hardly see or hear as he left the Immortals behind and trudged on, right around the curve of the ring street. He walked for a time and just held them until he saw the western gate looming over him once more.

There was no fighting there any longer, though there were armed men, standing in the livery colours of many of the Twelve Families of Darien. They made ranks around the officers and lords and royal guard captains, discussing what to do in quiet groups. Order was returning to the city, though the ground was still a wasteland of bodies and broken tiles. Elias saw Sallet green and gold was there amongst them, which brought its own guilt when he thought of the king. There was no sign of the Aeris colours. Perhaps there would not be twelve families after that night, but eleven.

Elias saw a bench at the foot of the gate. He headed for it, sitting down with a gasp and letting his girls settle on either side. They leaned into him, drowsy with exhaustion as he just breathed and breathed and stared.

23

Deeds

Lady Sallet had been surprised how relieved she'd been to find Tellius still alive. Whatever concern she'd had over her nephew's golem had been drowned in the greater trials of the small hours, but she'd felt her heart skip when she recognised the old man by the western gate, stern and confident. He and Captain Galen seemed more relaxed in each other's company as well, she realised. Whatever tension had been present before had been burned away by the experiences they had shared. Lady Sallet smiled at that. There was never a moment when she wasn't planning ahead, not really. She began to wonder if the old man might spend a few months in the Sallet estate, in peace and luxury. She thought he might enjoy the experience as much as she would.

As the street-clearing went on all around her, she saw Tellius was still surrounded by an odd-looking and ragged group at the bottom of the gate. They were clustered around the old man like boys with their father, clamouring to be the first to tell their stories to him. The visible delight in Tellius somehow made her heart skip again. It had been a strange day, she thought. The loss of half the Sallet Greens was a blow, but thank the Goddess, she had saved three – and that extraordinary young woman would seek her out in a more peaceful time, Lady Sallet was quietly certain of that.

A messenger from Gandis Hart had come without a box

or a sealed letter, but just a word from his master to say General Justan Aldan Aeris had been killed and his remaining men had surrendered. Lady Sallet had enjoyed the pride and satisfaction in the messenger's face. She shared it, though she would still oversee the decimation of the remaining legion, whether they had entered the city or not. Before the Twelve Families could appoint new officers, they would burn out the treason. The public execution of one in ten would be a salutary lesson, she thought. Blood could clean a wound. It had worked for Caesars. It would work for Darien.

On a sudden whim, Lady Sallet approached the knot of young men and boys around Tellius, seeking out the smallest of them and hoping. Captain Galen stood to immediate attention as he registered her presence. She saw with pleasure that one or two of the older lads tried to mimic her captain's stance.

'I have heard you played a vital part in closing the gate, all of you,' she said. 'And that several of your number gave their lives in the defence of this city. For that noble service, I will accept your applications to my house guard, if Meneer Tellius or Captain Galen can speak for your characters.'

A few smiled at the very idea and Tellius chuckled.

'They are good lads, my lady, one and all. Micahel here is a master of the Mazer steps, a form of fighting back east. He'd appreciate the chance to run a school to teach others – and in a few years, perhaps you might have a whole new guard.'

'Very well, meneer,' Lady Sallet said, inclining her head to the powerfully built young man staring in awe at the way his life had suddenly turned. He bowed in return and she saw there were tears in his eyes. It pleased her to be able to move others in such a way. It was the very heart and purpose of having power.

Her gaze dropped at last to the one who had the appearance of a small boy, watching her like an owl, solemn and silent as the rest of them grinned and joked with one another.

'And you, young man,' Lady Sallet said. 'What am I to do with you?'

'I am not a young man,' Arthur said. He smiled. 'I am a golem. Will you look after Tellius?'

Lady Sallet glanced at the older man and to her embarrassment found herself blushing under his gaze.

'I will, yes,' she said.

A slow smile spread across Tellius' face at her response and Micahel laughed and prodded his ribs with an elbow.

Arthur nodded.

'Then I would like to spend the summer with a man who lost his son. He has two daughters and lives in the village of Wyburn, to the east of here.'

'I . . . see. It will take that long to rebuild the palace. It is my understanding that you are an adopted son of an older nation. Is that true?'

Arthur hesitated, growing still. At last, he nodded.

'It is. My mother was queen of a dozen cities.'

Lady Sallet thought again, but the decision she had made before had not changed. Darien would have a king without greed or spite. An eternal king who would never fail or grow cruel.

'I am sure one city will do,' she said. 'For now.'

She leaned forward as if to kiss his cheek and whispered the words Tellius had revealed to her into his ear. Arthur stiffened as she pulled back. He bowed deeply to Lady Sallet then.

'I am yours to command, Lady Sallet.'

'You will rule in Darien, as a just king?'

'If it is your wish, I will.' Arthur glanced at Tellius, to find the old man's expression completely blank, as if he was controlling great emotion.

Lady Sallet watched them both.

'You may spend the summer as you planned, my lord,' she said softly, wondering, but deciding not to ask. It had been a long night.

Vic Deeds was weary and fed up with the spiteful anger all around him. He hadn't really expected to walk away from the Immortals, not once they'd surrendered and been rounded up. There were too many in the ranks of that elite cavalry whom Deeds had scorned or insulted, safe at the time in his position as the general's right-hand man. One or two suspected him, correctly, of having slept with their wives. Of *course* they would point him out, claiming him for their own as he scowled at them and wished for bullets he no longer had. That was one thing about a sword. It didn't run out.

The Hart guards didn't know exactly who he was, of course, nor what he had done. They were still happy to take his four pistols and tie his hands behind his back with all the other prisoners. They didn't care what happened to him after that, not really. Someone else would sort the wheat from the chaff as the city restored order.

Deeds had not even been too dismayed at being captured. Once the anger had settled, once all the passions of battle had eased, he knew the city would still need its Immortal legion, with hard, killing men in it. Perhaps more importantly, there would always be killing men in Darien who needed a legion. What fools they'd be if the Twelve Families destroyed their own defence in a fit of righteous retribution and were then invaded! No, as long as he kept his head down, Deeds thought he had a good chance to survive the cull and the floggings that would certainly follow.

He had not expected to be denounced a second time. He had never read a bible, but his mother had once told him some story about a fisherman who kept being accused, every time he turned round. *You were with him, weren't you? You're one of his apostles. He's the one. He's one of them.*

Deeds felt a little like that when half a dozen guards from the royal palace came down the line of prisoners, staring at faces, grabbing dazed and wounded men and peering at them before letting them fall back. Deeds had been in the process of being shackled to a slave chain with a dozen Immortals already slouching on it in their fine boots and white coats. He'd seen the guards coming and turned away on instinct. It was just bad luck that one of them seemed to recognise him, pointing a quivering finger like an old maid identifying the fellow who took her purse.

Deeds had done his best to look astonished at the awful accusations they were making, but his chances of living through it all had dropped considerably. There were still groups of men exacting revenge in a few places, dragging Immortal officers aside to be beaten and kicked to a pulp. No one was stopping them, Deeds saw. It was an ugly business, but not particularly personal. Darien was just a hard place and there was always a price to be paid.

Deeds had killed a lot of the palace guards, but not quite enough of them, it seemed. He said nothing when a burly fellow was called over, half his head wrapped in bloody bandages. The man bent to smell his coat, the cloth of it still thick with smoke. Deeds saw his own death in the fellow's one bright eye then and his heart sank.

'Yeah. He was there,' the man said. That was the end of anyone listening to his protests.

Deeds staggered as they shoved him along the road, away from the Hart soldiers and back towards the western gate. He saw sullen anger in the men who had failed to protect King Johannes. Shame and spiteful pleasure too, which did not bode well for him. He grimaced as he saw that one of them was carrying a coil of rope, loosening loops of it as they walked along. It seemed they were only looking for a place to string him up. Deeds could still not quite believe his mother had been right all along. He really had been destined to be hanged.

Despite his predicament, he could not help staring as he and his captors came back to the area by the western gate and saw the destruction there. Deeds had been right at the heart of the opening moments of the attack, but it had clearly grown much worse when he'd left in pursuit of Elias Post and the general.

He whistled in amazement at the fires and rubble strewn all over. One of his guards smacked him across the face in response, making his nose bleed. Deeds would have liked his hands freed then. Some men were ever so brave when they were dealing with helpless prisoners.

He looked across a scene of desolation almost like a painting. Bodies lay sprawled everywhere, right up the huge steps to the wall and the western gate. He could see soldiers standing in neat lines there around a noblewoman in skirts. He did not know Lady Sallet, though he recognised the colours of her men well enough. His eyes widened at the sight of the looming green warriors turning back and forth, watching for threats to their mistress. Deeds shook his head in awe. He knew the general had hoped to take them down with cannon fire, but that chance had been lost in the chaos by the gate.

Deeds sighed suddenly, so tired then that he could barely stand. Perhaps it was time to stop struggling. He recalled there had been some ancient fellow forced to carry his own cross to where they crucified him. The thought was in his mind from before, when he'd felt like an apostle. Deeds thought he might resemble the man with the cross then. He just wanted to put his burden down and go to sleep.

His swinging gaze sharpened and grew still when he saw three figures sitting on a bench in the shadow of the gate. Elias was looking straight at him, red as a devil and with his arms around his two daughters. A puddle of chains lay beside them on the bench, where he had placed them.

Deeds shuddered under that awful stare. None of his weary guards could stop the hunter if he chose to stand up and come over. Deeds tutted. It was that sort of thinking that had driven the general to the edge of madness and probably cost him the city. You lived or you died. There was no point worrying about it. He raised his head and nodded to Elias. In response, the red man stood up, one hand held out for each of his daughters. He made no sign he had seen and Deeds realised suddenly that he too could accuse.

He had not been alone in the palace, after all. No matter who had fired the final shots, the Twelve Families would be very interested in Elias. Deeds understood the man would be afraid of his own pointing finger and for a moment he considered dropping Elias as deep in it as he was himself.

He shook his head and turned away, leaving Elias to take his daughters through the gate. When Deeds looked back, there was no sign of them. They had left the chains behind, he saw.

One of the guards flung the rope he carried up over a balcony that hung above the street. Deeds watched them tie the famous long noose with scorn on his face, though he felt fear grow. There'd be no sharp drop and quick ending for him, not the way they'd arranged it. The thought of strangling and turning on the rope while they all watched him die was infuriating. He felt himself growing frantic as they took him by the arms. He had not found any last words worth saying.

The actions of that little group had drawn a Sallet soldier over from across the road. Deeds watched him come, trying not to hope, though the guards all stood steady and respectful in the presence of a house officer.

'Who is this man?' Captain Galen asked.

'He was seen in the palace, sir. One of the killers, as I heard it.'

'Has anyone even asked his name? Has anyone questioned him?'

The guards looked shiftily at one another and Deeds grinned at the man who had struck him. One extra day, then, surely.

'I am innocent, sir – and I fought against the Immortals in the end. There will be someone who'll vouch for me, I do not doubt.' It would not hurt to muddy the waters a little on that score, Deeds was certain. He saw doubt in the officer's face, but then watched the man shrug.

'Take that rope off his neck for now. He can wait with the others to be questioned. We can always hang them later, can't we?'

The lickspittle guards all smiled at that. Deeds rolled his eyes and found the captain's gaze still on him. One of the guards kicked him in his seat as he trotted away with the soldier, all the vengeance they could manage. He turned his head and winked at them. There was many a slip between cup and lip, his mother had always said. A hanging postponed was a hanging avoided. The woman had been full of stupid sayings. He missed her still.

Epilogue

Deeds sat up in the darkness, hardly daring to hope. The sound he'd heard could have been a man having his head knocked against a stone wall. That was the weakness of cells, even those beneath the Sallet estate. Every part of them, every flight of steps or locked door, was guarded by ordinary men, with keys on their belts. Elias Post had no better chance of getting through iron bars than anyone else, but he could knock the wits out of the man guarding it well enough.

Deeds stopped smiling when he considered Elias might also have come to kill him. He put that aside as mean-spirited. Yes, there was a very small chance the hunter had taken his daughters to a safe place and then come back to make an ending. Deeds could still betray him in exchange for his life, after all. He knew exactly where Elias lived and Deeds knew more about his knack and how to counter it than anyone alive.

Deeds raised his eyebrows in the darkness. It had not actually occurred to him to use that information to free himself, though he supposed it would have done by the time they got round to questioning him. He could not honestly have said if he would have betrayed Elias Post. The man deserved better than that from him – but Vic Deeds deserved to live as well, and if the choice was one or the other, he suspected he'd have sung like an opera.

Deeds pressed his ear to the door of the tiny cell in time to hear someone padding closer outside. It seemed the designer of those Sallet cells had thought light a luxury for prisoners. The bare stone rooms were so far beneath the ground that the air itself was thick, and so warm he sweated all the time, while thirst became its own torture.

Deeds licked cracked lips and stood back at the sound of a key scraping in the lock. He heard the hinges creak and felt air move across his face as the door swung inwards, yet he could see nothing at all. It might as well have been the door to hell and he had a terrible sense of Death standing there, come for him.

For just a moment, Deeds was caught in a state of frozen, supernatural fear, then he shrugged and walked out. Staying in the cell meant torture and public execution in front of the baying crowds of Darien. Walking out could hardly be worse.

He felt the air shift again as someone moved aside from the doorway.

'I hoped you'd come back,' Deeds said into the darkness. There was no response, though he imagined a scowl he had come to know well. 'Elias? I didn't set those palace dogs on you by the gate and so I hoped you'd get me out. That's why you're here, isn't it?'

'No,' Elias said at last, his voice hoarse and low. 'I remembered you knew where I lived.'

Deeds swallowed uncomfortably at the words spoken into his ear, much closer than he'd realised.

'If not for that, I'd have left you to hang.'

'We're friends, though,' Deeds said. 'I'd never have betrayed you! You're not intending to kill me, surely?'

There was a long silence and Deeds could feel his heart thumping. Then a sigh.

'No. If you promise to leave the city and never return, I'll set you free.'

'Done,' Deeds said immediately. 'I couldn't think of any last words anyway.'

He felt his hand guided to the other man's shoulder and followed him out until there was moonlight. A few sprawled guards lay still on the cobblestones. Deeds saw one of them groaning and trying to sit up. He hurried past.

They climbed over the gate on a piece of carpet laid across the spikes. Deeds eyed two more guards lying unconscious and shook his head at the hunter he'd first seen calling cards in a Wyburn tavern. As they dropped down to the street outside, he put out his hand.

'Thank you, meneer.'

After a moment, Elias took it.

'We're *not* friends, Deeds,' he said. 'Understand? This is me settling my debts, that's all.'

The man's grip was impressive and Deeds nodded, just pleased to be out.

The streets all around were quiet, nothing like the madness of the night before. That whole part of Darien had been battered still, stunned or dazed, like a sandy shore littered with sea-wrack after a great storm. Elias held his gaze for a time, then unclasped his hand. Deeds took a deep breath of cool night air. The two men set off together towards the western gate.